MOON LANDING

Podric Moon's Adventures
with
JFK and the Apollo Missions

Praise for MOON RIVER

"Barney Broom has written yet another cracking Podric Moon story: **Moon River**. Once again, the gripping account flies off the page and it's impossible to put down. The Podric Moon stories cry out to be made into movies! Tailor-made to become fantastically exciting computer games, these fast-paced adventures would translate beautifully onto the big screen..."
– Sarah Greene, British TV Presenter and Actress

Praise for PODRIC MOON

"An ingenious and imaginative adventure from Barney Broom whose first novel, Haute Cuisine, was hailed as a clever satire on the restaurant industry and a very good read."
– Tony Williams, Former Head of Film Production for The Rank Organisation

Praise for Haute Cuisine

"A lovely satire on the restaurant industry and the gullibity of 'foodies'. Highly entertaining read."
– A G Williams

"Brilliant Book. Barney Broom lets his imagination go wild in a dark and macabre way. Recommended."
– Lark, Vine Voice

"Fast paced and a narrative jam packed with goodies, I loved it."
– Stanford, Vine Voice

About the Author

Photo: Matthew Usher with kind permission, Archant

Barney Broom is a screenwriter and director with many years' experience in the film industry. Barney has worked in the USA, Europe and the far east including China.

His varied work includes music videos, commercials, corporate and educational films and documentaries for the History and Discovery channels.

Barney's theatrical short film *Knights Electric* is catalogued by the British Film Institute as an iconic musical memoir of 1980s Britain.

Barney Broom is a member of BAFTA and the Directors Guild of Great Britain.

He lives in London and North Norfolk.

Also by Barney Broom

HAUTE CUISINE

PODRIC MOON
and the Corsican Tyrant

MOON RIVER
Podric Moon's Adventures
in the American Civil War

MOON
LANDING

Podric Moon's Adventures
with
JFK and the Apollo Missions

BARNEY BROOM

Podric Moon Ltd
London

MOON LANDING
Podric Moon's Adventures with JFK
and the Apollo Missions

Podric Moon Ltd
Chiswick Park
Building 7
566 Chiswick High Road
London W4 5YG UK

First Published in the United Kingdom 2021

British Library Cataloguing-in-Publication Data.
A catalogue record for this book is available from the British Library.

ISBN 978-1-8380460-6-4
www.podricmoon.com

to David

"Who knows what lies beyond? What we discover in our lives is only limited by our imagination. Possessing Ultimate Alternative Reality – it knows no bounds..."

Prologue

The Ultimate Alternative Reality mind path state Podric Moon and his computer games writing partner Dr Archie Light have created is a revolutionary parallel existence. Developed using a programmed microchip, the minute processor inserted into the wrist linking a pulse to the brain and activated by a player's index finger, has already enabled them to experience adventures in Napoleon's world challenging the emperor in *Napoleonic Wars*. Their first sojourn inadvertent, their next adventure was stimulated by Podric's GCSE studies and chartered the computer wizard's escapades in another conflict – America's bloodiest, its Civil War.

During that period under pressure to close down UAR due to his twenty-first century friends becoming over reliant on the alternate existence available to them – Podric's decision to enter more recent times is influenced by MoonLight's lawyer. The legal representative in her thirties, Kaliska Monroe is profoundly affected by the aseity of her client's creation. A lifetimes obsession with President John F. Kennedy's assassination – Kaliska persuades Podric to position UAR in the 1960s. The Cold War and the decennary attempt to reach the moon – the challenge laid down by Kennedy during his presidency excites Podric and inspires him to expand *JFK Reloaded* into a broader picture that encompasses the decade.

Emerging from the dreary '50s the subsequent ten years began optimistically, but with JFK's and later Martin Luther King and his brother Bobby's deaths, along with America's increasing involvement in Vietnam, by 1970 the country seemed tarnished.

To paraphrase Jackie Kennedy – the 'only brief shining moment' came in July 1969 when man walked on the moon – achieving the goal her late husband's challenge had set his country's scientific community. The astronauts congratulated by Kennedy's nemesis President Richard Nixon – in the murk of the unravelled decade questions are asked. Did the astronauts make it? Was the Apollo program partly a hoax?

In the 21st Century – celebrating his 17th birthday is seminal for Podric Moon. Beginning to recover from the loss of his father (the reason he sought to create Ultimate Alternative Reality) and experiencing his first real girlfriend, UAR and its co-creator are maturing. Initially formulated for fun and escapism, the mind path state is increasing in its depth and meaning to participants – not because it can influence past events but the power it has to affect people privileged to experience the lives of others in their time. Those characters' actions – sharing their feelings with UAR parceners – tell of what they might have done and what they rue.

The increase in UAR's sophistication in no way reduces the intensity of adventure. JFK apparently surviving events in Dallas and now aware of the powers that be out to remove him, goes on the offensive reaching into the very heart of American governance. At home this involves the FBI as well as the underworld: Abroad – Khrushchev, the Cold War and the nuclear arms race. Featured in conjunction with Kennedy's determination for America to be first putting a man on another planetary body and returning him safely to earth make for thrilling excitement.

Engaged in their extraordinary parallel existence, it's small wonder UAR's adventurers are forced to face inadequacies in their real lives. But as Archie says, 'An alternate life allows you to make all the mistakes you'd otherwise inflict in your real one without the consequences'.

Who can argue with that?

Part 1
The Challenge

Chapter 1

Dallas 1
22nd November 1963

Standing in Dealey Plaza, Archie Light was as excited as anyone anticipating the presidential motorcade's approach. He'd been there with his wife and daughter since early morning, keyed up and tense at the volatile situation the city was experiencing. Dallas on November 22nd 1963 was in a strange mood. Exactly how much unrest and antagonism there was towards America's young charismatic president was difficult to gauge, but it was generally felt that feelings ran high – perhaps even ugly. Many disliked the eastern seaboard Harvard-educated Kennedy regarding him as a young whipper snapper who had only carried the state in 1960 due to his running mate – Texas' leading political son Senate Majority Leader Lyndon Baines Johnson, now Vice-President.

Kennedy had spoken at a breakfast held at the Hotel Texas in Fort Worth then flown aboard Air Force One to Dallas, landing with his entourage at Love Field a little before midday. After a drizzly start, the weather was bright and sunny – a brilliant Texas day with clear blue skies. Stepping off the plane those greeting the president and his wife seemed excited by the visit. Governor and Mrs Connolly were also riding in Kennedy's open-topped Lincoln. Once everyone had climbed in – with a wave to the crowd the motorcade began making its way from the airfield into the city.

*   *   *

The sixth floor of the Book Depository overlooking the plaza area below, was a mass of boxes housing school textbooks. Due to repair work, a plywood floor covering was in the process of being laid. Tools had been left out and the place was a mess.

Looking about, Podric Moon took in the dishevelled scene. At first he thought he was alone but standing quietly for several seconds, Podric caught glimpses of some men climbing up the rear stairwell. Moving forward from the depths of the building, he approached the front windows overlooking the street – part of the route President Kennedy's motorcade would be making in a few minutes time. Gazing across the half dozen windows, Podric saw the profile of a man shadowed in the one farthest away. He was slim, around five feet eight in height and of seedy appearance. Lee Harvey Oswald fiddled with a gun – a Mannlicher-Carcano rifle. Bolt action and magazine fed – the weapon had a 4-power Ordnance Optic scope sight fitted to it. Podric watched Oswald insert a 6.5-millimeter 161-grain six clip into the magazine, step back from the window and raise the fifle, fine tuning the sight calibration.

Set and ready, Oswald put down the weapon. Leaning it against the wall, he walked across the depository. Seconds later Podric heard him relieving himself. It was all the time the boy needed. Quickly reaching the rifle, Podric made an adjustment to the Optic sight, laying it off a fraction from Oswald's setting. Re-locking the preset adjustment, he replaced the gun where he'd found it and hid behind some upturned boxes. Seconds later Oswald returned.

The noise from the crowd was rising but somehow up in the dingy storeroom the excitement below seemed remote and far away from reality. Yet it was all too real!

The roar reached a crescendo. Podric watched Oswald pick up the Mannlicher and put it to his shoulder. Kennedy's would-be assassin moved the rifle back and forth settling down to aim. Large crowds had watched the presidential motorcade make its slow journey along Main Street before turning right into Houston Street. By the time the vehicles reached Elm Street the pace was very slow. Standing on the grassy knoll beside the road at Dealey Plaza, Archie, Charlotte and Cosima saw the advance car make its turn. Then the second pilot vehicle appeared followed by a lead car and the presidential limousine. Behind the Lincoln numerous secret service vehicles, the Vice President's car and other state dignitary's conveyances crawled along. Aware that JFK wasn't assassinated by Oswald – or at least if he was hit by him, only a single bullet from the ex-US Marine's rifle struck the president – Archie looked round at the fence running along behind them. He'd read that shots were likely fired from that direction but scanning it, could see no sign of anyone.

Because of the knowledge Archie, his wife and daughter had, that no others surrounding them possessed, they were especially keyed up by the events about to unfold. Yet even with their knowledge they were still captivated by the expectant atmosphere. Scrutinising everything his eyes could take in, the games creator found himself transfixed by the situation. Jackie Kennedy was a blur of pink, her box hat perched attractively on her head. With JFK's tan and relaxed demeanour – it was surreal. Archie's phone vibrated in his pocket. Operating on auto-reflex, he spun round just catching sight of several barrels poking through slits in the ribbed paling behind. Simultaneously releasing the smoke cannister, it immediately exploded. So did shots fired from the book depository – both on the sixth floor and the seventh. Archie felt rounds whistle past him from both directions.

Pandemonium in the street. Running back to the fence, Archie discovered several bullet casings lying on the grass, but the shooters had disappeared. High up above in the Book Depository it was eerily quiet. Emerging from the shadows, Podric heard fleeing footsteps descend the fire escape. Crossing the 6th Floor, he found Lee Harvey Oswald. Several spent cartridge cases were at his feet. Oswald wiped his brow and dropped his rifle. Picking it up, Podric studied the sights returning them to the would-be assassins presets.

"Missed."

Podric removed the remaining bullets from the magazine.

"Sights on an old weapon like this are critical. Shooting a moving target, even a slow one – if they're a fraction off, you won't hit a thing."

Tapping his wrist Podric deactivated *JFK Reloaded.*

Chapter 2

The Oval Office
23rd November 1963

Sitting in the Oval Office Podric Moon and President John F. Kennedy watched the president's assassination on television. The expression on Kennedy's face was one of bemused fascination. Not wishing to interrupt JFK viewing his own death, Podric looked round the room. Comfortable without being ostentatious, Podric thought back to his previous UAR adventures. When he'd visited Mr Lincoln at the White House in 1865 the Oval Office hadn't existed. It all looked very different now. The carpet a deep pile, the room was quietly refined. Several maritime pictures adorned the walls and Winston Churchill's bust brooded over the whole from a recessed alcove. The famous Resolute desk the president worked from – a present Queen Victoria had made to President Rutherford Hayes in 1880 – was positioned in front of the bay windows that overlooked the Rose Garden. Apart from a phone system, the desk's surface was relatively uncluttered. The only other things on it were a pen tray and several inscribed whale's teeth. On the mantelpiece stood a model of motor torpedo boat PT109, the vessel the president had skippered in the Pacific during World War II. It was a treasured possession (Kennedy had PT109 tiepins made for himself and his crew). As he turned to Podric – his cool green grey eyes appraising the boy – it was his tie clip Kennedy adjusted.

"The darndest thing."

Kennedy's self-deprecation was well known. America's young president and the seventeen-year-old creator of Ultimate Alternative Reality took the measure of each other. Podric being born early in the 21st century, Kennedy's notorious charisma had less effect on the computer games wünderkind than might otherwise have been expected.

"Fancy a swim?"

The president's question surprised Podric.

"You'll know we have a pool here."

"Didn't when I last visited."

It was Kennedy's turn to show surprise.

"1865."

"You met President Lincoln?"

Podric nodded. Kennedy said.

"Can we do that?"

This was something Podric hadn't considered – one computer games character meeting another in a different game. It could be interesting.

"Dunno. That's something I haven't tried."

The president smiled.

"The White House was a bit different then. Only part built."

"And no Oval Office."

Kennedy looked around the room. It was one he liked. They'd gone through by now for Podric, the usual rigmarole of establishing what Ultimate Alternative Reality was all about and how it worked.

"So, I'm only alive in this game?"

Like Napoleon and Lincoln before him, Kennedy was quick. Podric nodded.

"Better make the most of it then."

He got up impatiently.

"You might also know I suffer from a bad back. The exercise helps."

Podric didn't really know that much about JFK. He'd only found a computer game – and that a dubious one – because of Kaliska Monroe. Ever since returning from *Civil War* and Podric's seventeenth birthday party, MoonLight's legal advisor had been using her considerable powers of persuasion to get Podric to take her back into UAR with a game featuring Kennedy. At first Podric had desisted.

"Who is he?"

"Who is John F. Kennedy?"

Kaliska was surprised Podric didn't appear to know who JFK was.

"Oh, um – he was a president. Yuh?"

"Yes, he certainly was – and he was assassinated."

"Another one then. I'm not sure I want to get involved with anymore dead American leaders."

"You will with him."

"Why? What's so special about Kennedy?"

For several seconds Kaliska didn't respond.

"He was a very special person."

This seemed lame to Podric and he said so. However, he promised Kaliska he would look into it – as much as anything to get the solicitor off his back – and in the next few weeks, Podric began his research. He unearthed Kennedy's Bay of Pigs fiasco, but when discovering the terrifying Cuban missile crisis, Podric's interest shot up. Even to his young eyes, born at the beginning of the following century, the world in 1962 stood on the edge of a nuclear abyss – a potential end game. Podric also studied JFK's work desegregating American society – still extant 100 years after the Civil War – and the black leader Martin Luther King. But playing Kennedy's Rice University speech Podric's imagination was really fired by the young president's plan to put a man on the moon during that decade. From then on Podric's interest in Kennedy and the 1960s grew rapidly.

The weeks after his seventeenth birthday party had been particular for Podric. His girlfriend Catherine Halliday declaring her desire for him and wanting them to make love exploded their mutually intense feelings. Both were essentially shy people, and both were private. The experience they shared felt unique, and to them, it was. Still on their school holidays several weeks went by before either surfaced. Catherine's father and stepmother were away on an extended cruise which meant that the two had an ideal opportunity for privacy and they took it. Podric's mother Barbara, sensing what was going on – apart from enquiring whether her son and his girlfriend were taking appropriate precautions – wisely kept her distance. Barbara was fond of Catherine and when Podric finally began reappearing at home just before the beginning of his first term in the VIth form, she was welcoming and matter of fact. Barbara did, however, notice a change in Podric. Whilst it was subtle – he was an enigmatic character at the best of times – if anything Podric appeared more thoughtful and mature. Even when his sister Amy was at her most provocative he seemed to absorb her wacky behaviour. On her way out with her friend Lilian Bekes (aka Romany Mad Lilian – RML) Amy was particularly irritating.

"Mon bro – you are with us. Booked your driving test yet or have you been too busy Ultimately Altercating?"

Podric merely smiled.

"Me and Romad want to go on another Vertical Realistic trip. What about us heading for Outer Space with you and C. Halliday – if your time permits earthling? Young luurv."

Aware his sister sometimes referred to her friend as RML, Romad was a new one. Lilian gave Podric a Lilian look. Though she was a friend of his sister's (Amy was seven years younger than Podric) Lilian's Romany blood had given the girl a particular perspective on life. As they left Podric felt he couldn't fathom either of them. He didn't tell Amy he'd begun looking into the heavens for his next UAR adventure. He supposed now that his sister had experienced *Civil War* (she'd visited Abraham Lincoln with their mother) he'd have to let her have another UAR trip though he didn't feel she needed any kind of alternative reality. Amy's mind ran only loosely parallel to the rest of the human race. She lived in her own arcana dimension.

* * *

"Presumably you know a bit about me."

Swimming in the White House pool with Jack Kennedy Podric noticed there were several attractive young women present including Kaliska!

"Less than you might imagine. I haven't really studied you."

Kennedy's eyes had a sparkle of amusement. Podric continued.

"In fact, I only tracked you down because a friend wanted to meet you."

Podric nodded towards the girls at the far end of the pool. JFK's eyes followed. The four young women were all good looking, but Kaliska stood out. "I'm afraid she's spoken for."

Podric's words didn't seem to mean much to Jack who began swimming towards the women. Podric decided it was time to go.

Chapter 3

The Awakening

"What do you mean you've made love to her and that's changed everything?"

"Well... How else – what other way can I describe it?"

Standing in Archie's den Podric and Cosima were alone. Podric was a little tense, Cosima, very. She began pacing around.

"How could you? How could you? You've known how I feel about you. You're mine!"

Podric didn't reply to this astounding comment. Cosima was overwrought and behaving erratically.

"You. You – you know what you mean to me."

She turned to him.

"Why have you done this to me Podric?"

She came close to him.

"I love you."

Since the unpleasantness of their early days, the relationship between his business partner's daughter and UAR's inventor had developed considerably. Only recently Cosima had made advances towards Podric – most notably at his seventeenth birthday party. But there was always something – some concern lurking in the back of his mind that wasn't quite right. Podric had to admit that on occasion Cosima even scared him. It was her erraticism that was so disquieting. Now he said.

"You... I thought you were – you know.."

"Oh, that was nothing. I just wanted to try it.

Cosima's friendship with Louisa Davenport had appeared more than just friendship which, when he learned about it, completely freaked out her father, Archie Light. The American girl was now back in Charleston and the Lights senior weren't sorry to see her go. It wasn't that Louisa was unpleasant – her manners were exemplary. But in a deeper sense, Charlotte believed the girl was lesbian and that her daughter had only been experimenting sexually. Cosima turned back to Podric

"And what's wrong with that?! We're supposed to have advanced – have more liberal attitudes, though I admit sometimes one wonders.."

She wrung her hands.

"Oh, God Podric. I'm heartbroken."

Whilst concerned to see Cosima distressed, Podric doubted her sentiment. Hearing someone enter the tower and the lift summoned – the girl flung herself into his arms. The little elevator arrived, and the small glass door opened. Archie stepped out.

"Ah. Not disturbing anything am I?"

To Podric, one of the particular things about his business partner was the man's ability to sail through situations with apparent nonchalance. Walking into his den Archie seemed predisposed to ignore his daughter's histrionics.

"Coffee anyone, or there's something stronger if you like?"

"I've never seen you so much as go near the machine."

Supposedly désarroi, Cosima's equilibrium apparently rapidly returned.

"No? Watch me."

Archie began preparing the expensive-looking Italian coffee maker.

"Ooah!"

Cosima abruptly threw up her hands, walked over to the lift and left.

"What was all that about? Not declaring undying love for you, was she?"

Podric didn't reply. Prepping their coffees, Archie raised an eyebrow.

"I see. Well, 'shouldn't put too much store by it. She's always declaring her emotions for something."

Archie preoccupied himself with the Gran Gaggia.

"Charlotte's just relieved the American girl's gone home. 'Reckoned she was the genuine thing."

The machine made some positive noises. Archie opened the door of a cabinet and took out a tin of biscuits. Taking one for himself, he handed the tin to Podric.

"So, you came out of *JFK Reloaded*. Why did you take us all in?"

"Left over from the birthday extravaganza. Our legal lady had a disappointing time. Thought you might find it interesting."

"Ah, you promised her, and that's what she chose."

Podric nodded. Archie finessed his coffee creations.

"I have to say whilst it's a terrible game I couldn't help get excited at Dealey Plaza. The girls were fascinated too. Somehow compelling – almost more so because one knew what was coming. Weird. You obviously expanded the profile."

Archie handed Podric an espresso.

"Yuh. One thing Kennedy asked was if he could meet characters in other games."

"You mean him and Lincoln or even Napoleon?"

Podric nodded. Archie picked up his macchiato.

"I can see the appeal. Are you going to work on it?"

"No reason why not."

"Little UAR fest then – all the good and great we've hung out with joined together for one night only. With those egos, probably be a disaster."

"Don't think Mr Lincoln would be a problem."

Archie laughed.

"I wasn't thinking of him."

Archie sat down in one of his leather Charles Eames chairs.

"Imagine if we do a few more of these – Caesar maybe, the bad boys of WW2 plus a few others – can you imagine such a bunch of hedonistic SOBs?!"

He sipped his coffee and sighed with satisfaction. Archie continued.

"I've got a problem."

"Nothing new there."

The games creator sat back.

"If you remember just before your septima decima pars est natalis, I was unhappy about the state of our business relationship."

Sipping his espresso, Podric didn't reply. Podric's sometimes lack of response unnerved the older man.

"I felt it was lopsided."

"How?"

"You really want me to repeat the dialogue we had in here with your mama and our legalis consilium."

Obviously in a Latin mood, Archie appeared smug.

"You're a pretentious bastard Archie. Frankly, if you persist with this line, let's just finish it now."

Podric downed his coffee. Surprised at the forcefulness of his young partner's response, Archie was suddenly on the back foot. Podric went on.

"I'm bored with you and your attitude. We've got a good business – some might say a very good business going here. *Issandro Iguana's* selling well and both major companies are wanting more of what we can bring to market."

"Wrong. Given both games were picked up by Pasaro, Secorni are desperate for one, and both outfits are desperate for you. I'm an irrelevance. That's the issue."

"Archie, we've had all this. I can't make my position plainer. Anything I work on commercially goes through MoonLight. I've said so time and again. I've told Kaliska that's how it is. If you have a problem get over it or let's split."

"Kaliska. Miss Monroe. Fitting surname for a game featuring Kennedy."

Podric looked at his partner indifferently.

"You've heard of Marilyn Monroe I suppose."

Podric gave a slight shrug.

"Yeah."

"JFK had a number with her."

"What's this got to do with MoonLight?"

"Nothing. More to do with Kaliska wanting to go into a game in his world."

Seeing the latest copy of *Games & Gamer* on a side table, Podric picked it up. Archie said.

"Ever wondered about her?"

Podric briefly looked up from his magazine.

"Who?"

"Kaliska."

Archie took his coffee cup over to a small sink.

"Doesn't it strike you as odd how this uber bright, highly sophisticated and beautiful woman is so fascinated by our invention. One would have thought someone like her would have every sensation they wanted in this world's reality, not crave adventures in an alternative one."

Buried in his journal Podric expressed little interest. Becoming aware of the silence, he stopped reading.

"Sorry Archie. Your point?"

"My point is why's she so keen on UAR and particularly anything to do with Kennedy?"

"I do not know Archie. Why is she so keen on UAR and anything to do with President Kennedy?"

Archie was thoughtful.

"Apart from fancying him, I wonder if it's not bound up with the conspiracy theories surrounding his death? Her being the legal beaver I can see how that combo would interest her. It could be... compelling."

"Why don't you ask her?"

Archie and Podric's relationship worked because they were so different. If Podric found Archie's self-confidence – sometimes conceit, and even arrogance challenging – the older man often felt the younger's directness disconcerting.

"It has fascinated a lot of people."

"What?"

Podric resumed reading his computer magazine.

"JFK's assassination."

"Why?"

"That's a better question than you probably realise."

The internal phone rang. Podric heard Alannah's voice on

the line. After a few seconds, Archie hung up. Looking round he began to laugh.

"There's a surprise."

Archie walked over to a window overlooking the drive and looked down at a figure emerging from a car.

"Something you didn't know about. The games-writing colleague I had before you came along."

Now vaguely interested, Podric stopped reading and joined his business partner.

"George Benedict. Haha... Old George. I'd forgotten he was dropping by. Like to meet him?"

Podric shrugged.

"Can't see he'd want to meet me. You'll have lots to catch up on."

"Nonsense. It'll do him good to meet new blood – the voice of tomorrow."

Chapter 4

Conspiracist Theories and
A Meeting of Significance

Working in her penthouse apartment at Butlers Wharf overlooking the Thames, Kaliska Monroe gazed into her computer screen. Spooling through countless versions of the Zapruder film and yet another interview about the Umbrella Man, Kaliska was immersed in a subject that had long held fascination for her. Archie was right when he said Kaliska had a life-long interest in John Kennedy. He was further correct that it was partly to do with the Kennedy mystique and partly to do with his death. At one point in her developing years when studying at university (Kaliska read law at Oxford) she became so obsessed with JFK's assassination she nearly flunked one of her papers. Considered a solitary hiccup by her tutor, she re-sat Common Law Part 1, but it was with the greatest difficulty she set aside her Kennedy assassination treatise. For a while Kaliska considered making the paper she'd written part of her degree field work (to support her efforts she'd even taken a holiday in Dallas to pursue her study of the subject). After extensive research of the many conspiracy theories presented over the years – Castro/anti-Castro/FBI/Mafia – even Lyndon Johnson's involvement to name several – Kaliska had come up with her own hypothesis which she felt broke new ground in the cluttered and frequently fantasy world surrounding the subject.

Her mobile vibrated. Kaliska saw that it was the office. Now a senior attorney at Limmerson, Bart & Co her own surname had recently been added to the board. Professionally, she ought to be over the moon, but there it was again. Moon. Podric was just a boy but what he'd invented affected Kaliska more than she could explain.

Kaliska had her fair share of admirers. At 33 she was in no hurry to marry but her current beaux (Kurt Weismann was a partner with his own highly-successful City brokerage firm) was pressing.

Why did she feel so removed?

On learning about Ultimate Alternative Reality something had happened to Kaliska. Perhaps it was the fascination of an alternate life she responded so strongly to but whatever it was she supposed she'd have to snap out of it soon. Surely UAR was a passing fancy. But was it? What it offered was so out of this world she felt it really had changed her life.

The trouble was having persuaded Podric to take her into Jack Kennedy's existence she was currently even more in thrall to UAR than ever. Kaliska picked up her phone.

* * *

Late afternoon, Archie left Podric and George Benedict whilst he took a call. The boy and older man sat opposite each other on the chintz-covered sofas in the Light's drawing room. The day autumnal, the remnants of tea lay between them. Now he was in the sixth form Podric's school attendance was more flexible. It being a Thursday, he only had an economics tutorial in the morning which was how he came to drop by Archie's and get collared by his daughter.

Looking at George Benedict a more unlikely man for a computer games writer it would be difficult to imagine. Short and rotund, Benedict wore thick horn-rimmed glasses and had all the appearance of an owl. Podric immediately liked him.

"So, Archie never told you I co-wrote several of his games."

"No."

"Doesn't surprise me. He was never one to enlarge on detail where our partnership was concerned. I think he wrote about a third of *Knights of the Avenger* and *Krimon* less than half."

Podric noticed that Benedict spoke with a slight American accent.

"What about *Petra*, and *Marvin the Destroyer?*"

"They were mainly his and *Guns of Orion* I didn't have anything to do with."

"How come he took the credit for the ones you worked on?"

Turning back from the window, George Benedict's cherub-like face broke into a smile.

"'Tell you the truth I've never been interested in the limelight and it didn't make any difference to the money. In some ways it was better Archie handled the front end. I wasn't a marketing man."

Walking round the room, George stopped at the fireplace. Over it hung an oil painting of Charlotte.

"Whatever else he isn't, Lightweight – I used to call him that – is fundamentally straight. Sort of."

"Why did you split up?"

"Her."

Benedict pointed to the painting. Podric looked surprised.

"I didn't like the way he was treating her – or she, him."

"No..?"

"No."

George sat down. Podric was silent and Benedict continued.

"I've heard about you of course – not from Archie but Secorni. That ogre Cy Zaentz reckons you're hot."

"Haven't had much to do with them."

"No, you're more a Pasaro man. Guess you'll be doing the heavy lifting here."

Not having a ready reply, Podric was quizzical. Benedict said.

"Games."

"Oh, we've written a couple."

"I know – *Agrolution* and that weird named *Isandlwana Iguana* or whatever it's called."

"Issandro."

"That's it. Where the hell did that come from?"

"Where does anything come from?"

"Fair enough."

Podric looked thoughtful.

"Wait a minute. I'll bet... You're Benedict Gee. I've read about you. You're the guy who wrote that crazy interplanetary *War God* series. They were weird."

Taking off his glasses, Benedict carefully wiped the lenses.

"Did you enjoy playing them?"

"Bit psychotic. The levels seemed a bit strange."

"Ha! I wanted to push the challenge."

"Oh, I cracked them alright though it took a bit of doing."

Realising Podric was paying him a compliment Benedict smiled. Podric said.

"You're just catching up with Archie, then?"

Benedict put his glasses back on.

"I'm on skid row."

Before Podric could reply Dog barged into the hall going berserk barking at the front door. Alannah appeared and opening it welcomed Barbara Moon. Returning some books the housekeeper had lent her (the two were forever exchanging reading matter) Podric's mother breezed in. Alannah went back to the kitchen checking on some cooking. Though he didn't really know George it was left to Podric to introduce his mother to Benedict. They made small talk for a little while before Archie reappeared. Barbara asked Podric if he wanted a lift home and after a brief chat with Alannah on the way out, mother and son left the Lighthouse.

"Funny little chap."

They were in Barbara's old VW Beetle on their way back to Briony Close.

"I liked him."

"Strange fellow. You say he was Archie's co-games writer."

"Hmm... 'Said he's down on his luck."

"Then or now?"

"Ha."

"Is your partner likely to help him?"

"He could."

Barbara's car lurched over a bump and made an unwelcome

noise.

"Mum, I've been wondering. These games I've launched with Archie – we've made a bit of money. Well, quite a lot I think. How about a new car?"

They turned into the little 1960s close.

"And maybe we could move house?"

His mother laughed.

"Darling – are you really that rich?"

"Maybe. Yuh."

Podric laughed.

"Wouldn't you like a new car?"

They pulled up outside No 5.

"You know I had this old girl when your father got his last posting. We bought her off the station commander's wife. I somehow thought I'd never get rid of das auto der menschen."

"You don't have to. I need to learn to drive."

Laughing, Barbara opened the driver's door.

"Then I'd better get online. What do you think – a newer one of these or would your earnings run to a Faciella?"

Referring to one of the several Facel Vega's Archie Light owned, Barbara got out. Podric said.

"Two if you want. The call from Pasaro said they're pretty pleased."

Podric unlocked their house.

"You'll see the official returns when they come through in a few days' time."

Looking thoughtful, his mother followed her son inside.

Chapter 5

Successes and Concerns

Although Podric kept a low profile about his computer games earnings, not even his mother knew that with an advance he'd received on *Agolution* he was privately helping Barney Sturridge put a roof over his head. Since Wendbury High's ex-school bully had been disowned by his father who had sold their family house in Athill (a wealthy neighbourhood adjacent to Wendbury) he and his wife decamping to southern Spain, Barney had been living with their classmate Jason McBride. But this couldn't continue. The forces house the American boy lived in with his mother and two sisters on the local USAAF/RAF airbase wasn't over large even with Jason's dad away serving on secondment in the Middle East. It was while Podric and Catherine were enjoying their intimacy that the subject of what might happen to their complicated friend came up.

"He told me he can't go on staying at the McBride's. I'm worried he's got nowhere to go."

Ever since Catherine had got trapped inside UAR with Barney aboard a Mississippi riverboat during the American Civil War trying to help Jason McBride who was experiencing a slave's life in *Civil War* while he went in search of his origins – a particular friendship had evolved. Barney also having sexual identity issues – at seventeen Catherine didn't feel she possessed any motherly instincts but there was something about the ex-bully's bullshit that made him seem vulnerable.

"What about that flat your dad has?"

Podric had once visited the apartment Charles Halliday owned with Catherine.

"What about it?"

"It's still empty, isn't it?"

"Yes, but where's Barney going to get the money for the rent? I'm afraid my father would want a normal tenancy agreement. He's not just going to let BS live there free."

"How much is it?"

Catherine mentioned a figure she knew previous tenants had paid.

"I could cover that."

"What do you mean?"

"What I say."

"Wha-? How?"

"I could pay the rent."

Catherine was so aghast she got out of bed. Looking at her lovely figure Podric immediately lost his concentration! Catherine said.

"You'd pay his rent? I mean even if you could – why would you?"

"He hasn't anywhere to live. You're always worried about him and I can."

"How?"

"You've already asked me that and I could say it's none of your business."

"You could."

Putting a dressing gown round her shoulders Catherine walked to the door.

"Coffee?"

Podric nodded and got up. In the kitchen Catherine fired up a coffee machine. Podric appeared.

"I've got this money. It's the first return on one of the computer games I've written."

"But Podric-. No. You can't do that. It might have to be for a while."

Podric continued as if he hadn't heard her.

"And it's only the beginning."

"So?"

"So, it's quite a lot of money."

"How much?"

Podric laughed.

"A bit."

"Enough to pay his rent for a year?"

The return was a lot more than this and Podric just nodded.

"That's the most amazing thing I've ever heard."

"Why? I've got the money – he needs somewhere."

"Yes, but…"

"You brought it up. What else is he going to do? Go back to living rough?"

Catherine looked steadily at her boyfriend. She had lovely grey eyes that had a mesmeric effect on Podric. With great difficulty, he matched her gaze.

"It comes with two strings."

Catherine didn't respond.

"One – he'll have to get a Saturday job to pay for his food, beer and whatever else he spends his money on."

"And the second."

"He never knows."

"What do you mean?"

"He never knows I'm paying his rent."

"You're crazy. How are we going to not tell him that?"

"Easy. Say your dad isn't letting it because of some tax issue but thinks to have someone living there will stop it falling into disrepair."

"'Seems like you've already thought this through. You're a devious bastard."

"Is that all you've got to say about my generosity?"

She came over to him and they were quickly intimate.

"You know I'm in love with you, don't you?"

"Is that because I'm suddenly rich or are you fascinated by my other attributes?"

"What might they be? You're a geek."

"Well…"

There's nothing like young love! A little while later as they lay on the kitchen floor, Podric said.

"But you must forswear."

"Forsooth I must, must I?!"

Catherine giggled.

"I'm serious. If you ever tell him.."

"What? What would you do?"

She sat astride Podric, smiling.

"Why do you so not want him to know?"

"Because."

"Because what?"

"Because it wouldn't be fair. There would be some kind of debt situation and I don't want that."

Catherine got up.

"This is all very saintly Podric, very noble."

"No, it's not. Do you?"

He looked at her.

"Promise?"

Catherine watched as Podric stood up. Lithe and easy, they were close again.

"Alright. Promise."

They kissed. Catherine said.

"But in return for my silence you must forswear."

"What?"

"That you'll never make love to me in UAR again."

Podric's eyes narrowed. He and Catherine had first realised their desires in the computer game *Napoleonic Wars*.

"You couldn't remember it."

"Exactly."

*   *   *

Kaliska spooled through her e-mail In box. Seven from Kurt – a new one popped up. From Dallas112263 it read 'Lot's to learn. JFK and Moon landings – what moon landings? Interested in knowing more? Jackie'nJack12953'.

Kaliska had had contact with conspiracists before and received many such e-mails over the years pursuing her trail. But though this one wasn't any crankier than plenty she'd read it triggered the stimulus – who, why and how? Because she'd just been into *JFK Reloaded*, Kaliska was particularly thoughtful. She had seen her hero and wanted to see him some more.

Leaning back on her sofa Kaliska stretched. She'd have to learn how to get in and out of UAR by herself. That had always been her intention – to be able to enter and exit the state when she wanted. Right now, she didn't have the necessary knowledge. That meant getting hold of Podric. Kaliska would need his help to master it. She'd suggest they meet – maybe take him out for lunch with that girlfriend he was so besotted about. But get into *JFK Reloaded* again Kaliska Monroe would – whatever it took.

Chapter 6

Rack, Ruin and Confessions

"So, she's taking you to lunch. Interestinger and interestinger."
Early evening, sitting at a table outside the Trout & Eel – Archie and Podric's local Hampshire pub – the water flowing over its weir made a pleasant scene. The two sat opposite each other. A setting sun pierced through gathering clouds caused Podric to squint.

"Why?"

Looking at his young business partner over the rim of his beer glass, Archie drank.

"Because as I said the other day my dear Podric it's at the very least particular that the educated, attractive, highly successful and much sought after Ms Monroe should be so interested with the world of our little old alternative reality she's become obsessed by it."

"I think it's more the game and her preoccupation with JFK's assassination."

Archie smiled. "And JFK perhaps..."

Toying with his beer mat Podric said.

"I don't really know our legal lady but one day when we were in *Civil War* she said she felt she'd really come alive. Bit strange only feeling you're coming alive in a computer games world but she's not the first to feel that. Given Kaliska's clever – perhaps because she knows she's supposed to have everything in this world, she feels dissatisfied – with her life, her career – even with herself."

"This is deep and profound, Podric."

"Yeah."

Flicking the beer mat neatly between his fingers, Podric rotated it across the back of his hand.

"She also told me she'd been so bound up with Dallas stuff, she flunked one of her law exams and had to re-sit it."

Archie considered.

"That's an obsession alright."

Podric said. "What about your ex-games writing partner?"

"What about him?"

"Gather Mr Benedict wrote quite a bit of your stuff."

"Ah, that old gripe."

"He didn't say it was bad, just that he wrote some of your games."

Archie frowned.

"George Benedict turning up in my life again is the last thing I need."

"What happened?"

"What happened with me and George Benedict.."

For several seconds Archie was distracted.

"George is a clever bugger. He's not like you but he's off the wall. There's a darker side to him but there's a darker side to me too. We had a row – a big row. I was in a bad place. Charlotte was leaving me. Things got said."

More clouds gathered as the sun slipped over the horizon. The Trout & Eel's exterior lights came on. Archie drank his beer.

"And now he's down on his luck."

"I said George had a darker side. He's an inveterate gambler of endemic proportions."

Podric put some cash on the table.

"My round."

Taking the money Archie got up.

"Besides – I wasn't as successful with him as I am with you even if I do only contribute a timer or a transition here and there. But if I go down that road of inadequacy I'll end up flagellating myself and I can't imagine you'd want that."

"Oh, I dunno."

Archie strolled off into the pub carrying their empty beer mugs. Seconds later rain began to fall. Customers got up and headed inside. Podric joined them.

* * *

His collar turned up against the rain, George Benedict stood on the doorstep of No 5 Briony Close. Pressing the doorbell, seconds later a light came on and the door was opened by Barbara Moon.

"Er, Mrs Moon. We met earlier. I'm George Benedict."

"Yes."

Rain splashing into her hall Barbara wasn't keen to prolong the conversation.

"I was wondering if your son might be around?"

"He's out right now but he shouldn't be too long. Er, would you like to come in?"

"That's very kind of you."

Benedict stepped inside dripping rain on the carpet.

"Mr Benedict. If you're going to wait for Podric might I suggest you take your coat off?"

Seeing he was making a puddle George readily complied.

"Thank you."

Barbara took his coat and hung it in a little utility closet. The warmth fogging Benedict's specs, he took them off and wiped them.

"Would you like a cup of tea?"

"Oh, I don't wish to put you out."

Barbara smiled.

"Or something stronger? There are a few beers, some wine – even a little whisky. Podric made me get some for his partner."

"Ha. Yes, I understand your son's working with Archie games writing now."

"Amongst other things. What would you like?"

"A little of the auld and peat wouldn't go amiss."

"Scotch then."

Benedict looked at her.

"Sorry. Yes, I have these odd phrases."

"I'm aware of the Anglicised Gaelic for burn Mr Benedict."

"George, please."

Barbara went into the kitchen and produced a bottle of single malt.

"My, the Glenroamin."

Pouring a decent amount into a tumbler, Barbara re-stoppered the bottle.

"Water?"

"Er."

Reaching into the fridge, she took out a bottle of Highland Spring.

"Just a little."

Barbara handed the glass and bottle to Benedict.

"Please."

Benedict took them. Barbara said.

"Come through."

Leading the way to the Moon's living room, Barbara picked up her glass of wine and muted the television. Several of Amy's possessions lay on the sofa – some exercise books, a bizarre face mask and part of a computer game. Barbara gathered them up.

"I could wish for a tidier daughter. Have a seat."

"Is that *Flying Bats of the Hyper Galactic?*"

"Sorry?"

"The cover of that game."

Barbara picked it up.

"Two."

"I worked on the first."

Sitting down Barbara sipped her wine.

"I can't imagine what you wanted to see my son about."

Barbara laughed. A beat later, so did George Benedict. There was something about Benedict that intrigued Podric's mother – a certain quirkiness. Unlike the smooth Dr Light, there seemed a naïvete about Benedict. It was refreshing.

Over the next couple of hours their talk ranged from Sean's death, Barbara dealing with widowhood and working at Tweeney's Waste Disposal to George Benedict's gambling addiction and the ruin he had brought on himself. As they conversed it was the man's raw exposure of his character that Barbara appreciated. Benedict didn't hide behind any cloak of blaming others and admitted his inadequacies. So engrossed was she, Barbara quite forgot about her children. It was only their arriving home that brought her conversation with Benedict to a close. Barbara said.

"Didn't know you two were meeting up?"

"We weren't. I found him sitting in a cab outside on his cellulite."

"She means – to use the American term – cell phone. My daughter specialises in the misuse of words."

Barbara introduced Amy to George Benedict. The two were soon chatting away – the girl idiosyncratic, the man, wry. Although aware of Benedict's presence Podric had gone into the kitchen where his mother found him making coffee.

"Darling?"

Podric hadn't been overly teenage since his father's death – taking on the role of man of the house. But tonight, his manner was abrupt.

"'See he's making himself at home."

"What do you mean?"

The whisky bottle was back on the table. Barbara came and stood in front of her son.

"At my invitation while he waited for you."

"He hasn't borrowed any money, has he?"

"No Podric, he hasn't."

Podric poured water on his coffee.

"Archie's been telling me stuff. The guy's in real trouble. Apparently he's gambled away thousands."

"I know."

"What do you mean, you know?"

"We've been talking about it."

"He'll want some off me then. I told you MoonLight's returns have come in."

"You did."

Barbara moved a little away. Keeping her voice low, she said.

"Did Dr Light tell you why Mr Benedict came to see him?"

Barbara poured herself another glass of red wine.

"So frustrated are Secorni at not being able to secure your services and prize you away from the good doctor, they're threatening him with bully boy tactics accusing him of fraud. Apparently they claim not everything was as it should have been in their dealings with Messrs Light and Benedict and they're intending court action unless Archie agrees to part company with you. George came to tip him off."

Barbara drank some wine. Podric sipped some coffee.

"Do you want me to help him?"

"Who? Mr Benedict or your partner?"

"Ha. Archie doesn't want my help."

Amy came in.

"Mr Benedict then. He's starving and so am I. How about a Chinese?"

Half an hour later Amy, Barbara, Podric and George Benedict sat in the Moons kitchen devouring Peking Duck, beef and ginger with spring onions and Singapore noodles. All declared it hit the spot!

* * *

Sitting in his den, Archie re-read the Private & Confidential letter that a courier had delivered. Through their lawyers, Secorni intended to take legal action against him for misrepresentation and taking disproportionate credit for games he'd supposedly written. How much was his work and how much was George Benedict's? Archie thought this alone was a weak legal argument but as George had told him, compromising his ex-partner and putting him in the dock under oath would be another matter. It was hard to recall exactly what percentage he'd contributed and what George had. At the time of their partnership it hadn't mattered. George had never seemed bothered by who had done what by way of contribution, but that had all changed now.

The devious lengths these bastards would go to. He'd have to part company with Podric. It wasn't fair on the kid to drag him into all this. But George fessing up that Secorni were compromising his ex-partner into going against Archie – there might be an angle there, though if he made a formal challenge it would bring George down. What a bloody mess. Reaching for his whisky, Archie looked grim.

*   *   *

"Why didn't he tell me?"

Podric and George Benedict were sitting in Barbara's little garden studio – once Podric's computer workshop. The older man had another whisky (a lot of it was being drunk in Drinkwell that night!) and Podric a bottle of beer.

"You know what an ego he's got. Half the time with A L (George pronounced the letters separately) he's a conundrum wrapped up in an enigma or the other way round."

Benedict sipped his scotch. Podric looked at the computer games man.

"I thought you were coming here to tap me up for money."

Benedict laughed a sad laugh.

"You don't have enough."

Podric swigged his beer.

"So, what about this legal case?"

"Leverage Podric. I'm in debt up to my eyes. If I don't play ball in Secorni's legal action against Archie for taking the credit for games he didn't write, they'll foreclose on me."

"Mum thinks they're doing it to split him and me up – legally."

"That's not an impossibility. They think disgracing your partner will isolate him. Secorni are hell bent on securing your services."

Benedict had some more scotch.

"What's this other stuff your mum was telling me about – this alternate reality?"

Podric's face darkened. Benedict continued.

"It's alright. Don't blame your mother. We talked about everything – from the loss of your dad to gambling my life away."

Podric sighed.

"You can have my room tonight."

"Thanks, but I've got other plans."

"Are you around for a while?"

"Few days perhaps."

"You're not staying at Archie's?"

Benedict chuckled.

"I wouldn't accept if he invited me."

"Know people here, then."

"I do now."

Benedict finished his scotch.

"Mrs... Bickerstaff?"

"Ivy? You're staying with Ivy?!"

Podric was surprised.

"She's got this amazing macaw."

"Tell me about it. How do you know her?"

"When I left Grand Palace Light, I was walking across the village green and met her."

"And she offered to have you to stay?"

"Well, not exactly. It was the bird."

Podric stared blankly at Benedict.

"He seemed to take a liking to me – wouldn't let me go. It all got rather intense. She invited me to move in."

Chapter 7

Barney's New Abode
and the Stitch Up

"What do you think then Pod? Pretty cool huh?"

"It's great Barney. How are you going to afford it?"

They were standing in the living room of Charles Halliday's empty apartment in Athill.

"Cheeky."

Barney threw a pretend punch at Podric.

"Catherine's old man's decided not to let it. Some tax issue – but he wants someone to live in it, mind the place. Neat huh?"

"I'd say."

Podric was blandness itself. Catherine appeared from the kitchen carrying a tray. On it was a bottle of sparkling wine, three glasses and a cake with a single candle. Barney looked taken aback.

"Go on. Blow it out!"

Catherine smiled. Barney blew.

Catherine began pouring the bubbly. Barney said.

"I don't like the stuff."

"More for Podric and me then. You don't have to make a speech."

Barney reached into a shopping bag on the window sill and took out a couple of cans of larger. Catherine handed a glass of Prosecco to Podric and raised one herself.

"Na zdravi."

"If you say so."

Podric and Catherine had regained their intimacy. Barney pulled the tab off a beer can and took a swig.

"To the end of the Sturridge's."

Hearing this startling toast, his friends turned to him.

"Er-."

"I'm changing my name."

"Why?"

"Why? Why?! Cos I have no fucking family and I have no fucking parents that's why!"

Distressed, Barney walked around the room.

"What about..?"

Catherine was hesitant.

"You said they were paying you some money."

"Oh, they did that. Fifty measly grand. The price was to never see them again."

Podric was going to say that he knew some parents who never saw their kids and also never gave them any money. As if reading his mind, Barney said.

"Okay, fifty k is fifty k – I won't tell you what I should have got. Dad sold his business for five million plus."

He finished his beer and crushed the can.

"Anyway, it doesn't have anything to do with the money. I thought about sending it back with a note saying they can stuff it."

He began to cry. Because Barney was always so bully boy it was somehow doubly pathetic. Catherine put an arm round him. Grabbing the other can of beer, he pushed her away.

"Whatever – I'm gonna break in – take some furniture. Get the hi-fi and a TV."

"Thought they'd sold the house."

Podric was casual.

"They have but it hasn't been emptied yet and the new owners haven't taken possession. 'Need to get in quick though."

"Isn't that a bit dodgy?"

Catherine was concerned. Barney looked at her.

"Why should I care?"

"Well you don't want to get into trouble with the law – not with your track record."

Podric's comment sounded harsher than he meant it to. Catherine shot him a glance.

"Thanks Pod. That's what I like about you. A friend in need."

Refraining from comment, Podric gulped down the rest of his sparkling wine.

"I'd better go."

He glanced at Catherine.

"Tomorrow, 11.00am at the station."

Picking up his bag, Podric headed for the door.

"When are we going in again? You can do that much for me."

In spite of the good fortune that had come his way, Barney was querulous. Podric turned back.

"Soon Barney, soon. Good luck with your new home."

Catherine saw Podric out. She said.

"He can pay his own rent."

Catherine was upset. Podric adjusted his shoulder bag.

"No, leave the deal. Right now, that's his lot. Life's all about on-going income as I've been learning."

"You're very Mr Business these days. How much money are you making?"

"That would be telling."

*   *   *

September that year was hot and although the air conditioning in Secorni's London office was on full blast it was fighting a losing battle with the city's afternoon heat. Even the ever-cool Californian Carla Logan sweated, though her raise in temperature was due less to the wafts of hot air surging up from the street than the phone call she'd just heard. Playing back the recorded conversation between her boss Saul Prendergast and Secorni's CEO Cy Zaentz – Carla could hardly believe her head-phonic ears.

"How's it going with that deal?"

"I presume you mean landing young Moon."

There was an affirmative grunt at the other end of the line.

"Gertner's are on it serving papers to Light and the heat's on Benedict. I'll follow up shortly."

"Think he'll play?"

"He's desperate enough. The guy's in hock up to his eyes."

"Our people okay with the case?"

"Sure they are. Enough shit there to bury Light ten times over."

"Huh. He was never a popular guy."

"We just need sufficient mud to stick to make him untouchable. Then the boy'll have no choice but to drop him."

"High risk Saul. If... anything got out, backfired – it wouldn't be pretty."

"I want to nail the bastard."

For several seconds there was silence on the line. When Zaentz finally spoke, his voice was quiet. Carla knew that was an ominous sign.

"Let's hope your idea pays off then."

Zaentz rang off. Minutes later Prendergast emerged from his office and headed for his exclusive South West London sports club. Wishing him a goodnight Carla's cordiality was ignored. Getting up from her seat, Carla walked over to the air-con unit and stood under it. The appliance was pumping out hot air! Bloody UK. Nothing worked properly though like many of her fellow countrymen, Carla loved London.

What to do? Archie Light was an arrogant SOB and maybe he was past it. She and the Brit games creator had a partisan relationship not infrequently crossing swords. But stitching him up like that and driving a wedge between him and his young computer partner left a bad taste. She'd heard a lot about this wünderkind Podric Moon. Maybe she should find out more about him – what the fuss was all about and why her bosses were so determined to secure his talents? She'd make some discreet enquiries. Carla took a drink from the fridge. Adding cubes from the ice-maker – that at least worked and refreshed her.

* * *

Having gone by his school handing in a history essay on ancient Rome, Podric was on the bus coming into Drinkwell. Alighting at the village green rather than Briony Close – he decided he would go and see how George Benedict was getting on at Ivy's.

Although Podric knew where she lived, he had never been to Mrs Bickerstaff's cottage. Situated at the end of a long lane off the green, the tarmac surface gave way to a dirt track. Several hundred yards further on Podric heard a distinctive sound before he saw Ivy's dwelling. Eamon's squawk resonated across the countryside. The cottage was on the edge of a field, and the garden was overgrown. Podric approached its rotted front gate. George and Ivy sat in a couple of old chairs on the front stoep. A hot afternoon, Benedict was jacketless. Bright braces supported his trousers. Ivy wore a gaudy and none-too-clean Mother Hubbard. Both were laughing and enjoying a drink. Untethered, Eamon swooped into land. Perching on a rail, the macaw preened his magnificent plumage.

"Hi Podric. Wondered if you'd be coming by?"

Pushing open the gate Podric approached them. Picking up a plastic jug of Pimm's, Ivy refilled Benedict's glass.

"Like some? It's just the thing on a day like this."

Podric said he wouldn't mind a drop. Ivy raised her ample body and stroked Eamon briefly as she went into the house. George said.

"Sorry if I barged in on you last night. Truth be told things have been a bit stressful."

Ivy returned with a plastic beaker and poured Podric some of the fruit cup. Thanking her, Podric quickly drank it down.

"Thirsty, huh? It's deceptive."

Looking out at the recently cut cornfield, Ivy sighed. The late afternoon sun was beginning to dip. It had been a perfect summers day. Benedict stood up.

"Fancy a walk Podric? I could do with stretching my legs."

Eamon hopped along the fence towards the computer games man.

"I tell yer George, my bird loves yer. 'Never seen 'im like that. He likes Podric, but you."

Eamon nuzzled Benedict's arm. Benedict stroked the bird as if he was used to macaw assiduity. Then putting his wrist under its claws, he gently moved Eamon on to the arm of Ivy's chair.

"Anything I can get you Mrs B while we're out?"

"Godiver's don't stock Nutri-Berries. The rogue's got no taste has he my beauty."

Vociferating, the macaw pushed his neck into Ivy's hand for continued attention.

Crossing the track Podric and Benedict walked round the edge of the field. For a while neither spoke. Reaching a style – the English landscape stretched away from them.

"I love this country."

Benedict scratched the back of his neck.

"You sound as though you're visiting."

"I am."

They walked on.

"Ever been to Vegas?"

Recalling what Benedict had told him about his gambling compulsion, Podric replied that he hadn't.

"Ha. Everyone should once. Lost most of my money there."

"Reminds you of Vegas, does it this?"

Benedict laughed.

"I love being back in England. One of the reasons I love it is the use of language."

Benedict stopped again. He seemed to want to take in every last detail of the countryside.

"Nowhere else do people say something with such apparent innocence when they mean the exact opposite. You have to be English to get it. Ha. I can see why Archie rates you."

"Not on that basis."

Benedict didn't seem to hear. When he next spoke, his tone was different.

"They're bastards Podric. Rottweilers. Once they get their teeth into you they never let up."

They walked on.

"I was going to ask about this other reality stuff, but I guess you don't want to talk about it."

"Why do you want to know?"

"No reason. Just seemed... interesting. Having a lifetime in the games industry I've never been much of a player. Sometimes when designing a game though, one could sort of feel one was in amongst it – creating things that were so lifelike."

Podric didn't reply. It wasn't until they'd crossed another field that he suddenly realised they were approaching the Trout & Eel – the pub by the weir he and Archie sometimes went to. Entering the garden, who should Podric and George come across but Barney and Cosima sitting at a table. Addressing Podric, Cosima said.

"What did you expect me to do – give up on your blocking tactic?"

Podric smiled.

"Good move. With Barney's proficiency you won't have a problem."

Barney fired off an expletive. Benedict not understanding the conversation smiled at Cosima.

"You're Archie's daughter, aren't you?"

She turned to him.

"I can see the resemblance to your mother."

Cosima looked questioningly at Benedict.

"Did we meet?"

"It was several years back. You were twelvish I think."

"Whereas now I'm an old maid of eighteen!"

Introduced to Barney, Benedict volunteered to get a round and went off to the bar. Cosima said to Podric.

"What's the deal with him?"

She nodded towards the pub.

"'Came to see your dad."

"About?"

"See your dad."

"You're a close file Podric."

"Tell me about it. Never get anything out of Pod."

Picking up an old navy kit bag he used to carry his schoolbooks, Barney was dismissive. Benedict reappeared carrying a tray of drinks – a glass of white wine and three beers. Glasses were raised.

"You came to see pa."

George's eyes flitted to Podric then Cosima.

"I was in England and thought I'd look him up. We go back some."

"Based in America are you?"

"Have been."

Benedict drank his beer.

"Can't find that bloody book."

Barney tossed notes and files on the table. Podric said.

"Is it important?"

"Oah – I've got to get some work in."

"Doing it here?"

"Make a start when you lot piss off."

"Walking back to Wendbury are you?"

Cosima sipped her wine.

"Get a cab."

"Come in to the money, huh? – new pad and all."

"Ah, got it."

Barney took out a chunky volume on filmmaking.

"What are you studying?"

Trying to see the book Cosima was interested.

"Economics, Film Studies and History. Everyone in UAR's doing H. Crawford can't understand it. Your other one's Applied Maths isn't it Moonface?"

Ignoring Barney's euphemism, Podric drank his beer. Barney flicked open the book.

"Got to get something in on Stanley Kubrick. Unusual geezer he was. Amazing stuff. More your time I guess George. That *Dr. Strangelove* and *2001* – interesting flicks."

"I'm surprised you're not into *A Clockwork Orange* Barney. Surely Alex DeLarge is more up your street – all that ultraviolence and his little droogs."

Although Podric had seen *A Clockwork Orange*, he was somehow surprised Cosima knew the film.

"Didn't know you were into movies."

"There's a lot about me you don't know Podric."

Cosima finished her glass of wine.

"Dad is too – in fact we all are. We go over to the little preview theatre in the tower. Movies are a big thing in Light land."

"Once upon a time..."

George Benedict stared into his beer glass.

"You alright Mr Benedict?"

Cosima picked up her bag.

"Like another pint?"

"'Think I'd better make a move."

"I can give you a lift if you like. If Mr Films is starting his essay, I'm heading back to Drinkwell."

"I might go back to Wendbury and meet mum."

Podric finished his beer.

"Drop you there, then."

Cosima stood up.

"Be with you in a minute, gentlemen."

She went off to the loo. Barney began watching *Dr. Strangelove* on an iPad – George C. Scott muttering about foreign substances and precious bodily fluids.

"Sap and impurify... Far out!"

Podric and Benedict headed for the car park.

"I'll stroll across the fields to Mrs Bickerstaff's."

"Sure? Cosima's going to Drinkwell. She's just dropping me en route."

"No. I-. The walk's good."

"Like me to come with you? Meeting my mother's flexible."

"No. Er- you go on. My best to your mum."

Benedict turned away.

"Mr Benedict. George. Are you okay?"

Podric was concerned.

"Yes, fine. Something threw me a little, that's all."

"Something we said?"

Reappearing, Cosima rummaged around her bag looking for her car keys.

"No. Er-."

Finding them, she walked round to the driver's door. Benedict turned to Podric.

"The film studies.."

"'Nothing you can't do at A level now."

Benedict seemed agitated.

"Stanley Kubrick – some weird things."

Catching this, Cosima opened her car door.

"Great film maker wasn't he."

Benedict glanced at her then back at Podric. Cosima got into her Mini Cooper.

"Just... what I was saying about rottweilers and the evil world of business."

Benedict fiddled with his braces and continued.

"P'raps, p'raps we'll talk again."

"How long are you here for?"

"Oh, er-. Reckon a few more days."

"Seeing Archie again?"

George Benedict didn't reply. Turning on his heel he set off through the pub garden. For several seconds Podric watched him go. Archie's ex-games creator was certainly a rum cove. Podric wasn't sure he was getting the whole nine yards from him – or even the half of it.

Chapter 8
Legal Desires

"Going down the conspiracist road, are you?"

Sitting in Blairs – the same Mayfair restaurant Kaliska's senior partner Monty Limmerson had entertained Archie at when Ms Monroe first met him, Podric and Catherine were enjoying themselves. A number of patrons wore suits, but the dress code wasn't universal and the two young people in their smart casual clothes weren't out of place.

"I wasn't looking for it. Just seems there's a lot of this stuff around with JFK."

Their meal nearly over, a half empty bottle of Sancerre and a beer were left on the table. Kaliska eyed her guests.

"It's his assassination – that and the moon."

"Why?"

Catherine sipped her wine.

"The assassination – because there are so many conflicting theories as to who might have done it."

"And the moon?"

"Kennedy was the person who publicly kick started the project. After he was shot and the decade unfolded, it gave rise to all sorts of theories. Did the Americans actually land on the moon? Was there some kind of cover up? Most people think it's all crazy, but conspiracy theories abound."

"And you're interested in this stuff."

Catherine studied Kaliska. Her cool gaze gave nothing away.

"With Kennedy's assassination so much so it's the only time I ever flunked a law paper."

Looking at Catherine's concerned face, Kaliska laughed and

put a hand over hers.

"I was born twenty years to the day of his death – November 22nd."

"You're a Scorpio."

Kaliska nodded. Podric mentally worked out his solicitor's age.

"When I was ten, a news item came up on television. Thirty years since Dallas – I was transfixed. Somehow because it was my birthday I felt I had some strange affinity with it. Of course, rubbish – it doesn't matter. I was hooked. In my teens I got hold of every bit of information I could. What and who in America would want to murder Kennedy. Whether it was the work of a rogue government body, the LBJ/FBI theory, the Mafia or a lone killer. The CIA coverup. Influences from abroad – Castro and Cuba. On the day, lax security, absence of the secret service, trajectory of Oswald's rifle – the feasibility of hitting JFK. Other shots. I was consumed."

"And taking Podric and me to lunch today you still are – wanting to get back inside his world."

Catherine sipped some wine.

"Or desperate."

Podric drank his beer.

"What's the link with Stanley Kubrick?"

Kaliska smiled.

"Another conspiracy thing. I'm not so clued up on all that – something to do with faking the lunar landings I believe."

She finished her wine.

"'Still don't quite get JFK and peoples fascination."

Podric polished off his Peroni. Kaliska swept some imaginary crumbs from the tablecloth.

"An indefinable something – an intangible connection with the public."

"What, like Lady Di?"

"That's a comparison. Tends to involve people who sail too close to the sun if you'll pardon the galactic pun."

Her mobile vibrated. Kaliska checked a message then put down the device.

"When you look at that time – the late fifties – men and women seem dowdy. World War Two ending only fifteen years previously – its global effect was shattering. The world order changed. Two countries emerged as superpowers – America and the Soviet Union. The Iron Curtain, the Cold War, the nuclear arms race. Perhaps the planet was never in more danger because for the first-time mankind had the ability to destroy itself outright."

She fiddled distractedly with her iPhone on the table.

"Into this, steps Kennedy – good looking, intelligent, charismatic. A new decade – the world went crazy for him. Maybe more internationally than in America itself. A million people turned out to see Kennedy in Berlin. He had the Germans at his feet. We now know he was unwell, on high levels of medication and his private morality was at the least, dubious. His reputation's tarnished. But for a while – just a thousand days, it felt like someone special was around. He somehow lifted people and they saw a brighter future. That's a powerful elixir."

"Not convinced."

Catherine finished her wine.

"What I mean is I think what you're saying came about because he was killed. Gunning someone down when they're in their prime adds a dimension. It romanticises things. I read LBJ got a lot of social reforms through congress because while he was an operator on the Hill, America felt guilty about what had happened. It was a kind of a guilt trip, an absolution."

Kaliska was impressed.

"You two are formidable!"

Podric ignored her compliment.

"But what you really want to do is learn how to get in and out of UAR on your own."

"That's brutal Podric."

"And true."

"Okay. I would like to learn, yes."

Offering some wine to Catherine who declined, Kaliska poured the remainder of it into her glass. Podric looked at her.

"That's the second time in twenty-four hours I've had such a request. If I didn't know better I'd say people want me to become superfluous to requirements."

"Isn't that a military phrase?"

Podric smiled sadly. "Dad."

Both women knew Podric's father had been a serving officer in the RAF. It was left to Kaliska to break the silence.

"But to go in again. Are we soon?"

Catherine looked at her boyfriend. Podric sat back in his chair, his gaze shifting from his lawyer to his girlfriend.

"You both that interested?"

Catherine replied.

"Wouldn't you be if you had the chance to be the first women to walk on the moon?"

*   *   *

"What are you going to do?"

On their way home, Catherine and Podric sat in the train at Waterloo station.

"Archie's right about one thing. At thirty-three why would someone with so much going for her be so desperate about UAR?"

The train began to move. As it left the station Catherine gazed out at London.

"Do you think it's alternative reality or President Kennedy?"

Podric shrugged.

"One thing's for sure, she's in love with him – or thinks she is."

"How do you know?"

Catherine laughed.

"You don't need woman's intuition Podric when something so blatant's staring you in the face."

"Is that how you feel about me then?"

"No!"

She pushed him winsomely.

"So, you're taking me on the first woman's lunar landing."

"Uhuh."

Podric shook his head. Catherine was instantly on guard. Podric dead panned.

"Moon."

Chapter 9
Presents Past

Current costs running to several million dollars for a fully perfected game created with all the resources available to developers at the major computer companies – the fact that Podric and Archie had marketed two successful conventional ones – *Agrolution* and *Issandro Iguana* since their union said much about their abilities. With such skills it was perhaps not quite so surprising they'd been able to turn Podric's Ultimate Alternative Reality dream into its unique form of an alternate existence.

Given recent pressures and his own increasing interest, Podric decided to delve deeper into Kennedy's life using his mind path state. When he'd left Jack Kennedy in the White House swimming pool, removing Kaliska and himself from UAR, Podric had no idea if he'd ever return to JFK's world. With the many other options open to him, he wasn't sure if he particularly wanted to. However, more on a whim, Podric decided that before resuming adventures in early 1960s Washington he'd look at expanding *Reloaded* – broadening its scope to accommodate an enlarged period of Kennedy's life. In fact, all of it. Checking out Jack's birth, *JFK and His World* would commence 29th May 1917 and Podric would create an open-ended expiry date after 22nd November 1963.

Working in his partner's computer laboratory, Podric also considered creating a games situation that would see all America's presidents – from George Washington to Kennedy meeting at the White House. Those presidents JFK had wanted to be introduced to more personally Podric positioned in a folder and created private rendezvous opportunities.

Discussing things with Archie – as well as Lincoln they decided to add several other presidents to the list. George Washington and Thomas Jefferson were givens as well as Franklin Roosevelt. Archie thought FDR's distant cousin Teddy, twenty odd years senior might also be interesting. Although JFK had been excited by Podric meeting Napoleon, the computer games youth passed on including the French emperor preferring to make it an all-American affair. Although this work wasn't taken to anything like games level – both *JFK and His World* and *Presidents 1789-1963* were in effect files of metadata tacked into games such as *Power Politics* and *The Political Machine*. Not for public consumption, they would serve their purpose.

Studying their developing game creation Podric and Archie also considered presidents' wives and other characters who might add layer cake to the presidential format. Looking at the men's marital partners, two Marthas – Washington and Jefferson, Lincoln's wife Mary Todd Lincoln and Jackie, JFK's – by far the most formidable was FDR's wife. Eleanor Roosevelt was a powerful character who, whilst not serving in elected office, achieved a considerable political profile in her own right.

All the presidents were surrounded by some larger than life characters no one more so than Kennedy. His brother Bobby would come to play a leading role in US political life as Attorney General and then run for president himself before being gunned down. More contentiously, their boot-legging father Joe – one of the richest men in America and hangers on like the entertainment star Frank Sinatra with his Mafia connections – all laid claim to a place at JFK's computer games table.

"Along with that FBI bastard J. Edgar Hoover."

Archie was forceful.

"There's so much sleaze in these administrations."

Then came Podric and Archie's partners and friends.

"I presume my co-party organiser would like some adventure in this."

Aware Archie was referring to Catherine, Podric said.

"If I ever forgive her – and you."

"Hmm... I'll ask Charlotte if she's interested though I know what the answer will be. Likely she'll want to meet Jackie."

"And Cosima an intern?"

"What?! Not on your life – not with that randy goat around."

Archie got up and went to the fridge.

"If he had half the women he's supposed to it leaves about five nights in a thousand when he wasn't screwing someone."

Podric wasn't very interested in discussing JFK's sexual she-nanigans.

"So, what then?"

Returning with a couple of cans of beer, Archie tossed one to Podric.

"Didn't you say part of this adventure will involve a trip to the moon?"

"Haven't got there yet."

"Maybe they didn't if you listen to the conspiracists."

Pulling the beer tab, Podric took a swig.

"You're kidding? You really believe that stuff?"

Archie opened his beer can.

"I'll find her a nice little niche down there in Houston and make sure I have control."

"Who's to say something wouldn't happen to her in Texas?"

"You're a little ray of sunshine."

Archie drank deeply.

"What about Limmerson Bart's new senior partner?"

Podric had his own way of phrasing things. Less original than his sisters word creation, it was still distinct. He continued.

"Her surname being what it is – I watched Marilyn sing the president 'Happy Birthday' on *YouTube*."

Some performance."

"Yeah, and three months later she was dead."

Chapter 10
From Clean to Murky Waters

Opening his eyes, for several seconds George Benedict didn't know where he was. Normally a light sleeper and a man with much on his mind, he'd slept surprisingly well. The night had been mild and George had opted to kip down on Ivy's veranda. Sitting up on his camp bed in the early light of dawn he gazed out at the recently harvested cornfields. In the few days he'd been staying with Mrs Bickerstaff it was a view he'd come to be fond of. The peace, the natural rhythm of life – it was good for the soul.

Eamon choosing to spend the night in his mistresses' room, Benedict padded round to the back of Ivy's little habitat untroubled by the scarlet macaws' interruptions. Raising the handle of an outside pump, he splashed water over his face. Reaching for a none-too-clean towel, Benedict dried his face and went into the kitchen. Preparing coffee – the proper stuff – it was while he was cleaning an old percolator that he chanced to look through the serving hatch. Its view through the house and lane beyond – George watched an SUV with blackened windows slowly making its way down the track. Instinctively certain it was bad news he silently left the kitchen. Going into the garden, Benedict darted to the hedge. Peering through a gap, he saw the vehicle was having trouble turning round. Taking a pair of small field glasses from his pocket, George watched as two men get out. Sporting earpieces – Benedict had dodged too many figurative bullets as well as the odd literal one not to know Agency operatives when he saw them. The stupid bastards. It was time to go – and sadly without saying goodbye to his hostess. Packing up his few belongings George disappeared into Ivy's overgrown garden. When he'd gone, there was no trace of Benedict ever having been at the property save a small badge he'd hidden in Eamon's cage. Extremely rare, only twelve were ever struck. Possessed by those dozen men who claimed to have walked on the moon, its face featured what looked like an inch of rock. On the reverse was the motto 'multi autem sunt vocati pauci vero electi'. Many are called, but few are chosen – it was Benedict's prize possession.

* * *

At school that day, Podric was absorbed in his maths tutorial. Although his algorithmic abilities were phenomenal, Podric's overall mathematical talents varied. Applied maths came naturally to him, but pure he found challenging. His main maths teacher Mr Ravenglass was a boffin and though some students had difficulties understanding some concepts, Podric found elegant solutions satisfying. It was his maths talents that enabled him to write computer games and had been so critical in creating the codebases necessary to formulate Ultimate Alternative Reality.

It was lunchtime before Podric checked his phone and picked up the message from his mother.

"Mrs Bickerstaff's just left the office with Dr Light."

It amused Podric how sometimes his mother referred to Archie more formally – as if his doctorate had significance.

"She's extremely agitated. Apparently George has disappeared."

Not overly fazed, Podric called her back. "What did Archie say?"

"He's been concerned from the moment I called him."

A little later Podric received a text from Archie. His business partner said that he would be at Catherine's at the end of the afternoon and to meet him there after school. Podric knew that his girlfriend didn't have any tutorials that day and was working from home. It was all a bit strange.

Leaving school at the end of the day, Podric made his way to Dearbourne. No car was parked outside the house and walking up the drive, everything looked very shut up. Arriving at the front door, it was opened before he pressed the bell.

The scene that greeted Podric could best be described as incongruous. Sitting in the Halliday's living room Ivy Bickerstaff was drinking a cup of tea. Eamon's portable cage was on the floor beside her and the prince of macaws had perched himself on a tree-like lamp stand. Carved in wood, it could have been made for the bird. Sitting in another chair Archie was drinking whisky. Podric accepted a beer from Catherine.

"Hi Podric."

Smiling her single tooth smile, whatever adventures Mrs Bickerstaff had had that day she outwardly appeared none the worse for wear.

"'Knew sumthin' wos up. I don't rise early but I could tell in a flash 'e'd gone."

Ivy drank her tea.

"It weren't just everythin' folded up – it wos like 'e was never there."

Eamon squawked. Mrs Bickerstaff belched.

"Not 'alf an hour later I'm makin' me breakfast noggin. This 'ere vehicle come lurchin' along. Cor, they don't 'alf look daft. Wearin' dark glasses, radio'n each other. 'Ad a chuckle when their big motor got stuck."

Ivy finished the rest of her Lipton's.

"I'm sittin' watchin' 'em make a pig's ear of it – finally, they come through the gate. Talkin' all American, my boy'ud bin flyin' about 'an 'e come back buzzin' the critters. Ooaah they didn't like that. When folks start criticisin' me, Eamon gets upset. Bombin' 'em 'e wos. Got a drop of whisky luv?"

Catherine smiled and went over to a drinks' cabinet. Taking out a crystal glass, she poured a healthy measure of Glenlivet and handed it to Ivy.

"'The ticket. Ta."

Recharging Archie's glass, Catherine put the scotch away.

"They're bangin' about gettin' all hoity toity – 'you've 'ad someone stayin''. 'We're on to you' so I let's 'em rant a bit till they start gettin' threatenin'."

Ivy enjoyed her whisky.

"'E's a funny old stick is Eric Paxman, but a while back 'e give me 'is number. When these johnnies show up I had a feelin' they'd get pushy an' I sent 'im a text. Blow me down if little Ravelious don't appear in 'is Vauxhall. Nice inside - heated seats 'an all."

"Guess he needs them in this weather."

Archie's dig and the fact that it was 80° Fahrenheit outside wasn't lost on Ivy.

"Yeah, likely."

She had some more scotch.

"All very plod like - 'Just passin'' 'e says. 'Just passin' my eye. No one passes my gaff. Anyway, these yankee geezers don't like it - the old Brit bill pokin' around, an' pretty soon they hop off. But Ravelious givin' me a lift, I see 'em in the village."

"So have I."

It was Archie's turn to have some whisky.

"Did they follow you?"

Podric swigged his beer.

"Not as far as I could tell. Ravi - 'e got all Maigret like - check-in' and double backin'. Right little Luther."

"Where did he drop you?"

"Your mum's work. We'd agreed. Doc met me back of their loading bay. Ravi loved it. 'Don't get a lot of this cloak an' dagger stuff around 'ere' 'e says. 'Why I joined the force.'"

She finished her whisky.

"I don't want nuthin' 'appenin' to Mr George. We likes Mr George, don't we Eamon?"

Cawing his agreement, the bird adjusted himself on his perch.

"Anyway, Podric what I want to know is when are we goin' into your computer world again. Take Constable Ravelious along for one of your adventures. Be fun for 'im. 'E might even make sergeant!"

Leaving Catherine to fix Mrs Bickerstaff another drink, Podric and Archie went out into the Halliday's garden. Ivy's story and her handling of the situation didn't surprise the young computer champion. Podric's belief – accurate or otherwise – was that Ivy hid a lot about her past. Being one of the first people he profiled into UAR he had seen her resilience in alternative reality. When in Paris freeing some royalists in *Napoleonic Wars* Ivy was housekeeper at the unoccupied British embassy residence. With an array of home-made defences at her disposal she had been formidable – holding off numerous French revolutionary forays and showing them no quarter.

"This is serious."

Archie looked tense.

"These goons are heavyweight."

"What do you mean?"

"I mean this isn't just some company rights ownership row. Gorillas like this are the dark force."

"You're talking games speak. Anyway, what has these people turning up got to do with anything?"

Archie scowled.

"Maybe nothing, but George appearing unannounced, me being served with legal papers – and now these punks arriving at Bird Woman's place doesn't bode well."

"Hold on Archie. This last lot maybe nothing to do with you or George."

"Oh? You really think these tree huggers in their blacked-out Chevy SUV sporting short wave radios and likely semi-automatic firearms just dropped by?"

Archie paced up and down.

"You heard the aged ornithological wonder – they knew George had been there and turned the heat on her."

"Sure you're not paranoid?"

"No I am not sure!"

Archie was nervy.

"These types don't piss around Podric. Undercover secret service operators aren't people you want to mess with."

"Are you serious?"

"Deadly."

"What government and stuff?"

"Yeah, likely American."

Because he was only seventeen, the seriousness of the situation didn't alarm Podric quite as much as it might have done.

"What to do then?"

"What to do indeed, Podric."

Archie took a turn around the Halliday's neat back garden which was bordered by tall trees. He said.

"I'll think about that. George has obviously gone to earth. For his sake I hope it's a deep burrow."

*   *   *

"There's been some developments. Our man's disappeared."

There was silence on the other end of the line. Looking out of Secorni's penthouse office in Berkeley Square, Prendergast was agitated. Though he'd known Cy Zaentz for a number of years he still found his CEO intimidating.

"You've made enquiries?"

The voice was quiet. It was barely a question.

"Limited. The authorities here – it's thought intervention's foreign."

"My side of the stream."

Zaentz referred to the US. Prendergast waited for Zaentz to continue. He never did and rang off. He was a specialist at that.

Chapter 11
An Interesting Meeting

It was a triumph – JFK in his element. Not only as current president had he spent time with his hero, Thomas Jefferson, but Jack had also had tête-à-têtes with Lincoln and George Washington! Kennedy was in lively banter with Theodore Roosevelt who he got on surprisingly well with – as it turned out more easily than the younger Roosevelt cousin, Franklin Delano. It wasn't that JFK disliked Franklin, or that he felt Franklin disliked him. More, because the four-term elected president had zero respect for Kennedy's father, Joe. Having made Kennedy senior ambassador to the Court of St James in 1938, JPK's craven behaviour towards Hitler's onslaught brought about his abrupt resignation from the post. This made things initially awkward between the two presidents. Though Kennedy couldn't help but respect FDR's titanic achievements – the New Deal and guiding America through World War 2 – his own legacy gnawed at the younger man: What he would leave? How would he be remembered?

"Mixed."

Presidents past having retired, JFK sat in his rocking chair – Archie and Podric on sofas opposite each other.

"Who the hell are you?"

A little older than Kennedy, Archie explained that he was a computer games creator and Podric's partner inventing Ultimate Alternative Reality. There was a slight atmosphere in the room and Podric felt friction between Archie and the president. Archie said.

"You wanted to know about legacy."

JFK took a long look at Dr Light who continued.

"You'll forgive me Mr President. We have the benefit of history."

Kennedy appeared to relax a little.

"Well?"

"Like I say, sir, it's mixed."

That was a first. Podric had never heard Archie call anybody sir.

"Looking back, you inspired people as few other presidents have. However, several things come to light."

"Only several?"

Podric caught a twinkle in Kennedy's eye.

"Well three big ones with your assassination."

Kennedy rocked in his chair.

"Your medical history and your private life. People tend to accept the secrecy surrounding your ailments. It explains why you had to run in 1960. Longevity wasn't likely to work for you."

"It didn't."

Kennedy stopped rocking. Archie continued.

"As to your private life-."

"Which is mine."

"Not deemed so when you're President of the United States. With the perspective of history, it tarnishes you – considered unacceptable behaviour by later standards."

"And the third?"

"There's no doubt your legacy is strengthened because of your assassination. People were so shocked that you had been killed – pretty much all you'd wanted to get through congress, did. Social welfare, segregation reform...The Civil Rights Act of 1964 was landmark legislation."

"As a result of. Huh. Fitting, with Lyndon taking the credit. 'Sons of bitches."

Jack stood up.

"What are the reasons given for my assassination?"

"Some say Dallas was a coup – that elements of government wanted you got rid of and Johnson in the White House – even his implication in your removal."

Kennedy exploded.

"Lyndon? Pchwa! If he had the balls."

"Jealousy is a powerful thing."

His back giving him pain, JFK moved round the room.

"Who else? Angleton at the CIA or that bastard Hoover?"

"Depends who you listen to, but it appears you had a lot of enemies."

At first Kennedy didn't react then said.

"Difficult to grasp – being removed so... abruptly."

Archie was considered.

"Your rows with the intelligence agencies – potentially bypassing them. The military pressing for greater involvement in Vietnam and your hesitation."

"Bastards. After the Bay of Pigs-."

"They blamed you for the failure to depose Castro."

Archie actually cut in!

"Then there's your desire for improved relations with the Soviets. Your antagonists couldn't have you for weakness after the missile crisis but it's solution wasn't how they wanted it."

"Quite a list."

"That's just the governmental stuff."

Archie sat forward.

"Others being involved in some kind of plot – and a lot of people think there was one – you entered dangerous territory having an affair with Judith Campbell. Her connections with the Mafia, the mob and organised crime."

Walking over to the Resolution desk, JFK looked at some papers. Archie continued.

"Then there's family antagonisms. While many areas of the country regard your family as some kind of American royalty, others dislike the Kennedy's."

JFK looked up.

"Surely we're bullseye with the immigrant story."

"Not so much you, but your father was pretty much loathed, and your brother's tough talk and aggressive attitude alienated him from a lot of people though that changed some after you were shot."

"Politics is a rough business."

"Given looks and talent – a theory I have is that some people in government felt threatened by your family – that the Kennedys could take over the country. Your brother in congress, others one day in the senate – another attorney general maybe – in time more Kennedy presidents.."

"What's Bobby's take?"

"Publicly he never said. He and Martin Luther King were assassinated themselves within months of each other a few years after you were. King – April '68 in Memphis. Your brother, June 6th in Los Angeles that same year."

"Grim decade."

JFK was extraordinarily philosophical. Archie nodded to Podric who using UAR, projected a holographic screen on to an Oval Office wall. The imagery that played out revealed King's assassination and Kennedy's brother, Bobby's. It made harrowing viewing. The clip continued with JFK's arrival at the Dallas Trade Mart where he was to have spoken after his motorcade through the city. Using voice recognition techniques of the speech he never gave, Kennedy heard it.

"Had your life continued that day... It's been put together from thousands of recordings of your voice."

Podric deactivated the screen. Archie continued.

"As to your future it's debatable whether you could have kept the lid on your private life through '64."

Kennedy looked at them and flicked a switch on his phone system.

"Mrs Lincoln – I'll be dining with my wife this evening. Please ensure my visitors have everything they need."

Kennedy came round the desk.

"Gentlemen. Do we have the particular experience of meeting again?"

"Depends if we follow through with your adventure."

Archie stood up.

"Are you interested in tracking down your killers?"

Kennedy shrugged.

"Doesn't make a lot of difference to me. I'm dead."

Because they were in a game, items of the future were featured. On a coffee table lay a copy of Jed Mercurio's *American Adulterer* published in 2009. Archie said.

"Your well-known speed reading skills would have digested this pretty quickly."

"The use of 'subject' is interesting."

Walking to the door of the Oval Office, Kennedy turned.

"Is there anything else you want to tell me?"

"Is there anything else you want to know?"

For several seconds JFK stood deep in thought.

"Guess it's tempting to ask about one's family – my son and daughter."

For once Archie didn't reply.

"President Kennedy."

Kennedy looked across the Oval Office. Podric stood up.

"I lost my father. He was killed in a flying accident. I'd been a computer games champion. Missing him desperately, it's why I dreamed this up – UAR I mean."

Kennedy came forward.

"I'm sorry. Losing a parent when young is difficult. Have you found your alternative reality beneficial?"

"It's been the best thing I ever created."

JFK studied Podric.

"I can understand that. You've made another world for yourself. I wouldn't have minded having it available sometimes."

Kennedy smiled.

"Thank you for telling me Podric. Dr Light."

JFK turned away.

"President Kennedy."

There was an intensity in Podric's voice. Kennedy stopped again. A look of irritation flashed across his face.

"President Kennedy – if... There maybe some things we want to look into, find out about and help someone in trouble. Would you help us if we needed you?"

Kennedy's eyes locked with UAR's young creators.

"You mean use this time – 1963 to learn about something that happens in the future..?"

"Yes."

Kennedy grinned his Irish smile. Watching him Archie suddenly saw how infectious his charm was.

"Why Podric I think that would be very interesting, very interesting indeed."

JFK turned away.

"And Mr President."

Podric had difficulty keeping his voice steady.

"If you're with us you're going to find out. Your son is killed in a flying accident in 1999."

The colour drained out of Kennedy's ever-brown face.

"That made him 38 – younger than me."

"He'd been married for three years. No children."

"And Caroline?"

"She's alive and well. Married with two girls and a boy. He's known as Jack."

Chapter 12
The Secrets of Secorni

Carla Logan wasn't one for conspiracy theories. Working as American PA to the European head of the world's second largest computer games company and based in London, she had recently experienced disquietude with her employers. Although Carla had antipathy towards Archie Light who historically had been very successful for Secorni – learning of a subterfuge being played on him, she was uncomfortable with proceedings. Deciding to research matters on her own, it was a surprise that the research came to her.

Living in an expensive apartment complex in Kensington, Carla was late in that night. A nervy Saul Prendergast had demanded some work be completed for submission to their masters in California which kept her at the office. Kicking off her sling-backs as the buzzer went, Carla hadn't been advised by reception anyone was visiting her. Looking up at a security screen whose camera covered the hall, she saw George Benedict standing on the mat. Opening the door with the chain still in place, Carla peered out. Benedict said.

"Er-. We have met."

The two stared at each other.

"Yes? What can I do for you?"

"I'm not sure."

Several seconds went by before Carla undid the door chain. George Benedict didn't move.

"You do know-, know who I am?"

"Yes."

Benedict entered hesitantly. Never one to appreciate his surroundings much, he followed Carla into her apartment.

"Would you like a drink?"

"That would be very kind."

"Scotch?"

"Thank you."

Carla busied herself getting her guest his refreshment. Handing a glass of whisky to Benedict, she poured herself a Drambuie.

"Nearest thing I get to the hard stuff."

She raised her glass.

"If we have something to drink to. By the by – how did you get in?"

"They had a fire alarm."

He smiled. Carla smiled. Standing in her open plan kitchen, she indicated a seat in her living area. The room was comfortable – two leather sofas and a matching chair, a large wall mounted television screen along with several tasteful but uninspiring pictures. Benedict stayed where he was. Carla did too.

"So, you know what your bosses are up to – or have an idea..?

"That's a big supposition."

Carla moved into her living area.

"Mind drawing your curtains?"

"You're kidding me – cloak and dagger."

Benedict still didn't move. Carla pressed a switch and her curtains began to close.

"Go on."

"The legal thing they're trying to work is only the surface. There are longer tentacles."

"Hey now. How delusional are you?"

Carla put down her drink.

"Insufficiently not to know armed goons when I see them. Yesterday half a dozen turned up in Archie's little Hampshire village enquiring after my whereabouts."

"And why would they be doing that?"

"Like I say, what's going down company wise skims the top."

"What do you mean?"

"I mean that some members of Secorni's management are in

cahoots with the government."

"CIA? Intelligence? Why?"

Benedict finally moved away from the wall and came and sat down. He still looked ill at ease.

"That's a good question. I believe it has to do with a game I did some analysis on. It was a while after I'd finished working with Archie."

"What's a computer game got to do with anything?"

Benedict sipped his drink.

"Ever heard about innocents who stumble on things they didn't know they had?" Carla looked doubtful.

"The game I was involved with had several strange characteristics about it. Developed by the firm you work for, you never heard of it."

Carla didn't react.

"You never heard of it because it never came out."

Carla sipped her drink.

"Called *Moon Landing* – weeks after I started on it, helping the team who'd begun its development, people seemed to disappear. Not only were they on other assignments, their employ was apparently terminated."

George Benedict had a slug of scotch.

"Secorni had decided they only wanted technology available in the '60s to be featured in the game. They thought it would add authenticity. One of the challenges *Moon Landing* offered was flying a lunar module and landing it on the moon's surface. An icon that kept reappearing on the menu while building the game was 'Failure'." The games man finished his whisky.

"You've got to remember the algorithms I was working with were pretty primordial. In spite of over riding the math to create the contest, the more one analysed the figures, the more one wondered how man ever landed on the damned place."

Carla got up and took Benedict's empty glass.

"This all sounds ludicrous. You really that paranoid?"

"Yes."

* * *

"I don't think it's a very good idea Mrs Bickerstaff goes home this evening."

Standing in the Halliday's kitchen, Archie took some cutlery from Catherine who was busy cooking.

"Neither do I."

"Really?"

"Well it wouldn't be, would it? If all this is as serious as you say, people will be looking for her." Catherine said.

"What about you? Won't they be watching your movements?"

"Likely. Can I crash here tonight and figure out where to take her in the morning?"

"Be my guest. Now go and set the table will you?"

Catherine adjusted the heat under a saucepan.

That evening at supper the atmosphere was thoughtful.

"It's been decided you'll stay here tonight. It's for your own safety Mrs Bickerstaff."

Ivy's only molar slowly masticated its way around a mouthful of macaroni cheese. Sipping some red wine, Archie continued.

"In fact, I'm not sure when it will be safe for you to go back to your house."

Ivy, Catherine, Podric and Archie were sitting in the Halliday's dining room enjoying their supper. Presiding over them all, Eamon perched on the arm of a chair at the head of the table.

"Can't stay 'ere forever."

"Can't stay 'ere forever."

The macaw was in a cheeky mood.

"Nor will you Ivy – or Eamon." The bird cocked his head.

"You've got to give us a little time to shift the trail."

Podric raised a finger at Eamon 'shift the trail'.

Eamon looked put out. Ivy asked.

"How are you gonna do that then?"

"Carry the fight to the enemy."

"Bold's always best."

Podric couldn't stop Eamon repeating that one.

*   *   *

Standing in her kitchen Carla recharged George Benedict's glass.

"So, you really think your working on a lunar landing computer game led the authorities to come after you."

Carla handed Benedict his drink.

"Through Secorni – yes. Believing someone – me – had discovered something they didn't want people to know about they squashed *Moon Landing* being released."

"Was that so serious?"

Benedict looked at Carla archly.

"You're not that naïve. Even then games costs could run into millions."

"Why's this re-surfacing now do you suppose?"

Carla sipped her drink.

"Because they're trying to pressure me into screwing Archie."

"What's Archie Light got to do with any of this?"

"Nothing except he's working with this boy wonder Secorni are desperate to secure the services of."

Carla studied Benedict.

"Supposing any of this fantastic story had credence – what exactly do you think they thought you'd found out?"

"That the whole Apollo mission project – man walking on the moon never happened."

"That's rubbish!"

"Call it that if you like but there's some very strange stuff that's occurred."

Carla sipped her Drambuie.

"Given such gobbledegook – I still don't get Archie Light's involvement?"

"Because there's rumour he and this boy have discovered some other type of reality."

"What do you mean?"

"A form of reality inside a computer game – some kind of alternate reality."

"And that would be threatening because it would blow every

conventional game out of the water."

"Not only that – think if they got into the matrix of *Moon Landing*."

"You mean then get access to what you say people are so frightened of being found out about."

"Uhuh."

"Ridiculous."

Carla finished her drink.

"What's the name of this boy partner of Archie's?"

"Moon. Podric Moon."

"You are kidding. Perfect name. Sums up all this craziness."

Chapter 13
Carrying the Light

Taking a taxi to Wendbury station, it was unusual for Archie Light to travel by train to town, but particular times required particular transport. It being necessary to keep a low profile – for all Archie's love of them, on the road Facel Vegas stood out like a jewel in the crown.

Grabbing a cab at Waterloo Archie crossed the Thames to Berkeley Square. Arriving unannounced at the offices of the company he now regarded as his nemesis, he approached the reception desk. Fiona finished issuing a pass to a visitor and smiled at the computer games creator.

"Dr Light."

"Good morning."

Archie was coldly polite.

"Before you ask, I don't have an appointment with the odious Saul, but he will see me."

Recognising Archie's mood, Fiona smiled nervously.

"I don't think Mr Prendergast's here. Let me check."

In his desire to come face to face with the reviled Prendergast, Archie hadn't considered the man might not be at his office. Fiona tapped into her internal phone system and spoke in that subdued tone receptionists have. Finally, she said.

"He's not in the building Dr Light, but Ms Logan's coming down."

Prepared to let his anger erupt, Archie was surprised when Carla appeared a few minutes later with her bag and jacket slung over her shoulder.

"I can't be long."

Without waiting for him to respond, she led the way across the foyer and out of the building. There was little time to talk as making a hard-left turn into a side street, Archie and Carla arrived at a café. A macchiato and double espresso ordered, they squeezed into a booth at the back.

"God I could do with a cigarette."

Tense, Carla put down her bag.

"Don't have to ask why you're here. Your pal was at my place last night."

Archie raised an eyebrow.

"He's hardly that. Anyway, it explains the off campus. He took a punt."

Carla looked at Archie.

"Didn't he." Their coffees arrived. Archie said.

"So, this isn't just about Secorni trying to screw me to get at my new partner."

"It would appear not though Mr Benedict's claims seem so far-fetched as to be almost unbelievable."

"And Cy and Saul will pay off his gambling debts if he complies."

"That's not why he's frightened."

Archie sipped his espresso while Carla began telling him about George's concerns. Though it seemed like only five minutes, they spoke for nearly half an hour. Accepting what she said more readily than the American girl might have supposed, what Carla told Archie was worrying. She looked at her watch.

"Christ – I've got to run! Saul's due in at midday."

Carla began scrambling out of the booth.

"What? Where? How?"

"GB's alright at mine for another night. Tomorrow you'll have to get him somewhere else." She turned to leave.

"Any suggestions?"

"Not right now."

Carla spun back and leant over the little table.

"Just one thing. For my silence I want some of whatever this alternate reality thing is. In this bleak world it sounds fantastic. Okay?!"

And with that she was gone. Archie ordered himself another coffee. What Carla had told him and knowing George Benedict, Archie didn't doubt the seriousness of the situation. And what would this do to Podric? Through no fault of Podric's own he was now caught up in something that was way out of either of their depths. Secorni being after Podric's services was old knowledge; he swatted their advances away on a daily basis. But Big Brother having fingered Benedict because of the reach he might have to something they thought could somehow compromise them was another matter entirely.

Sipping his espresso Archie reflected that however they'd got wind of UAR – whilst he was fairly certain the authorities wouldn't understand it – he was equally sure the powers that be wouldn't rest until they'd discovered what it was all about and had the people who created it under their control. Their concern would be that if any such entity could potentially expose their secrets it was something they simply could not afford to let happen. But exactly what were those secrets and why was it such a big deal? One thing was obvious. Whatever it was, it was of sufficient concern to have forced Secorni to close down its game, have George tracked down, and come after Podric and himself. All this was heavy fare and Archie really felt like a drink!

Chapter 14
A Trap is Laid

Whenever he thought about his subsequent actions – meeting Kaliska Monroe and getting George Benedict out of Carla Logan's apartment Archie Light could never quite believe how the series of events unfolded. At Kaliska's insistence they called Podric and it was decided the lawyer and the two partners would meet at Catherine Halliday's. Although this meant Benedict making a return to the Hampshire neighbourhood it was deemed safer that Podric and Catherine stayed where they were in Dearbourne. Neither had been into school during the last couple of days and whilst they had no proof the two pupils had been identified being linked to Benedict no one wanted to take any chances – particularly as the goons had been sighted in and around Drinkwell.

"I've seen those bad men bandits Podric stooging about in their big smokey smoke-glassed fed bed."

Reasonably up on urban slang, Podric surmised his sister meant 'fed sled' which he knew was street speak for a US government owned vehicle. As usual, Amy was sort of right.

"Waved at them."

Podric felt she was pushing her luck. He'd never been able to handle his sister and recently had given up trying.

Hiring a cab from town, Archie and George arrived at the Halliday house that afternoon. Reunited with Ivy and Eamon, Benedict was delighted and supper that night began light-heartedly. As the evening wore on Archie took the lead suggesting to his ex-games creating partner and Catherine they entertain Ivy and Eamon. He, Kaliska and Podric needed some serious discussion.

"We'll test you on Pieces of Eight later Eamon."

Podric appeared jocund as he followed the other two into Charles Halliday's study.

"Bit characterless" was Archie's verdict on Halliday senior's den.

Considering the dilemma, the first item on the agenda was to spirit Benedict away to safety. This seemed more challenging to Kaliska and Archie than it did Podric.

"With these guys around, you won't do it."

The lawyer and games creator looked at the boy.

"They're watching everything and reporting in to big brother. The only thing to do is carry things to them."

Kaliska and his business partner were non-plussed.

"If we give them the slip them now they'll keep probing about. The thing to do is get them on our side or at least neutralised."

Picking up a Playstation, Podric fiddled with the controls and fired up his laptop.

"I've been doing some work on this JFK game – expanding it."

On the laptop calculus flew across the screen. Peering at the data, Archie was gobsmacked.

"I'll say. What haven't you included?"

Podric had taken *JFK Reloaded* and written criteria that far exceeded the limited spectrum of the original game. Expanding its narrative to include a profile of Kennedy's family background and presidency plus the assassination in minute detail – under Potential Assassins as well as the usual Mafia, Castro, Maverick Government Options Podric had included Rogue Elements into the Menu.

"So, we put these SUV zombies into UAR."

Archie stared at his young partner.

"Then we do to them what you did to your Colombian friend and I did to the Romanians. Turn them around."

"O-k-a-y..."

Archie was beginning to get it.

"But José – hardly a friend you'll recall – we put into *Civil War* throwing him into its grizzliest aspects."

"Your point being?"

"With the training the bunch of operatives tailing us have it's likely they'd want to take a pop at JFK themselves if they had the chance."

"Not if they become sickened by everything they do professionally."

"How will that be achieved – making them little bunny lovers?"

Podric laughed.

"We hurl them into this."

Pulling up a game on the Playstation, Podric activated *CIA – Secret Agent* and clicked on Training.

"Adjusting their profiles to make everything they do that's violent – hit killings, aggressive physical combat, corrupt psychological analysis, lie detector tests – you name it, they react to negatively."

"They will be zombies if you do that."

"It's a great idea."

Kaliska got up.

"You guys think it's weird I'm so taken with UAR. I know you do but listening to Podric, how can you be surprised?"

Kaliska turned to look at them both.

"I wonder if you're not becoming blasé about what you've created."

Archie looked at her. Kaliska continued.

"As far as this story's concerned, it's only the beginning."

Podric continued adjusting calculus as Kaliska went on.

"All the research I've done on the assassination and other cover ups around this time – there's so much subterfuge its obscene. Can you imagine what it'll do if things are exposed through UAR?"

Kaliska was passionate. Archie said.

"It won't make any difference to the outside world. We can't change history."

"We're not trying to change history. I want to know what the authorities kept hiding and why – now. If UAR gets us into that world we can discover what their dirty little secrets were once and for all."

"Hmm... It's true these sort of guys get excited by shadows – even their own."

Podric hit his Return key.

"Time for some fun then!"

*   *   *

The weather staying fine Podric and Ivy Bickerstaff sat on the village green bench. It was early the following morning and playing a conventional computer game using an Xbox and VR visor, Podric had his school bag with him.

"Best time of the day I reckon."

Ivy waggled her lonely tooth.

As the sun rose, a faint mist began to evaporate. Eamon swooped down and landed beside them.

"What do you think about all this Ivy?"

"As long as George don't come to no 'arm blooody great."

"You just want to get into UAR again."

Podric smiled.

"Too right I do. Aye aye – that didn't take long."

Out of the corner of her eye Ivy watched the Chevy SUV trundle up towards the green. Stopping nearby the electrically operated side door opened and two agents got out.

"That's very annoying!"

Podric vented his frustration at the computer game.

"Hey kid. You got a problem?"

The speaker had an American drawl. Podric lifted the visor above his eyes.

"Any of you play computer games?"

"Computer games? Why Ethan here's uncle invented the darned things."

Although he thought this unlikely, Podric didn't respond. Wearing dark aviator glasses the archetypical agents ambled over.

"What'ya playin'?"

"Some secret service thing. It's not very difficult."

"That so? Mind if I take a look?"

Podric handed the computer kit to the agent. Sitting forward he took out his iPhone and was quickly engrossed.

"My, my – this is one of ours. Agent trainin'."

Ethan laughed. Podric said.

"I've got others."

"Have you now?"

The second agent whose name was Deke was faintly hostile.

"You interested in secret agents?"

"Not particularly. I just like winning games."

"You two know each other?"

Deke nodded at Ivy.

"How could we not, living in the same village? Eamon's a local star."

Deke looked at Podric quizzically. Ivy stroked Eamon's neck.

"You seem like a bright kid. Play a lot of games, do you?"

Podric didn't think these guys knew who he was.

"Some."

"We're lookin' for someone'."

"Yuh?"

"He's in the business."

Picking up that the men had inferred they were security agents, Podric said.

"What, spying?"

Deke laughed.

"Computers."

"Yuh?"

Deke looked at the boy and said.

"Recently arrived here."

Podric shrugged.

"Maybe the big man around here knows him?"

Deke's eyes narrowed. Podric continued.

"A computer games bloke lives in the village."

"Yeah?"

"I'm going that way. Want me to show you?"

Chapter 15
Passive Subjunctive

Whatever happened to the four agents admitted into Archie Light's computer den – the men who left several hours later were very different mentally to the aggressive operatives who walked through the door. Outwardly, they remained highly trained killers who had been tasked with an overseas mission, but after witnessing Podric's re-programming – checking their responses to aggression, deception and all kinds of interrogation – the computer games creator doubted if they'd swat a fly so passive had they become. Archie fired questions at them.

"A target's running away trying to evade capture. Your reaction?"

Deke looked queasy.

"Don't sound like sumpthin' I'd want to get involved with."

"You're primed to take out a target. You know nothing about him, but you're instructed to liquidate."

"Don't wanna know nothin' about that stuff."

Pale, agent Ethan was subdued.

Watching the vehicle go down the drive, Archie was reflective.

"Incredible. About as proactive as a bunch of conscientious objectors."

"I read some of them weren't so peaceful."

"Podric, remind me to never debate anything with you."

"They'll be contacted."

Podric clicked out of UAR. *CIA – Secret Agent* vanished before his eyes.

"And in twenty-four hours people in Langley are going to know something's up."

"So will we. Good idea of yours to tag them."

Reaching the end of the drive, the SUV turned on to the road and disappeared from view. Reflective, Archie looked down at his garden below.

"It'll be interesting to see how the powers that be react."

He went over to the Gran Gaggia machine and began to prepare coffee.

"We know about the game being stopped way back when. We also know about Secorni wanting you."

Archie pressed a button and noises began emanating from the machine.

"But UAR – what do they know about that?"

Closing out some data, Podric put the machines on standby.

"I don't think the agency knows much though they're about to learn we possess something. Sending their boys home brainwashed might suggest we have serious coercive powers of persuasion."

"Coercive powers of persuasion, huh? Your vocab's expanding."

Archie laughed. Podric ignored him. The games creator took two small cups out of a cupboard and placed them under the machine's filler nodules. Archie said more seriously.

"Podric, I'm not sure you realise what we're dealing with here. What we've done is ease pressure away from George and dump it on ourselves – big time."

Archie removed a cup and putting it on a saucer, gave it to his partner.

"I'll tell you now – whatever plan we come up with from here on had better be better than good. The folk we're up against make company shenanigans chicken feed and I don't fancy ending up supporting a motorway."

Taking the other cup of espresso, Archie didn't bother with a saucer but downed the little drink in one.

"What about a flyover?"

"This isn't funny Podric. These undzer shtik play dirty."

"Then we'll find something with tunnels and bury them. That's not funny either."

*   *   *

"Podric and you."

"What about us?"

"He's an interesting young man."

"He's different."

Catherine and George Benedict were standing in the Halliday's kitchen. Catherine was emptying the dishwasher.

"His mother's a nice woman."

"And his sister's crazy."

The kitchen being part conservatory, Benedict walked over to some double glass doors which opened into the garden.

"Must have been difficult for them all when Mr Moon was killed."

"Yes."

Catherine put items away. Benedict said.

"These couple of games he and Archie have created are doing well."

"Mr Benedict, you're fishing."

They looked at each other. Benedict smiled.

"I'd really like to know about this other thing, this other reality."

"I can't really talk about that."

"Why not?"

"Because only Podric and Archie can tell you about it."

Benedict wandered around.

"Have you... experienced it?"

"That would imply it exists."

Catherine removed some plates from the machine and began putting them away. Benedict sighed.

"I can't stay here."

"Dr Light said they'd be in touch when it was safe."

"It's never going to be safe."

The sound of a vehicle was heard coming up the drive. Catherine looked up at a small closed-circuit TV monitor.

"Shit."

"Unexpected appearance?

"'Say that again. My dad and stepmother weren't due back for several days."

"That settles it."

George turned a key in the conservatory door.

"I saw you had a side gate."

"Where are you going?"

"Not sure right now."

"I can blag my dad."

"How? I'm a private tutorial or something? The fewer people who see me the better. Any introduction to your parents can wait for another occasion."

Catherine came over to Benedict.

"You can't disappear George. We can't help you if you do."

"Maybe I can't be helped."

"That's not how they see it."

Benedict smiled.

"You've already been more than kind. Rekindled my faith in human nature."

He twisted the door handle. Catherine put a hand on his.

"There's no other experience to compare with it."

Half out the door, Benedict turned back. Realising what she was talking about, he paused. Catherine said.

"If you lose touch with us, you can't know."

"Ha. I'll bear that in mind."

"Do that. It's what Ultimate Alternative Reality is all about."

Chapter 16
Defender of Information Technology

Whether Podric had been able to secure the last Land Rover Defender ever built at Solihull for his mother prizing the treasured vehicle away from its only owner in Norfolk for an undisclosed sum, it was the model Barbara Moon had wanted all her life and would always cherish. Its livery the classic original 1948 pale green spec with a canvas rear cover, Barbara couldn't believe her eyes when the loader delivering the Defender turned up at Briony Close.

Having recently overseen a launch campaign at the company she worked for – Tweeney's Waste Disposal, Barbara had been given a few days leave. Both her children at school she couldn't wait to get behind the wheel. Patting her old multi-coloured VW Beetle (Podric had announced he intended to learn to drive using it) Barbara's first trip in BM 1 (Podric had also bought his mother her own number plate) was into Drinkwell to show off her new car to Alannah Brodie. The housekeeper made all the right noises, but Barbara quickly realised she wasn't very interested and departed.

That day she motored all over Hampshire – down to the coast and back across country. Barbara intended picking Podric and Amy up from school. Driving into Wendbury, it was whilst waiting at some traffic lights she thought she caught sight of George Benedict. The glimpse fleeting, Barbara pulled over. She looked around, but George was nowhere to be seen. Finding a parking space, Barbara got out of her Defender. Inspecting her vehicle – as possessions go, Barbara felt she'd hit the jackpot. Climbing back behind the wheel she was surprised to hear a voice.

"I love these."

It was George.

"Can I take you somewhere?"

Pleased at seeing Benedict and excited at having her Land Rover, Barbara's eyes were bright. He said.

"Well, er-. Not really."

"Hop in then."

Laughing, Benedict walked round to the passenger door.

* * *

"What am I going to do mum?"

Sitting in Hazlitt's coffee house in Banedon, Cosima looked at her mother.

"Podric's mooning over his girlfriend and I can't get back into Ultimate Alternative Reality!"

"At least you're acquiring wit."

Her daughter's brow furrowed then clearing, the girl smiled.

"Yeah okay, mooning. Haha."

Charlotte Light (she had reverted to using her married name) sat back.

"I think it's about time you started concentrating on other things in this life and not be so preoccupied with an alternate one."

"Why?"

"Because strictly speaking one has to ask one's self if it's entirely healthy. Podric is."

"What do you mean?"

"Asking the question."

"Podric's not always right."

"In my experience he's not usually wrong."

"Oh Podric, Podric, Podric. I've had enough of Podric!"

Not believing her daughter for a moment, Charlotte didn't respond. Reassessing her thoughts, Cosima continued.

"I reckon Ultimate Alternative Reality was entirely healthy for you. Perhaps even saved you. Surely that's not insignificant."

"No."

Looking out of the coffee house window Charlotte was thoughtful. The scene of her being followed by her Colombian ex-lover José was still strong and whilst a remarkable denouement had been achieved, the emotional scar it had left was far from healed. What was her daughter saying?

"Anyway, I need to learn how to get in and out of it on my own. I'm going to study IT and I'm going to find the best teacher."

"Then-."

Charlotte looked up.

"George. George Benedict. And Barbara. Lovely to see you both."

Charlotte smiled. Although Benedict and her husband had fallen out – like Podric's mother, Charlotte had a soft spot for the man.

"Didn't you know I was around?"

"Archie didn't tell me, but you know what he's like."

"Do I?"

They both laughed. Charlotte stood up.

"We're just on our way."

Looking at the state of their coffee cups, they hadn't been.

"Remember our daughter, Cosima?"

"Er-. Yes."

Benedict looked momentarily embarrassed. Cosima wasn't.

"It's alright George. Mum, George and I bumped into each other the other night."

"Oh."

Ignoring her mother, Cosima addressed the computer man.

"George. Would you be interested in teaching me IT? More specifically computer games technology?"

Eying the young woman, Benedict knew she had a history of being spoiled and was non-committal. He said.

"You already have better skills available to you than I can provide."

"But I don't! Dad's not in the league I'm looking for and Podric-."

Barbara raised an eyebrow. Cosima continued.

"Podric's otherwise engaged."

"Nice line Cosima."

Barbara laughed.

"Though I don't think they are yet."

As the Light women prepared to depart, Cosima turned back to Benedict.

"I'm serious. Mum's been at me to get myself a career and I want it to be in your world."

"Not mine. Don't go into that."

Benedict was surprisingly forceful.

"Your dad's better than you think but if you want the future, Podric's your man."

This wasn't what the girl wanted to hear but her reply was unexpected.

"The 1960s was the moon decade wasn't it?"

"Amongst other things."

Benedict was subdued.

"Then somehow it's got to be with Podric. He'll want to walk on it."

She turned away to follow her mother out of the coffee house.

"According to some, he'll be the first."

Cosima didn't catch Benedict's comment.

*   *   *

Working from home that day, Catherine reached Podric at school and told her boyfriend about George Benedict's departure.

"Hmm... Fancy meeting up? Actually, I want to use you."

"That's new."

"Twenty minutes?"

"Good job my parents are back."

"Meaning?"

"I'll be seeing less of you."

Chapter 17
Revelations at Hazlitt's

In the coffee house Barbara Moon and George Benedict took a table by the window.

"That'll set tongues wagging."

Barbara sipped her latte. Benedict said.

"So the daughter fancies your son."

Having tea, George Benedict was drinking a herbal infusion. Barbara said.

"More, she tends to want for things she hasn't got. I like her."

"Trust?"

Barbara smiled ruefully.

"That's something different. I don't trust many people."

Sitting companionably, George watched the Chevy SUV pull up and park behind Barbara's new Land Rover. No one got out.

"You're the first man I've been able to talk to like this since Sean died."

"I'm sure I won't be the last."

The two looked at each other.

"Please don't treat it lightly."

"I'm sorry. I didn't mean-. Barbara, there's something I've got to do."

"That sounds dramatic." George smiled and sat forward.

"Inside that vehicle over there are some men who've been tailing me ever since I arrived in the UK."

Barbara looked across the road.

"Black glass?"

"Uhuh."

"Who are they – debt collectors?"

Knowing George Benedict had gambling debts Barbara assumed the operatives were some kind of international bailiff outfit. Although he was tired and tense, Benedict couldn't help smiling.

"In a manner of speaking."

"What are you going to do?"

Pushing back his chair, he stood up.

"Have a chat."

"Won't they come to you?"

"They already have."

"Like me to come with you?"

"Better not."

Benedict looked at the vehicle – sinister and ominous.

"If they want me to go with them, it's okay."

He began to move away. His statement apparently minacious, Barbara was taken aback.

"Odd way to part."

"It was an odd way to arrive."

Normally, Barbara would have disregarded what she'd just heard and followed Benedict outside but something in his manner made her stay where she was. From her vantage point Barbara watched him cross the road and approach the vehicle. The electronic sliding door was on its far side and George disappeared from view. Seconds later, Catherine's little lime green Vespa appeared, her son riding pillion behind his girlfriend. The scooter pulled up in front of the SUV. Throwing down some money Barbara left Hazlitt's. Jaywalking across the street, she was in time to see Benedict talking to Deke who seemed shy.

"Er-. We've had orders."

"Yes."

George was taut. Pulling off his crash helmet, Podric appeared.

"To do what?"

Podric looked into the SUV then back at Benedict.

"Hullo George. Everything alright?"

If Benedict was surprised by Podric's appearance, the vehicle's occupants were dumbfounded.

"Ha. You guys – not recalled yet?"

Podric was conversational. Deke, Ethan and their two compadres appeared at a loss.

"If you people don't get out of our hair now it'll be all out warfare and you know what that means. Requiring you to interrogate, assigning you hits and liquidating targets."

The occupants of the SUV looked as though they were going to throw up. Podric continued.

"Okay? On your way. Go and report."

He reached inside the vehicle and pressed a button to close the sliding door. The Chevy departed.

"What the hell's all that about?"

George was incredulous. Podric smiled. He noticed his mother standing beside her Land Rover.

"Pleased with your new wheels mum?"

Chapter 18

Conspiracy Theories – True or False?

"I'm glad things worked out for you Archie. Love this tower. Quirky."

George Benedict, Podric and Archie were back in the latter's den. Podric and Archie had decided to tell Benedict about Ultimate Alternative Reality and what the mind path state was all about. They'd also explained how Podric had been able to track Benedict's recent inquisitors and what they'd done to the agents. Once the games writer got over his amazement at their invention, he was quicker than most at being able to grasp its rudiments.

"Would it be possible to have another cup of that excellent coffee?"

Having made a percolator for him, Podric got up and refilled Benedict's cup. Benedict continued.

"I saw Secorni's lawyer. They dragged old man Gertner himself into it. They said-."

"They? Whose 'they' in all this?"

Of the three people in the room, Archie was by far the twitchiest.

"People you only see once with faces you forget."

Podric handed Benedict his coffee refill.

"Thank you Podric."

The guest cleared his throat.

"'They' could get the tax rottweilers off my back but needed answers to some questions. Talk wasn't the problem. It's when things started to get more.."

"Threatening?"

Benedict nodded.

"That my real concerns began."

He sipped his coffee. Archie said.

"So, what's your take lying behind all this George – the American government getting worked up about the machinations of a kids computer game and forcing its termination?"

Benedict put down his coffee cup.

"As you well know Archie, games aren't just played by kids. If you study sales profiles the increase in adults' participation is massive."

"I never thought marketing was your thing George, but the lesson's noted."

Podric said.

"What's odd is you worked on this game yonks ago. It got pulled for weird reasons, but then nothing more. Now suddenly all this kicks off."

Benedict sat back.

"When Secorni started pressuring me a few months ago they told me it was because they wanted to badmouth Archie and get to you."

Neither Archie nor Podric reacted. Benedict continued.

"But that was only part of the reason. Word was that you two had created something new, some amazing new games dimension which they wanted to find out about."

"As does big brother."

Benedict nodded. Intense, Archie continued.

"And this could somehow threaten them – maybe expose them in some way.."

Benedict had some more coffee and said.

"I've never gone for conspiracy stuff. Not my thing. But I've started making enquiries."

He stretched and got up.

"Can you imagine what it must have been like for the infant NASA to be on the end of JFK's clarion call putting a man on the moon – throwing down the gauntlet with a ten-year target."

Enjoying Archie's den, Benedict strolled around.

"What if it just couldn't be achieved – they just didn't have the technology or the capability. Kennedy had pissed off both the internal and external agencies something rotten."

"So what?"

Benedict ignored Archie's question.

"The issue of man in space. Can he actually survive in such an alien and hostile environment? Do we have the technology available even today to put a human being on the moon?"

Archie said.

"Yes, we do."

"Okay, but did we then?"

Benedict stared out of the window.

"Let's say for argument sake, they couldn't achieve it. They just didn't have the ability."

Podric and Archie didn't respond.

"Imagine if they rigged the greatest cover-up to ever take place. One that was so audacious it fooled not only the American people but the entire planet."

Benedict sat down.

"The landing on the moon was completely fabricated."

"You're kidding?"

Archie burst out laughing.

Benedict shrugged.

"I don't know whether it's true or not but I'm not kidding."

"Never heard such tosh."

UAR's co-creator was dismissive.

"Are you saying all space flights didn't happen – Russian or American?"

Podric seemed more interested. Benedict said.

"Not necessarily. Look, I don't know much about this stuff. I've just rooted around – met people, asked questions."

"What about photographic evidence – bits of reflectors and old rovers they left on the moon."

Cynical, Archie was becoming irritated. He continued.

"Where these things are concerned, conspiracy theories abound."

"Some people feel the word conspiracy is bandied about far

too readily. People I've talked to reckon it's more that a deception was carried out at a very high level."

"By agency masked tomb raiders, no doubt."

Benedict looked at his ex-business partner and said. "Ever heard of Lookout Mountain Laboratory?" Archie shrugged.

"Or Graphic Film Corps?"

Again, Archie appeared dismissive. Benedict continued.

"Both outfits had military involvement and alternative modus operandi."

"Alternative?"

Podric was inquisitive.

"Developing particular technologies with a twist."

"Creating fake news, no doubt!"

Archie rolled his eyes.

"You have lost it George. Sure it's just caffeine in that coffee Podric?"

"And that film director Stanley Kubrick was involved working with them."

Archie made a mocking sound.

"Oaah, with my old mother flying around on a broomstick."

Archie got up.

"Listen George, we've got to make a move shortly. I just need to pop across to the house. See you in five."

With that he walked over to the internal lift. Opening its little glass gate, Archie pressed to descend.

"Do da de de do da." Archie whistled the *Close Encounters* riff.

"We are not alone." When he'd gone Podric said.

"Kubrick's the guy Barney's learning about in his A level Film Studies."

Benedict nodded.

"Look, I don't know whether there's a shred of accuracy in any of this. Flags on the moon, footprints, co-ordinates stacking up – I don't know. But things we do have a handle on include the technology they had available then which was at the very least, crude. It's also odd that after man had got there, exploitation was never developed. It was as if that goal having been reached suddenly stopped. That seems strange. You'd have thought having made it they'd have wanted to exploit things, develop it."

Benedict picked up his coffee cup.

"All the effort, all that work – then nothing. Anyway, whatever it is something spooked these people to follow me over here and have me tailed to your door."

Benedict drained his coffee.

"I can't wait to try UAR Podric. When can I go in?"

George Benedict's request joining the ever-increasing line of others had already come to haunt Podric Moon, who said.

"I read they're looking to put women on the moon by '24."

Benedict smiled.

"Do you have anyone in mind to make the visit?"

"Want to see the queue?"

Chapter 19
Challenges all Round

For a while after Archie and Benedict had left for town to go and confront the computer company they had done so much work for and who was now compromising them both, Podric sat on in his partner's den. Reflecting on the bizarreness of what he had just heard and the current situation, it was several minutes before he became aware that someone was in the lab. Getting up, Podric left the den and put his head round the laboratory door. He discovered Cosima sitting at the bench, deeply immersed studying the screens in front of her. She looked round.

"Oh, hi Podric."

"Didn't know you were up here."

"Didn't want to disturb things."

Entering, Podric sat down in one of Archie's Eames leather chairs.

"Hear it all?"

"Most."

The girl continued looking at the on-screen calculus. Putting a foot on the footrest, Podric sat back.

"What do you reckon?"

Having her concentration temporarily broken, Cosima turned to him.

"I wouldn't know. It all sounded pretty crazy."

Seeing the rudimentary algorithms displayed Podric glanced at them.

"You serious about learning IT stuff?"

"I said I was."

"What exactly do you want to study?"

Cosima tapped a space bar.

"I've already told you and why. You not wanting to help me – I think George would, but he's got other things on his mind."

Podric got up and went to the lab's side window.

"Haven't we all."

He stared out at the woodland below. Running alongside the drive, the copse led up to the road.

"Suppose I agree to teach you."

Podric turned back to Cosima.

"The thing is you know all this computer work is built on maths, don't you?"

"Well, yuh."

"I'm serious Cosima. Quite apart from anything to do with UAR, if you do want to learn Information Technology and more specifically, the science behind writing computer games – make a career of it-."

Podric paused.

"You've got to have the mathematical ability. It's not all arty creative."

Podric sat down beside her.

"It's great declaring you've made up your mind, that you're sincere. Right now, I'll believe you are. But this stuff's dry Cos – its algorithmic, its calculus, its writing formulaic data. That's what builds electronically to create a game."

Podric tapped several keys. The mathematical screed was replaced by stratospherically more complex hieroglyphics.

"Once you've had the idea – be it fantasy, a war game or sci-fi orientated – it's all this that actually makes it happen."

"And UAR?"

"UAR makes a conventional game 11+ to a double first at Oxbridge! It's off the scale."

"How come you can do this?"

"I'm a genius."

Podric stood back.

"Want a coffee?"

"Don't know."

"How about yes, no, or maybe?"

In spite of feeling dejected, Cosima couldn't help but laugh.

"Okay then."

Podric went through to the little kitchenette. Cosima got up and followed him.

"We already know you know how to hurt a girl. How about destroy?"

Prepping the coffee machine, Podric began emptying the mini-dishwasher underneath it.

"Rubbish. But the reality is that's the reality."

"What, that you're a genius."

It was Podric's turn to laugh.

"Yeah, I got a C in Geography."

"Big deal."

He placed a mug under one of the Gran Gaggia nodules and a cup under the other.

"Some people can write, some can paint – not all my maths is that sharp. But I have enough grounding plus a zillion hours playing games to my credit."

Waiting for the machine Podric put away some cups.

"Sure, I wanted to get inside and explore them, and it was their adventures that excited me. But I also had to learn how games were created, how they were constructed."

"So you'd be able to invent UAR."

"So I would be able to invent UAR."

The machine made some satisfying gurgles and coffee began dripping into the mug and cup. Cosima adjusted the pipette dripping coffee into hers. Podric continued.

"Things didn't advance to that point entirely logically but after years of being surrounded by them – well you know the rest. I was obsessed about finding another life for myself."

"It's still fantastic."

Cosima removed their coffees and handed Podric his. Podric went on.

"And your pa contributed more than he realised though I admit some of his contribution came in the form of bloody mindedness. The more he disbelieved, the more determined I became to make it work."

For several seconds they were silent then Cosima said.

"It's not just the adventure that does it for me but the fact that whatever it is, it's an alternate reality. That's my trip."

"And time we were off on one. I want to check something."

"You serious? Now?"

"Never more so."

Carrying his espresso, Podric went through to the den. Cosima had a gulp of her macchiato. Podric said.

"Coming?"

"Only if you agree to re-programme my brain to understand maths."

"No problem. We'll just reconfigure your dorsal parietal."

Cosima looked at UAR's creator uncomprehendingly. Podric continued.

"It's the maths part."

"You'd really do that?"

Sitting in the den, Podric readied himself to go into UAR.

"You'll need a surgeon and it's pretty dangerous but if you're that determined."

Cosima sat down beside him.

"Any other options?"

"Yeah. Skip all this talk of maths and let's get into Ultimate Alternative Reality."

Podric finished his coffee. Cosima said.

"But you know what I really want is to get in and out on my own."

Podric took a sharp intake of air.

"Ooh, tricky that. Better have the operation then."

Chapter 20
Secorni v Moonlight

Sitting in Secorni's Berkeley Square office was a strange experience for George Benedict and Archie Light. Not since they were partners in crime several years previously, had the two men sat side by side with representatives of the company who had been their employer. At that time Cy Zaentz was operational head of Europe before he made his final bid for the top as president and CEO of Secorni Games Global (SGG) based in Silicon Valley. With Zaentz's departure his right-hand man Saul Prendergast stepped up to become Vice President Europe.

The London office's boardroom was a chrome and steel affair. Alongside Archie and George sat Kaliska Monroe – immaculate and business like. Opposite them was Saul Prendergast, and beside him Simon Meyer, head of Gertner Hirschowitz – Secorni's law firm – along with his colleague Mia Haas. The four men and two women turned to a large wall mounted screen at the end of the room. A Zoom call revealed a severe looking man with cropped grey hair sitting in an office on the other side of the world. His image in medium frame, the executive suite he sat in was stylish and several works of contemporary fine art could be seen behind him. Zaentz wore a white collarless shirt done up at the neck à la Steve Jobs and a casual jacket. Though it was known Zaentz had an ability to piss ice and was regarded as a remote cove, Archie had always had a secret soft spot for the Chief Executive. Tough he may have been, but Archie was pretty sure Zaentz hadn't liked what he'd tacitly approved. The same couldn't be said for the man sitting opposite him. Prendergast could barely disguise his dislike of the two men – especially Archie Light! Far from feeling threatened Archie relished the VP Europe's antipathy. Saul was a bully and there was nothing Archie enjoyed more than challenging his type. Aware of Archie's contempt only aggravated Prendergast's mood. It would be a contentious meeting.

It hadn't been a difficult one to set up. Bypassing Prendergast, Archie went directly to Zaentz citing that he and George Benedict rather than comply with Secorni, intended challenging them. Zaentz suggested the two parties meet.

"Sorry you're not in town Cy. I'd have thought something of this magnitude might get even you on the private jet."

Zaentz grunted. Archie smiled.

"Guess we'll hear it from Saul, then."

Simon Meyer cleared his throat.

"My client intends pressing charges on the basis that several computer games supposedly co-written by yourself, weren't."

Meyer adjusted some papers and continued.

"Having established proof that assigned copyright did not reside with yourself, you knowingly declared co-authorship and fraudulently accepted payment for this work."

He referred to his notes.

"On *Knights of the Avenger* and er, *Krimon and the Undersea Invaders*."

"And who might I ask contests this?"

"Don't be dumb, Archie."

This from the only person outside the room.

"The assertion being obtained under duress is-."

Kaliska was cool.

"Not so."

Interjecting, Mia Haas was also. Kaliska raised an eyebrow at her legal adversary who continued.

"The plaintiff signed the declaration incriminating the accused full in the knowledge that doing so authorised the company bringing the charges met with his approval."

Eerily, a recording of Benedict signing the document with Gertner's US people began. 'You're quite clear what you're signing Mr Benedict? The fact that this document states Dr Light did not write the relevant games is in breach of contract and liable to prosecution.' 'I understand.'

Benedict's voice wasn't loud, but it was clearly audible.

'And that the company has claim on you to testify against Dr Light as and if it sees fit.' 'That's acknowledged.'

Mia Haas resumed.

"It's entirely clear that Mr Benedict was in complete under-standing of what he was signing."

Kaliska said.

"We all know this is subterfuge. Your intention to pressure Mr Benedict into compromising his ex-business partner is in order to get access to his current one."

Kaliska sat back and continued.

"In support of this claim, Mr Benedict further asserts that he understands any incrimination made against Dr Light by himself prosecuted by Secorni could be dropped if certain conditions are met regarding Dr Light's business partner, but perhaps you wish to contend the point..?"

"Will that be forthcoming?"

Simon Meyer's voice was soft but cold. Looking at Prendergast Archie smiled and ignoring Meyer's question said.

"What interests us more is Big Brother sitting on you."

"You're implying pressure from an outside party attempted to influence my company."

Cy Zaentz's cadence was neutral. Archie laughed.

"That's exactly what I'm implying, Cy."

"But that hasn't happened."

Meyer again. Kaliska eyed Gertner's senior European lawyer. Rather than call him out as a liar, Kaliska took another approach.

"You'll be aware Mr Benedict has been hounded since he arrived in England. We've ascertained these people are federal agents."

Mia Haas said.

"What's that to do with us?"

Archie got up and began pacing around.

"Let's quit sparring. It's all over the business Cy that Secorni had pressure put on it, forcing the company to stop work on *Moon Landing*. No lawyers need tell us otherwise. This inevitably leads us to ask the question, why?"

No one responded.

"George here, would never have been working on *Moon Landing* if it hadn't been conceived by Secorni. In fact, he only began researching the game when it was some way down the road. You can explain to us why he ended up being the Lone Star on it."

Still silence. When Archie next spoke, it seemed as if it was partly to himself.

"Why would the American government be so worried about a computer game that it forced the company developing it to stop work and kill its release? If something important had been discovered – presumably inadvertently what had been stumbled across?"

Archie's rhetorical question was received in silence.

"This all taking place years ago – now suddenly George reappears in my life."

Archie turned to face the room.

"This little charade isn't to do with me Cy, except for your puppet here's dislike of moi – something incidentally that's reciprocated."

"Looks like we'll be seeing you in court then."

Simon Meyer closed a file. Ignoring Meyer's comment, Archie continued his stroll around the boardroom.

"Let's say the goons are nothing to do with you and this is just a pathetic attempt to get your hands on my new partner. In the process you've dragged poor George into something he had no desire to be a part of. Whether we decide to expose you for what you are, remains to be seen. But beware all. This matter won't be going away, and I suggest Cy we might yet have the pleasure of your company on this side of the pond."

With a look to Kaliska and a glance at George, Team Light headed for the door. Archie continued.

"If they are putting pressure on you Cy, I'd watch out. Big brother is frequently off the pace but invariably gets there in the end. Anyway, he's relentless."

The recording of Prendergast's conversation with Zaentz outlining their intentions – the stitch up – began playing. It rendered the remaining people in the room mute. As he closed the door Archie said.

"Touché."

Chapter 21
Lunar Madness

Podric felt as though he was falling through space. Seconds in this state seemed much longer – indeed the sensation was strangely timeless and reminded him of the first accidental experience he'd had with Archie and Dog when they entered Ultimate Alternative Reality. Their conscious selves had recovered their senses in a stable on the Rock of Gibraltar circa 1793!

Images flashing by included a graphic depicting the Van Allen radiation belts, a moonlike surface on Hawaii, Nevada desert lunar landscapes, film facilities at Lookout Mountain Laboratory in Laurel Canyon and studios in places like Huntsville, Alabama. A director resembling Stanley Kubrick identifiable by his beard and sunken eyes stood on a set directing a scene involving astronauts apparently gathering rock samples. Behind them was the Eagle landing craft. The kaleidoscopic montage concluded in NASA's Building 9 at MSC (Manned Spacecraft Center later the Johnson Space Center) in Houston. Walking along a corridor, NASA media relations personnel Podric Moon and Cosima Light wore white overalls with the NASA logo on their chest pockets along with an array of security badges.

"What was that all about?"

Cosima was dazed.

"I think it was the multi-programming option I selected. Haven't come into UAR like that since the first time."

The studio light went from Red to Green. Podric swiped his ID card and pushed open a door. The set revealed a vast lunar landscape. Expanding the *JFK Reloaded* computer game creating *JFK and his World* and deciding to make a visit to 1960s NASA,

Podric had upwards of a hundred computer games to choose from. Selecting an amalgam of several brought Cosima and himself to the Houston Space Center during the early months of 1969.

Walking onto the set swarming with technicians they were in time to see Neil Armstrong and Buzz Aldrin take off their headgear. Podric flashed his NASA media pass.

"Difficult to feel what it'll really be like I should think Commander..."

Armstrong looked round at Podric.

"Podric Moon. Media."

"You serious?"

Buzz Aldrin looked at Podric's accreditation.

"Podric MOON. Why aren't you on the mission?"

"Who's to say I'm not?"

The astronauts smiled.

"With a name like that you certainly ought to be."

Armstrong fiddled with an O_2 socket on his space suit.

"You're the guys doing the interview."

"'Sir."

Sitting in a briefing room adjacent to the lunar set, Armstrong and Aldrin sat in overalls not dissimilar to Podric and Cosima's.

"So what story are we telling today?"

Buzz Aldrin was cynical. Podric shrugged.

"Whatever's required be put out. Your mental state. Any issues."

"Crap. Do that and you ain't got a mission."

Now Aldrin was acidic. Cosima said.

"Anything the public can engage with."

"Like we're heroes. How wonderful our wives and families are. What they mean to us. Da di da. ZZZ."

Aldrin again. Armstrong sat back.

"There's a lot of things about being an astronaut that run counter to being a fighter pilot. The adrenal rush of combat or testing an untried prototype – pushing it to the extreme bouncing around at the top of earth's atmosphere. The feeling you're still in control – just. That's the kick."

Smiling, Armstrong glanced at the disgruntled Aldrin before

continuing.

"People have suggested we don't really fly the spacecraft – that we're passengers sitting on top of the Saturn rocket – dummys blasted into the sky. But for humans to make this trip our very existence and experience in the capsule is a unique one. It's a human voice that reports back, it's a human being staring down at earth and it'll be a human being that walks on the moon's surface."

"The technical controls you have are pretty crude."

Armstrong studied Podric.

"You implying the G & C Optics and Computer Command Module in our Columbia capsule aren't state of the art..?"

Podric didn't reply. Armstrong continued.

"Something I have got to practice handling is that."

Armstrong nodded through the interior window overlooking the lunar set. At the front of it was a full-size mock-up of the Eagle landing craft.

"The LLV – we call it the Flying Bedstead."

"And it's a bitch."

Aldrin injected. Armstrong went on.

"Teach you anything about fly-by-wire in media?"

Living fifty years ahead of 1969, Podric didn't like to say too much about NASA's 1960s media department or the fact that even as a layman playing computer games in the twenty-first century, he knew quite a bit about fly-by-wire and what it did. He just said.

"That's how it'll fly."

"Going where no man's gone before."

Buzz and Neil were amused. Podric and Cosima didn't respond.

"You watch Star Trek?"

For several seconds Podric and Cosima looked nonplussed then Cosima said.

"Oh, er yeah. Captain Kirk and all that.."

"Ha – and all that... Where they go on TV we can only dream of in reality."

"Reality. Hmm.."

Podric seemed momentarily lost in thought.

"What if your mission was just that – a dream?"

"Not with you son."

"Well, what if it couldn't be achieved."

Aldrin had already got up and was getting ready to leave. Looking thoughtful, Armstrong didn't move.

"Then we'd be the biggest suckers this side of paradise."

The astronaut smiled and continued.

"Like to be coming with us?"

He stood as did Podric and Cosima.

"Everyone'll be with you in spirit Commander Armstrong."

Podric fiddled with his security pass.

"Like you said Colonel Aldrin, Moon being my surname, maybe one day I'll get a chance to walk on it."

* * *

Archie Light, Kaliska Monroe and George Benedict left Secorni headquarters and crossed Berkeley Square walking into St James's where the games creator had parked his Facel Vega in his club's underground carpark. On the pavement and about to part company with MoonLight's lawyer, Benedict took his leave and excused himself entering the club for nature's call. Kaliska turned to Archie.

"That wasn't a bad performance."

"Ha. Thanks. Where to now do you think?"

"Surely time to go exploring."

Archie looked at her. Kaliska continued.

"Starting from JFK's inauguration through to his assassination and the Apollo Space Program."

Archie chuckled.

"Just what you always wanted."

The lawyer smiled.

"I've a hunch UAR could help with all this."

Archie said.

"You'd better come down."

"Tomorrow night work for you?"

"The sooner the better."

Chapter 22

George Missing Again
and Stanley's Shining

Having taken his leave of Kaliska Monroe minutes later Archie walked into his club. Looking around there was no sign of George. Archie spoke briefly to reception and enquired if they had seen his friend. The house manager recalled George Benedict who as a non-member, had advised the desk who he was with and that they were collecting Archie's car. He'd then gone to the Gents. Making his own way there Archie met a couple of acquaintances but there was no sign of Benedict. His irritation turning to concern – Archie realised something was amiss.

His first thought was to contact Secorni. Perhaps for some reason Benedict had returned to their offices? On reflection he decided not to pursue that line of enquiry. Instead, he phoned Kaliska. Had he somehow missed George coming out of the club? Might his ex-partner have gone back to her offices? Kaliska advised him that wasn't the case. Finally, Archie called Podric. Unbeknown to him, his young colleague had only just returned from 1960s Houston with his daughter. Briefly outlining what happened in the Secorni meeting Archie explained that George had disappeared again. Chatting things through – their having recently proved the effectiveness of using UAR to neutralise the agents Podric didn't believe the US secret service would be so quick to immediately put a replacement SWAT team in to abduct Benedict.

"More likely they'll wait a little to see how things develop. Isn't that what you'd do?"

Archie replied that what he'd do and what the security services might hardly compared. With Kaliska coming down to Drinkwell the following evening, MoonLight's directors decided that a council of war could take place then.

*   *   *

Lunchtime at school the next day Podric and Catherine sat in their privileged GCR (Groundsman's Common Room) enjoying a coffee. Podric said.

"Very inconsiderate your dad and step-mum coming back early."

Catherine smiled.

"Tell me about it."

Podric folded the newspaper he'd been half-reading.

"Haven't seen your dad's new tenant at school recently?"

"He's been away on a field trip. Visiting some studios – part of his course work."

"You're well up on the reformed one."

"Given he is dad's tenant that's hardly surprising plus I fancy him rotten."

Catherine put down the textbook she was studying.

"You won't believe how great he and dad are getting on. Right mates they are. Dad was even taking him down the pub the other night."

"Sure he's alright your old man?"

Podric got up.

"Maybe I should put in an appearance given financial responsibility actually rests with me."

"You want to see my father?!"

Catherine was incredulous.

"Isn't that what boys do when they ask for a girl's hand?"

Podric kissed Catherine's.

"Pchwa!"

Podric laughed.

"I need to see BS."

The school bell rang at the end of the lunch break.

Catherine said.

"UAR stuff?" Podric smiled.

"Maybe I just want to get in with your dad."

* * *

After school that night Podric and Catherine mounted Catherine's scooter and rode out of the gates. Arriving at Mr Halliday's rental apartment in Dearbourne, they parked in the little crescent. Banging on the front door, it was opened by the new tenant. Catherine and Podric followed Barney into the living room. Squatting amidst papers, DVDs, film posters and media books, Jane Cartwright was making notes. Sitting in the only spare chair a hockey stick between her legs, Carol Jensen looked bored. Podric said.

"Don't tell me you've actually got him working Jane."

Looking up, Jane smiled. Carol said.

"All she does these days."

Clearly put out Carol sulked.

"How's Sports Psychology Carol?"

Podric was friendly.

"Fat lot you're interested."

Grabbing her sports bag Carol headed for the door.

"I'm off."

The comment really aimed at her best friend Jane made no acknowledgement. Expecting a reaction, Carol was poised for a second or two before continuing.

"Bloody films. Bloody computer games – morning and night."

She looked back at the scene.

"What about some proper sport – physical? Something worth winning!"

Carol slammed the door.

"Do you think she means that computer games aren't, Podric?"

Jane, who had never been disloyal to Carol, closed one book and opened another. Barney squatted down and picked up his iPad.

"Disturbing our studies, you don't make a visit without wanting something Moony."

The beginning of Stanley Kubrick's *2001: A Space Odyssey*

started playing on a blank wall at the far end of the room. Catherine sat down to watch. Podric walked over to the French doors, opened them and went outside. The small balcony had a table and a couple of metal chairs on it. Podric sat down and activated his iPhone. Barney came out with two beers. He handed one to Podric.

"To get rid of you."

Barney opened his beer and took a swig. So did Podric.

"How's it going with Jane?"

"What sort of a question is that?"

They both had some beer.

"Quite a shift for her."

Barney didn't reply. Podric continued.

"Gather you're sucking up to my would-be father-in-law."

"Steady Pod. Sure UAR isn't doing funny things to you?"

Podric smiled. Barney drank again.

"You've been in recently."

Podric nodded and replied.

"And you haven't been bothering me."

Barney shrugged.

"I've kind of got interested in things."

"I knew you'd lock on to A levels."

"Result then smarty."

"It's not so much *2001* I want to talk about but *The Shining*."

"Why? Ah, don't answer. Conspiracist."

"What do you reckon?"

"It's not in the syllabus. What game are you into?"

Podric told his singular friend about his latest UAR adventure. It was dark when they came inside. Catherine and Jane had gone. Podric checked his phone.

"Trout & Eel."

He turned to Barney.

"Didn't know they were pals."

"You don't know everything Podric."

"Sometimes Barney I don't think I know anything."

Barney deposited several beer cans in a bin.

"Enough of the false modesty crap."

He picked up a set of car keys lying in a fruit bowl. Podric had forgotten Barney had already passed his test (he hadn't a year previously when he'd tried to run Podric down – an act for which Barney had ended up doing a spell in a Young Offenders Institution). Locking the flat, they crossed the road and Barney unlocked an old Rover 3500. To Podric it seemed a most unlikely vehicle for Barney to drive.

"Saw you more as a Mustang man."

Getting into the car, Barney laughed.

"When my folks were selling up it was still in the garage. I thought I'd remove it. Part of my settlement. Bastards."

Starting the Rover, they moved off.

"My mum had it. Only ever drove it twice."

They cruised along.

"Remember my old man had these dealerships – he was always coming back with motors. Had a Bentley Continental for a couple of weeks."

Barney negotiated a bend.

"It's got a load of poke this old girl. Ideal for me don't you reckon? Plenty of oomph but un-flash. In anything else there'd always be the revolving blue light in the rear-view mirror."

*   *   *

Sitting outside in the Trout & Eel's garden, Jane was on her own. Barney went to get drinks. Jane said.

"Your girlfriend's in the loo."

Not replying, Podric sat down. Jane continued.

"I've only ever been into your alternative reality state by accident."

Turning over a book Barney had left on Stanley Kubrick, Podric glanced at Jane.

"What about Abe?"

"That was different. You brought him to us."

Podric said.

"*Skice Ball* on my birthday..?

Jane fiddled with the toggle of her hoody.

"I was thinking more of Gibraltar."

"You remember that? You weren't programmed then."

"Dribs and drabs. I was in a bar - working.."

Jane smiled and looked around. Podric had always rather liked Jane. She'd been considerate to him when he first arrived at Wendbury High getting him into the unofficial school common room after he'd helped Jane and Carol with some IT issues and the dodgy school janitor. Barney appeared with Catherine. He put a pint of beer down in front of Podric.

"So he wants a list of all the anomalies in *The Shining*. Room 237 and all that."

"Anomalies? You're getting an education Barney."

Catherine smiled and continued.

"Didn't see you as a conspiracist Podric."

Jane sipped her lager. Barney said.

"The Forest Ranger equating to Houston, character Stuart Ullman being Werner von Braun."

"The NASA rocket guy?"

"And ex-Nazi. Yuh. The kid Danny wearing an Apollo 11 sweater - Kubrick faking the moon landings. There's all kinds of stuff surrounding the picture."

Barney drank some beer. Catherine was amazed.

"How come you know all this?"

"Well I don't know it, do I? There's just a lot of stuff out there about it."

"Why?"

Catherine seemed genuinely interested.

"That's a very good question."

It was Jane who spoke, and she continued.

"*The Shining* was made long after the moon landings."

Barney said.

"Yeah, years later. People who believe this conspiracist shit say it was Mr Kubrick's way of giving his audience clues about what happened."

"He felt it necessary to do that?"

Jane was cynical.

"People studying the conspiracies read it that way."

Podric said.

"Kennedy challenging his country – more particularly the scientific and space community – to put a man on the moon, reckoned it would establish America's pre-eminence in the new world order. But then he was assassinated. After that wheels began coming off."

Podric quenched his thirst. Picking up on Podric's comments, Barney said.

"Giving rise to every covin theory under the sun. From a double playing Jacky boy in Dallas taking Oswald's and anyone else's bullets to Stanley filming the lunar landings in top secret locations. Cover-ups of Oscar winning proportions."

Barney finished his beer. Catherine turned to Podric.

"What do you think?"

"I think we're off again."

Chapter 23

Supper at HQ and a Surprise

It was a surprise to Podric arriving at The Lighthouse that evening not to go up to Archie's den. Intercepted by a genial Dr Light, he was shown into the dining room where Kaliska was having supper with the family.

"We tried calling but you didn't answer."

"There's a surprise."

Cosima was pleasantly waspish. Podric muttered something about having had things to do.

"I'm sure they were pressing."

This from her mother who offered Podric a plate of spaghetti which he readily accepted.

"Yes, one of them was very, though I can't quite figure it out."

Podric sat down. Archie immediately filled a wine glass for his guest.

"You always know how to make an entrance Podric."

Smiling, Kaliska sipped her wine as Podric picked his up.

"UAR's been hacked."

Charlotte out of the room attending to Podric's food, this news brought the rest of the table to a standstill.

"What exactly do you mean?"

Archie was serious. Podric said.

"I mean someone's tried to get into Ultimate Alternative Reality who isn't profiled by us. They're trying to access it using some warped adaption of our codex."

"Without success?"

"I'm not sure."

Charlotte re-entered with Podric's plate of vermicelli.

"What have I missed? You all look strangely hipped."

"That's because we are. Someone's hacked into Ultimate Alternative Reality – or trying to."

Getting up, Cosima went out carrying an empty water jug. Charlotte said.

"The hazards of uniqueness."

She smiled brightly. Archie said.

"It's serious Charlotte."

He leant back and opened a French door.

"Is there any corruption?"

Podric attacked his food.

"Not from what I could tell. It was only an initial check."

"What do you reckon though?"

Kaliska looked across at Podric. Finishing a mouthful, the boy said.

"First I wondered about Secorni but somehow I think it's unlikely. Then these security dodos, but we're still speculating how much they actually know about UAR."

"So..?"

"Somebody who knows a bit more than that."

"And they've disappeared."

In the kitchen Cosima was filling the water jug. The front door opened, and Alannah entered.

"Good movie?"

"We tried to get into that new Scandi thriller, but it was full. Ended up with some comic strip thing. I find all the effects lull me to sleep. One kapow after another."

"Thought you might bring Barbara back."

"Oh, she had a call and things to do."

Cosima returned to the dining room to find her father had gone over to his computer laboratory. He'd left a strangely neutered mood, the atmosphere only broken by Podric's eating.

"This is fantastic Mrs Light."

"How many times have I told you Podric, it's Charlotte."

"That's right mum – flirt with him. Can't get enough flattery can you Podric?"

Ignoring her, Podric finished his spaghetti. Kaliska and Charlotte caught each other's eye. "You going over to the lab?"

Addressing Podric, Kaliska finished her wine.

"He'd better. Dad'll never figure it out."

Pushing back his chair, Podric got up.

"That was delicious Charlotte. Will you give me the recipe? I want to learn to cook."

"Do that and you'll be completely perfect."

Capable of charm, Cosima was a contrary being particularly where Podric was concerned. He turned to her.

"Let's go then."

"What do you mean?"

"We'll put you in as a decoy. 'Have to activate things anyway, to find out what's going on."

"You'll make a wonderful guinea pig darling."

"Treadmill's already rolling."

Podric and Cosima left the dining room.

"She's crazy about him." Charlotte began clearing plates.

"Unusual tactic." Kaliska helped.

"Not uncommon – a front. Takes after her father."

"You handle it well."

"I handle it."

*   *   *

A key in the lock and seconds later the front door of No 5 Briony Close was opened by eleven-year old Amy Moon. Followed into the house by her friend Lilian Bekes the two girls went through to the kitchen. Amy opened the fridge and took out a big bottle of coke. A note was placed on the kitchen table. Addressed to her brother, Amy glanced at it then activated her mobile. Getting her mother's answerphone, she didn't leave a message.

"Mum didn't say she was going to be late, but you never know."

"What's with the note?"

Amy shrugged.

"Want something to eat?"

"Wouldn't say no. What have you got?"

"There's a nearly whole pizza in the fridge."

"What is it?"

"Fussy are you? Capricciosa."

"Olives?"

"You can take them off."

"Do me then."

A few minutes later the microwave pinged, and the two girls began tucking in. They had almost finished their meal when the front door opened and Podric came in.

"You should be in bed."

"We've been out doing some chovexani."

Podric looked at his sister. Although he was possessor of an original mind, Amy was in another league altogether.

"How did it go?"

Laughing, Amy got down from the table and went to put her plate in the dishwasher.

"You don't know what that is, do you?"

Podric ignored her question.

"Mum not home?"

"There's a note."

Podric turned to Lilian.

"Best you stay over Lilian."

"Soske?"

If his sister was eccentric, to Podric Lilian Bekes was strange. Though he liked her, at times her Romany ways seemed peculiar.

"I know you're a wild gypsy girl Lilian but you're not wandering around out at this time of night."

"Don't go all phal on me."

"Go all what?"

"You don't know the lingua. Phal – brother."

"Okay I won't go all phal on you or chop suey or whatever else you've been up to."

Both girls burst out laughing.

"It's me who makes up words Pod. Chovexani is a witch. We've been witch hunting!"

Podric picked up the note his mother had left him.

"Find any?"

"Loads. Then we went to see some detlene."

"Oh, spooky spirits, no doubt."

"Hey – you know the Romanes. He knows Romani!"

The girls disappeared into the Moon's living room. The note Barbara Moon left her son was the strangest piece he'd ever read from her. Concerning him deeply, it read.

Darling,

Although you're going to find these lines disturbing, you're not to worry – I'll only be away a few days.

Coming out of the cinema with Alannah this evening George Benedict called me. Getting the train from town to Wendbury, he said he'd run out on Dr Light – pressures inside him exploding. Suffice it to say his indebtedness is nothing to the difficulties he's facing Podric. The kind of trouble George is in is so serious he believes he may not come out of it alive. I offered to hide him locally, but he wouldn't hear of it. He only asked if he could talk to me but as he went on I realised the poor man was bordering on deranged and that if he wasn't helped, he'd likely do himself in let alone anyone else get to him.

You'll think my actions the craziest your crazy mother has ever done but honestly darling I wouldn't do this if a) I didn't think it necessary to preserve life, and b) I didn't think I could help George. Everyone will think what I'm doing is not only irresponsible, its unhinged and maybe even you will think so my darling Podric. All I can say is it's my decision and mine alone – indeed, George is unhappy I'm doing it. xxx

Love you darling – there's food in the freezer and please make sure Amy does her homework – particularly maths. Sadly, she doesn't have your abilities in that subject!

PS: I won't be answering my phone. If I don't appear in three days, contact Tweeney's. Owed stacks of leave, everything's up to date on my computer.

Hugs and kisses to you and your sister.

Your ever-loving mother. xx

Chapter 24

Lunar Landing – or Not

The following day being Sunday, Amy and her friend Lilian had been invited out for the day by the Veeraswamy's, Petal's family taking their two guests to the circus. Podric decided it was time to revisit President Kennedy. Texting Kaliska, he went by the Lighthouse where he activated UAR. The lawyer said.

"I'm honoured. I thought Dr Light's daughter would be accompanying you."

"Oh, she was just a test checking out the hacking attempt."

"And?"

Podric shrugged.

"It hasn't been penetrated yet. Be even more difficult now we've added an extra firewall."

* * *

In the White House theatre located in the East Wing, Podric Moon sat in the dimly lit preview cinema with Kaliska Monroe.

Kaliska said.

"I'm even more privileged to be here then."

Podric smiled.

"For this trip, I thought you'd be best to have tag along."

"Tag along? Flattery for you. Why?"

"Because you have an interest in these times – some might say an obsessive interest."

Kaliska smiled. Podric continued.

"And you have a lot of knowledge. Besides, you got me into

this adventure."

At that moment a door at the rear of the theatre opened and President Kennedy entered. Brisk as ever, he walked down the aisle. Podric and Kaliska stood. Both shook hands with the president. Podric introduced Kaliska who had narrowly avoided meeting him when Podric removed them both from their first foray at the outset of the adventure. JFK gave a brief glance of appreciation in the young lawyer's direction. Ms Monroe shone. Kennedy walked to a small podium positioned at the side of the screen.

"So Podric, we meet again. I recall we're here via a computer games program."

Podric smiled. More than Abraham Lincoln who Podric felt was a genuinely humble man, Kennedy could be an intimidating presence but having met before, Podric didn't allow JFK's aura to affect him.

"That's it Mr President. I've come to ask some questions."

"Technology must have advanced phenomenally. I know my day today has involved meetings with the Defense Secretary and Joint Chiefs chairman, a cabinet meeting, discussions with the Italian foreign minister and some civic leaders from Birmingham."

"As well as time with a new Marine Corp commandant and the Laotian prime minister. You've just left a meeting with two men who are departing for Alabama. We're inside a game I've created called *JFK and his World*. It's day specific."

Kaliska said.

"Sadly, Blaik and Royall turn out to be unfortunate appointments. The ball coach never had a black player in any of his teams and the general fought black integration in the army."

"As I said, technology must have advanced phenomenally."

Kaliska gave a sad smile.

"What's personally upsetting is that last weekend aboard the Honey Fitz you shot a movie which is staggeringly prescient."

Kennedy gave an impatient shrug.

"The hindsight of history. If I understand correctly it's of little consequence to me in er, sixty days' time."

"Except your legacy."

Jack smiled at Kaliska.

"History will have its say."

Podric said.

"On Friday you gave a speech to the United Nations in New York. The rhetoric seems to have altered since your congressional one two years ago and the Rice University speech last year."

Kennedy moved around the podium.

"The space program is losing impetus. Costs are exorbitant and the public's waning interest questionable. Soviet rhetoric is aggressive. Unlike my apparent civil rights error today, testing the water is rarely a mistake – it's sometimes even successful."

"Victory has a hundred fathers and defeat is an orphan."

Kennedy glanced at Kaliska.

"That's one episode of my presidency I'd happily have expunged."

"Is CORONA working as satisfactorily as you'd like?"

Having already acknowledged the advancement technology had to have made in the fifty years since his assassination, Kennedy didn't turn a hair.

"Damned sight better than using U2."

Podric said.

"You're aware just how enormous the challenge was that you put before America's scientific community – the moon challenge."

Podric dimmed the house lights remotely.

"After 22nd November things change and conspiracy theories kick off. Your assassination is one of the biggest of all time, but another involves the Apollo space program which you initiated."

Images appeared on the screen in front of them involving Apollo 11's blast off. They watched as seconds later the first and second separation of the giant Saturn V rocket parted company from the remainder of the craft as it entered orbit around the earth. The mission unfolded; the lunar landing and return to earth. Kennedy was transfixed only speaking when the sight of a smiling President Nixon appeared welcoming Armstrong, Aldrin and Collins home.

"That bastard made president."

"Things go very wrong. What with Vietnam, America enters a dark place. He resigns the presidency pending impeachment."

Kaliska spoke quietly.

"There are those who question whether everything you've just seen, happened. Whether man actually made it to the moon."

"Having just seen that, what evidence is there to the contrary?"

"The game the ex-business partner of Archie's was working on several years ago was entitled *Moon Landing*."

Ignoring etiquette, Podric stood up and began pacing around.

"A computer game is made up of calculus and algorithms. It seems that some people in the team discovered that working with technical information available at the time, the game wouldn't function. The commissioning company wanted to only use technology of the '60s believing it would add authenticity. This games writing colleague who had been put in to help its development suddenly realised technicians were being abruptly withdrawn from the project. It's now established the game never made it to market due to government pressure."

"On whose authorisation?"

"That's the question."

Podric and JFK made eye contact.

"The more one looks into your presidency the more one discovers the feathers you appear to have ruffled. It's as if during your thousand days in office, global and domestic issues exploded."

"It's certainly felt like that."

Kennedy prepared to leave. Podric said.

"I want to explore things."

"Using this... state?"

"Uhuh."

"Well, I said if I can help."

"Thanks."

As Kennedy headed up the aisle, Kaliska said.

"Ask not what your country..."

JFK nodded to Kaliska.

"My legacy doesn't appear entirely forgotten."

Chapter 25
Nada to Search and Rescue

After he received his mother's note explaining that she had gone into hiding with George Benedict, it may seem strange to readers why Podric Moon didn't immediately go in search of his errant parent.

Poring over his mother's letter – reading and re-reading it several times, Podric thought hard about what he should do. Should he try and find her straightaway or respect her wishes – leave her alone for a couple of days?

Out of UAR and his meeting with JFK that Sunday night, the following morning Podric got Amy and her friend Lilian Bekes their breakfast. Telling his sister their mother was away for a few days met with a remarkably relaxed response.

"All okay with you Podriquil – all okay with me."

Podriquil? That was another new one. Lilian said.

"Chindilean raklo?"

She and Podric eyed each other. The gypsy girl continued.

"Dya slobuzenja."

School bag in hand, Amy went to the front door.

"She's just asking if you're fed up and mum wants some freedom."

"You majoring in Romany?"

"Honours mon bro. I might – it's fun!"

Watching the girls skip down the path and head for the school bus stop, Podric went back into the house. Having no lectures that morning he read his mother's note again for the umpteenth time. Checking his phone, Podric discovered several messages from his business partner increasingly urgent in their request he contact him.

An hour later sitting in the Moon's kitchen, Barbara's note in front of him Archie Light was for once dumbstruck.

"Christ."

Podric put a mug of instant coffee in front of him.

"Which means outside efforts to enter UAR could involve my mother."

"God."

"You can leave deities out of this Archie. Obviously my mother wanted to help George."

Podric went over to the counter and picked up his own coffee. Archie tried his but it was too hot.

"You seem remarkably relaxed."

"I've had time to think about things."

"And?"

"Her whereabouts will be on her office computer."

"Certain?"

Podric nodded.

"Let's get over there then."

"Uhuh."

Podric shook his head and drank his coffee. Archie said.

"Podric we've got to get to the bottom of this once and for all – checking on your mother and finding out a bit more about George and why he's here."

"I'm not interested."

Archie snorted.

"You think *I'm* callous?"

"I don't mean that. Mum, yes, but George is a side issue."

Archie managed to swallow some of his drink.

"Go on."

Podric looked out at the Moon's little garden. The old shed where he'd semi-invented Ultimate Alternative Reality – now his mother's painting studio and their little lawn which was in need of a cut. The terrace had recently been adorned by two gnomes Amy had come home with. 'Some of Lil's people were moving on. N and B. Cool.'

Chipped and discoloured, Noddy and Big Ears were now a

feature. Archie said.

"I guess it's pretty certain it's George who's trying to hack us."

Podric nodded.

"You're right when you say Secorni were using him to get to me, but we agree what lies behind all that is much more significant."

Podric turned back to face his business partner.

"Unfortunately, we have to reckon a tiny amount of knowledge about us having some kind of alternative reality has reached the security people. George attempting to hack into UAR whether for his own interest or more likely, to get these people off his back – the authorities are going to come after us."

Finishing his coffee Podric put his mug in the dishwasher. Archie said.

"I'll run with that. I told you, these bastards don't mess around. Anyway, if you're disinterested in finding your mother and my erstwhile ex-business partner, I'll do it."

Podric reached for his school bag lying in the hall. Archie finished his coffee.

"You won't Archie because you'll be with me."

"What do you mean?"

"I mean we're going inside Ultimate Alternative Reality for a while. We're going to find out why Kennedy was killed and why the moon landing was faked if it was. We're going on the attack."

Podric collected a couple of books lying at the bottom of the stairs.

"Can you spare half an hour?"

Archie looked at Podric quizzically.

"I need someone to come with me in Wombat to the driving school. It's my first lesson."

Wombat was the name his mother had given her VW. Archie shrugged.

"What else would I be doing?"

Podric locked the house. Archie continued.

"Want to write anymore conventional games?"

"What's the account looking like?"

The games creator burst out laughing.

"I told you Pasaro have been on. Fred S never lets up. Who could have believed that Iguana game would take off?"

Giving his business partner an old-fashioned look, Podric took out the car keys of his mother's Beetle and opened the driver's door. They got in.

"Your mum's got the car of her dreams and you're keeping this."

"Got to learn on something. I thought it might be safer than one of your Facel Vega's. Thanks for offering though."

Archie not having done so, laughed.

"You're one particular guy Podric, that's for sure."

Podric moved some clobber of Amy's on to the back seat. Archie said.

"That's a point – with your mother away on her tryst what about 'Double A' as the junior Moon sibling insists I call her?"

The vehicle sporting L plates Podric started the Volkswagen.

"She'll be with us."

Archie looked at Podric for a second then it dawned.

"No doubt along with my brood, other sundry ne're do wells and any other transitory fainéants you decide to add to the team for reasons known only to your dark and disturbed self."

Avoiding Archie's Facel Vega, Podric reversed reasonably smoothly into Briony Close.

"Anyone ever tell you what a creep you are?"

"More stars than there are in the heavens."

"That's exactly where we're going."

Part II
Total Immersion

Chapter 1
In Which We Server

Although state of the art for its time, the dubbing theatre at Shepperton Studios in December 1963 didn't possess the audio mixing facility it does today. As the director of *Dr. Strangelove or How I Learned to Stop Worrying and Love the Bomb* Stanley Kubrick was known to push all aspects of his profession to their limits and beyond. But in that pre-digital age magnetic audio spacing, laying up reel upon reel to create a film soundtrack was still the time-honoured process in use. Only when it was completed was the audio mix transferred via inter positive and married to the final neg-cut picture for cinematic release.

Because of the tragedy that had recently occurred in Dallas, the distributors of *Dr. Strangelove* – Columbia Pictures decided Major T. J. 'King' Kong's line in the film that 'A fella could have a pretty good weekend in Dallas with all that stuff' should be altered substituting the word Dallas for Vegas. Sitting in one of the studio's recording booths, the actor playing the role, Slim Pickens was dressed Texan style – leather tassel fringed jacket along with cowboy hat and boots. Pickens looked at the line he was to re-record. Even with Kubrick's perfectionism the job was done after a number of takes and the session concluded.

Parting company with the actor, Kubrick went across to his office. Adjacent to the *Dr. Strangelove* Pentagon War Room sound stage – although the film had wrapped weeks ago Kubrick had demanded stills images capture the empty set before it was taken down in the new year. Seeing it was lit, he looked in and for several seconds watched stills photographer Arthur Fellig aka Weegee at work. The War Room's design was fantastic. Concrete sided and geometrically styled as a bunker the set was enormous. Ceilinged, it was some hundred and thirty feet long and nearly forty foot high. Along the front facing wall massive electronic strategic maps looked down on a vast circular table, overhead lamps suspended above it.

Leaving his stills equipment in situ, Fellig prepared to depart for the day. Sitting at the table flicking through a file, Kubrick requested he had one of the studio gaffers kill the house lights on his way out. Alone on set – hearing voices above, Kubrick glanced up to see several people on an overhead gantry. Standing with Podric Moon and Dr Archie Light the late President Kennedy surveyed the make-believe world below. Whilst used to the remarkable – even Stanley Kubrick did a double take. Although now domicile in the UK, Kubrick was American by birth and like many of his countrymen had been affected by the young president's brutal assassination. The house lights dimming – only the conference table's overhead spots remained. The effect was surreal. The man standing beside the late president waved and the little group moved into shadow. Seconds later it appeared on the floor accompanied by two secret service agents assigned to protect the president. Not a man easily impressed, Kubrick stood up.

"Mr Kubrick."

JFK put out his hand which the stunned director shook.

"I saw your previous film. Interesting."

Referring to *Lolita* Kennedy glanced at the cavernous set.

"This is... something different. Care to show me over?"

"Er.

JFK laughed.

"These gentlemen can explain if anyone can."

Referring to Podric and Archie, Kennedy wandered off talking to Roy Kellerman, one of his security agents. A few minutes later Kubrick was reeling. What Podric and Archie told him was so staggering, so his thing, the director couldn't wait to have further discourse.

"So he's only here inside a computer game."

"As are you. Likely you'll know computer games weren't big in the early sixties – just crude beginnings."

Archie was casual.

"And given we're now in the first quarter of the twenty-first century and you're also no longer with us – we've made you part of his world."

Kubrick thought for a moment then laughed – something that was quite unusual for him.

"In his game then he's still the president."

"You got it. Guess we could programme an election, but-."

Kennedy called across the set.

"Think this up before Cuba?"

The president stood beneath a giant map of the USSR. Kubrick said.

"It was being worked on."

Looking around Kennedy was thoughtful.

"Any chance I can see the film?"

"It's being released next month. Right now, I'm afraid the final print is with the lab."

Not one to dwell on something he couldn't experience, Kennedy gave the set a last look.

"Pity."

"We can show you."

Producing a MacBook Pro Podric activated it. Fascinated by the device JFK looked over the boy's shoulder and watched an edited clip of the Doomsday Machine scene. Then flicking his finger across the 16-inch screen, Podric produced Buck Turgidson and Miss Scott - the Brigadier General's secretary and mistress in their bedroom. JFK impressed with what he saw, the last sequence viewed featured Major Kong straddling the H bomb. Kennedy highly amused, Kubrick was staggered - not by his imagery but Podric's MacBook Pro!

"The picture quality."

"12mp on the back, 5 on the front. Dr Strangelove's based on Werner von Braun then."

Archie's statement struck a jarring note.

"Riding the Paperclip line Dr Light..?"

Kennedy had a twinkle in his eye. Itching to get his hands on the MacBook Pro, Kubrick was hesitant.

"Er-. Amalgam.."

"The Teller, Kahn, von Neumann mix? Always struck me as strange bedfellows for a movie character."

"In German, merkwürdigliebe translates 'strange love'.

Kubrick looked from Kennedy to Archie.

"After this."

Archie gazed around the set.

"You develop a penchant for space. Already thinking about *2001: A Space Odyssey*, does the US government hire you to fake lunar landings in '68 we wonder?"

"Why would it do that?"

"Because NASA couldn't actually get men to the moon and back – or so the conspiracists speculate."

"'When state intent is deemed a necessity..'. Isn't that the reason you believe is behind my abrupt removal from office..?"

JFK and Archie's eyes locked for a second before the computer man continued.

"Then in *The Shining* – a film Mr Kubrick makes in 1980 all kinds of codes appear. From Danny's Apollo 11 sweater to Room 237."

"11 I get from watching the clip with Podric. 237?"

"A hotel room number. There supposedly weren't so many rooms and the number's a throwaway reference to the mean distance in miles between the moon and earth."

"What's it about?"

"Horror flick with psychic tendencies."

"Guess that's as good an analogy of the government as any."

John Barry's James Bond signature tune began playing on Podric's MacBook Pro followed by Shirley Bassey singing *Goldfinger* – another Barry composition. Watching the imagery, JFK was transfixed. So was Stanley Kubrick.

"That doesn't start shooting till next month."

"You have to remember Mr Kubrick this experience is inside a computer game. We can go any which way time wise within the game we've created. I read you're a Bond aficionado Mr President."

Kennedy was engrossed in the *Goldfinger* pre-title 'Shocking' scene. Kubrick was inquisitive.

"How do we play?"

"You don't. We do. You're characters we come across."

"And to win?"

Podric handed President Kennedy his MacBook Pro.

"For that you need a licence to kill."

Chapter 2
Reflections – Podric, Archie and Jack

Viewing via the upper section of his eyes and using the cursor in his wrist Podric Moon spooled through the menu of *JFK and His World* – the game he and his business partner Dr Archie Light had created.

The game constructed around JFK's life both political and personal – the latter less for salacious reasons but included because of where it took Kennedy into dark and dangerous waters – enemies the president had made both in official circles and the criminal underworld were proving an interesting backdrop for a computer game. In the corridors of government – globally, all the well-known difficulties – Cuba, The Bay of Pigs and the Missile Crisis as well as Vietnam and space exploration were featured. Domestically, challenges Kennedy faced during his presidency included Civil Rights and the movement that was led by Dr Martin Luther King. By 1963 tensions were running high, and Kennedy was forced to threaten Alabama governor George Wallace calling out the National Guard in order that African American students could register at the state university in Tuscaloosa. The game *JFK and His World* also featured the administrative side of Kennedy's presidency. His relationship with his cabinet, and particularly Lyndon Johnson. J. Edgar Hoover was another prominent figure. Given JFK's private life, the FBI's probing into his risqué world – Sam Giancana and the Mafia were also incorporated.

Using these events as a structure, the game set a variety of alternate options for a player challenging Kennedy's actions. In the Cuban Missile Crisis – the decision to create a quarantine zone around the island being the solution in reality – in the game

Khrushchev attacks America using nuclear missiles thus forcing
the player into a dangerous position. How to respond? What
course of action to take? Upping the ante – defeat or victory? In
Vietnam options included greater involvement by China in support of the north's Ho Chi Minh threatening global war. Another had the south's Ngô Đình Diêm uniting with the north and
America declining its involvement in the region only for Vietnam
and its South East Asia neighbours to rise up against the West, its
weaponry supplied by the Eastern Bloc.

Pausing the menu – Podric sat back in a chair in his mother's garden studio. He reflected yet again what a wonderful thing
UAR was. The more he thought about it the more he felt that the
ability to remove oneself from everyday life and enter new and
different adventures in another world in another time was truly
wondrous. Their first exploits in *Napoleonic Wars*, then America's
Civil War and now experiencing life in the 1960s – the possibilities Ultimate Alternative Reality opened up were never ending.
Right now though Podric knew he had challenges closer to home
that would need addressing, but before leaving the state, he'd just
check on what his UAR partner was up to.

*   *   *

Sitting in one of his Eames chairs high up in his den Archie Light
was also spooling through *JFK and His World*. Within its Menu
– under an Option marked 'Recreation' then 'Date', Spring '64
was highlighted. UAR being fully engaged – the late president's
sailboat Victura tacked across Nantucket Sound. Jack was at the
helm, and Archie was crewing. The Victura was a weatherly little
vessel and the afternoon lovely, the sailing was excellent. By early
evening the yacht's sails were down, and she was moored on a
buoy in Hyannisport harbour. Sitting in the cockpit JFK and Archie put the boat to bed.

"Not a bad crew."

"I've sailed a bit in the old country."

Archie smiled – so did Kennedy.

"You have Irish blood?"

"Not a drop, but in spite of the Brit thing, there's usually a warm welcome in Kerry's harbours especially if ones buying a round."

Kennedy laughed.

"That's the English for you, cynical to the end."

"Thought you liked the Brits."

"Did I say I didn't?"

Archie coiled some rope.

"President Kennedy, sadly not having the pleasure of knowing you in real life, I've felt since Podric and I met you in our alternate one, you haven't taken to me. I appreciate that's likely because I'm a contradictory son-of-a-bitch, but whilst I'm not one for international Who's Who sycophancy you're already proving one of history's more interesting characters."

Kennedy chuckled.

"My computed self will bear that in mind, Dr Light."

Archie smiled.

"At the point we're meeting today just months after Dallas – I've got the benefit of history. You'd have been taking on Goldwater in this year's elections right now had it not happened."

"Surprised you haven't programmed the election for me to challenge the Grand Old Party."

The late President Kennedy eased his aching back against the boats combing. Archie hung the rope he'd been coiling on a cleat.

"In this computer game we've created, I sense you're not very interested knowing who killed you or who might have done let alone some of the other things Podric and I are looking into."

"Whoever it was, whatever the background – 'could have been any nut. In the end, it still ends up to a bullet."

"But if it was organised crime or even some lone star government maverick wouldn't you want to know?"

"Hmm... Perhaps."

Kennedy seemed slightly impatient.

"People will do as they will. My being around's likely of little consequence."

"You don't believe that Mr President. You believe your being around made every difference. It's why you ran. It's what drove you."

Kennedy didn't respond. Archie went on.

"Let's skip over brother and father Joe's – sad loss to you that your elder brother was. But you were the one who was going to do it. None of the others were you – though Bobby would have made The White House in a few years' time."

"The Attorney General would make a good president."

"Such is history."

"As you say, you have me at a disadvantage."

Taking out a packet of small cigars, JFK offered one to Archie who accepted.

"For some particular reason you're a catalyst. Your presidency threw up more questions in its short span than it answered – more than others do in eight years."

"It's been a turbulent time."

"You can say that again – but by your questioning, pushing and probing and your other behaviour were you in some particular way its cause, one wonders?"

"That now surely is for me and my maker."

Lighting his cigar, Kennedy tossed a box of matches to Archie.

"It strikes me that for lots of reasons you were a man in a hurry. I think you felt you'd never make old bones so used every hour."

"You have a criticism of that?"

"No, but with your family so young – I'd say not easy the life you led."

Archie puffed on his short corona.

"When Jackie came back from Greece just a few weeks before your assassination people said they noticed a difference."

"That's a private matter." The two men looked at each other.

"I speak from an historic perspective Mr President."

"History is a fine thing doctor and I commend your interest in the subject, but I'm not much concerned with personal analysis."

"Surely it's the personal element that makes history so interesting."

Kennedy looked at Archie shrewdly.

"A hundred years from now if historians have any interest in my presidency it sure as hell won't be because of the number of broads I've screwed."

Archie looked at JFK.

"No. You're probably right. If it's a single thing it'll be the Missile Crisis – though there is a fascination with what you got up to privately."

"You seem to have the answers doctor."

The two men puffed their cigars.

"You often spoke of being assassinated. You even talked of it early in the morning it took place."

Kennedy tapped a length of ash from his corona.

"We'd gone into nut country. It's well documented."

The late president drummed his fingers on the tiller handle.

"Right now, I'll admit from my point of view posthumously existing inside a computer game has its limitations."

JFK looked across the harbour.

"As you relate – apart from some vicarious interest in what a group of undesirables did for me, I'm not much concerned with exactly who pulled the trigger."

Archie Light was surprised at the detached manner JFK spoke of his demise. Kennedy went further.

"To my way of thinking it's of more interest the programs my administration began, the bills brought before congress those sons of bitches did their best to frustrate."

"As you now know, it all got passed. The Civil Rights Act sailed through congress and Johnson signs it into law July 2nd this year."

Kennedy finished his cigar. "Lyndon will enjoy that."

The late president tossed his cigar butt over the side and continued.

"He knows how to work the hill, I'll give him that. Lyndon was always at his best up there."

"Yes. Historically LBJ is remembered for being masterly with the legislature. As a politician reaching out to the electorate though he didn't have that indefinable something that people want to relate to." Archie stood.

"Whoever or whatever you are President Kennedy many people around the world mourned your loss. The American people felt an overwhelming sense of guilt when you were shot."

"Quite a speech. At least it laid my spoilt rich kid image to rest." JFK laughed and continued.

"One way to dispel a myth. Anyway, not everyone was sorry I'd gone. Some hated my guts. Let's get ashore."

Archie reached over Victura's side and pulled a little dinghy attached to their buoy towards them. JFK made his way for'ard.

"You going to handle the oars?"

Archie got into the dingy. Kennedy climbed in after him.

"The moment the shot went into you – was there a split second – just a moment?"

"For what? Pondering life's injustices? It was a bit late for that." They pushed off. Kennedy said.

"If there was a moment it was so brief as to be infinitesimal. It certainly wasn't shining if that's what you mean."

Archie began to pull for the shore.

"If existing inside a computer game has its limitations – why are you doing it?

"Because I'm interested in how things move forward."

"Even though you can't influence them."

President Kennedy looked at Archie Light. One felt he was recognising what an awkward cuss the computer games man could be. JFK smiled. "As I said, it has it's drawbacks, but I'll ride with it for the moment."

Picking up a tin lying at his feet, John Kennedy emptied some rainwater over the side.

"Besides, it beats being dead!"

Chapter 3
Inside Out

Five hundred yards above the farmhouse, the man put down his field glasses and leaned back against the flint wall. A baseball cap pulled low over his brow his face was difficult to discern. The man activated a cell phone.

"Pilgrims confirmed."

The call concluded. Dark now – a vehicle made its way along the valley and parked. Shadowy figures disembarked, melting into the night as they moved up the lane.

In the farmhouse known as Bwthyn Anghysbell George Benedict was making supper half listening to the radio. Having had a shower, Barbara Moon appeared. Dressed in jeans and a sweater, she combed her hair.

"A cook too. You're a man of many talents George."

Benedict looked round.

"Ah, you've surfaced. Sleep well?"

"I always sleep well but there's nothing like mountain air."

Benedict tipped vegetables into a stir fry pan.

"There's wine open."

Seeing the bottle of red and a half-drunk glass, another unused one stood beside it. Barbara poured herself some wine.

"Hmm... With such domestic bliss no one's going to believe I've spent the best part of a week with a strange man in the name of friendship."

Preoccupied with cooking Benedict didn't immediately hear the little device vibrating on the windowsill beside him. Checking it, he saw that the south side of the mobile triangulated security system he'd set up had been penetrated. Several figures were inside the invisible cordon. Turning off the stove George took Barbara's arm.

"Intruders are thirty yards from the door. They're armed."

His voice level was low but clear. Picking up two sets of ear defenders that he'd hung on the back of the kitchen door, George placed a set over Barbara's ears. Putting on the other, he took out his phone and selected a newly-installed app which he placed on Standby. George made a sign to Barbara that she should follow him. The two made their way through to the back of the cottage and used an inside door to get into the shed where Barbara's Land Rover was parked. In darkness, George peered through a gap in the shed doors. Turning to her, he put a finger to his lips then moved his hand in an ignition sign. Barbara pulled off her ear defenders and pulled one of George's away from his ear.

"What do these people want?!"

"Me."

He was equally quiet but intense. Barbara said.

"Who are they?"

"American goon squad. If we've any chance of getting out of here we've got to go now."

"I thought Podric had neutralised them."

In spite of the tenseness of the situation, George turned to her.

"Do you know Barbara it's amazing, but they've got more than one team."

Barbara stifled a giggle.

"Why have we got these on?"

"You'll see. Wait till I give you the thumbs up to start the engine."

Putting her ear defenders back on Barbara quietly unlocked her Defender. George took another look at his security app. He could see that the beam he'd angled across the rear of the building hadn't been disturbed. The shed being nearer to the hillside, a track climbed steeply away from the property. The route was badly rutted, but it would be their only chance. At least they had the perfect vehicle. Activating the radio app, a programmed sound pulse was emitted which affected the SWAT team. Dropping their

weapons, men put their hands to their ears. George threw open
the doors and Barbara having started the Land Rover, reversed so
quickly, he had to jump clear to avoid its wheels. Leaping into the
passenger seat beside her the Defender set off up the hill. In spite
of the gradient they made good going. After several hundred yards
Barbara checked her rear-view mirror but no lights were tailing
them.

"Somethings wrong."

George craned round. Barbara continued.

"We're not being pursued."

"That's wrong?"

A mile or two further on lights flickered in front of the Land
Rover. Seconds later they were in the full glare of a searchlight.
Soldiers revealing themselves, Barbara said.

"Depends if you prefer a British army unit to whoever those
agents provocateurs were, we left behind."

*   *   *

Aware Podric had things to do and having a line of action he
wanted to pursue on his own, Archie Light checked out of *JFK
and His World*. Activating WW2's *Call of Duty*, he opened a sub-
section – *The V2 Rocket*. Spooling through its list of characters
various names featured in Operation Paperclip – the codename
the Americans gave to spiriting Nazi scientists out of Peenemünde
in the Pomeranian region of eastern Germany to New Mexico
at the end of the war. Operation Osoaviakhim was the Russian
equivalent (perhaps the race into space started from this point?).
Leaving Ultimate Alternative Reality on standby, Archie sunc the
game up to it.

*   *   *

In an army barracks in Herefordshire Barbara Moon sat opposite
a slightly built but extremely fit-looking captain. The interview
room stark and unwelcoming, the door opened, and a soldier led

in George Benedict.

"Sorry about that. Nature's call."

Durrant opened a file. Barbara said.

"A file on us already?"

Barbara was watchful.

"It's only details we immediately obtain."

"From my license number. You probably have my blood group by now."

Durrant smiled. He looked across at George.

"You though Mr... Benedict. Drawn a big blank."

Benedict's look was neutral.

"I haven't been living in the UK."

"But you are a British citizen."

"I was."

You don't travel under a British passport?"

"No. Irish."

Durrant raised an eyebrow.

"You're from the Republic then."

"I wasn't born in Ireland but I took Irish nationality after the referendum."

"Why?"

Benedict shrugged.

"Same reason many people did. Easier travelling in Europe. I've been living abroad for a while now."

Durrant sat back.

"And you're staying in the Brecon's.."

"We are."

This from Barbara. Captain Durrant sat forward.

"Look, you're only here because I have to caution you. Whilst there's no accusation of trespass, you blundered into the middle of our exercise. You could have suffered injury or even worse."

A knock and the door opened. An NCO entered and whispered something in Captain Durrant's ear.

"Excuse me. I won't be long."

With that he got up and left the room. Following Durrant out, the sergeant closed the door. A second or two went by.

"Why do you think he's been called away?"

"To do with me."

"Might be something else."

Benedict shook his head.

"Uhuh. Tentacles will be spreading."

Barbara got up.

"What's to stop us walking out of here?"

"Several hundred-armed soldiers."

She smiled at Benedict's comment.

"But they can't hold us for no reason. Driving into their shooting match was an accident."

"Barbara, with what I'm up against they can do anything they like."

George sighed.

"I should never have let you come along."

"That was my decision."

Benedict looked at her.

"This isn't funny. It's deadly serious."

"It's alright George. You made that very plain."

Barbara smiled. Benedict got up.

"Anyone ever tell you what a warped sense of humour you have?"

"Yes."

"Somehow I thought so."

Chapter 4
Peenemünde, Mittelwerk and Reutte

Coming out of an office building that evening the view welcoming Archie Light was incredible. It was autumn 1944 and the Peenemünde rocket facility was busy preparing that night's launches. The launch sites being located within a series of grassy depressions vehicles were pulling V2s into their allocated positions. Each rocket was hydraulically erected vertically and a simple gantry held it in place. Beside the emplacements was a small control shed. Technicians swarmed all over the site. The rustic base with its futuristic projectiles was a hive of excited activity.

Something nudged Archie's leg. He looked down to see Dog beside him. What the-?! What was he doing here? How come he'd entered Ultimate Alternative Reality? Archie's UAR entries had always been erratic, and this was no exception. As if to support this, the Irish Wolfhound gave an underwhelming yawn.

"Someone's impressed then."

Archie turned to find his sister-in-law Belgian countess Dinah de Vries standing beside him.

"Wha-? Dinah?"

Archie was incredulous. He didn't even know she'd been programmed into their alternative reality computer game state!

"Archie."

Seemingly unsurprised, Dinah kissed him on the cheek. Dog nudged her leg and she ruffled his shaggy coat. Archie said.

"You haven't changed."

Slightly shorter than her sister and less statuesquely beautiful, Dinah was sexier.

"But you have."

She looked at her brother-in-law.

"A lot to deal with by the sound of it."

She put a hand to Archie's cheek and held it there for several seconds. A German soldier approached.

"Deine Pässe."

A rifle slung over his shoulder the man put out his hand. Without missing a beat, a torrent of German invective flowed from Dinah's lips. Taken aback, the soldier began to retreat but then repeated his request though less demonstratively. A truck pulled up. Men got out and the soldier was called over to them.

"Didn't know your German was so fluent?"

"There's a lot about me you don't know Archibald Light. What a name – Archibald? Wonderful. Who gave it to you? Family member with a grudge?"

"That describes my mother handsomely. What did you tell him?"

"Amongst other things that I was your mistress."

Watching the soldier talking to the men who were a mixture of civilians and military, Archie recognised Werner von Braun. The rocket scientist was good looking in a heavy-set way. Several SS officers appeared, and the mood became convivial.

"We need to get moving."

"Am I that unalluring?"

Neither Archie nor Dinah had taken note of their dress. She was expensively clad in a woman's hunting attire of the period – fitting tweed jacket, jodhpurs and riding boots. A rakish tweed hat with a feather in its band completed her wardrobe. Archie wore military uniform – a captain in the Abwehr. The soldier accompanied by two SS men turned to look at them. Dinah returned their gaze.

"Where are we going and how?"

Archie moved his right hand over his left wrist. Activating UAR he spooled through the menu of *Call of Duty – The V2 Rocket* and selected Mittelwerk.

"I'm currently pursuing a line of enquiry. I'll explain things to you more fully as we go along."

*   *   *

Located deep underground and protected by the Thuringian Harz mountains, the Mittelwerk factory was a twenty-four hour a day operation. Row upon row of V1 flying bombs and V2 rockets were stored in tunnels carved out of rock by the slave labour force taken from the nearby Mittelbau-Dora concentration camp. Whilst the works were clinically constructed, the state of the workforce was shocking. Skeletal and malnourished many men could barely walk let alone function. Railway trucks loaded with weaponry had been specially designed to distribute their precious cargos as expeditiously as the Third Reich demanded. It was the Fuhrer's belief that his wonder weapons would win his terrible war for him, a war whose tide was turning against the madman's evil regime. Archie and Dinah's UAR arrival saw the computer games creator part of a visiting team from Peenemünde. Having managed to leave Dog off the participant list, Dr Licht and his assistant Fräulein de Vries toured the complex. As he walked around Archie wondered just how crazy Hitler was. He could apparently be sane enough to take over a country and to many of his governed populace, rather than certifiable, the man's ambitions seemed alarmingly credible – evil and bizarre that they were.

A meeting held in offices at one end of the underground works between scientists and engineers was winding up. Both the Peenemünde and Mittelwerk participants included some fine scientific brains but neither the chemists, the rocket experts nor those in production responsible for driving the workforce to build them seemed to notice the dead and dying prisoners being employed. It was as if dealing with these poor decrepit people daily in some strange way rendered their overseers immune to the horrors before their very eyes. A prisoner collapsing at a bench was walked past – the Braun brothers Magnus and Wernher sharing a private joke as they went by.

Now waiting for their cars to arrive, Archie and Dinah looked at each other. In a few hours they had seen the horrors of the world. Separated from his sister-in-law who climbed into the car ahead of him with Wernher von Braun and other scientists, Archie's companions included Arthur Rudolph who ran the Mecklenberg research centre's rocket and fabrication laboratory and Ernst Steinhoff who managed flight guidance and telemetering devices essential to control a rocket's path.

"How good is he?"

Several people in the Mercedes limousine looked up. Archie hadn't realised he'd spoken out loud.

"von B."

'Papa' Reidel put down some documents and began cleaning his spectacles. A brilliant man himself, he was a leading rocket designer.

"Presumably you don't refer to Sigismund or Magnus."

Rudolf and Steinhoff smiled. Arthur Rudolph sat back.

"No single person is responsible for the creation of the V2 or any of our rockets. It's teamwork."

"Is that Wernher's strength then?"

The other scientists looked at each other.

"Why this interest in von Braun?"

This from a steely Steinhoff.

"When the war is lost others will want your skills and people will try to get out. The two powers who will control things will be the Soviets and the Americans. Do you go west or east?"

This really alarmed the scientists sitting in the car.

"That's treasonous. You can be tried for any one of those statements."

"Where are you from Herr Dr Licht?"

Steinhoff appeared the more committed National Socialist. Before he could answer, the car abruptly came to a halt at a roadblock and two SS officers climbed in. The atmosphere was tense except for Herr Dr Licht who ignoring the soldiers, continued as if they hadn't joined.

"Oh, I'm the lowest of the low studying the human condition. The Fuhrer likes to know what's going on in the minds of his subjects."

The scientists were suspicious. The SS officers smiled.

"And the striking young woman, Frāulein de Vries? I don't recollect seeing her before. Is she a member of your psychoanalysis team?"

Steinhoff was more hesitant now.

"Oh no. She's busy telling everyone she's my mistress."

The scientists sat open mouthed. The SS officers laughed. Archie sat back.

"How good are Gröttrup and Putze?"

Now convinced he was part of the secret service the scientific occupants were mute. Finally, Arthur Rudolph spoke.

"They do different things. Gröttrup's a remote guidance man. Putze is a technical director on combustion chambers."

Steinhoff looked hard at Archie.

"Why do you ask?"

"Because they're looking east like the Fuhrer."

The SS men interpreting Archie's comment related to Operation Barbarossa launched two years previously, nodded.

*   *   *

A rainy afternoon on Wednesday 2nd May 1945 saw a dilapidated army truck wind its way down Adolf Hitler Pass having travelled from Oberammergau towards the little Austrian town of Reutte. Inside the vehicle were seven men including the von Braun brothers Magnus and Wernher and Walter Dornberger – military head of the V2 program. The army vehicle trundling its way towards the border, two American jeeps suddenly appeared on either side of the road forcing it to stop. Some dialogue took place as well as a body search of the occupants and a check of the vehicle. The Germans were told to follow one of the jeeps. Forming part of a small convoy, arriving in Austria that evening the scientists were taken to a meeting room in the American mess. US intelligence decided they would interview the men individually. Wernher von Braun was shown into a suite and told that an American de-briefing team would be interrogating him. Left on his own Wernher wandered around his accommodation and was surprised to come across Archie and Dinah chatting in his sitting room.

"Ah, the wondering minstrel."

Von Braun looked at Archie.

"My English.."

"Will improve in America."

"I would like that."

"I'm sure you would. It's richer than the Soviet Union."

Archie got up and walked up to the German.

"So, you're the great Wernher von Braun. I'm interested to know just what a dodgy bastard you are."

Dinah translated but not literally. Although Wernher was in a tight corner and his future far from secure, there was something about this von Braun brother – an assuredness that spoke volumes. Archie continued.

"I've had my doubts about you being the great rocket scientist people say you are but perhaps that's your secret..?"

Archie looked penetratingly at von Braun.

"You're the arch manager bringing these eccentric and disparate group of scientific brains together. That's no mean feat. I'll give you that."

He turned away.

"Is the German word for disparate, difficult?"

Dinah smiled.

"Yuh. Disparat."

So did Wernher. Being a man able to turn on the charm himself, Archie was unimpressed by Wernher's.

"At least now I know you really are the duplicitous SS grifter I always suspected you to be."

"Ich weiss nicht, was grifter bedeutet, aber ich nehme an, dass es abfällig ist – weil ich so ein bastard war, wurde ich wegen meiner anti-Nazi aktivitäten verhaftet."

Dinah translated von Braun's reply – of his arrest and imprisonment by the Schutzstaffel.

"You clearly understand more English than you let on Wernher, smart fellow that you are."

Archie sighed.

"But we know all about the female dentists so called betrayal of you – Himmler, Speer, your release."

Archie looked tired. His recent experiences with Dinah in *Call of Duty – The V2 Rocket* had affected him.

"If one believes in your rocket and space ambitions – it's not the tightrope stuff you've been walking I'm concerned with. I get that – 'been doing it all my life."

He turned back to von Braun.

"But you lost all sense of morality. You knew what workforce was being used and frankly Wernher, you didn't give a damn as long as nothing got in the way of your rocket dreams."

Archie looked at von Braun dispassionately.

"But then in your mind that's a small price to pay."

Voices were heard in the corridor outside.

"Rocket obsessed you surely are but you're also a Nazi."

Chapter 5
Bwthyn Anghysbell

Sitting in the semi-darkened living room of the Welsh cottage Podric Moon looked at the two men in front of him. Setting up the meeting within the computer game he'd created *JFK and His World* – in their time James Angleton as head of the CIA and J. Edgar Hoover, the FBI's director, were America's highest-ranking security officers. One managed overseas issues and counter intelligence, the other, domestic policing. From their respective positions they jointly had a sizeable say in homeland security. Neither held the other in particularly high regard and though their interests sometimes crossed both Angleton and Hoover were naturally suspicious people, who privately disliked sharing information. Picking up a jug from the windowsill, the Welsh dragon proudly emblazoned on its side, Angleton said.

"Quaint little place."

He put the pitcher back and studied a photograph of the Brecon Beacons.

"So we're in the Land of My Father's. I was at school just over the border."

Addressing Angleton, Podric said.

"Your man Whitten – and Helms along the way... Yuri Nosenko."

He turned to Hoover.

"And you – the wire you received warning of the assassination and did nothing about. Double-Chek Corp and your Mexican assassins – seeing LBJ into The White House. The conspiracy rolls on..."

Hoover rolled his eyes.

"You cannot still be seriously interested in who pulled the trigger on that little playboy."

"I'm not. And neither is Kennedy which is why the public's continued interest fascinates. It doesn't go away."

The two men didn't much impress Podric. Angleton said.

"And with history's hindsight, people think we know."

Taking off his glasses, he wiped their thick-lenses. Podric said.

"They're certain you do – either the action, the reason or both."

James Jesus Angleton removed a last fleck of dust from his spectacles.

"And by such implication half the American government including you suggest, the man who replaced him."

Angleton put his glasses back on and continued.

"As well as underworld interests and Mr Castro. Surprised you haven't summoned the NSA and Secret Service. Maybe your James Bond did it? An overseas contract. Doesn't his 007 status licence him to kill?"

Looking about the room, Hoover said.

"Kid, just about everyone in the goddamn world had a hand in killing Kennedy. Books about his checkout rival Bible sales let alone those of the Quran."

A fastidious man, Hoover adjusted the lapel of his suit.

Podric said.

"I'm interested in the moon."

Not knowing what to make of this J. Edgar chuckled.

"You're different boy, I'll say that. Come at stuff in a lively manner."

"And Kennedy."

Whereas Hoover was earthy, James Jesus was more cerebral and noted the implication.

"You're asking if the moon landings were faked because of his challenge."

"Were they?"

Angleton said.

"I didn't walk on it myself."

Podric got up and went over to the window.

"How many people would have to be in on a cover up like that?"

"If it was managed by senior operatives – the fewer the better."

Hoover erupted with laughter.

"I always knew the CIA were a crazy bunch, but I didn't know they were mad. Almost worth coming out of retirement."

Angleton turned on his internal security equivalent.

"You're so mired – Nagy, Permindex..."

Then looking at Podric, he said.

"Tell me about computer games."

Angleton sat down. Initially Podric spoke with his back to them as he looked out at the evening.

"Early games were coming on the scene during your lifetime though they were crude, elementary."

Podric walked around.

"They're sophisticated now. What we call High Definition – even 3D. Again, you're aware of the concept."

UAR's creator felt charged.

"Played on a conventional screen – in effect like viewing television. Several years ago, Virtual Reality appeared. You wear an eye mask which assists entering a virtual world. I've created something else that takes things further. People experiencing Ultimate Alternative Reality are in a state that allows them to be in another pre-set existence sunc up to any particular game. They see, feel and live it. In this adventure I entered the world of *JFK Reloaded* – a game that was already on the market. Since then I've expanded the scenario writing *JFK and His World* – which is the game adapted by UAR that enables us to meet now."

Podric sat down.

"Sounds a little juvenile."

"If that's the case such juvenilia has changed people's lives."

He stretched.

"I became interested in the 1960s. Starting so positively, it ended in failure."

Angleton said.

"Except the moon landing."

"If that happened."

"What's your verdict?"

Angleton pushed his heavyweight specs back up his nose. Podric said.

"It's out right now but there's also talk the film director Stanley Kubrick shot sequences for the supposed landing."

"Where? Where did he do that?" Podric shrugged. Hoover said.

"If he worked on them in the States, I'd know."

"Which leaves..." Angleton was thoughtful.

"Went to live in your neck of the woods, didn't he?"

Incredulous, Podric said. "What filming lunar sequences in England?"

"Why not? No crazier there than anywhere else."

"He's the guy that made that space movie. Right?"

The FBI man was dismissive.

"And *The Shining*."

Angleton gave the movie title particular emphasis. Podric responded. "That was after Mr Hoover's time."

"So what does it all add up to?"

"Right now, a games writing colleague of my partner's is being hunted down by your people because they think he has an angle."

Podric sipped a half-drunk mug of coffee.

"Pressured by the agency to find out about my invention, this guy has been trying to get into it."

"And the relevance of that?" Angleton sounded cynical.

"Because how we are now – UAR could be the entity that exposes people who covered up what really happened. The assassination, Apollo – the lot."

"Hmm... This is very interesting Mr..?

"Moon. Podric Moon." Angleton laughed.

"You've got the right name alright. But will the world be a better place when you make this knowledge public?"

"Likely not, but its right people know the truth."

James Angleton smiled. J. Edgar Hoover laughed and said.

"The truth... The truth is only ever anyone's perception. We've spent our entire lives dissembling the truth."

"And you made the world a better place, did you?"

"Podric Moon - when you work for a government you do what you think best to serve that government. Nations don't have friends, they have interests."

"So, you're not in favour of truth, then?"

"I'm in favour of reality - what goes on in the real world."

"That does rather run counter to this then - your being in an alternate one."

*   *   *

Night, rain swept across Hereford barracks as the little convoy prepared to move out. It consisted of three vehicles - two military and one civilian though the middle Land Rover had a service look, its colour being a paler version of British Army green. Barbara Moon sat in the front alongside a driver. In the canvas covered rear George Benedict peered through a plastic window.

"Where's the nearest army base from here?"

"Back over the border in Wales."

Standing by the passenger door Captain Durrant was slightly hesitant.

"I'm sorry you were detained. As I advised, you were only brought here because it was our manoeuvres you stumbled into."

In the interview room, Benedict hadn't been able to discern what regiment Durrant was from but the badge on his wet maroon beret denoted the SAS. Durrant continued.

"The couple of security issues were just a formality. Anyway, my apologies. One of my corporals will drive you home. Mrs Moon. Mr Benedict."

Wet now, Durrant gave a brief salute. Walking over to an office building he was met by an American officer. The convoy moved out, the middle vehicle a little jerkily. Barbara turned to the driver and did a double take. She looked at her son's sleeve.

"How long have you been driving, corporal?"

Out of UAR and back in the real world, Podric was concentrating.

"Not long ma'am though when buying one of these for my

mum recently, they let me have an off-road test."

Barbara laughed at his incorrigibility.

"Where are we being taken?"

George was tenser.

"US people are standing by to lift you from a Brit base in Brecon."

"So how are we to escape?"

Podric picked up an infrared headset.

"I just said I've done some off-roading."

"So where to?"

"Briony Close seems as good a place as any."

As the leading truck swung down a lane, Podric turned off it along a smaller track. The second vehicle followed them. Putting on the infrared headset, Podric killed the lights and several twists and turns later Barbara's Land Rover crossed a cattle grid and headed out on to the moor. Podric driving without lights they quickly escaped the beam of the second army vehicle and minutes later had disappeared into the night.

Chapter 6
White Sands and Apollo 1

Evening now, and mercifully cooler, the afternoon of 24th August 1946 had seen temperatures in the remote part of Doña Ana County, New Mexico known as White Sands rise to over 120° Fahrenheit. It had been so hot in the dust bowl the soles of men's boots had melted. The location behind barbed wire, a few shanty military huts were scattered about and in the distance the strange structure of an elementary launching gantry complete with rocket poked its steel nose skywards. Accompanied from Fort Bliss, Texas by a member of the US military, Major Jim Hamilton, Wernher von Braun conferred with several of his German rocket scientist colleagues. The technicians having been sprung from Nazi Germany via the United States security services at the behest of the American government, US rocketry was largely progressing thanks to Yankee funding and German technology.

Looking at the rocket on the pan von Braun was in a spirited mood. High ranking American military and scientific personnel were much in evidence amongst them Dr Archie Light and his colleague Dinah de Vries. Bearing the appropriate accreditation, quite what they were doing there no one bothered to ask but they appeared conversant with the surroundings. Major Hamilton was talking to Dinah as Archie wandered over to the Germans. Colleagues came and went asking von Braun questions. In a lull Archie said.

"Got away then?"

von Braun turned.

"Ah, here you are. I've been wondering when you'd show up."

"Sorry to be so obvious."

"Don't apologise Mr-."

"Doctor. Light."

"Ah, you're a medical man. What are you doing here?"

"I am not a medical man. In a manner of speaking I'm an engineer. I create computer games."

von Braun didn't register.

"I won't explain how I come to be here but being the brilliant man you are, fast forward 50 plus years."

von Braun drew on his cigarette.

"Games with computers?"

"People love them – in fact they're obsessed."

A colleague of von Braun's approached with a question. The scientist snapped out an answer. Archie continued.

"Subjects are unlimited. Anything you can think of. The computation power I possess in this microchip-."

Archie held up his left wrist.

"Has more computing ability than every computer in America today. The secret's in micro circuits."

"But you here now – is this a game?"

"The biggest."

von Braun looked thoughtful.

"What have you got against me?"

"You know the answer to that."

Archie looked at the white sand covering his boots. It got everywhere.

"The fact that you're a Nazi bothers me."

"Ah. Well now I'm a prisoner. We're known as Prisoners of Peace."

A claxon sounded. They watched as in the distance men began leaving the gantry.

"I'd suggest your existence has little similarity with Nordhausen."

"Bah. You concern me with that?"

Incredulous, Archie's face was inches from von Braun's.

"Concern you? Concern you?! You being involved with the biggest set of gangsters the world's ever seen. Concern you? You disgust me!"

Von Braun was silent for several seconds then his face took on a look of superiority.

"The vision I have knows no boundaries. Nazism was an irrelevance to me. America is my country now, the country that's going to fulfil my dreams."

He turned away.

"It's you who's naïve friend – you and your beautiful assistant."

von Braun became contemptuous.

"You really think your wonderful United States, your land of the free – Uncle Sam would have bothered with me if he hadn't wanted what I possess and wanted it so badly he'd do anything to get hold of it."

"Even a deal with the devil – yes I'll believe that. Don't hold America up as a symbol of moral rectitude. How's your belief in God doing?"

von Braun didn't reply. Calmed now, Archie looked straight into the German's pale blue eyes.

"When meeting truly great men Wernher – scientists, mathematicians, or artists – they will tell you a belief in a deity bigger than themselves, space and the heavens is a requisite for their existence. Without that, man has no morality. You have no morality Wernher. That's why you'll not only never be a great man but remain in a gutter where you belong."

von Braun shrugged.

"We will see. We will see what I achieve and the respect I receive."

"Yes we will. And whatever heights you reach you'll know that someone out there sees into you – sees you as being the moral bankrupt you are."

The modified V2 rocket blasted off and climbed into the clear evening sky. Watching its trajectory for several seconds von Braun was preoccupied.

"Pure German genius."

He looked round but there was no sign of Archie or Dinah – only some tumbleweed gently blowing across the desert.

*   *   *

Sitting in Control Center 2 in NASA's Launch Control Center

on Merritt Island configured for the Apollo missions, Pilot Roger Chaffee, Senior Pilot Ed White and Command Pilot Virgil 'Gus' Grissom watched a tape of their deaths trapped inside the command module of Apollo 1 perched on top of the Saturn 1-B rocket, on Launch Pad 34. Chaffee had his head in his hands, White looked dumbstruck and Grissom was angry. Sitting nearby Dr Archie Light and his sister-in-law Dinah de Vries looked on appalled at what they were viewing. When it was over Grissom turned to Archie.

"Who are you?"

"I'm a twenty-first century computer games writer."

"What the-?!!"

Archie got up.

"You're able to see this because of a computer game."

Grissom also stood.

"What the hell are you talking about?"

Archie's shoulders sagged.

"It's a story."

"You'd better start talking then."

Archie told his tale taking them into computer games worlds – from *Super Mario* to *Sonic the Hedgehog*, *Teenage Mutant Ninja Turtles* and *Grand Theft Auto*. He explained what his current adventure involved. They skirted through *Call of Duty* which Archie and Dinah had already experienced in their quest to know more about Wernher von Braun.

"We see him from time to time. Plenty of Germans at NASA."

Ed White was neutral.

"What a great world man. I could have some of that!"

The youngest of the three astronauts Roger Chaffee was exuberant watching *Space Invaders*! Although untrained in their art, Chaffee being an aviator, quickly locked into the games concept and began showing Dinah their finer points.

"So apart from letting us view our own deaths, what are you doing here?"

Whilst he found Archie's story interesting Grissom was more serious. So was Archie.

"I want to check out the state of play at NASA in 1967 from your perspective. What the atmosphere was like. Many people felt that the congressional hearing after you died was a whitewash."

"Wouldn't surprise me. Nothing was ever straight with this project."

"What do you mean?"

"I mean there was a lot wrong with it."

"Isn't there always when things are pioneering?"

"Sure – but there's pioneering and there's downright incompetence."

Ed White was bitter, Grissom restless.

"But that doesn't answer why – why you want to do this?"

Archie appeared reflective.

"I'm exploring the possibility man never made it to the moon in '69 and that the world was duped in the biggest deception of all time."

Grissom burst out laughing.

"That's when they did it, huh?"

This from White.

"Supposedly." Grissom stared at Archie.

"You don't think they got there."

It didn't seem a question. Archie was equivocal.

"If you'd asked me a few weeks ago I'd have laughed. The idea of Armstrong and Aldrin not walking on the selenic satellite never crossed my mind. But since starting this adventure which kicked off with JFK's assassination – it's opened up a can of worms. Subterfuge and duplicity in every direction.

"'Reckon."

Ed White walked off. Grissom moved around impatiently.

"JFK didn't really know what he was doing setting up the challenge. That's okay – he didn't care. It was shooting a goal to beat the Russians who by the way, were way out ahead of us at the time." Grissom paused.

"Saying that we'd have someone up there walking around in ten years – that was really a problem."

Grissom sat on the edge of a table. Archie said.

"Getting a human being into deep space – are you talking

about the Van Allen radiation belts, effects on the body?"

"Let alone technical foul ups."

"Like."

"How many d'you want? As the world now knows – from the the comms and the wiring to the hatch, our module was completely unsafe. I told 'em but it made no difference. That's why I hung out the lemon."

Grissom shrugged and went on.

"What you're talking about, debates have raged how to get round the VA belt problem. My take's been to punch right through 'em fast. It doesn't eliminate the danger, but one might have a chance."

Grissom scratched his head.

"As big a problem is no module's gonna make it home through the atmosphere unless it adopts a skip re-entry – like a stone skimming water. Duck and a drake. Then there's body protection. Without some kind of shielding, radiation'll likely do for us. At best we'll be laid out sick."

Tense, the colonel forced himself to relax.

"What you got to realise though fella is there's no shortage of us aviator test folk who want to sign up for this stuff. We all want a trip to the moon, go walkabout. It's been motivating us for years. It's the technology or lack of it that's screwball." Archie said.

"Listening to you is getting to the moon feasible then?"

"If by feasible you mean it's damned difficult, well-nigh impossible, and we'll probably end up meat, then sure."

"But did th-?"

"Ask me that again and you'll be."

Grissom smiled. Gus got up and addressed Archie directly.

"Archie Light I do not know if Neil, Buzz and Mike got up there. All I'll say is that if they did NASA would really have to have upped its game."

Grissom looked across at Roger Chaffee and Dinah de Vries who were laughing.

"You can leave her behind." He was rueful.

"I heard you and Betty – love of your life."

"It's not just love fella. How about life?"

Chapter 7
Reality Checks

"So what the hell were you doing in all those places with Dinah?"

The Honourable Charlotte Light wasn't in the best of moods with her husband.

"I told you. I was in *JFK and His World* and wanted to find out more about Wernher von Braun."

"Who's he when he's at home?"

"He was big in rocketry and people believe a leading brain behind putting a man on the moon. That's all."

"And Dinah was important to this?!"

"I explained: I didn't plan on taking Dinah."

Archie was for him contrite, but Charlotte wasn't listening.

"Gallivanting about Nazi Germany – if you're going to make such idiotic trips why not take me?!"

"You know me accessing UAR is-."

"Erratic."

His sentence finished by his daughter, the three of them were sitting in Archie's den in the Lighthouse. Charlotte said.

"I couldn't care less. It's more you and she. You know I've always wondered."

"For heaven's sake."

"Morning all."

Stepping out of the lift Dinah de Vries joined them.

"Hi Aunt D. Sleep well?"

Cosima got up and greeted her aunt.

"Coffee?"

Without waiting for a reply, Cosima went to work with the

Gran Gaggia.

"Do I sense I've entered a contretemps within the bosom of the Light family?"

Dinah laughed.

"I said I was coming over sis. With all this other world excitement with your husband, thought I'd better put in a real life appearance."

For all her sophistication Charlotte felt vulnerable.

"What is it Lottie? The usual worry about me making off with your Archibald?"

The only person to call Charlotte by her abbreviated name, Dinah hugged her sister.

"I can understand your concern. He is rather gorgeous."

"Don't tell him that. He'll be insufferable!"

"But I don't fancy him."

Dinah walked up to her brother-in-law and caressed his face. It's something she'd done in UAR. It was familiar but somehow wasn't provocative.

"That chiselled jaw, straight nose and manly physique just don't do it for me."

"Obviously."

Archie was arch.

"You refer to my penchant for chubby cuddly Mediterranean types."

"Is Uncle Leo Mediterranean? I thought his blood line was north European."

Cosima handed Dinah a macchiato.

"Don't let all that 'trace me back to Charlemagne' stuff fool you. All families, whatever their claimed pedigree, have a bastard streak."

"For some it isn't just the blood."

Charlotte looked at her husband. Archie rolled his eyes.

"I'm going out."

"Anywhere I should know about?"

Reaching the lift, he turned back.

"I'll be in the village. Okay? You work it out."

"Godiver's shop or tea with Mrs Bickerstaff..? I know how you get off on her macaw."

Cosima was having a lovely time. Archie departed. Dinah sat down with her coffee.

"Anyway, meine grosse schwester – you told me this weird invention of your husbands not only saved you but was one of the most incredible experiences of your life."

She sipped the caffeine.

"I disagree. Never mind men – it's not one of. It's the most amazing experience of my life."

The three women quickly buried themselves in their fascination with Ultimate Alternative Reality.

*   *   *

A mile away across the village of Drinkwell, 5 Briony Close was surfacing. Off school with a summer cold Amy appeared in the kitchen where Barbara was making a morning cup of tea.

"Hi Momph."

Amy sniffed.

"Had a good holidashe?"

"Darling. You sound sniffy."

"I amsh."

"How long have you been off school?"

"I haven't till todashe."

"'Sounds as though you need me to make you a nice honey and lemon drink."

The doorbell rang.

"Who could that be?"

Barbara went through to the hall and opened the front door. Archie Light stood on the doorstep. Unusually for him, he'd walked.

"Archie. Hi... To what do we owe the pleasure?"

"I've just got back."

The man and woman looked at each other.

"So have I though mine was real."

"We were all a bit surprised you took off."

"George was desperate – he needed help."

Barbara rubbed her left wrist. Archie said.

"You considered the danger."

"No I didn't really and as for it being any of your business we won't go there. It was my call. George was against it and I was never in any danger. Hi Mrs Rajpundit."

Basanti's mother was reversing the Rajpundit's people carrier out of their short drive on to the road. Her attention taken up with the goings on in No 5, she clipped her own low wall. Liking the R's, Barbara gave a theatrical cough.

"I can't work out whether she despises or is jealous of the number of men callers I get. Tea?"

In the kitchen Archie looked out at the Moons little garden. The kettle clicked off.

"Why don't you go and take him one?"

Archie turned to Barbara questioningly. Podric's mother was making two mugs of Lipton's English Breakfast.

"Your ex-partner's asleep in my studio. Made him up a camp bed."

*   *   *

Half an hour later George Benedict, Archie and Podric who had also risen, sat at the Moon's garden table. Tea, coffee and toast were in front of them.

"So, Germany, Redstone and Mercury – you were taking a look at Wernher."

George sipped his tea. Archie sat back.

"I wanted to check him out, yes."

"Why?"

Podric sipped his coffee. Archie continued.

"Because he represents just what lengths the US will go to in pursuit of all this."

Archie looked at Podric.

"You may have heard of Wernher von Braun – the acclaimed

German rocket fundi and ex-Nazi the Americans brought over from the fatherland after World War 2."

"Operation Paperclip."

Benedict interjected. Archie continued addressing his fellow UAR creator.

"Was a US government operation in 1945. The Germans were way ahead on rocketry. The Americans wanted their technology so slipped sixteen hundred of these Hitlerians with their wives and families into New Mexico. It was, frankly, completely illegal. At any rate it seriously bent things around the State Department. Took years to officially assimilate them."

Archie poured himself some coffee.

"If they were prepared to go to the lengths they did over that, they certainly won't think twice about the little stunt they're currently playing on us."

George Benedict picked up a bit of toast. Archie continued.

"I also visited Apollo 1."

"Gus Grissom's feelings acid were they?"

"You can say that again."

"What was his take?"

Benedict spread some marmalade on his wholemeal slice.

"On the fire?"

"I can imagine that. The moon."

Archie was reflective.

"Grissom reckoned that if the Americans did make it they would have had to have upped their game some from '67."

Archie sipped his coffee.

"You know as well as I do there's going to be no quick fix to all this. What lies behind the situation is long and dark and deep. Was Kennedy killed in part because of his Man on the Moon promises? I still think that's far-fetched but so's everything about his assassination."

"Or not."

Archie looked at George.

"Fair enough. You mean the lonely, failed marine Trotsky-ite – except most people now reckon that even if Lee hit him, it was just the once. JFK's brains blown out backwards there has to have been some other gun fired from a different direction to have killed him."

Archie put down his coffee mug.

"Then there's Kubrick's part in this fantastical tale – his supposedly faking the astronaut's moon walks. The whole thing stinks."

Podric suddenly said.

"Why did you try and hack into UAR, George?"

Podric wiped his fingers from a particularly juicy piece of toast he'd covered with homemade apricot jam. Although his tone was bland it was deadly. The atmosphere became charged. Speaking in little more than a whisper, George said.

"You really need to ask me that?"

"Yes, we really need to ask you that."

Archie was more obviously uptight. When he replied, George was remote.

"You know about the pressure I'd been under. First of all from Secorni to compromise you because of their wanting to get to Podric and since the security people got involved, their desire to know what you and Podric were working on."

"Who, Secorni or the Satan's of Louden?"

George didn't reply. Podric said.

"You've been in touch then."

Podric sipped his tea.

"Operatives tailed me after the meeting Archie and I had in town."

All colour had drained from George's face.

"Ah, new battalions."

Archie was disgusted. Podric said.

"Did you tell them we had UAR?"

"I did."

The three of them sat in silence. Finally, Archie said.

"Well that at least is honest."

Podric put down his cup.

"Why didn't you just say we were working on conventional

games? We've created two. They didn't have to know about alternative reality."

George looked at the ground.

"I don't know I can answer that clearly. Maybe I just wanted to blow them away, get them off my back – impress them with something so amazing they'd leave me alone."

"You must have realised how stupid that was, that it was never going to happen."

"I don't know what I thought."

Archie said.

"This is very disturbing George."

Benedict muttered.

"What are you going to do?"

"I'm not sure. We obviously can't trust you. Any suggestions?"

Archie's anger had changed to cynical dismissal.

"I might have."

Benedict and Archie looked at Podric. After what seemed like an eternity Benedict enquired.

"What is it Podric?"

"For that George you'll just have to wait and see... P'raps you should go take that shower you wanted."

Benedict stood up.

"You know they'll kaput me."

Podric and Archie didn't respond. When George had left them, Podric put the top on the jam. Archie said.

"I can't believe it."

"You can."

Archie snorted.

"Where's your youthful optimism? You've got some cynicism for a seventeen-year-old."

Clearing up the breakfast things, Podric said.

"Who do you think's driving unter operativ Benedict?"

"Likely some element of the CIA or the NSA or a combination of. Could even be a rogue outfit – operatives directed by a maverick controller with their own agenda. Either way I think while they originally set out to harry, things will get more sinister."

Finishing his coffee, Archie was subdued.

"Have you actually got a plan oh wünderkind?"

"Sure."

Podric licked the last jam from his fingers.

"Walking on it ourselves."

Archie coughed causing him to reflux coffee.

"You can't be serious."

"Why not? It's got my name all over it."

Chapter 8

Back to School

"Are you sure she's pregnant?"

Talking to his friend Billy Johnson in their GCR common room, Podric was concerned.

"Well yeah – I think so Pod. She says she is."

The girl in question Carol Jensen had started a relationship with Billy not long after they had both enjoyed an Ultimate Alternative Reality experience at Podric's seventeenth birthday party. Playing *Skice Ball* – a computer game involving football played on an ice rink – Billy's naïve innocence apparently melted Carol's tough indifference – to Podric's way of thinking, all too rapidly! As mistress of the common room which she had procured, Carol wandered in with her best friend, Jane Cartwright.

"Okay?"

"Yeah."

Podric was neutral.

"Not you Pod face, my man."

Carol sauntered up to Billy.

"Want to feel it? You can."

This very particular offer threw the diffident Johnson.

"Go on Bill. You'll be a dad soon and life's over!"

Barney had appeared with Catherine and Miles Willoughby. Podric thought he caught a fleeting moment of intimacy between Jane and Miles.

"How far gone are you?"

Carol turned.

"What are you lot doing here?"

"Miles is-."

"Oh I know about him Carty. That's alright. But thuggy and Miss Goody Two Shoes... Who said you can be in our club?"

"I can't speak for thuggy as you call him but for myself – you did."

Carol looked at Catherine.

"Master Moon's party. Throwing your arms around me, you told me I was your best friend."

"Hmph."

"And me? I'm just thuggy and I've got a thing about pregnancy."

As bold as brass, Barney took Carol's arm.

"Now when you have baby, are you thinking of a water birth, LeBoyer?"

"Wha-? Get off me."

"It's very peaceful. Baby appears all calm and collected."

"What are you on man? Months to go yet!"

"Well, you've got to look after yourself, not overdo things."

Barney's concern was apparently so knowledgeable Jane and Catherine had a hard time not to laugh out loud.

"I-. Look. C'mon BJ we've got things to discuss. In private!"

"BJ. Particular initials.."

Barney was incorrigible. Carol took Billy off.

"Wow. What's she going to do?"

Catherine was considerate but practical.

"She'll have it."

Jane was matter of fact.

"But that's going to-."

"Effect things, careers? Yeah."

For several seconds no one said anything.

"And he'll sign up."

Barney was surprisingly sensitive.

"He's a good Injun."

Catherine, Miles and Barney went to get coffees from an urn the GCR had installed. Podric checked his iPhone.

"We're privileged to see you."

Jane sat down nearby.

"Back from your exotic world no doubt. Where is it this time?"

"It can be anywhere any time."

Jane wanted to say 'take me with you' but desisted. Podric said.

"The 1960s. President Kennedy's assassination and man on the moon stuff."

"Why that?"

"Good question. Archie and my legal lady is obsessed with JFK's murder. Who did it? How? Why? She's also become a UAR junkie. After my birthday Kaliska pestered me. It's turning out to be a pretty interesting decade."

Podric clicked off his phone.

"You and Miles then..?"

"Couldn't wait for you forever, could I..?"

Clearly tense, Jane got up.

"Well could I? That is even if you were interested – which you're not."

Jane touched Podric's hair. She was going to say a lot more but just blurted.

"Oh Podric!"

She went out. Barney returned with a cup of coffee and had seen Jane's distressed state.

"What did you do to her?"

Podric didn't respond.

"Don't tell me she's pregnant as well?!"

Barney sat down. A second or two later, Miles left them.

"Ah. Seems like love is all around us."

He swilled his coffee.

"So you want to go hustling Stanley again?"

Taking a sip of the lukewarm liquid, Barney immediately spat it out. "This stuff's disgusting."

Sipping her cup of the urn's best, Catherine made a face.

"It is pretty awful Podric."

"Glad we agree on that!"

Barney poured the remainder of the contents of his mug down a drain. He said.

"It happens that my schedule can accommodate this alternative reality wish as long as we take in *The Shining*. We're studying it right now."

Barney rinsed his mug and continued.

"Why this further interest?"

Podric stood up.

"It's not because I necessarily think Mr Kubrick filmed fake moon landing sequences – in a funny way, if he did it would only enhance his brilliance. But if he ever was compromised I'd like to know what people inside the American government had on him."

"That's not a dumb reason. When?"

"Yes Podric, when?"

Catherine looked at her boyfriend with her steady grey eyes. Podric shrugged. "How are we all fixed for the weekend?"

*   *   *

"But why Russia?"

Charlotte Light was irritated watching her husband pace around their bedroom.

"Because I'm trying to get a feel of the whole thing – some background."

"Archie, will you please sit down? You're making me dizzy pacing around like that."

Their bedroom possessing a chaise longue, Light flung himself on it. Charlotte softened some.

"Are you enjoying this adventure? You seem rather tortured."

Archie looked at his wife.

"Not sure whether enjoying is the right word. It's different to the others..."

He sat forward.

"You know I've been poking about the 1960s seeing what went on. If you're remotely interested I think NASA might have got Neil and Buzz staggering around up there at the end of it though more by luck than judgement. It was damned hairy. But if there was 'one brief shining moment' something went very wrong in America during that decade – something sour and bad – the beginnings of Pax Americana's decline..."

"Don't you think that's the way mankind is usually screwing up?"

"Yes, but this time is was particularly intense."

Archie got up.

"Whatever Jack was or wasn't – political lightweight, rich play-boy charmer – he had something that connected with people – more than most presidents and not just Americans. The height of the Cold War – it was the first time man had the power to completely destroy himself and the planet. Sure, Abe had terrible difficulties and civil war is the worst, but it was only America. Their war in the 1860s couldn't kill off mankind. Neither could the Great War and neither did World War 2 – though it very nearly could have. Plans for space rocketry were only envisaged because of military missile development – and that came from Germany circa '44/'45."

"My father once told me military things always drove civilian."

"Your father wasn't wrong."

Charlotte, who had been sitting on their bed, got up.

"But why the Russian steppes?"

Archie looked at her.

"Unlikely you've heard of Sergei Korolev."

"You know I'm crazy about all things Russian. Did his daughter go to Cosima's school?"

Archie burst out laughing.

"What's so funny?"

"I can't begin. Apart from anything else the man's been dead fifty plus years and anyway unless you were into such stuff you would never have heard of him. In the most senior circles of So-viet space then he was only ever known as Mr Chief Designer."

"Why is it so important you meet him?"

"Because when all this was at its height Korolev drove Russia's space program, and at the time they were ahead of our Ameri-can friends. He was also a charismatic man who I'm interested in meeting."

Charlotte was reflective.

"When are we off then?"

A look at his wife told Archie it was pointless challenging her UAR inclusion.

"How are you fixed for the weekend?"

It seemed as though the upcoming one would see a lot of UAR activity!

Chapter 9
Breaking and Entering

Activating UAR and trying to enter *JFK and His World*, the would-be player faltered. The menu appeared blocked and having made a couple more attempts, the effort was terminated.

"Damn!"

Kaliska Monroe sat back. Opposite her Cosima Light sipped some wine.

"What is it I'm not doing?"

Kaliska got up.

"I've seen Podric do it countless times."

They were in Kaliska's Butlers Wharf apartment. Staring out of the window at the lighters and riverboats below, Ms Monroe was agitated.

"It drives me mad! WHAT IS IT I'M DOING WRONG?"

If Cosima had a role model she looked up to, Kaliska was the nearest thing. The eighteen-year-old admired the stylish thirty-three-year-old gazing out of the window. Cosima got up, came over to her, and put an arm around her. A little shorter than Cosima, Kaliska briefly laid her head on the girl's shoulder.

"God! I must be cracking up – getting in a state about such a juvenile thing."

Cosima said.

"You think UAR juvenile?"

Kaliska looked at her.

"No, I don't."

She turned back to the river which she always found endlessly captivating.

"What is it about Ultimate Alternative Reality? Why are you so desperate for it?"

Cosima was matter of fact.

"You think I am?"

Laughing, Kaliska walked away and picked her glass of wine up off the coffee table.

"I am, aren't I. But aren't you?"

"Yeah. But not just for itself. Like you, what I'm about is getting in unaided. Me, myself – doing it on my own."

"Exactly!"

Kaliska drank.

"God I could do with a cigarette."

"You smoke?"

"Did. Smart girl like me – not in years."

Sinking on to one of her matching sofas, Kaliska activated her laptop. Cosima sat down beside her.

Discarding the computer device, Kaliska sat back. She stroked Cosima's hair.

"There's a lot you don't know about me."

"Want to tell me?"

They kissed. Kaliska abruptly got up.

"Oh, I don't mean that stuff. I can get that anywhere."

"No, you can't."

The two looked at each other. Kaliska took Cosima's hand.

An hour later they lay on Kaliska's bed.

"I thought... You and Podric."

"Ha. You and Podric."

"Me? What – a great aunt?!"

Cosima looked at Kaliska. The two burst out laughing.

"No. Podric. Podric's something else."

"What do you mean?"

They sipped wine. Kaliska caressed Cosima's back.

"You're beautiful."

Cosima turned to her.

"So are you."

They kissed again. Cosima lay back.

"Ha. He's certainly created something out of this world."

Kaliska had some more wine.

"He's got a girlfriend."

"Yup, he has. And as much as I'd like to stick pins in her eyes – Catherine's a cool lady."

"'Love Barbara and that sister of his. Crazy."

"Well that's Podric and his clan then."

Kaliska drank.

"Not really."

"No."

She replaced her glass on a bedside table.

"They're something else alright, the Moons."

Naked, Cosima got up and walked through to the main room. Seconds later she returned carrying a small backpack. She opened it on the bed.

"When Podric put you into UAR he sunc you up using what he and dad call Premium Profile Participant. I don't understand how they do that without any data insertion linking a person into a game in a programmed state. It's something to do with the synapse being aligned to the games electronic cycle but that's beyond me."

Cosima took out a little container.

"You might have a better chance if we use this though."

Kaliska stared at the plastic sleeve which housed a tiny microchip.

"I know what it is."

"Sure you do but what you don't know is that its programmed for you."

The older woman sat up.

"Why? How-?"

"When they were still looking at people they considered programming as opposed to profiling, you were on the list. Podric wasn't for creating a chip for you but Dad persisted. I watched Podric do it."

Cosima and Kaliska took another appraising look at each other. Cosima reached into her back-satchel again. Taking out the

G-Byte gun, she began preparing it for a microchip insertion.

"Getting kinky on me, are you?"

"You'll love it. Then you'll be like me."

Cosima brandished her left wrist with the microchip just visible below the epidermis.

"Where did you get hold of it?"

"Dad's lab."

"What an afternoon this has turned out to be."

"You ain't seen nothing yet!"

She cocked the G-Byte gun.

* * *

Close Up of a typewriter, its keys clacked metal letters on to paper writing the sentence 'All work and no play make Jack a dull boy' over and over again. The camera pulled out to reveal Jack Nicholson playing Jack Torrance trying to write his novel. Using newly-invented Steadicam, its creator Garrett Brown framed up on a wider image of the Colorado Lounge in the Overlook Hotel.

"Cut."

The film crew relaxed. Stanley Kubrick began conferring with Brown as First AD Brian Cook called a break for lighting adjustments. Nicholson left the set accompanied by an assistant. Standing behind the technicians Barney Sturridge turned to an associate producer who had been watching proceedings.

"How many takes on this set up?"

The producer looked at Barney, who continued.

"I'm studying at Film School."

"Twenty-two last count."

"Plenty more to come then."

Barney smiled.

Outside one of three sound stages *The Shining* had taken over at Elstree Studios people gravitated to the catering wagon. Tables and chairs nearby, cast and crew grabbed a break. Sitting amongst them Podric, Catherine and Barney sipped coffees. Wendbury High's ex-school bully was restless.

"'Won't get anything like this."

He looked around.

"Let's go walkabout."

Barney led his friends through a myriad of vehicles into a building attached to the sound stage housing the Colorado Room set. Walking along a corridor, Shelley Duvall's door was partially open.

"I can't work with him anymore. He's driving me crazy. The guy's an obsessive nut!"

Sounds of commiseration from Ms Duvall's assistant were interrupted.

"Even my hair's falling out! I'm having a fucking breakdown!"

"P'raps we can help?"

Putting his head round the door, Barney smiled.

"Who the-?"

Askance, Shelley Duvall dropped into a chair.

"What seems to be the problem?"

"Who the hell are you?"

"I'm a film student."

Barney was his usual publicly confident self.

"Well film student, you can get out of my fucking dressing room!"

"Miss Duvall. Shelley, I understand you need some assistance."

Catherine walked in wearing a white doctors coat. She had also donned a pair of professorial glasses which in spite of her age, made her appear more commanding. Shelley's assistant beat a hasty retreat.

"I'm here to help you."

Catherine stood beside the prostrate Shelley and began taking her pulse.

"You're... a bit young aren't you?"

Catherine didn't immediately answer.

"Little erratic. Yes, I graduated top student out of med school two years ahead. You'll be taking some time off on health grounds."

"Er, well-."

Several black and white stills pictures of Shelley on the set of *The Shining* were stuffed against her light-bulb-edged make-up mirror. Barney had a good look at them.

"Is this as spooky a picture to work on as the story comes out?"

Already in a distressed mental state, Shelley Duvall's face became expressionless as she mutely curled up in her chair. Catherine picked up a near empty bottle of pills – the label read phenobarbital.

"Film history folklore has it that around this time and on this picture, Stanley's losing the plot. Obsessed with the significance of the number 42 and Room 237, he leaves these weird coded lunar messages around the set. Given the guy's the ultimate obsessive for detail and June Randall's no continuity slouch – what we ask, was occurring? Things in one shot deliberately left out of another – what is Stanley trying to tell us?"

Passed out in her chair, Shelly Duvall slumped forward temporarily gone from the world.

"'Must say Barney, you've really got the touch."

"Yeah I know. It's my sensitivity."

*   *   *

The viewing theatre at Elstree Studios was in darkness. The days rushes playing out, Stanley Kubrick sat alone in the theatre. No actors or producers were present – not even continuity lady June Randall. Having had the projectionist re-run the material several times, Kubrick made notes. The director finally finished his work and carrying some cans of film, left the preview theatre. Walking to his adjacent office suite, one room housed some editing equipment. Although it was the middle of the night and his editing team had not long departed from their eighteen-hour working day, Kubrick opened a can of processed film and threaded it into a Moviola. The machine began to whir, viewable images rattling through its gate.

"How did they get to you?"

At first, Kubrick's attention was so absorbed by the pictures, he didn't seeem to hear and paid no attention. Podric emerged from the shadows.

"We met on the *Dr. Strangelove* set."

Kubrick stopped the machine; the film froze mid-frame.

"You had that i, i-."

Podric produced his MacBook Pro which he handed Kubrick. It already being on standby, the title sequence of *The Shining* began playing. Kubrick was transfixed. Podric let the download run for half a minute, then stopped it.

"You use that thing?"

Podric nodded at the Moviola.

"Like the Ark. Amazing what you did."

Moving his fingers across the MacBook Pro screen, Podric made several edits to a project he had on the stocks. It appeared effortless. He said.

"Forty years of technology later."

Handing the MacBook Pro to Kubrick, Podric looked round the room. Turning the Apple device over in his hands the director was transfixed.

"You'll be thinking about what you could have done had you had tools like this at your disposal."

Podric studied the posters of Stanley's work that adorned the walls. From *The Killing* in '56 through *Paths of Glory* '57 to *Spartacus* – Kirk Douglas exchanging his French Great War uniform for a loin cloth followed by *Lolita* and *Dr Strangelove*. After it, *2001: A Space Odyssey*, *A Clockwork Orange* and *Barry Lyndon*.

"Do you work all the time?"

Kubrick didn't reply. Podric considered then continued.

"I don't normally do this."

Syncing Stanley to UAR as a Premium Profiled Participant the director suddenly saw everything Podric could through the upper part of his eyes. A computer games Menu appeared, and Stanley watched as Podric moved the cursor. Selecting Options, Podric exited them from *JFK and His World* and entered *Ludification of Modern Cinema*. He took Kubrick on a comprehensive tour of contemporary and advanced computerised stop motion cinematic techniques – technology that created FX for films such as *Gravity*.

"I'm not taking film studies, but my spies tell me 80% of this picture was Visual FX."

They watched a scene with George Clooney zooming around in space as Sandra Bullock attempted to enter the defunct space station.

"To accurately simulate the reflection of unfiltered light in space a manually controlled lighting system of 1.8 million LED lights was created. All individually operated – your sort of thing I believe."

Kubrick fingered Podric's MacBook Pro. Podric continued.

"Plus of course the state you're currently in. That's my contribution to the future – enabling someone to be sunc up to a computer game – experience its world, appear to live in it. Well, one is living in it in one's head."

Podric brought them out of *L of MC* and returned to his JFK adapted game. By now around 3.00am in the morning and Stanley having worked twenty hours non-stop – Kubrick was looking bleary-eyed.

"So long ago..."

His voice was quiet.

"At first... reasons were elusive, but it didn't take long to figure. My wife's German."

Podric was still.

"That was a factor..?"

Kubrick laughed a hollow laugh.

"Check out the participants. The whole Apollo program was Teuton driven. I was a casualty by association."

"The authorities were... selective."

More silence. Then Kubrick continued.

"Knowing my interest in technology – the claim that advice was needed – lens strength, ratios, low light levels."

"You mean the speed of the lens – how little light was necessary to capture an image."

"That's one relevance of lenses."

Kubrick was mildly sarcastic. Podric turned from the posters to face Stanley.

"I'm interested in the moon."

"Aren't we all?"

"Conspiracists believe that Apollo 11 couldn't make it and that you were involved in filming faked sequences."

"Do they?" More silence. It was a very silent night. Kubrick said.

"I've just told you."

Podric said. "Around the time of *Space Odyssey* in '68 there was a lot of speculation."

"I heard you fell out with Arthur C. Clarke."

It was Barney who interrupted. Standing nearby with Catherine, Kubrick hadn't heard them come in.

"Who are you?"

"We're friends of Podric. I'm studying Film."

The situation was surreal even for Stanley Kubrick – a film maker who encompassed surreality.

"What's Clarke got to do with anything?"

Ignoring Barney and Catherine, Kubrick eyed Podric who replied.

"Mr Kubrick, you'll appreciate all I'm trying to do is find out what really happened."

"What really happened is I was asked a lot of questions. The work I'd done on the lunar surface for *2001*-."

"You mean terrain? What the landscape looked like."

Barney's voice interjected.

"If you're doing film and studying me, why are you asking?"

"Fair enough."

Barney turned to Podric.

"Mr Kubrick is detail obsessed."

"Of course I'm detail obsessed! I only do detail!"

"Perhaps your pictorial descriptions were modelled?"

Catherine could always be relied on to ask a pertinent question. "'Perfect guy then." No change from Barney.

"If the powers that be knew things were going wrong and they couldn't pull it off, you'd be the ideal person to consult."

"Except my images would be better than theirs."

"Even if theirs were the real thing?"

"Far better."

Kubrick picked up the other two 300ft film cans he'd brought in and headed for the door. Barney said.

"Work in your bedroom?"

"Sometimes."

Podric said.

"You know some people thought you were involved. They thought that during your life-time."

"It irritated me then and it seems I can't escape it even in this existence." He went out.

"Better than the real thing."

Barney laughed.

"That Stanley Kubrick!"

Chapter 10

Frozen Wastes
a Wrong Game and Secorni

The dawn air was bitter on the frozen steppes of Kazakhstan temperatures many degrees minus Celsius. It was a desolate scene, but man was here. Recently starting to build the Baikonur Cosmodrome – the USSR's equivalent of Cape Canaveral, several concrete launch sites had been constructed and a giant Vostok 1 space rocket was being worked at on a pan. Different in design to the USA's Saturn 1 series – the Russian craft possessed four flanged tubes and looked more aeronautic than its American equivalent. However, the Cosmodrome itself didn't appear much more advanced than Peenemünde some fifteen years before it. The buildings were nondescript, several little more than wooden huts. Into the early light a giant Sikorsky helicopter appeared thundering low across the wastes. After circling the Cosmodrome it landed near the buildings. Several men got out and hurried inside escaping the extreme cold as quickly as they could.

One area of the site that possessed some life was the restaurant/café. Whilst dark timber panelling and heavy furniture were prominent, the atmosphere appeared light-hearted. The room was filled with cigarette smoke, and vodka was never very far away! Several young military men were clowning about, apparently ignoring two people who sat at a large table normally reserved for top brass positioned away from the friendly fracas. The door opened and the helicoptered visitors entered. Even in their short dash an icy blast had left a covering of white rime on their coats. The newcomers obviously senior people, the young men immediately ceased their clowning and came to attention.

One of the arrivals in particular had a commanding presence. Stocky, he must have been good looking in his youth but was now jowly and had a poor pallor. The group made their way over to the table where the two parka clad people were sitting. Cigarettes lit, and small vodka glasses placed on the table along with several bottles – the stocky man looked around.

"I'm not sure I've had the pleasure."

Realising one of the hooded figures was a woman and beautiful, he inclined his head slightly.

"I'd have remembered if I had."

The woman smiled and pushed back her mink-lined cowl. Charlotte Svet looked stunning.

"No, you haven't Mr Chief Designer, but my wife and I look forward to spending some time with you."

Exhaling a lung full of cigarette smoke, Sergei Korolev turned to Archie. He gave a slight shrug.

"Married to this beautiful woman you are a lucky man."

"Is that Yuri Gagarin I recognise amongst your young heroes over there?"

Charlotte smiled. So did Korolev.

"You know him?"

"The whole world will know him soon."

Korolev frowned.

"How might that be?"

"Come now Gospodin Korolev – not so coy. My wife would like to meet Mr Gagarin. Could you and I adjourn for a little? I think what I have to say will interest you."

In spite of his age, Korolev looked as though he'd far rather spend the next hour of his life in Charlotte's company than her husband's.

"I'm not a professor and what's so interesting about Gagarin?"

Korolev was casual but his eyes were sharp. Archie took out his iPhone. Already opened at a Wikipedia history of the rocket engineer, Dr Svet passed his device across the table. Minutes later he was in Korolev's office where the komp'yuternyy dizayner began to tell his tale.

*   *   *

Spooling through the menu at the top of her eyes, Kaliska Monroe clicked on Options. Highlighting *Secret Service*, then Assassinations and Dates – the cursor hit Enter.

"We're going to be late Abraham. You must hurry and dress now."

In an anteroom off Lincoln's first floor office in the White House, Mary Todd Lincoln was hassling her husband.

"I'll be along shortly my dear."

Mrs Lincoln went to the door that accessed their private quarters.

"Ten minutes then. We're cutting it mighty fine."

When she'd gone Lincoln left his office and walked through to his secretary's room with some papers. He was surprised to find Kaliska Monroe and Cosima Light sitting there! For a second Lincoln looked nonplussed. So did the young women.

"I've met you."

Kaliska and the president took the measure of each other.

"Yes sir. We did briefly. In Clay Street. It was the end of the war and I was looking after things temporarily when you came by to visit."

"I'll be darned!"

Lincoln put the papers he was carrying on John Hay's desk.

"You're – ah... How's young Podric? Still out roaming around in his different worlds I've no doubt."

Kaliska was impressed at Lincoln's rapid recollection.

"Yes.."

"And you're back here. Weren't you done with the Civil War?"

"Well, er-. I've made a mistake. I'd been looking up Assassinations. Our current adventures involve being in the world of one of your successors who sadly met the same fate."

"Sorry to hear that. As an ending to life it's not one I would choose."

Lincoln was sombre. Kaliska said.

"As a point of entry into UAR I'd also been researching the

Secret Service. There are theories..."

Kaliska was tense. She seemed to be trying to view something in the top of her eyes.

Lincoln said.

"Point of entry. Ultimate Alternative Reality – that's the thing! What an invention."

The 16th US president stroked his chin and smiled.

"The Secret Service you say. Come with me."

He led them back into his office. On the desk lay one of the last documents he would ever sign. Dated 14th April 1865 it was a draft to establish a national secret service for the United States of America.

"This document is looking at such an inception."

Kaliska and Cosima were amazed. There were sounds of activity outside the office.

"I suspect that's how you made your mistake."

Kaliska could have hugged the president. Lincoln said.

"Yes, yes, I know what happens to me in-."

Lincoln glanced at his pocket watch.

"... A couple of hours' time."

He turned to cross the room.

"If you adjust that and check the date – adding what, a hundred years or so – you should get into the correct game in your – what did Podric call it – computer world..?"

Lincoln smiled faintly.

"Funny, I could almost feel he was here..."

The door closed quietly behind Abraham Lincoln.

*   *   *

Having made his daily round of checking on Ultimate Alternative Reality activity – something he was even more attentive about since the attempted hacking, Podric was in his bedroom on a Zoom call with Kaliska who was at her Butlers Wharf apartment. Podric said.

"So you can get in and out on your own now.."

Cosima's face appeared in shot.

"Hi Podric. Yeah we've cracked it!"

She held her wrist and taking hold of Kaliska's put it in front of camera.

"You got hold of the G-Byte gun then."

"Girl power!"

Podric smiled.

"How was President Lincoln?"

Kaliska looked a bit dazed.

"We're still not completely sorted. I only just managed to get us out and here you are."

"I saw. I came in..."

"Ah, he said he felt you might be around.."

"Big brother, huh Podric? Keeping an eye on us."

Obviously excited, Cosima was her usual caustic self.

"Would you have it any other way?"

"I wouldn't!"

This from Kaliska.

"Keep an eye on us Podric. I'm not completely confident."

"But I am! You just see!"

Cosima waved at UAR's creator and the screen went dead.

Chapter 11

Mr Chief Designer
and the Wing Commander

"Me and Braun?"

Korolev omitting the von, the Russian rocket scientist walked over to the window. His first-floor office pokey, the glass was frosted. Korolev still wore his coat and Archie his parka.

"Me and Braun..."

Korolev scratched away some ice and looked out at the building site that represented the beginnings of the Cosmodrome.

"Ignoring his National Socialist involvement, the Americans made off with Dr Wernher while I rotted in a gulag. Now here we are – he's chief engineer of the Saturn program and me, Vostok."

The room was already clouded with cigarette smoke, Korolev lit up another Belomorkanal.

"You don't seem very inspired about it."

For a long time Korolev didn't reply.

"Inspired. That's a word – 'inspired'. When you've been through what I have words like inspired don't feature large in one's vocabulary."

The Chief Designer exhaled and turned to Archie.

"Dr Svet if that's your name – my interest in rocketry is my interest in space – its travel and exploration. In that sense perhaps I share something with the German."

Korolev strolled to the other side of his office where a larger window looked out internally at the bar/café scene below.

"Your wife. She is very beautiful."

"So you've said."

Korolev watched the young astronauts including Gagarin and Gherman Titov fussing around Charlotte. Still sitting at the table Archie continued.

"You have beautiful women in Russia."

"Perhaps, but not on this base!"

Korolev had a long pull on his cigarette.

"So this Absolyutnava Al'ternativnaya Real'nost' – I am in a computer game. It is fitting."

"Finishing his smoke, he tapped his packet of Belomorkanal.

"Computers must have really advanced in the next – what did you say – fifty years for you to create this... state?"

Korolev gave a hollow laugh. Archie said.

"Computers have advanced – a revolution!"

Returning to the table and sitting down, Korolev chuckled at Archie's use of the word. Light produced a tiny microchip in a small sachet which he passed across the table to the Russian space scientist.

"That can hold your entire Soyuz program."

Studying the chip, Korolev shook his head in genuine wonder. Archie continued.

"But it's not just computers. The mindset you talk of – Ultimate Alternative Reality takes things to an entirely different level. The menu I showed you viewable at the top of your eyes – how all that works is another dimension. Very few people possess it."

"And you created it with a boy you say."

"Yes. Podric's just seventeen."

"Ha. What's his name – Podric?"

"Moon. His name is Podric Moon."

Korolev burst out laughing.

"Podrik Luna?!"

Archie nodded. Sergei was amused.

"That's this lad's real name?"

"I'm not aware he has any other."

"Fantastic! This adventure is made for him."

Neither spoke for a little while. Korolev put another of his vile cigarettes between his lips and lit up again.

"This game being fifty years from now you know what happens to the Russian space program."

"Yes."

"And no doubt my demise."

"If by demise you mean mortality – yes."

Slightly uncomfortable, Archie moved in his seat. Korolev had a long pull on his Belomorkanal.

"And Gagarin will be the first astronaut?"

"Would you like to see the flight?"

"Yes."

Activating UAR, Archie played Korolev an edited version of Vostok 1's flight.

Korolev sat back.

"So we do it."

Happy, he smacked his thigh.

"And the program?"

Archie exited them from UAR.

"There are reasons perhaps you don't want to see everything."

"Difficulties ahead huh? No surprise there."

Korolev got up.

"Difficulties, always difficulties."

Archie said. "You know right now Russia has a lead over the Americans. You also know of Kennedy's challenge."

"Ah, that boy – propaganda. His program is driven by the military just like ours is, but at least the moon isn't a military target – at least not as far as I know."

"Khrushchev comes to love the Vostok success."

"Of course he does today – or as long as it suits him. The people in Moscow are only interested in rockets for military reasons to be ahead of the Americans. Except for the publicity, Khrushchev couldn't give a night at the Bolshoi about space. Not that he ever goes there. Drunk in his dacha most evenings like the rest of them." Korolev stubbed out his cigarette.

"If you've finished telling me about the future, shall we go down?"

He got up and walked over to the door. Standing, Archie felt

Korolev had been underwhelmed meeting him and whilst impressed at the technological advances that had taken place, wasn't overawed by them. Archie admired him for that. The Russian expected them to happen. Archie wouldn't accept though that the man hadn't been secretly amazed by UAR. So few people had that dimension in their lives even in the twenty-first century. As they went out the Chief Designer put a hand on Archie's arm.

"One can never forget – to the politburo my work is a cost it would prefer to do without. And you still have a beautiful wife!"

*   *   *

"You're going to write a new game with our name on it and a UAR dimension then, son?"

Having finished his Ultimate Alternative Reality participant patrol, Podric had gone into the state himself and was now with his father. Given his dad's tragic death in a flying accident eighteen months previously had been the driver for Podric to create UAR – now that it was extant and Podric and Sean could communicate the boy's frame of mind had improved. Inserting his father's profile into the mindpath had been easy. Sharing a common DNA personal details weren't a problem and programming his father into the computer game *Fastjet!* nothing else was needed. The extraordinary thing was how quickly Sean accepted their electronically created relationship as if it was the most natural thing in the world. Talking to his dad about Ultimate Alternative Reality, Sean's only comment had been what had taken Podric so long?! Father and son now happily reunited in their games world, Sean sat in the cockpit of his aircraft, a Typhoon T3.

"It's a good idea. It's also your only option if you want to pursue the lunar issue."

"What do you think about man not reaching it, dad?"

Sean Moon laughed.

"If he didn't it would be the biggest cover up ever."

Sean adjusted a couple of controls in the cockpit.

"Reckon Armstrong and Aldrin made it, though it was much

riskier than the public knew. Lack of computer power, infant technology – JFK's challenge having man walking around up there
and bringing him home – they were lucky to get away with it. But
why should that worry you?" Podric said.

"It's part of the adventure."

Sean tapped a screen on his console.

"Hmm... And you're looking into it via UAR..?"

Sean thought for a minute before continuing.

"Should it be an issue – remember how smart generals oper-
ate. If you can't take something head on, go round. 'Same applies
to problems. Think outside the box."

Some intercom squawk came through for Sean.

"Okay... Ops. Got to run."

Podric watched as the polycarbonate canopy gradually closed
over his father who sat solo in the front seat. Through the intercom Sean said.

"Write the game and go find out."

The cockpit hatch locked shut and the Typhoon T3 rocked
forward as Wing Commander Moon released the brakes. His father continued talking through the intercom.

"Then go walk on its surface yourself. Plant that flag! That'll
liven things up. Roger control. Z8815 rolling."

Watching his father climb into the sky, Podric was certain of
one thing. A Union Jack on the moon really would be a first!

Chapter 12
The Two Monroes

"Happy Birthday to you
Happy Birthday to you
Happy Birthday Mr President
Happy Birthday to you."

Morphing into her own adapted version of 'Thanks for the memories', the husky tones of Marilyn Monroe's voice purred out across Madison Square Garden to an empty auditorium. Rehearsal day, Ms Monroe stood onstage breathing her sultriness into the mic. Unlike the shimmering skin-tight sequined number she was sewn into the following evening Marilyn wore slacks, a loose top, headscarf and sunglasses. Apparently relaxed, she joshed with the stage manager and crew running through her performance again and again. A break for lunch was announced and host Peter Lawford hurried away to make calls. Leaving various coaches and hangers on, Marilyn made her way to the powder room. In front of a mirror fixing her face, Kaliska Monroe appeared beside her and began doing the same. The English lawyer a striking looking woman, Marilyn glanced over at her and smiled.

"That's a great lip gloss."

Kaliska didn't do a double take and behaved naturally. Taking out the stick, she opened it and turning to the star, put a little on her wrist.

"I love the colour."

Marilyn purred in that breathless way she had. Kaliska said.

"For you."

Slipping the top on the lipstick, Kaliska gave it to Ms Monroe.

"We share the same name."

Marilyn was impressed. Kaliska continued.

"Oh, no-. I didn't mean-."

Marilyn smiled and said.

"My real name is different."

"Not your first name or Mortenson."

Marilyn laughed. Kaliska said.

"Monroe's much sexier."

She prepared to leave. Looking into the mirror, Marilyn tried the new lip gloss.

"Are you around for the show tomorrow night?"

"I haven't got tickets if that's what you mean."

"Would you-? Why not come as my guest?"

"That would be lovely. Would two be possible?"

Seeing Marilyn's face alter a little, Kaliska said.

"I'm in town with a girlfriend."

"That's fine. And come to the party afterwards. We'll have a girl's night."

Believing this to be highly unlikely Kaliska was about to leave.

"I love the way you talk. You know I was in a movie in England with Sir Olivier."

"*The Prince and the Showgirl.*"

"You know it?"

Marilyn was childlike in her enthusiasm.

"I do. My favourite's *Some Like it Hot*. Brilliant. How's it going with your current shoot?"

"Oh... not so good."

The English lawyer looked at her watch.

"I've got to run. Mustn't be late for a meeting."

"When did you get in?"

"This morning. Truth be told I'm a bit jet lagged."

"You flew over? That's so much fun."

A potential gaff – Kaliska was pretty sure jet passenger aircraft were crossing the Atlantic by 1962.

"What do you do if you don't mind my asking?"

"I'm a lawyer. Big case over here. London client American company."

"A lawyer? My. I might be needing one soon. It would be so good if we could talk."

"I do corporate work."

Marilyn smiled.

"That's what I need. Divorce attorneys are a thing of the past for me if that's what you're thinking."

Kaliska smiled and said.

"Good luck tomorrow night."

"Oh, how will I get the tickets to you?"

Fascinating – it was Marilyn who seemed keen not to let the other go. Kaliska turned back.

"Why not leave them at the door for Ms Monroe?!"

*   *   *

Glancing through gaps in the partially frosted styled glass that made up one of Secorni's London board room walls, Carla Logan saw that the meeting called by her boss Saul Prendergast was in full swing. In response to a directive from the company's CEO in California, Cyrus Zaentz - Head of European Marketing Jean Baptiste had flown in from Paris that morning. London based FD Colin McFadden was also present as was Mia Haas of Gertner Hirschowitz, Secorni's law firm. Although the meeting was a private one and Prendergast had given Carla no indication of its content, the PA had pieced together it had something to do with George Benedict. It was the lawyer's presence that was the giveaway – George, Archie and MoonLight were currently Secorni's preeminent legal preoccupation. Working in her office when the discussion finished – McFadden and Baptiste filed by her door with it appeared, a reluctant Mia Haas. Prendergast called Carla into his office.

"Likely you'll know what that was about."

He was offhand.

"If I link the meeting time to some notes you gave me from Mr Zaentz…"

Ballsy and intelligent, Carla was smart. Prendergast turned

back from the window.

"Yeah. Okay."

He sat down at his desk. Carla said nothing. Prendergast fiddled with a Rubik cube his wife had bought him to help her husband de-stress. It appeared to have the reverse affect. Not only had Carla never seen Prendergast solve it – failure to succeed with the brightly-coloured square invariably put him in a bad mood. Today was no exception.

"The meeting with George Benedict and... his ex-partner."

Prendergast so loathed Archie Light, he preferred not to speak his name.

"Oh, Dr Light. He's now working with that young guy Podric Moon. They say the kid's a genius."

"That so?"

Prendergast well knew of Podric's prowess, Secorni being desperate to sign him. His face hardened.

"We're looking at how MoonLight had all the cards. It was as if they knew each move we were making before we made it."

Prendergast tossed the unsolved Rubik cube on to his blotter.

"The feeling is there had to have been a leak."

He looked directly at Carla who met his gaze without a flicker.

"You have any take on that Carla?"

"Do I... have any take on what..?"

Speaking very slowly, Carla's face was equally set. Secorni's Head of Europe picked up the cube again.

"You know.."

"I know what?"

"Oh come on Carla don't play the innocent!"

Prendergast's anger erupted. Carla stayed cool.

"Mr Prendergast. Are you suggesting that I would have somehow accessed your private and confidential 'In' file which one assumes anything so sensitive would be handled through?"

Prendergast twisted the Rubik cube more aggressively. Carla continued.

"Were I to even contemplate such a thing, your security code as you well know I don't have access to."

The colours of the Rubik cube were all over the place. Carla said.

"Are you making an accusation against me?"

Prendergast twisted the cube so aggressively something in it snapped. He threw the broken bits into his trash bin.

"Bloody thing."

Saul sat back in his executive chair.

"No. No, I am not making that accusation."

A temporary loss of control he might have had but Prendergast wasn't stupid.

"What are you saying then?"

"Others..'"

Stressed, Prendergast stood up.

"You were the only person outside myself who-."

"What Mr Prendergast? The only other person who what?"

"Could have had prior knowledge of all this."

Surer of her ground now, Carla went on the offensive.

"Dr Light, Mr Benedict and their legal representative – a Ms Monroe I believe, had a private meeting here with you and Gertner Hirschowitz – Mr Zaentz joining on Skype. I organised the link. You're suggesting I advised MoonLight prior to the meeting of this company's position entrapping Mr Benedict and attempting to compromise him. Is that correct?"

"No. Well, we-. The board are wondering..."

For once Prendergast appeared to be in a bad place and was squirming.

"Directors even inferring this are making a serious accusation."

Carla turned to the door.

"If there's nothing else?"

Prendergast sat in his chair flummoxed by what had happened.

"Where are you going?"

"That Mr Prendergast is none of your business."

"But-. What do you mean?"

"I mean it's none of your business."

"But-. You work for me."

"Not anymore. Because of these assertions, that's temporarily rescinded – at least on my part."

"You can't just walk out."

"Can't I? Try me."

"But it's mid-afternoon."

"Tell me about it. All that slaving away – never out of here before mid evening."

"You'll be in breach-."

"Ha!"

Carla cut in.

"I'll be in breach?! If you're suggesting I did as accused the legal department here is going to get even busier."

Leaving the room, Prendergast heard her clearing out the few personal things she had in her office. Re-emerging minutes later with her jacket over her shoulders and carrying a box, Carla put her head round his door.

"Your legal fundi Miss Haas hasn't long gone. I'd get her back here. You'll certainly be hearing from my solicitors soon enough."

And with that she was gone. Prendergast noticed a strip of yellow Rubik cube lying on his desk that hadn't made it to the bin. Picking it up he broke the threads bonding it and hurled the lot at the window. He'd certainly handled that well. Carla was the best PA he'd ever had. Non compare. Sitting there, he also remembered that she had originally worked for Saul Zaentz, and rumour had it the CEO still liked to keep in touch.

Chapter 13

Happy Birthday Mr President

The crush that night – 19th May 1962 in Maddison Square Garden was extreme. It seemed the whole of New York City wanted to wish the 35th president of the United States a happy forty-fifth birthday but as the celebration involved a Democratic fund-raiser, admission was by ticket only. The meeting between the two Monroe's – Kaliska and Marilyn the previous day had been so casual the English lawyer was dubious whether she and Cosima would be admitted. However, they had gone along to the main doors an hour or so before the event was due to begin. The dress code being lounge suits, some women were in cocktail dresses and knowing how Marilyn would be looking performing as she was, Kaliska and Cosima had opted for identical little chic black numbers slashed at the thigh. The two of them looked stunning.

"We're collecting tickets. Two for Monroe."

The security man scrolled down a list of attendees and sure enough two tickets had been left in that name. Admitted, both women were surprised how close they were placed to the dais where artists were to perform. An enormous round of applause went up when the president arrived, and the entertainment got underway. Hollywood glitterati were out in force. The line-up included Henry Fonda, Mike Nichols and Danny Kaye who performed along with Harry Belafonte, Ella Fitzgerald and Maria Callas. The African singer Miriam Makeba was also on the bill. But the highlight of the evening was Marilyn's appearance singing her rendition of Happy Birthday. Watching her closely, Kaliska realised that Marilyn was barely able to hold it together so far gone was she on drugs. Part of the sultry whispery delivery was due to her being more than slightly out of it. However, the performance was sensational and brought the entire audience at Maddison Square Garden to its feet. JFK made a brief speech of thanks and suddenly the show was over. Two bodyguards appeared.

"Miss Monroe?"

Kaliska nodded.

"This way please."

Kaliska and Cosima were ushered from the building to a limousine for the short trip uptown to Hollywood executive Arthur Krimm's Manhattan town house where an after-show party was being held for the select few. Photographers' cameras clicked catching one of Kennedy – his head bowed and back half-turned talking to Marilyn as his brother Bobby looked on. Forty minutes later the president left. On his way out and surrounded by other well-wishers, JFK caught sight of Kaliska and Cosima. His eye couldn't help but be arrested.

"You're back."

Kennedy came over buoyed by the evening's celebrations in his honour. Kaliska said.

"I would say happy birthday but its ten days yet."

"Ha. So you can come in out of life's sequence in this games world... Of course you can. Where's Podric?"

The two women glanced at each other.

"We came on our own."

Kennedy studied Kaliska.

"You're... a lawyer I recall."

Kaliska nodded.

"And you?"

He glanced at Cosima.

"Lawyer's friend."

They all laughed.

"I don't believe you're here just to congratulate me."

"After such a rendition that's something we couldn't possibly match. Going to retire?"

More laughter. Kaliska said.

"I wanted to see you about my Dallas obsession."

"That was one thought I hadn't bargained on having this evening."

Kennedy gave a wry laugh.

"But seeing as how you're here I did think of running something by Podric if I met him again."

"Won't we do?"

Kennedy's entourage approached.

"How do you rate your alternative reality skill sets?"

Did Jack actually have a twinkle in his eye?

"Call my office in the morning."

* * *

Although she had divorced playwright Arthur Miller two years previously, Marilyn brought his father Isidore along to the party that evening. She thought that Miller Senior being an immigrant, meeting the President of the United States would be something special for him. A kind gesture, after JFK left Marilyn was subdued.

"Are you okay?"

Sipping champagne, Kaliska was attentive.

"Yes. No. I don't know. It's like the light goes out when he's gone."

"He has that effect on people."

"Are you in love with him?"

Cosima's clipped English tones and direct question permeated into Marilyn's fuddled head. Cosima smiled.

"I'm the other ticket."

"Oh sugar of course I am but so are most women in America."

Marilyn gushed her breathy whisper.

"Most women in America aren't you though."

"I'm just a small-town girl.."

The star swayed against a pillar. Kaliska said.

"You look a little flushed. Can I get you some water?"

"I want to go to bed. Will you go to bed with me?"

Seeing the state Marilyn was in, a couple of Krimm's minders quietly positioned themselves nearby.

"We could go on to dinner somewhere first if you like."

Kaliska's offer seemed to appeal to Marilyn.

"That sounds great! I just need the powder room."

When she didn't return, Kaliska and Cosima left.

*   *   *

"I was wondering how difficult it would be for me to remain alive in this game – what did Podric call it, *JFK and His World..?* Podric seemed to indicate my life in it could be extended."

"You mean your games life wouldn't end on 22nd November 1963."

"That's what he said."

"Why are you interested living after that – I mean in the state?"

Starting nervously, Cosima was considered.

"Good question and I'm not entirely sure. Your UAR creators have been on about who killed me but from my point of view, that seems academic."

Given this statement largely rendered months if not years of Kaliska's own life – researching and delving into assassination possibilities irrelevant, she was shattered. JFK continued.

"Of course, I haven't figured how it would function. I guess I'd be witness to events playing out. Perhaps I could be a shadowy presence watching Lyndon make a hash of things?"

The thought obviously appealed to him, and Kennedy laughed. They were sitting in the Oval office – JFK in his rocking chair and Kaliska and Cosima on the two sofas opposite. Kaliska said.

"So you're not worried about who kills you."

Kennedy looked at her.

"You've made quite a study I believe..."

"It's consumed me."

Kennedy adjusted his posture.

"We can look at it, but you'll appreciate it makes little differ-ence to me. I was concerned about going to Dallas, but I didn't know I was going to get shot."

There wasn't anywhere for this topic of conversation to go and JFK brightened things.

"Anyway, how are you girls positioned to make my extension in this computer games world happen?"

"We can try."

Kaliska was bright eyed.

"No. No we can't."

It was rare to see Kaliska thwarted but Cosima was firm. Amusingly surprised, JFK turned to the younger woman who said.

"No, President Kennedy, we don't have that ability."

"Thought not. You're that other fellow... Dr Light's daughter."

Cosima smiled.

"And he doesn't have it either."

"Familiarly ruthless."

"Just honest. The only person who can create what you're talking about is Podric."

"And I have no control as to when he might show up."

"There I believe we may be able to help you – find out when Podric plans to see you again."

Kaliska who hadn't got over her agitation at JFK's lack of interest in his assassination, went on.

"If he says those are the plans he has for you if you want them, then he'll make it work."

A buzzer sounded on the president's phone system. Rather than pick up the extension beside him, Kennedy stood and went over to his desk. Both women noticed the momentary stiffness in his movement.

"Thank you. I appreciate your candour."

He didn't dismiss them, but the feeling was that the meeting was over. Kaliska and Cosima also rose. An aide opened the door and they made to leave. Cosima turned.

"Why do you want to?"

About to pick up the phone, Kennedy paused.

"Be around in some way after the event?"

Jack smiled. He could be so winning.

"Wouldn't you if you knew what was going to happen in eighteen months' time?"

Holding the receiver, Kennedy pressed a button on the phone system which enabled him to hold the call.

"And it could be fun to see how things turn out."

"Maybe not."

"Well I'll sure as hell not be able to do anything about it."

He laughed. Cosima said.

"Won't that irritate?"

Still holding the receiver, Jack turned away to the Rose Garden. "People have no idea what it's like to do this job."

Then he was light.

"Besides, the experience will be a new one for me if it comes off." The buzzer went again. As they went out Kaliska thought. 'Whatever you say – even if you don't care who did for you, you love new sensations. That's your thing. And whether it was a lone nut or some dark conspiracy, I want to know...'

With her mind mulling these notions Kaliska followed her friend along the hall, away from the Oval Office and out into the Washington sunshine.

Chapter 14
To The Lighthouse

The gathering in Archie's den was sizeable. Recent Ultimate Alternative Reality participants had all returned from the state and were back in their real-world existence. The suggestion for the meeting had come from Catherine Halliday. Podric confiding to his girlfriend that he was going to write a new game which would be called *Moon Landing* and that this time it would come to fruition – Catherine thinking about the concept realised how critical it would be that Podric had his select band of brothers and sisters around to support him in the adventure. It would be some game and no doubt all his friends would want to be involved. As discussions developed those in the room felt they were actually going to make the 237,000-mile trip to the earth's nearest neighbour – and in their minds they would be. Billy Johnson not included in the meeting, Podric had met his friend privately.

"Are you sure about this, Billy?"

"Yup. Nope. I dunno Pod. She's determined to have it."

"That's as maybe."

Podric looked at his friend.

"Your facing responsibilities is great, but it's going to affect your life forever."

"I know that. But what am I going to do? She's adamant she wants the baby."

"A young Billy, huh?"

"Or Carol."

The two boys were silent. Then Podric said.

"What about school and stuff?"

"Reckon I'll have to leave and get a job. There's always the round though dad's not keen."

Billy referred to the local milk round he did with his father though it was winding down.

"You've told your parents?"

Billy nodded.

"How did they take it?"

Billy shrugged.

"Not good. Mum was worst. 'Said I was throwing my life away."

"Has she met Carol?"

"Oh yeah. Didn't go well."

"I don't think you should leave Wendbury, Billy."

"I'm gonna have to Pod. I'm gonna have to provide."

Whilst impressed with his friend's sense of commitment Podric wasn't satisfied.

"Billy, I've come into a bit of cash-."

"Stop right there Pod – if you're gonna say what I think you're gonna say the answers no thanks..."

Podric looked at his friend. He was very fond of Billy.

"I couldn't do charity Pod. Just couldn't."

Billy fiddled with his smart phone.

"There's some things you got to do. I got into this. It is what it is."

This slightly downbeat comment led Podric to consider asking Billy if he loved Carol, but he thought better of it. His friend seemed so determined, Podric could only admire Billy's sense of commitment. Parting company Podric said.

"Well even if we fall out, I don't think you should leave school."

*   *   *

When word of the *Moon Landing* meeting got out it spread like wildfire amongst UAR aficionados. The usual suspects had ensured they would be present – Cosima Light and Kaliska Monroe both now back from their first unaided experience and Barney Sturridge – all committed to UAR in their own particular ways. Barbara Moon attended, and Charlotte Light made the cut. Although she hadn't consulted Podric, Barbara had asked Alannah Brodie if she was interested in more Ultimate Alternative Reality adventures, but the Lights' housekeeper passed.

"If he can put me back into Dublin 1916 I'll go and live there forever. That's what I want. That's all I want."

Barbara didn't tell her friend she thought this next adventure not only didn't include historic Eireann but wasn't even on this earth – others were keen to be included. Most of Podric's class wanted in, and a surprise attendee who turned up at the meeting was Denise Mullins – Podric's ex-form teacher.

"I've experienced Ultimate Alternative Reality. Would you deprive me of being included in this new adventure?"

It was a litany Podric had heard before, but Miss Mullins wasn't the most unexpected person sitting in the room. That honour went to Carla Logan. Podric and Archie had decided that George Benedict should be involved. Having worked on the original *Moon Landing* game that failed to come to fruition, if he was in theirs it would be easier to keep an eye on him. It was Benedict who recommended Carla's attendance. Archie agreed.

"She's gone out on a limb for us – quit her job."

"I heard she was fired."

"For being accused of something she did for us."

If Archie could sometimes irritate Podric, on occasion the reverse applied. Podric ignored his older partner's dig.

"Can we trust her?"

Podric was sceptical. Archie said.

"One way to find out."

Archie and Podric were talking privately in the computer lab. The games creator sipped some coffee.

"It could be a ruse on her part but somehow I don't think so. From what I've seen of Carla she's a passionate girl if she believes in something – or someone."

"So passionate she previously disliked you intensely."

"She told me even more than that."

Archie finished his coffee. In the den all were waiting. With Dog in their midst – his boisterousness tiresome as ever – the meeting got started. Given the disparate nature of the group, it was interesting to see the chemistry between Kaliska and Cosima. There was no special intimacy. It was as if the events in the afternoon a few days previously hadn't happened. Perhaps their desires had been short term and temporarily satiated?

"So what adventures are we going to have?"

Bullish as ever, Barney was as rumbustious as Dog if slightly less physically disruptive. Podric said.

"Sometimes Barney I wonder, I really wonder."

Podric took a sip of coffee.

"It's self-evident where we're going."

"Yeah but what else man?"

"You mean it isn't enough for you that this is the first intergalactic adventure?"

Catherine was sipping white wine.

"No. I suppose it wouldn't be."

"The key is the search for proof. Did the Apollo missions make it or was it a con?"

Archie wandered around his den and continued.

"And us spooking the authorities... We want to find out what they know."

Archie took a couple of beers from the fridge and handed one to his ex-business partner.

"We still come back to what the original games team might have touched on George. That's got to be the key."

Whilst Archie paced about, George Benedict pulled the tab of his beer can.

"It was the technological crudeness that was the problem. The initial thrust of a Saturn 5 was unstable – we know some of the rockets blew up – and the adapter section housing the LIM didn't always function properly. In fact, a hell of a lot of the Apollo craft stylised for the game I ever experimented on didn't seem to function at all – or if they did, at best only erratically. I could never get a whole range of its functions to work. For example, the S4B orbital section and linkage to the Lunar Landing Module would never hook up. As a result, I had serious doubts about any Apollo mission ever actually making it."

"Had. You said had."

Before he could answer Archie, Catherine interjected.

"Are you suggesting Secorni's research into the Apollo program meant they might have stumbled on the fact that NASA didn't, nor ever could have got to the moon with the technology available then?"

"That's exactly what I'm saying."

"And these would support that."

Carla Logan took out a couple of files from a slim briefcase along with a USB drive.

"It's everything I could find about the company's winding up development of *Moon Landing*."

She laid the documents and memory stick on the table beside her. Archie quickly gathered them up.

"This is all bullshit man. What's all this got to do about us being here?"

Barney brought everything down to earth as only he knew how. Looking preoccupied, Archie left the room.

"If you don't understand that, why don't you go home?"

Barney scowled at Catherine's reply. Others knew Barney was as obsessed with Ultimate Alternative Reality adventures as they were.

"Whilst he's wrong about bullshit, our UAR philistine has a point."

Several quizzical looks were trained in Podric's direction.

"We are here Barney to discuss designing a game that was once started but never completed and one that I intend finishing. As UAR cognoscente we knew you'd all want to be involved so we're telling you about it now rather than any of you suddenly turning up in it."

"At your beck and call."

Barney's riposte met with a stunned silence. Podric considered.

"Is that how you view it Barney – that you're just inserted at our bidding?"

"Well we are, aren't we."

The way Barney spoke it wasn't a question.

"Oookay. So you're not in for the upcoming game and won't be in it."

"My point. You get to choose."

"Barney, I think we might be at cross purposes."

Podric looked round the room.

"How Archie and I came up with UAR and the subsequent clamour from you all to be included in our Ultimate Alternative Reality adventures which you Barney have been at the spearhead of..."

Podric had some more coffee then continued.

"If you want out, split. In fact, if any of you are unhappy with UAR I will personally ensure you're not involved again."

One could hear a pin drop.

"Barney?"

"Can we have any input?"

Barney Sturridge was unfazed by Podric's challenge.

"Sure. What suggestions have you got?"

"A shuttle ride."

Podric laughed.

"That's not really a challenge."

"Isn't it?"

George Benedict had another swig of his insipid larger and grimaced. Podric responded.

"Point taken. I meant game. We're really looking at games' challenges."

"You mean on the basis of the previous effort a games task could actually be getting to the moon?"

Denise Mullins was excited. Podric nodded.

"And back."

Cosima was Cosima - cool and cynical.

"Yup. As Kennedy said - return a man safely to earth."

George Benedict finished his unsatisfying drink and dropped the empty can in a bin.

"If that challenge is surmounted, can it be programmed to spend some time on the moon?"

"You mean like create a base? We know no ones done that."

Kaliska caught Denise Mullins mood and continued.

"Do you think we'll find the Lunar Rovers?"

"If they're there." Podric finished his coffee and continued.

"Don't suppose you have any of your old codex workings George?"

"Carla, we owe you." Re-entering, Archie waved a sheet of paper at them. "A link. I'm just downloading all the original metadata."

"You'd better get started then."

Barbara smiled and picked up her bag.

"Guess you'll let us know when everything's ready – given you still want us to come along."

Not having heard the recent debate Archie couldn't imagine any one of those present wouldn't give their life savings for the chance to be part of the adventure. Kissing her son lightly, Barbara walked over to the lift.

"Why Archie, we'd all of us give our life savings not to miss it."

A murmur of agreement went round the room and a 'whoop' from Barney caused some mirth. Dog charged about as the meeting began breaking up. "Taking him, are we? The Russians did." Barney was unbowed. Archie replied.

"With mixed results you'll recall."

Archie and George came over to Carla who was standing beside Podric and Catherine. Handing her the USB stick Archie said.

"Carla, we owe you. Company data that had gone missing and US authorities subsequent raison d'être.."

The two smiled briefly to each other. He continued.

"We haven't always seen eye to eye."

"Or game to game." Carla raised an eyebrow. "Some riddle though." She looked at Podric who appeared preoccupied. He said.

"Some sands..."

Chapter 15
Back in the Lab

In spite of George Benedict's recent actions and Podric and Archie's uncertainty about his honesty, UAR's creators decided to avail themselves of Benedict's games writing skills. 'Keep your friends close but your enemies closer' had been Archie's attitude. Now working in the lab with George Benedict – the next few weeks were the most rewarding Podric had ever experienced professionally. Not only were they creating a new computer game – they were building it to include Ultimate Alternative Reality which would give a playing participant that additional dimension. Because of UAR's uniqueness Podric insisted a number of components he'd generated for *JFK and His World* were incorporated in the new *Moon Landing* game. US and Russian societies – leading figures both political and scientific were featured as well as NASA and the Soviet's use of German rocketry that kick-started both countries' space programs. The controversy surrounding these origins as well as the political turmoil after JFK's assassination: Flagging American interest in the space race as the 1960s progressed and US unrest: The Civil Rights movement, the Vietnam war and subsequent administrations' relationship with the National Aeronautics and Space Administration: Lyndon Johnson and Richard Nixon plus Soviet issues – Khrushchev and Brezhnev. It was a multi-layered scenario.

George Benedict being a more intuitive games' creator than Archie, Podric found him interesting to work with. Whilst the two laboured over their efforts, Archie was busy dealing with other issues one of which was Carla Logan's safety. When the senior Secorni personal assistant came over to them there had been much discussion about her safety living alone in her Kensington flat. Whilst it wasn't believed that the company would resort to abducting Carla, her security could not be guaranteed when it came to lurking security agencies. MoonLight and those connected with them, felt there was sufficient potential risk to ensure that she initially stayed at the Lighthouse. For a variety of reasons including Carla's own protestations this was rapidly rendered as impracticable. George Benedict also wanted a move from his garden lodgings in 5 Briony Close so it was decided that the two of them would share a place. Choices in Drinkwell appeared minimal but the unlikely solution came from a most improbable source. Lilian Bekes turning up at the Moons one day to see Amy overheard George on the phone looking for accommodation.

"I got a place."

Podric said. "I don't think that would work Lilian."

"Don't mean the trailer, twat. And I'll be on yer next adventure."

The two statements not obviously linked, Podric liked Lilian. Before binning the idea, George and Podric agreed the Romany would take them to see whatever it was she was suggesting. George immediately fell in love with the dilapidated 1930s horse drawn caravan, and very surprisingly when she saw it, so did Carla Logan! Parked in a field off the Wendbury road a few miles from Drinkwell, the broken-down vehicle was a sorry sight.

"Doesn't it belong to anyone?"

Although the caravan was in need of repair, George was entranced. Lilian said.

"What this heap of shit? I was 'avin' you on!"

Guffawing with mirth, Lilian suddenly realised George was serious.

"Dumped wannit. Zag the Slitter left it and he's banged up for a stretch."

"How long?" Podric enquired. The girl gave the young UAR maestro a look.

"Ten."

"Months?"

Lilian snorted.

"Get more than that for murder – even these days."

This ghoulish information didn't put George or Carla off. After paying Lilian's family some money as a finders fee the following weekend saw them both hard at work. Carla Logan turned out to be quite skilled at woodwork ('Dad had a lumber business') and with others turning up to help, the caravan was rapidly transformed. Deciding on a hard top rather than canvas, wandering into their renovating midst Barney Sturridge proved a real craftsman 'I did pay some attention in Woodwork, Pod'. Along with Miles Willoughby, Jane Cartwright and Catherine and Podric's help the caravan was made habitable. A couple of days later Barbara Moon showed up and took it upon herself to adorn the waggon decoratively. Her swirls and crests were elaborately exotic and gave the horse drawn conveyance a romantic touch. George would have the upstairs bunk, Carla's below. Hers was reached through some neat little double doors making the quarters snug and private. It was an amazing transformation.

Owning a small orchard next to the Lighthouse (it had been the location for the Field of Dreams marquee hired for Podric's seventeenth birthday party) Archie suggested that for safety reasons the caravan should be moved there when it was finished. A loader was brought in and with some ceremony the Romany fiacre was winched aboard.

"Only nag we've got wouldn't pull a milk float let alone that thing."

Lilian looked on dismissively as the truck carrying its fantastic cargo disappeared from view. Relocated at its new site, Carla was heavily quizzed about her sincerity choosing to live in such a dwelling but with the arrival of a portaloo positioned judiciously nearby she announced it was the home of her dreams! On their first night in their new habitat George and Carla hosted a campfire party which went on late into the evening. All the usual guests were present including Mrs Bickerstaff and Eamon.

"You've fixed this up nice George. Eamon still misses yer though. All the excitement you brought."

The parakeet swooped and dived over them flaunting his brilliant red plumage. Mrs B sounded quite wistful. In charge of the barbecue Benedict handed Barney yet another hotdog.

"Anymore onion George – and a bit of mustard? I do like some of the yellow stuff with a dog."

Watching Barney shower mustard all over his hot dog and shove the bun and giant sausage into his mouth, George Benedict reflected on mankind and the human condition. It invariably left him wondering and it did now.

The creation of the new *Moon Landing* computer game quickly accelerated. Much of George Benedict's original codex being accessed, layer upon layer of data was rapidly inserted. What took time to install were Podric's additional dimensions. *Moon Landing* would be a highly complex challenge with far more elements than the average game. It was a comprehensive profile of not just America's Apollo space program, but the country's socio-economic situation and how the desire to get to the moon first sat within that.

The most potentially innovative decade of the 20th century – the pill, flower power, rock and roll and originality of contemporary music along with Andy Warhol, avant-garde art and risqué living – anything and everything was to be tried and experimented. It was a refreshing explosion of liberal thinking after near global destruction in the Second World War. However, only a few years into the 1960s this pantheon outburst of creativity was hit by a series of crises that undermined its initial confidence. In Podric's mind *Moon Landing* would explore this and provide him and his friends with unparalleled adventure. That was sufficient motivation for Podric to drive himself and his computer games colleagues to intensify their efforts and create an ultimate game for Ultimate Alternative Reality!

Chapter 16
Space Odyssey and
a Quiet Weekend

Sitting in a preview theatre in Elstree Studios at Borehamwood in Hertfordshire a small audience including several members of *2001: A Space Odyssey*'s production department, co-writer Arthur C. Clarke and director Stanley Kubrick watched a clip of the Apollo astronauts rehearsing for their walk on the moon. Their LM was visible behind them. The piece finishing, the house lights went up.

"Realistic."

Arthur C. Clarke put down his notes.

"Could be the real thing."

"Better than the real thing."

Kubrick was curt. The group began to leave the theatre. Clarke said. "They look a lot less advanced than Keir in that gear."

He was referring to Keir Dullea, the actor playing the lead in *2001*. Clarke and Kubrick reached the theatre door.

"Think they'll do it?"

"How the hell would I know?"

A disgruntled Kubrick left. Clarke shrugged and followed.

"Okay Stanley.."

One of the sets of *2001: A Space Odyssey* involved a giant revolving centrifuge, the interior of which depicted part of a space craft. It was an incredible piece of film construction. Painters, prop designers and set decorators were hard at work as Kubrick made an inspection of the set.

"What did you think of the clip?"

The director looked round to see a young man working on

an electronic panel he was fitting into the command module. Kubrick came over and inspected Podric's work.

"What do you mean 'what do I think of the clip'?"

"The Apollo guys."

Kubrick turned and realised who he was talking to.

"Ah. Visiting me on this picture now, huh?"

Podric made some adjustments to the controls display. He had decided to make a few entries into UAR by himself before official-ly launching his *Moon Landing* game and this was one of them.

"You go back and forth in time then. I made *The Shining* in 1980 and *Dr. S* five years ago. This is '67."

"Mr Kubrick, you know I have something you just love. In my reality I can move about as I want. It beats TV, motion pictures – even computer games. It's the ultimate form of an alternative reality. What you create on steroids."

Podric and Kubrick looked at each other.

"*2001: A Space Odyssey* is released next year – a year before July '69."

Kubrick flicked through a series of storyboards, studying their depiction against the actual design.

"If you're using your alternative reality for all this you must be pretty obsessed."

Selecting a frame, the director took the cardboard mount out of the file and rested it against a props strut. The set was a perfect reflection.

"Met my match there, then."

Podric Moon and Stanley Kubrick took in the scene.

"And you believe I shot these lunar sequences commissioned by the American government."

"Perhaps agencies for them as an insurance policy in case of failure. Why would you not?"

"Why would I?""

Kubrick was quietly angry.

"You really think I'm an Uncle Sam stooge?"

"Not deliberately. You told me how you were pressured and the reason they got to you."

Podric stood back and checked his recent work then turned to Kubrick.

"Look, I'm about to launch into another adventure. The computer game is called *Moon Landing*. I wondered if you'd like to come along – be a part of it?"

"So you can check me out and see whether I did what you think I did.."

"No."

Podric put some tools in a bag and stood up. He looked Kubrick in the eye.

"You're one of the greatest film directors of your time – all time. You're fascinated by space, mankind and the future. You already know the kind of sensations you can experience in the UAR state I've created though that's nothing to outright Ultimate Alternative Reality adventure. I just thought maybe you'd like to live some of that."

For a long moment the boy and man studied the set. Then Kubrick turned to Podric and smiled.

"Put like that..."

* * *

Their mother away in Greece enjoying the largesse of Greek shipping tycoon Aristotle Onassis with her sister Princess Lee Radziwill and other guests, six-year old Caroline and nearly three-year old John Kennedy Jnr had been flown to Camp David from the White House on Thursday 11th October for a weekend with their father who followed them up there after a day of meetings in Washington that Friday night. John Jnr was at the helipad to welcome his dad and the atmosphere was a happy one. When Jackie was away Jack tended to spoil his children and things in general were more playful. Caroline would be big sister to her little brother and JFK enjoyed his private moments with his offspring.

Camp David – the official American presidents' retreat set in a couple of hundred acres of Maryland countryside just sixty miles from Washington had a relaxed atmosphere and was a pleasant contrast to the hurly burly of the nation's capital. Originally converted from a camp built for federal government agents and their families it was converted to a presidential retreat by Franklin Roosevelt. An early guest of his had been Winston Churchill. During Kennedy's presidency – when he wasn't using the place JFK let members of his staff frequent it from time to time.

A magazine photoshoot with his son on Saturday morning while his daughter was out riding her pony was the height of the weekend's excitement. Kennedy had the usual phone calls – there was always some government business, but things were pretty laid back.

That evening after a day with John and Caroline – both now in bed, Kennedy settled down to a book, a modest whisky and a small cigar. It was a rarity in his life that he was ever alone. It wasn't that Jack had a particular problem with his own company but given his penchant for living every moment as if it was his last – by anyone's standards, this was an unusually quiet few days for him.

People had noticed a certain change in Kennedy in recent months. Whilst his roving eye would lessen little, since the recent death of their prematurely born second son Patrick who lived only a few hours, he and Jackie appeared to have grown closer which is why eyebrows were raised when her Greek trip was announced.

"Things must be a bit quiet for you here."

Sitting in one of his many rocking chairs in the Camp David living room, Kennedy was in silhouette. Exhaling his panatela, he looked across at Podric who stood by the window.

"Ha. Wondered when you'd fetch up."

"Did you? You always seem vaguely irritated whenever I appear."

Kennedy looked at Podric and smiled.

"Only because I never know when you're going to."

He puffed his cigar.

"Interesting moment you've selected."

Something that could be said of Kennedy, he didn't miss much. Podric glanced around.

"Official retreat. Relaxed vibe."

Kennedy didn't reply. Podric looked out at the rolling Maryland countryside.

"Yes, I could see it's a particular weekend – just you and your children. I was sorry to hear of your recent loss. I know I'm viewing things from the perspective of history, but it must be very raw for you right now."

Kennedy's face betrayed nothing. Podric continued.

"I don't think you go much on intimacy. You're always a bit apart."

"I consider a person's private life to be their own affair. Everyone should be entitled to that – even public servants."

"I can only say that the times you're living in – such a private life becomes increasingly difficult to maintain. The advances in technology mean that everyone knows everything about everybody nowadays."

"I very much doubt that."

Podric shrugged amiably.

"Okay. Most things about most people and some things they don't even know about themselves!"

"That's nonsensical."

"It is, but you might catch my meaning."

Kennedy who never suffered fools gladly wasn't used to being spoken to in such a way least of all by a seventeen-year-old English schoolboy. It wasn't that Podric was rude – his character meant he just said things in a naturally forthright manner. In a sense Podric met Jack Kennedy's well-known charismatic charm with his own idiosyncratic one. Kennedy liked him for it. Podric said.

"Dreadful and difficult though it is looking ahead a few weeks' – after the shock waves finish reverberating around the world – rumours subsequently begin surfacing about your potentially being exposed in '64."

"There are always rumours."

"Yes, President Kennedy, but it's the level of them. Your dalliances are seen to be on something of a grand scale."

Did Kennedy's eyes actually twinkle?

"That has a touch of Irishness, Podric."

Given he was facing death in five weeks' time JFK's sangfroid was remarkable. Podric went on.

"In fact, presidents in the future who play away on a much smaller scale are seriously exposed with the threat of impeachment. Then there's a period of POTUS's brazening things out. Believe me the sleaze gets murkier."

Podric turned back from the window.

"I gather you'd like to be a part of a computer world after November 22nd."

Kennedy finished his panatela.

"It could be interesting."

JFK stubbed out the butt. Podric said.

"Interesting is an interesting word."

Jack laughed.

"You're an old head on young shoulders, Podric. Is it so daunting?"

"I'd say that would depend. You'll likely be okay because you have a certain detachment about life, but for anyone with much emotion it could be difficult."

Kennedy chuckled.

"You may have some Irish blood but you're also British. 'Difficult'. The British use words like that when their world is falling apart."

"You like the Brits?"

"I partly grew up in London."

"Your father.."

"Is a complicated man."

The way Kennedy spoke closed the topic. Ignoring presidential protocol however informal, Podric wandered around.

"My explaining about Ultimate Alternative Reality previously – how you're able to see me – there have been some issues recently in my contemporary real life. They've involved branches – perhaps maverick cells of the US Secret Service compromising a colleague of mine for his involvement in a computer game."

"The one that somehow exposed the space program..."

JFK sipped his whisky. He hadn't offered Podric a drink. Seeing a drinks tray and continuing to ignore decorum, Podric poured himself a glass of water.

"Weirdly, yes. The moon challenge you laid down as an inspiration to your country poses a big headache to your National Aeronautics and Space Administration. Do they have the technology? Can they achieve the task you set them?"

Podric sipped his water.

"The technology available to the science world in your decade is frankly infantile by comparison to the advances made over the next fifty years."

Podric walked over to JFK and placed his wrist in front of the president.

"That's a microchip buried just below the surface of my skin."

Podric removed his wrist.

"It has more processing power than all the technology the United States possessed in 1963. That technology still wasn't so brilliant in 1969 when men supposedly walked on the moon."

Podric drank some water.

"It may sound far-fetched but there are schools of thought that query this ever happened – that the landing was some kind of giant hoax. Society in general considers it was real but who knows? When you're assassinated most people originally believed you were shot by a crazed killer named Lee Harvey Oswald, but now the feeling is that others were involved."

"So I gather."

"Your FBI chums have been back to the book depository in Dealey Plaza and tried the shots using a rifle of the same type Oswald used – an old bolt action Mannlicher-Carcano. They also added the 4-power Ordnance Optic scope he'd had fitted to it, but they still had mixed results."

Podric finished his water.

"Something else that's highly suspicious is that Oswald was shot dead himself whilst in custody just 48 hours after he supposedly killed you. Its suggested Oswald was taken out before he could open his mouth."

"The implication being-."

"He needed to be silenced."

Kennedy finished his drink. This quiet weekend wasn't turning out to be quite so quiet after all.

"You seem to know a lot about this."

"A lot of the work in computer games is research. I become a geek about a topic. I have to know everything or as much as I can to program it for accuracy."

Podric replaced his empty glass on the drinks tray.

"So, the game. It's called *Moon Landing* and is a rebuild of one my colleague worked on but was forced to quit by the commissioning company."

"Why?"

"Because it's thought they got too near something. Somehow touched a nerve – discovered a flaw in the real space program from data they were using. Anyway, he had to stop work on it and the game was never released."

"But the computer game couldn't have affected the National Aeronautics space program. It came years after."

"Correct. There was a big gap timewise and yet more years before the goons now showing up. They're trying to find out about UAR and the possibility it'll expose their cover-ups."

"As you say you have me at a disadvantage."

Kennedy got up and like Podric, gazed out at the evening countryside. Kennedy continued.

"Accepting that, you're including me in this situation because I started it."

"The comparisons interest me. What did you possess that was so threatening to people in the county you're head of that you were so violently removed? What is it the computer games technicians touched on re the moon project that so worried the authorities they closed it down? You're the common denominator."

Kennedy shrugged.

"Couldn't you be over analysing this? If this Oswald guy was simply a nut, he could have just done for me."

"And these agency gorillas and the game could be the same.

You're right – it could all just be castles in the sand."

After a second or two's reflection President Kennedy and Podric turned to each other.

"Given I'm dead, what the hell?"

"More like the heavens President Kennedy. You get to walk on the lunar surface all the fuss is about!"

Kennedy laughed.

"One way to see it I guess."

The president's weekend had turned out to be livelier than he could possibly have imagined.

Chapter 17
Lift off and GCR

The occupants sitting inside the command module on top of the giant Saturn V rocket listened to their launch countdown. The three people – astronauts Moon, Light and Benedict were impassive in their white space suits. The right-hand seat was occupied by Dr Archie Light. As Lunar Module Pilot he checked a switch in front of him. Unnecessary, it was the only sign of nervousness on board. The Command Module Pilot George Benedict was centre and although he was by far the youngest, Commander Podric Moon's position was on the left side of the capsule. Whilst shields covered the tiny windows prohibiting any view, the three knew exactly what the rocket looked like outside. A clear bright dawn, the massive projectile sat on the Florida pan, fuel vapour flowing down its sides, streaming away from the craft.

Podric couldn't speak for the two men in the capsule with him but his own mind was contradictory. Professionally he felt an inner calm, but it sat challenged alongside palpitating excitement. As the seconds ticked by – Mission Control's inexorable countdown – Podric's disciplined self subconsciously processed the mass of data that was continually fed to them. He also found another part of his brain thinking about his aviator father. How excited Sean would have been knowing his son was breaking out of earths' atmosphere, pioneering his way to the heavens.

The final ten seconds of the countdown began. Then at T minus 8.9 the ignition sequence started. Having flown in his father's Typhoon T3 variant which had the most powerful sense of thrust Podric had ever experienced – the shattering, almost primal roar from the five Rocketdyne F-1 engines that exploded below him was so earth-shaking as to be seismic defying any other experience. It certainly put the Eurofighter's thrust in the nursery! Temporarily blotting out all else, it became possible to hear the countdown resume through his headset – six seconds, five, four, three, two, one. Lift off! The gantry swung back, and the giant rocket – the largest ever made to transport man – inexorably began what seemed for a moment or two its slow climb up the side of the tower – all its thrust pushing the giant tube skywards gradually gathering speed as its trajectory pointed towards the upper atmosphere.

On board, though G increased with accelerated speed it was amazing how quickly the earth-shattering vibrations quietened as sections of the rocket parted company. Eighty seconds in the first and largest S-1C section fell away, the smaller S-II section continuing to propel the craft for six minutes taking it upwards another hundred and nine miles. Then the third section – S-IVB carried the spacecraft into orbit around the earth as it prepared for its translunar injection and pushed it on its way towards the moon. Half an hour later Archie managed the separation of the Command and Service Module and the Lunar Module from the spent S-IVB section – uniting the CSM and LM heading them on their way. It was an adventure that thrilled the boy and two men. It was the experience of a lifetime.

*   *   *

Catherine Halliday had only gone into school that day to deliver a maths paper to her tutor Mr Ferwig. Knowing Podric had left to travel to Archie's rented cottage in Wales from where he intended to enter his latest Ultimate Alternative Reality adventure with his business partner and George Benedict, things in Wendbury felt very pianissimo. Not even Barney who she'd had dinner with the previous evening at his flat could lift her spirits. Barney himself appeared deflated.

"All a bit bozo right now. Dunno what it is. Just feel a tad entmutigt."

He enunciating the word germanically, Catherine riding home

knew why their circle was deflated. Such had been the high learning about Podric's new UAR adventure – the wait before they all had the chance to experience it inevitably left them with a deep sense of anti-climax.

The few hours Catherine had spent at school hadn't helped her mood either. Having briefly seen her maths tutor and leaving her work with him, Catherine had been heading back to the bike sheds where she'd parked her Vespa scooter when she bumped into Billy Johnson. Equally dejected but for a very different reason, the two had fallen into desultory conversation. Catherine liked Billy who she felt was a genuine person. With the impending arrival of his girlfriend Carol's baby, Billy had taken on responsibilities and was intending to leave school in order to get a job and support them. Podric had told her that whilst admiring Billy's sense of duty, he didn't think this was right and privately, how he'd like to help his friend with some of his computer games earnings. Billy would have none of it.

"Fancy a coffee? I don't really have access to the GCR though we can risk it."

Catherine's suggestion met with a positive response from Podric's friend.

"I do!"

Aware of Billy's girlfriend's involvement in getting the selected few pupil's access to The Groundsmen's Common Room, Catherine smiled.

"So, going to get married?"

"One thing at a time... No hurry for that is there?"

Entering the GCR, the place was empty. A water urn was always on and they made themselves some coffee.

"Has Pod told you how he offered to help me?"

Catherine was non-committal. Billy continued.

"He wanted to give me some cash to help. He doesn't think I should leave Wendbury."

"What do you think?"

"I think... I know I'm going to be a dad."

"How do you feel about that?"

"Excited."

Billy sipped his brew.

"Well, okay I guess.."

Catherine sipped hers. It was pretty disgusting stuff.

"It's a big thing Billy. In fact, it's more than that – it's life changing."

"Like UAR."

"No, not like UAR."

Billy had some more coffee. He seemed to like it!

"Pod's really pushing it now. 'New adventure sounds fantastic. Must be amazing to go on it.."

Billy couldn't keep the wistfulness from his voice. Finishing her coffee, Catherine put a hand on his arm. "Billy, I'll tell you what I think."

Emptying her half-drunk mug in a sink, Catherine rinsed it out and turned back to Billy.

"Podric's made a barrel load of cash from his computer games and if he genuinely wants to help you I'd let him. You can always do a deal, sort something out but you shouldn't leave school. Even if you just do your A's – do a job for a while and then get back to college. But you need the best education you can get."

"Oh, well. Carol."

"Carol's not daft Billy – far from it. Would you like me to talk to her?"

"No need. I'm here." As if on cue, Carol entered. Signs of her pregnancy were now visible. "Pleased to hear I'm not daft." If she'd been surprised by Carol's arrival, Catherine didn't show it. Carol said.

"If you're trying to get Billy to stay on at school, forget it. He's got other things he's got to do now."

Picking up her bag Catherine approached them.

"You're right Carol. He has got other things he should do and he's going to. But if you love him – really love him, you won't make him leave school. We've been talking about an alternative. There is a way he can stay on and do his A's at least. You should let him explore that option not only for his sake, but also for yours."

And with that she left them.

Chapter 18

Romany, Lighthouse and
a Lunar landing

The Apollo craft travelled behind the moon and firing its service propulsion engine, entered lunar orbit. Looking out of one of the now unshielded windows Podric saw the grey undulating surface. The moon a foreign body – this was adventure most people of any age could only dream about. Here he was about to enter the LM and descend on to the lunar surface. It was taking UAR to new levels alright. The solar system now – one day maybe another galaxy and beyond!

* * *

"All very rustic Carla."

Standing in front of the Romany caravan positioned in her father's orchard, Cosima Light watched Carla Logan take a boiling kettle off a portable Gaz unit. Since being fired as PA to the European head of the world's second largest computer games company with swank offices in London, the young American woman had taken to the nomadic life with surprising alacrity.

"It'll be herbal tea next."

"I already drink herbal tea."

Carla began pouring hot water into a mug. Picking it up, she handed it to Cosima.

"Hot chai with vanilla. Try it."

Cosima put the tin mug to her lips.

"Hmm. Different."

"Good for you. Cloves, nutmeg, ginger – even some cardamom."

"Wow. What about you?"

"That is me."

"Oh-."

Cosima attempted to hand the mug back but Carla put up her hand. Taking a chipped Duralex glass from a shelf, she poured some red liquid out of a kilner jar.

"Sloe G. George made it. The best."

Cosima laughed.

"Certainly. Fastest way I know to happy oblivion."

"Don't need that. Just like the stuff."

Cosima sat down at a picnic table Benedict had placed in front of the caravan. Carla sat on a step.

"Big change for you."

"Long overdue."

"Seriously? Why did you do it?"

"You mean, get fired?"

"Yeah. I mean especially as you and my dad weren't exactly bosom buddies."

Carla Logan laughed.

"'Say that again. He's a strange one your old man."

"Tell me about it. Try having him as a father."

They both laughed and drank. Then Carla reached for the kilner jar behind her and handed it to Cosima.

"Well... As to getting fired, I didn't like what they were doing to him... using George."

Swilling out the dregs of her mug, Cosima poured herself some sloe gin.

"Strange how he turned up. Strange really he and Archie worked together."

"Which they did surprisingly well."

"Cosima shrugged.

"If you say so."

Carla sipped her drink. She said.

"As far as George goes, you say turned up. He was set up and likely there's more behind it. There's dirty and dirty. I've closed my eyes over the years to some of the tricks they play but this was a bridge too far."

Cosima had a swig of her drink. Having finished hers, Carla poured herself some more.

"Funny little trio aren't they – those two and boy wonder."

"Ha. There you touch their nerve. George is more original than pa, but pa had the dialogue. Both helped each other in their games world. Podric coming along is someone neither can figure. He's in a realm all his own."

"'Making' it would seem."

Cosima looked at Carla.

"You wait."

"I am. All a bit dramatic."

Cosima finished her drink and stood up.

"You're right. The experience is."

"Why did they go to Wales?"

"Podric said he had a lot to do prepping for all this. It's by far the most challenging UAR adventure ever."

"But why there?"

"It's very quiet. My parents have a rented place. They've had it for years. He and Archie have been down before."

"But we're not... 'going in' from there."

"No. Everyone's rendezvousing at the Lighthouse. Make sure you're on time – to avoid disappointment."

* * *

"Lunar Module in final stage for separation."

Inside the LM Archie Light went through rotation procedure in preparation for separation from the Command Module.

"Okay, we're good to go here."

Some sixty nautical miles above the moon's surface Podric and Archie detached the LM from the CSM. George Benedict who was commanding the CSM gave a visual inspection of the lunar craft as it rotated in front of him. Then the two directors of MoonLight performed a Descent Orbit Insertion burn putting the LM into a sixty by nine nautical mile orbit. They would start their powered descent from its lowest point.

* * *

One of the developments Archie Light was proudest of was a small theatre he'd had created below his computer museum. That space in the Lighthouse having previously been spare now housed a sixteen-seat presentational room and cinema. It was here that participants arriving at the Lighthouse met. They arrived quietly in dribs and drabs. Such were the feelings of heightened expectancy, few had much to say. Barney Sturridge attempted to lighten things with a Mars bar quip 'Work rest and play, 'in it?' but the slogan referring to the wrong planet he was promptly told to shut up. The UAR conquistadors were a disparate crowd. Podric's younger sister Amy and her friend Lilian Bekes – eccentric children. Podric's equally unconventional mother Barbara Moon and Archie's enigmatic wife Charlotte Light. Their headstrong daughter Cosima and Podric and Archie's lawyer, the unusual Kaliska Monroe. Also present were Carla Logan their recent computer company compadre and Podric's ex-form teacher, Denise Mullins. Everyone arrived fired up and ready for their new adventure into the unknown. What would it hold and what alternative reality challenges would they face?

* * *

The CSM Archie had called Albion orbiting above them and Hermes, the name he'd given the LM – began its descent towards the lunar surface. Archie had chosen Albion as being appropriate for their capsule and according to George Benedict, Hermes was as fitting a Greek god as any to call the landing craft! Podric had been indifferent to either. If it made the men happy it was fine by him.

Hermes was going too fast! As the LM pilot, Archie was due to 'fly' the vehicle in but his skills in training had been found wanting. Although his program knowledge was good, Archie's practical abilities reflected those when playing the games he'd written. He clearly had little feel for mastering the craft Neil Armstrong and Buzz Aldrin had nicknamed The Flying Bedstead! It therefore fell to Podric to also act as pilot of the LM. Looking down at the moon's surface the site that had been planned for their landing didn't appear to be as smooth as it had looked on the photographs they'd studied prior to departure. Showing some of his bravura playing skills, Podric guided Hermes with an apparently assured hand, heading away from the original site of Pentagonal Bay across undulating terrain towards Alamo Ridge. Alarms went off from the limited on-board computation equipment – red lights flashed and a tiny siren wailed. Archie looked tense but Podric was concentrating so hard he didn't seem to notice any warning signals. Forcing himself to stay calm, Archie called out navigation data as they drew closer to the surface. At just over two hundred feet and with fuel fast depleting (they had less than a minute's worth) Podric grabbed a glance outside. Although still boulder-strewn the surface appeared flatter. A little away to the right it looked clearer. At one hundred feet the LM's engines caused surface dust to kick up which blotted out their view. Trusting his instinct more than data, Podric landed Hermes.

"Descent engine stop. ACA – out of detent."

Archie could barely speak he was so excited. Adjusting some switches, Podric replied.

"Out of detent. Auto."

"Mode control – both auto. Descent engine command override off. Engine Arm – off. 951 is in."

They were on the moon.

Chapter 19
Unchartered Waters

Taking a holiday because of her employer's alternative reality adventures 'They prefer living in that world to this!' – the Lights' housekeeper packed her car. As keen as anyone on her own particular Ultimate Alternative Reality adventure, Alannah was only interested in Ireland 1916. The Easter Rebellion. Because of her heritage she was obsessed with it. She thought about going over to the lab and trying to gain access to *Erin Freedom!* the game Podric had so wonderfully put her into at his seventeenth birthday party, but on reflection decided against it. She didn't even know how to turn on a computer! Brodie also wasn't keen to see the alternative reality participants in their state. 'Lot of zombies, they've even taken Dog!'. She would go to Ireland. Her home. Land of her dreams. She would go there and bathe in its rebellious history. One day Brodie told herself she would get back into that Irish game. Podric had promised her. And when she did she'd decided she would disappear inside it never to return.

* * *

Their boots leaving neat treads on the surface, most of the moon's covering appeared to be rough grey soil. Portable Life Support Systems on their backs, Podric and Archie set off across the Alamo Heights towards a ridge in the distance bearing the same name. Strange to walk on another world – Podric didn't quite know how he felt. Euphoria yes, but also the feeling that he was standing on the edge of a new beginning. It gave him a feeling of optimism – the start of a new dimension in the history of man's exploration. Breathing steadily, Podric didn't find the pack on his back cumbersome; it was a necessary extension of himself. Reaching the bottom of the escarpment, Podric stopped. Archie approached and turning, both looked across the thousands of miles of space at the earth. Although they knew this was the tiniest of journeys in galactic terms it was still the most extraordinary experience.

"One small step Podric."

"Think they made it?"

"That's what we're here to find out."

The boy and man started up the incline.

Aboard the CSM orbiting the moon, George Benedict stared out of Albion's little windows at the lunar surface below. Glancing at a digital clock he was still several hours away from the planned rendezvous with his colleagues. Making the usual checks Benedict contemplated what had gone on since he'd shown up at Drink-well, threatened as he was by Secorni and the more powerful shadowy forces behind them. Benedict had asked himself a thousand times what he could have stumbled across working on the original *Moon Landing* computer game. His mind racing, George thought about his escape – what he owed the several people who had his back when he was on the run. His ex-business partner, Carla Logan, Podric and Podric's mother. What had Barbara said that day in the café in Banewell? That 'he was the first man she'd been able to relate to since her husband died'. Those words affected Benedict who wondered if hers offered the beginnings of intimacy. So warped had his attitude to personal relationships become, Benedict didn't trust himself to make a balanced judgement anymore. Twice married his first had been one of convenience. Leaving university with no job and desperate to get into the American computer scene, he'd spent what few funds he'd had marrying Tammy. She had helped him get a precious green card and US social security number. How that had come back to bite him. His second wife Zena had left after several years of marriage. The union bearing no children Benedict felt that ironic considering he was writing computer games for kids. Although Zena had been serially unfaithful, he'd reached a kind of emotional immunity with her. It wasn't that Benedict considered her behaviour accept-able – she was immoral, but when she wasn't running fast and loose they got along. Their odd partnership gave him a bond. An unusual one perhaps but she was a part of him and at least he had some purpose in his life providing for them both.

Benedict smiled. Earthly existence. Considering where he was now – how fitting that was. There followed a series of unsatis-factory – well he could hardly call them relationships. One-night stands more like and the odd weekend with a woman in a hotel or resort somewhere. Half the time he didn't want to be there and was pretty certain the women didn't either. In some weird way one felt one was on a treadmill. Conventional society suggested it was desirable having a partner, but growing weary of such antics, Benedict decided that whatever happened from now on he'd be done with it all. Better by far to be on his own wherever his life might lead him.

A light flashed on the console. Adjusting Albion's trim, George settled down to another orbit. Each one taking just a couple of hours, he'd be into the last few soon and the countdown would begin. He had to get ready and prepare himself. In this new game far from returning to Earth, it was his responsibility to dock the craft and begin their new adventures. It would require all Bene-dict's programming experience and the hours of concentration he and Podric had put into the sequence to manage the manoeuvre.

* * *

Standing on a broad ledge halfway up Alamo Ridge Archie's ox-ygen supply began to plummet alarmingly. Suddenly, what had seemed an afternoon stroll on the moon was life-threatening. Looking at the ridge top it was still several hundred feet above them. Podric checked the connections on Archie's pack. Strug-gling to breathe, Archie gasped.

"Al-r-ead-y ch-eck-ed... th-em."

Podric indicated to his friend not to speak. Adjusting a fix-ing, a little more air flowed into Archie's lungs, but the gauge remained terrifyingly low.

"I've ju-st... Should-be-enough... make-it.."

And with these words the computer games creator collapsed. Podric bent over his business partner and using a small emergency device, plugged it into his system. Then, checking a programming unit on his wrist, he activated it.

* * *

JFK's October weekend with his children at Camp David was turning out to be far from dull. Sunday had been another enjoyable day. He'd loafed with his kids in the grounds of the presidential retreat, Caroline riding again and John playing hide and seek. They'd eaten ice cream and when heading for bed he'd read to them – Caddie Woodlawn and Country Bunny. The children were now asleep, and Kennedy sat downstairs relaxing in a small den. He couldn't remember the last time he'd spent so much time on his own but with all he had on his mind it was for once preferable. There were any number of people he knew he could call for a chat – his friends Lem Billings or Dave Powers and company could be provided for him. But for once President John F. Kennedy chose to stay home and stay solo.

Staring at the television screen watching his assassination – images Podric had left with him – was a surreal experience. What had the boy said? They had been 'stabilised': Kennedy assumed that meant steadied from the rough grainy imagery taken from someone's amateur 8-millimetre movie camera. Playing and replaying the few seconds – he saw Jackie in a pink outfit sitting beside him. He watched himself slump over when the first shot hit his neck then his head snapping back from another bullet half a second later – the one that blew most of his brain away. Kennedy and Podric had discussed how the findings of the Warren commission – the enquiry set up by his successor Lyndon Johnson to look into his assassination had to be flawed. The Lee Harvey Oswald character. Killed himself hours later – Oswald was a fall guy. No other explanation made sense.

Although Kennedy had been philosophical about the risks he ran going to Dallas that day along with the belief that he would never make old bones, part of JFK's mind found his assassination difficult to comprehend. It was one thing to dismiss the risk in life and even appear flippant about it. It was quite another to see one's demise so gruesomely played out in actuality. Even so Jack was not a man to dwell on things. Turning the television off he sat back. He decided he would enter Podric's post 22nd November 1963 world. If it gave him some strange and unique perspective – how many of history's characters were ever allowed that? It would be interesting to see Lyndon in the top job lording it with his boorish behaviour presiding over his cabinet. It would be a stark contrast from Kennedy's own more urbane style.

What gnawed at Jack was the legacy he would leave. It was all very fine having grace and glamour but in the end it was the effectiveness of one's presidency that counted – and recognition of his achievements was something John Kennedy craved – at this point in his rapidly diminishing life, more than anything else. Maybe Johnson would be more effective than he was? Maybe he'd be a better president? Jack couldn't deny Lyndon had great skills with Congress and the Senate. But Kennedy's legislation currently frustrated in the House getting passed into law in part because of his assassination – a result of the nations political representative's guilt at what had happened – the loss of his life would be the ultimate price to pay.

Chapter 20
Moon Landing

The moon base Podric and his computer games colleagues Dr Archie Light and George Benedict created in *Moon Landing* wasn't vast or grandiose – more a research station from which they could pursue their task of exploring the lunar surface and attempt to discover if anyone had been there before them.

Located on the far side of Alamo Ridge they had named it Luna. The complex was sufficiently comfortable to house several dozen people. With the exception of its canine member whose role was mainly one of entertainment and getting in the way, every person was required to contribute individually as well as assist in practical tasks that were common to all.

The domestic quarters were styled as a functionally futuristic hotel and the working environment was comprehensive. It included a laboratory, a medical unit, kitchens, a gym, a library, classrooms and an internal horticultural area. Although everyone was able to view media wherever they wanted (programs screened via their eyes) a theatre was extant which also served as a main lecture hall. A subterranean pressurised walkway linked the station to the servicing area where space shuttles and rockets were housed. These had been designed in a longer-term plan for deep space exploration.

Those included on the mission were:

Denise Mullins	Teaching
Barney Sturridge	Space craft technician
George Benedict	Space craft technician
Archie Light	Space craft technician

Podric Moon	Space craft technician
Amy Moon	Pupil
Lilian Bekes	Pupil
Barbara Moon	Horticultural
Catherine Halliday	Pharmacological
Cosima Light	Assistant chef
Kaliska Monroe	Space craft technician
Carla Logan	Space craft technician
Charlotte Light	Chef de Cuisine – cook!
Dog	Entertainment value!

Of the twelve participants in *Moon Landing*, spacecraft technology and exploration occupied five members of the team. Podric managing to get Archie to the Lunar Station and George docking Albion at a much more advanced space station he and Podric had created in the game – the others had arrived in a passenger shuttle.

Without exception everybody loved their lunar existence. The complex was big enough not to be claustrophobic and people constantly spoke of discovering new things about themselves. Never seeming to tire of the stark moonscape vista, there was something spectacular about looking across space at mother earth. Sometimes one felt one could reach out and touch her; sometimes earth seemed much more than its two hundred and thirty-seven thousand nine hundred miles away. Whatever the sensations experienced, it allowed one to reflect. It certainly helped people put their thoughts into perspective.

On his way to the medical area, Podric bumped into George Benedict.

"All worked okay George."

A fact not a question, Benedict smiled.

"Like a dream."

Podric looked at the original creator of *Moon Landing*.

"Well, you're living it. Glad we came up in the old Apollo?"

Benedict kept smiling.

"For me it was everything. I can't begin-."

"Then don't. See you at supper."

Entering the medical area, Podric found its only patient sitting up in bed in the small ward. Archie was spooling through data on an iPad.

"How are you feeling?"

"Miraculous. Your girlfriend can be bossy."

"Tell me about it."

Light put down the device.

"When are we starting?"

"Couple of days. George and Kaliska are getting all the kit sorted."

"Still think it best we go in separate teams?"

Podric shrugged.

"With two groups we can cover more ground. Anyway, you're not going out first."

"What do you mean?"

"One technician must always stay back at base. We agreed that. George and Kaliska can go as one team and I'll take my luck with bully boy."

"'Still sure about bringing him along?"

"No. But that's my problem."

Archie snorted.

"Well I'm going anyway."

Catherine appeared. Archie continued.

"Ah. Perfect timing."

Activating an electronic medical chart, Catherine spooled down the screen. Podric said.

"Your having experienced hypoxemia Doc Halliday's been running checks on your heart and brain."

"And neither of those organs has been affected."

"Long term that's true but a few days managing base operations won't do you any harm."

"You two deserve each other. Doc my eye."

Temporarily released from Catherine's medical clutches Archie sporting a natty dressing gown went looking for a book in the base's little library. Glancing into a computer workstation, he found a preoccupied Stanley Kubrick sitting in front of a bank of screens talking to Barney! Archie sat down.

"I'd forgotten Podric intended programming you into this."

"Allowed up are you? That's a quick recovery."

"Your concerns' appreciated."

Barney turned back to Kubrick.

"Still amazes me how you created those sequences in *2001*. Didn't have any of this kit fifty years ago."

Archie said.

"Barely had any computerised kit fifty years ago. A year after its release man was supposedly walking about up here. Mr Kubrick's unlikely to get much technical know-how from you though Sputnik Sturridge."

Not liking Barney much, Archie's unnecessary sarcasm was wide of the mark. To his credit, Barney didn't bridle.

"I've seen every one of Mr Kubrick's films at least five times – his early work through to *Eyes Wide Shut*."

"Whilst I'm sure Mr K's impressed by your film studies, that's not what I said."

Continuing his work, Kubrick responded.

"The kid's got talent."

"My, my. Praise indeed. You'll be driving the rover next."

"Already been out in it. Piece of junk. I've had it back in the repair bay for a complete rebuild."

Barney got up.

"If you want in on that trial engine test Stanley I'll see you in RB3 15.40."

He went out. Archie shook his head in disbelief. The casualness of youth. Immersed by matrix on the screen in front of him, Kubrick grunted his acknowledgement. Archie said.

"As a director with an interest in space and the future, out of your time weren't you?"

Tapping a keyboard Kubrick said.

"'You deliberately trying to irritate me?"

"Nope. I can see you're preoccupied. Lot of catching up ahead if you want to master data."

Archie looked along the bank of computers.

"There'll always be questions you know."

Kubrick sipped a mug of cold coffee and said.

"Do you know how the fifteen-foot Discovery model was made to look half a mile long?"

An admirer of Kubrick's work Archie was interested to observe the American director's intensity. Kubrick continued.

"Or a man falling through space."

Kubrick fiddled with the handle of his coffee mug.

"Or riding a nuclear bomb into oblivion."

"You didn't have computers that's for sure."

"No. I didn't. I had illusion – the way film is made and something we're experiencing in a far more advanced state now. Podric explained Ultimate Alternative Reality to me. Not fully comprehending the calculus that created it, I understand its principle. It's more amazing than anything I ever did. It's an outstanding breakthrough."

Apparently unmoved, Archie said.

"So, the moon landings could have been faked."

Like Barney, Kubrick didn't lose it with Archie who continued. "Global media would have to be controlled to an unparalleled extent."

"While its of little interest to me, technically it's possible."

Closing down his work Kubrick turned his full attention to Archie. The computer games man found it unnerving.

"If I'm a person who is out of his time and you've had a hand in creating this new form of alternative reality – meeting the historic figures you have, one would think you'd possess more empathy."

Kubrick stood up and went on.

"The preoccupation about whether man has been here before is not why I'm here. Podric invited me to come along, and the experience was too good a one to miss."

Archie said.

"Several people's lives have been at risk in recent weeks worrying about this 'preoccupation'."

The two men considered each other. Kubrick smiled.

"Didn't anyone ever tell you that nothing is sadder than the death of an illusion?"

Kubrick went out leaving a thoughtful Archie sitting in the computer workstation.

"But is it worth someone's life..? Open the doors HAL."

Chapter 21

Exploration

Gusting sleet swirled about the night as turning off the highway, the SUV began making its way along the narrow lane deep in Virginian countryside. Having travelled the forty miles from the National Security Agency at Fort Meade, Maryland, the vehicle had gone by the CIA headquarters at Langley and was now heading for a secret security complex.

An agency associate sitting beside the driver, their rear passenger stared out at the night. Head of Secorni Cy Zaentz had a broad and varied experience of life but nothing could have prepared him for the grilling he'd received at the NSA. Interrogated rather than interviewed, Zaentz had been subjected to hours of questioning which included a polygraph test but had not learned why he was being cross examined. Bizarrely things stopped as abruptly as they'd started. Zaentz was escorted to the vehicle he was now riding in and summarily dispatched.

The SUV stopped in front of the compound's main building. Zaentz could just make out the shapes of several smaller single-story structures. Ushered into one he was advised to rest and told that he would be called in the morning. Zaentz decided during the trip he would go into neutral mode. Tired from the day's unpleasant exertions, the computer marketing chief grabbed a few hours of fitful sleep.

On waking Zaentz shaved and ate the breakfast that had been left in his suite's adjacent living room. Later that morning he was taken across the compound to an office building. Left for a while and certain he was being watched by a remote camera Zaentz continued his passive demeanour. Afternoon now, the sleet had turned to rain which continued to beat down. Zaentz sat staring out at the sodden countryside.

"Can it ever rain in these parts."

He turned to see a slightly built, featureless man of indeterminate age standing behind him.

"You?"

"Surprised? We've never seen each other."

Zaentz shrugged.

"If you say so. I seem to recall when we didn't meet, you were keen for me to inveigle an ex-employee."

Zaentz referred to George Benedict and the pressure Secorni had been put under to comply with the agency's directive. The agent said.

"An operation that so far's been overwhelmingly unsuccessful. Come through."

The man made Zaentz no apology for his ill-mannered treatment nor did he re-introduce himself. Indicating a chair, he offered him coffee. Zaentz chose water.

"Get some rest? Good."

Zaentz's host didn't wait for a reply.

Electrically-operated curtains began shrouding the office in darkness. Simultaneously a screen on the far wall activated. Zaentz was aware of someone else quietly entering the room. The picture displayed was the moon's surface. A voice behind him said.

"Thirty-six hours ago, we suddenly started getting strange signals. They appear to come from outside our atmosphere. More specifically, here."

Magnifying the moon's image, the six areas of the listed Apollo landings were brought into focus – from Mare Tranquillitatis, to Oceanus Procellarum and Frau Mauro then Apennines, Descartes and Taurus-Littrow.

"Mare Serenitatus."

"Mean anything to you?"

This from featureless man.

"You dragged me across country to ask me this?"

"For any exploration, the site is ideally placed to study all the

Apollo landings."

"You've got to be kidding." Zaentz stood up.

"What cloak and dagger idiocy are you guys up to? You hijack me – the CEO of a computer games company to talk about receiving strange signals from the moon?! In my business I'm used to crazy ideas, but you guys are off the scale. Never mind extra-terrestrial – your mindsets got to be inhabiting some parallel universe!"

"There being no official current lunar landings scheduled by any country, anywhere."

There was a moments silence before Zaentz replied.

"I'm thrilled to know that. What am I to do about it? Invent a new planet?"

"You know very well."

Walking round the room, Zaentz stopped.

"Are you seriously telling me you brought me here because you actually think these signals are somehow linked to a computer game that you forced my company to shut down work on seven years ago?"

Zaentz resumed his pacing.

"I've heard of some extraordinary scenarios gentlemen – like I say in my world I'm used to eccentricities... Neither am I normally a man who takes to swearing, but apart from being wacko if you'll forgive the vernacular I can only say you guys are fucking nuts!"

"Tracking down the lead games creator."

"Don't patronise me. The technique of singing your own song and ignoring the other is old and tired."

Zaentz sighed and continued.

"You're suggesting failure of an operation you drove and which you've botched."

He held up his hand as if to prevent either of the men speaking.

"I have a question and one that you will be answering. How do you link random signals coming from the moon to a computer game?"

Zaentz looked from featureless man to the other individual who was half in shadow.

"I mean fellas get real here."

He turned away from them.

"I surely don't have to spell this out. A computer game's something that for all its imagination is very much earthbound. Signals from the moon's surface..?"

No one spoke. Finally, featureless man said.

"It's believed some new computer dimension has recently been created. Some other form of reality."

"A different reality? And what might that be when it's at home?"

Neither agency man spoke. Zaentz was exasperated.

"This reality beams signals from the moon, does it?! Guys again I suggest you get some rest. Take the strain off. Whatever it is it's a computer game for chrissakes!"

"Not this one."

Half-shadow man spoke quietly.

"This one reaches another dimension."

"You'll be right there if it's sending signals from another planet!"

Half-shadow came nearer to Zaentz, but because the lighting was low he still couldn't be seen clearly. He said.

"That's the point dumb wit. It's the dimension that somehow gives it that ability. And the moon's a satellite, jerk"

Unused to being spoken to in such a way Zaentz felt angry. Before he could respond the curtains drew back. The rain-battered countryside was still rain-battered. Zaentz was aware the man he never saw properly had left. The other said.

"You'll be contacted. For your information I'm director of this operation and the other gentlemen is lead source for code named Lodestar."

A sliding door opened and the Director as Zaentz would now call him, disappeared through it. Left alone in the room the computer man couldn't quite believe what had taken place. He sat down, his head in a spin. Zaentz' overwhelming sensation was one of fatigue. What had he said? Old and Tired. For once that's how he felt.

*　*　*

"Pass your test then?"

Wearing space suits Podric and Barney were out for a spin on the lunar surface. The rover seemed stable enough though every now and then it appeared to drift.

"You haven't, have you – passed? Still a learner. Ha! That's a good one. Learner driver takes test on moon. When interviewed for the six o'clock news the galaxy's newest motorist said. 'Negotiating lunar rocks and boulders are nothing. What's a stellar slide causing congestion? You should see Wendbury High Street on market day!'"

"Ha ha. Regular wag, aren't you Barney?"

"That's it – eye on the road Pod. Ha ha!!"

They drove along.

"Did you take a reading for the Sea of Tranquillity?"

"The Apollo 11 site? Take several days to get there mate. We'll need two teams. Lot of kit."

Concentrating on his steering, Podric didn't reply.

"Besides, plenty of work to do on these before we can go exploring. You should have seen some of the flimsy welds on 'em. And the shocks. Terrible."

"Good job you're with us then."

"I'd say. Without me *Moon Landing* would be in a fix. No doubt about it."

"Where are the indicators?"

Chapter 22
The Meeting

When he got back to the Coast Cy Zaentz didn't go directly to his office preferring to hunker down at his beach house north of Santa Monica. His children having long grown up and his wife away, Secorni's CEO sat on the exterior deck that fronted the sea. Evening now, sipping a bourbon on the rocks he stared out at the Pacific coastline. Zaentz had plenty to think about. With the London office uppermost in his mind normally he would have called Prendergast, but recent events had shaken Cy. It wasn't so much being abducted by America's security services that bothered him. Those weird bastards were nuts. It was unpleasant but in spite of their threats Zaentz didn't harbour fear. Not yet. It was his Carla Logan's dismissal that troubled him.

Carla had been with Zaentz for several years, originally serving as his PA. When he was appointed CEO he only left her in London because he wanted someone in that office who could be trusted. Carla had become his eyes and ears. That Saul fired her without telling him wasn't the issue – he had the right. It was the fact that Carla had gone apparently without a murmur and hadn't contacted Zaentz about her departure which gave Cy cause for concern. The implication had to be that Carla accepted her dismissal which suggested some form of guilt on her part. Activating his phone, he selected a number he very rarely called, a number that in ninety-nine cases out of a hundred meant confrontation. Zaentz wasn't altogether sure why he felt the need to make it. Pasaro was the largest computer games company in the world and its chief executive Fred Schepesi was his arch-rival. Having pressed dial, Zaentz guessed it was instinct – instinct that had seen him through fifty-seven years of a roller coaster existence.

"I'm cooking" was Schepesi's answer. Zaentz waited a beat and was about to enlarge on the reason for his call when the man from the Bronx continued.

"Wanna come over?"

Given they were very different types of operators, Zaentz had to concede that communication with Pasaro's CEO was never dull. The man was 5ft 4ins of raw energy.

"Wouldn't want to intrude."

"You won't be. Another steaks going on."

The phone went dead. It wasn't perhaps surprising that although the two men came from different backgrounds their company headquarters in Southern California placed them geographically near to each other. Schepesi had a beach property ten minutes from Zaentz up Pacific Coast Highway towards Malibu. A short while later Secorni's chief executive arrived at Schepesi's gated house. A voice admitted him.

"Park and come round."

Zaentz left his Porsche in the drive and walked past the house to find a scene similar to the one he'd left a few miles away. Schepesi had a gas barbecue going on which two enormous steaks were sizzling. Zaentz said.

"Thought you might have company."

"Did you now?"

Then as an afterthought Schepesi said.

"Marie's away."

Zaentz vaguely knew that the Schepesi's didn't have any children. The Pasaro man handed his Secorni equivalent a beer.

"*Guns of Atlantis.*"

"*Exterminator Eleven.*"

Drinking to each other's latest games, Schepesi prodded a steak and both men took in the ocean.

"Saturday night and the heads of the world's two largest games companies are hanging out."

Schepesi sipped his drink.

"Guess you haven't dropped by for me to make you an offer.

Take a seat."

Zaentz sat down.

"It's been an interesting twenty four hours."

"Must have been for you to call. What yer do? Sell yer stock? Guess not. I'd know."

Zaentz smiled slightly.

"Conducted to Maryland then some spook hideout in Virginia." Schepesi scowled.

"Extreme even with your tax bill."

Realising the seriousness of what Zaentz had said, Schepesi parked his flippancy.

"You've got no call with HUAC."

"Tell that to those goons. Paranoia rules their world."

For a smart man who frequently spoke faster than his brain could keep pace with, Schepesi was silent. Zaentz stood up and walked over to the deck rail.

"You'll know a few years ago we had a particular game on the stocks. *Moon Landing* was what it said on the tin.

"Yeah. Heard it got shut down."

Zaentz sighed. Schepesi continued.

"Unprecedented."

"By those type of authorities – yuh. Least I never heard it happening before."

Schepesi didn't reply and waited for Zaentz to continue.

"The lead writer who was working on *Moon Landing* was a fella by the name of Benedict"

"Archie Lights ex-partner." Zaentz acknowledged such.

"A few months ago, we got leant on again by the forces of darkness. They'd found Benedict and put some phony tax screw on him. Told him his only way out was to sue his old brother in arms. If he did that, they'd do a deal."

Zaentz sipped his beer before continuing.

"Piled pressure on the company too insisting this little fandango would go through us."

"Which you kicked back on."

"Sure we did. Soft peddled for a while but these guys can get nasty."

"What have they got on you?"

"That our game contravened laws threatening to the government."

"How did it do that? It's a fucking computer game!"

"Tell me about it – and as you said, we had to shut it down. Now they're dragging the whole thing back into the arena saying issues remain of governmental concern."

"Crap."

"Of course it's crap. The whole thing is."

"Take 'em on then."

Zaentz didn't say that he had his own reasons for temporarily running with the agency. Aware MoonLight's games went to Pasaro and their success – while he didn't like the lure Prendergast had come up with, trying to drive a wedge between Archie and Podric and influence the boy bringing any ideas he had Secorni's way – all was fair game in the highly competitive computer world. He said.

"Likely we will."

Zaentz swigged his beer. Schepesi lined him up with another.

"We also wondered at the timing. Why was the hydra rearing its many ugly heads again now? Benedict doesn't have a pot to piss in. We figured it had to be for other reasons. Anyway, Light showed up at our office contesting things and since then he and Benedict have gone to ground."

"So what's with callin' me?"

"You have two new games Light's written."

"What's that got to do with anything?"

"Maybe nothing."

Zaentz looked at the ocean. Schepesi grunted.

"Neither of them are his. You had the best years of Archie Light. His beams faded."

"But that crazy sounding name... Iguana something."

"*Issandro Iguana*. Cleaning up as did its predecessor *Andromeda Volcanism* – both the work of a young games' genius who Archie's now in business with."

Fred Schepesi picked up a box of Cuban cigars and offered one to his guest who declined. Schepesi selected a Romeo Y Julietta.

"So Spooksville and your game."

The Pasaro man rolled the cigar in his fingers. Zaentz said.

"They pressed about Benedict. They're obsessed with the fact he might have found something."

"What do you mean, 'found something'?"

Zaentz shrugged.

"Whatever it was he touched a nerve in *Moon Landing* – something they want to hide. Something big."

"And they're gettin' one over you because of a game?"

Opening his new beer, Zaentz didn't immediately reply. Schepesi said.

"So why'd they bring you in?"

Zaentz chuckled darkly.

"'Said they had a signal."

Schepesi looked at his counterpart.

"Uhuh. What type of signal?"

"Electronic."

"From don't tell me – outer space."

Zaentz paused for a second.

"The moon."

Schepesi part hiccupped, part laughed, part gulped.

"Guess that's nearer home."

He made a last inspection of his cigar.

"What's any of this got to do with a goddam shigeru miyamoto?"

Schepesi put the cigar in his mouth but didn't light it. Zaentz said.

"We heard.."

He stopped then started again disjointedly.

"There's a lot of secrecy surrounding MoonLight."

Schepesi fired up his lighter and lit his cigar. Zaentz said.

"We began to wonder... Maybe, maybe they only want to get to Light because of his new partner?"

"How'd they know about him?"

"That's the one thing that isn't a secret."

Schepesi smoked. Zaentz shrugged and said.

"Benedict's now with Light and kid wonder. The goons think something's going down."

Zaentz was hesitant then continued.

"Some new brilaf Light's outfits created, something with another dimension."

"Yeah right. I've been smelling something's on the cob. Podric's clever and he's been bored with conventional squares for a while."

"So what might he have put together?"

"Search me. It would have to be somethin' special though to beam signals from the moon!"

A flame shot through the barbecue; the steaks little more than cinders caused Schepesi to give the food some long overdue attention. He held up a burnt offering.

"Like 'em well done?"

Schepesi discarded the two cindered pieces of meat.

"Guess not."

He began to prepare new steaks. Zaentz said.

"This is all pretty crazy stuff."

"We're dealin' with some pretty crazy people."

"Games writers or spooks?"

Schepesi laughed.

"Likely there wouldn't be much to choose between 'em."

Zaentz smiled. The head of Pasaro produced two bowls of salad from a side table.

"Salad to start."

Zaentz applied dressing to his tomato and raw onion. Schepesi flipped the steaks and continued.

"We know who we've got to get hold of."

Zaentz sipped his beer.

"Reckon the boy'll be the key?"

"As certain as my aunt May's poker game."

Zaentz assumed Schepesi's aunt was a committed punter and said. "His name amuses me."

"He's an amusing kid."

Schepesi plated two prime filets. Zaentz said.

"Podric Moon. That's a very pertinent name."

Pasaro's CEO served his rival.

"He's also a very pertinent one."

Chapter 23
Selenic Life and a Trip to London

At the same time as the heads of the two computer games companies sat enjoying their delicious meal overlooking the Pacific Ocean in Southern California the participants of *Moon Landing* were doing the same in their space station on the lunar surface!

Setting up their latest adventure, the games creators had stocked their kitchens extensively, the Options menu having sensibly planned for long term food supplies. Mealtimes would be important – a coming together to compare notes about the challenges of living in their quarters and an opportunity to discuss every element of life in such an alien environment. Debates ranged from the technical to the mundane – had Dog's weight been affected since he began living his Nebulan existence? Female members wondered if more face cream was needed in such a dry climate? However, as plans advanced for the departure of the rover teams exploring the moon and going in search of the first Apollo landing site, discussions inevitably became more focussed.

"Can we take some of this cassoulet with us Charlotte?"

Whether he was on the earth or the moon, Barney remained his incorrigible self.

"Lunar lunch boxes – we're gonna need plenty of those."

In spite of their different backgrounds and contrary attitudes The Hon Charlotte Light had a soft spot for Wendbury High's ex-bully.

"Not a problem. Would the driver of Rover 1 prefer sweet pickle or English chutney with his foie gras?"

"Hmm... Brown sauce more like."

The two looked at each other and burst out laughing.

As well as Charlotte and Barney's unlikely friendship *Moon Landing* threw up other evolving relationships. Discovering a mutual interest in obscure rock bands Catherine Halliday's rapport with Cosima Light developed. Becoming more involved with rover planning and placed in charge of charting the teams' routes to the Apollo sites Kaliska Monroe and George Benedict drew closer. When determining their central location from each of the six Apollo locations the lunar camp's position meant that Theophilus – the region Apollo 11's site should be located at would be a 400-mile journey. Ptolemaeus – Apollo 14's stated landing area would be an 800-mile sojourn. The teams intended a return to base between each trip.

Beginning with local exploration acclimatising themselves and getting used to their vehicle – maintaining a Greek connection they nicknamed the first rover Calypso (the nymph connotation amused the classicists amongst them) and for no apparent reason Archie gave the other two vehicles the Roman sobriquets of Romulus and Remus. Driving around the immediate terrain Kaliska and George worked through teething issues. Given how sophisticated the rovers were supposed to be some of their construction was surprisingly basic. Barney Sturridge may have had a cavalier attitude to life, but his knowledge of metalwork was comprehensive. He stripped down the three rovers completely (one would serve as a back-up vehicle) – his work involving new axles and fitting improved electronic equipment. Not everything was left to Barney. As their departure date approached, Podric spent long hours in the station's workshop with his friend. Podric's concerns about the state of the equipment became increasingly focused as the two boys strove to ensure the vehicles were made as reliable as possible.

A key factor in the rover's exploration involved their power source. Modifying the electrical system, the lunar rover's original format used two 36-volt silver-zinc potassium hydroxide non-rechargeable batteries which gave a top speed of less than 10 mph and a very short functioning area. This would be no good for the trips the teams had in mind. Podric, Archie and George Benedict worked on creating a recharging plutonium/uranium unit which would give the vehicles much higher speeds and greater operational range. They also worked on a mechanism that used an adapted solar panel as well as creating a regenerative power system for the rover when it was on the move. Further developed was the vehicle's ability to handle steeper inclines using gears and an adjustable chassis system. This was operated by computerised hydraulics which would enable it to cross rough terrain at speed. Taking all these improvements into account the rovers would explore the moon extensively.

Most problems seemingly ironed out it was while making a longer foray involving the first overnight away from the station that disaster struck. Forty-three miles out from Lunar Base Calypso's battery system began acting up. George Benedict got out to check what the problem was. Staying in the vehicle Kaliska Monroe sat analysing data from one of the numerous on-board computers when the rover started rolling backwards causing its trailer carrying their supplies to yaw. Kaliska applied the footbrake but nothing happened. Attempting to steer as the rover and its trailer gained speed she was thrown off. Managing to intercept Calypso, Benedict grabbed the steering wheel and centralising it, brought the kart to a stop. Checking his spacesuit and that of his partner their apparatus didn't appear to have suffered any mishaps. Radioing base it was decided they would stay put that night, set up camp as planned and Podric and Barney would rendezvous with them in 24 hour's time.

One of the greatest inventions Podric had developed was the portable lunar cabin they called CabStar. Flat packed, it could be erected in seconds and provided with its own one-week air supply cylinder, enabled space explorers to remove their helmets and suits when inside its confines. Provided with a small cooking device and portaloo – while one wouldn't choose to make the CabStar a permanent home it made life on the trail much more tolerable.

"These rovers are the devil."

"Boy thugee's been working hard on them."

Kaliska and George were sitting at a lightweight fold-up table enjoying a supper of noodles and rice prepared by Charlotte Light.

"You suggesting its deliberate?"

Kaliska laughed.

"Actually, I think he's had to rebuild the damned things."

George played with a set of sealed condiments.

"Several times!"

He was non-critical.

"How are you finding life in *Moon Landing?*"

Saving data on a device, Kaliska pulled her legs up round her body in a semi-lotus position.

"What do you know about me?"

"What do you know about me?"

Both were relaxed. Kaliska spoke.

"I wouldn't normally accept that but okay. Only what Podric and Archie have told me."

"Succinct at any rate."

George sighed.

"There's not much to tell. I made a lot of money with Archie, but it disappeared."

"That's unfortunate. Wine, women and song?"

"Two wives. There was some wine and no song."

"I'm sorry."

Kaliska unwound herself.

"Coffee? We have on board lunar latte, moon mochaccino.."

"How about coffee?"

Kaliska laughed.

"Arabica or Robusta?"

So did George. She began to set about the caffeine's spatial preparation.

"Why d'you think all this happened?"

"What do you mean? Us being here or the other stuff?"

"The other stuff has bearing on us being here."

"True."

Picking up a data unit he'd taken from the rover, George

spooled through its menu.

"It had something to do with not being able to get the Apollo program to work in a games context using the original formula. Secorni wanted it to be authentic – make it part of the challenge."

"Even with modifications its certainly that alright."

Finishing her coffee preparations, Kaliska held up two beakers of hot liquid. "Black as the devil, Strong as death!"

"Sweet as love, Hot as hell!"

They laughed and sipped their scalding drinks. Benedict said.

"When commissioning the game, Secorni were innocent. I'm certain of that. Then all of a sudden people started asking questions."

"Think we'll find the landing sites?"

"Your guess is as good as mine."

"Maybe it isn't..?" Both thoughtful, they drank their coffee.

"At least the new game got created and with such additional dimensions."

"Like living here. That's both awesome and challenging."

Kaliska looked at Benedict who continued.

"You think the intelligence services won't be scouring every avenue, every angle to know about this – 'defending their nation' using their intelligence sources with 'fidelity, bravery and integrity' – to bastardise their agency mottos... They're more than desperate. They're obsessed with what they don't know and when people are like that they're dangerous."

"Deus autem in fide."

"If that's what you believe in."

*   *   *

Whilst not having the knowledge Benedict was espousing eighty miles north of the Sea of Tranquillity on the lunar surface, the fact that his beliefs coincided with those of the two games company executives back on earth comforted neither.

Although their information was more limited than the *Moon Landing* participants, Schepesi and Zaentz's decision to travel to the UK to see Podric Moon, Archie Light and George Benedict was significant.

Landing in their private planes on quiet airfields outside London several days later and checking into their company apartments in town – both men were quickly on the phone to each other. Schepesi said.

"Reckon you do Light and I contact the boy."

Zaentz grunted.

"I'd better do Benedict as well. We go back some. Hell, I commissioned *Moon Landing*.

"Parley in the morning then."

Their lines went dead. These guys never wasted words – not even on goodbyes.

Chapter 24

Lunar Base – Berkeley Square

"What do you mean – they know?"

"Signals from *Moon Landing* have been beamed to the moon and directed back to Earth."

"Oh, moon bounce. EME."

Sitting with Podric and Archie in the station's computer lab, Stanley Kubrick was studying calculus. Watching Kubrick now Archie realised what a technophile the man was. In an age of more advanced technology than his own, the film director had embraced developments with his well-known obsessiveness. Addressing Archie, Podric said.

"Exactly. Well, a variant of. You help write it."

What was that? Archie was temporarily thrown.

"I what?!"

"It's a tiny part of the codex formulation in the game."

"Why the hell did we do that?"

The fact that Archie was party to a detail of a game he had supposedly co-created yet was unaware of wasn't lost on Podric. Neither was it on Kubrick. Whilst the film director knew little about computer games or Ultimate Alternative Reality, his meticulous eye for detail was all too accurate.

"To deliberately let them know you're here – or something is."

Though he might respect Kubrick Archie wasn't too sure whether he liked the director coming up with his smart-arse replies.

"How'd you know a receiver wouldn't identify it as coming from us?"

Archie still had some ammo in his verbal armoury. Podric said.

"Better."

Podric tapped some more data into one of the computers and continued.

"The encode is encrypted in such away as to look as though a lunar expedition has arrived on the moon – as in our minds, it has. Hopefully, it will freak them out."

"Who? Who are we actually trying to provoke?"

"Archie has your head taken a bashing? We can get Doc Halliday to check you out for concussion."

The look Archie gave his young business partner made no difference to Podric who continued forcefully.

"The people who are after George, that's who! I've tracked various sites and the signal is being fed specifically into their system."

Completing an encode, Podric began programming another.

"We also want to check out the Apollo landing sites."

"How are we going to do that? We're inside a computer game for chrissakes!"

"Indeed we are – and whether we find them in our game or whether we do not the whole point of this exercise is to flush out whatever the cover up has been if in fact there was one. If the security arm these operatives are under is rogue or officially sanctioned we want to see what they do. That's what this is all about Archie."

"What are you going to do if you get a reaction?"

Stanley Kubrick turned to speak but Light held up his hand. Podric said. "Depends what their response is."

"They're not going to believe we're on the moon."

"Agreed. We just want to see what cards they're holding."

"Which means they'll visit Wales and the Lighthouse."

"Exactly. Which is why we'll need something to outflank them, throw them off balance."

Podric was heeding his dad's advice. Kubrick said.

"A news exposé could be useful."

Archie said.

"I was thinking that Mr Kubrick."

Then turning to Podric he continued.

"No doubt you have ideas maestro Moon?"

Archie cynical, Podric replied.

"Bring them into UAR."

Podric completed the codex he'd been inputting and stood up.

"Whether these people had any part in getting to the moon or were involved in covering up NASA did not – an Ultimate Alternative Reality lunar adventure ought to be a whole new experience for them."

* * *

"Why'd you fire her?"

Sitting in Secorni's London office boardroom, Zaentz's question to his European head was terse.

"I didn't. She left but she was duplicitous, deceiving and found wanting."

Unapologetic, Prendergast's reply was equally. Zaentz sighed.

"Found wanting. That's good."

He got up and gazed out at Berkeley Square.

"You mean she didn't support our skulduggery."

Prendergast didn't respond. It was Sunday morning and he resented being summoned to the office missing his usual tennis session.

"Does it matter?"

"Sure, it matters."

Restless, Zaentz began pacing about the room.

"There's something very wrong here Saul – something I intend getting to the bottom of."

Zaentz stopped mid stride and returned to his window gazing. Having spent much of his early life in Europe beginning his professional computer career as a technical operative in a small start-up company based in Hoxton Zaentz was particularly fond of the city.

"Those goons didn't take me halfway across country for the sake of my health."

Zaentz watched a man get out of a cab and pay it off. Recognising Monty Limmerson – he recalled Limmerson Bart represented Archie Light. For years under contract Light had been incredibly successful for Secorni though latterly he had been regarded as a nemesis. So Limmerson was working on a Sunday. Zaentz bet that made a change. He said.

"But sitting in their grotesque company it wasn't their threats that bothered me."

Prendergast fiddled with a nail file.

"It was Carla."

Zaentz resumed his pacing.

"Though she may have been a lot of things, Carla's no coward. I would never have thought to doubt her word, nor did I ever find her loyalty wanting as you put it. Which means.."

Zaentz sighed.

"She's guilty as charged. She knew she'd done something sufficiently significant to get herself compromised which is why she never contacted me about leaving her job."

"You mean had she thought otherwise she'd have done so?"

"Damned right she would. I'd have expected her to."

His face set in a fixed grimace Prendergast put down the metal nail file.

"So why would this wonderful Californian girl, this perfect PA behave in such a way?"

Saul was getting twitchy now.

"That Saul is what I intend discovering. I'd suggest given our recent activities an angle could lean towards George Benedict and the *Moon Landing* game we were forced to drop."

Zaentz walked towards the door.

"Talking of lunar landings, I believe not only has Benedict gone to earth since you met with him here but also his ex-business partner."

"Whose current one has also disappeared."

"Quite a party. Any idea where they are?"

"Archie and Boy Wonder live in a village called Drinkwell in Hampshire."

Zaentz said. "You've made enquiries?"

Prendergast replied noncommittally and stood up.

"What would Carla want with them?"

Zaentz shoulders momentarily sagged.

"You're not stupid Saul. If the train of thought has any potential the thread would also make sense to the goons."

"You mean she could be on the run from the security services?"

"If that's what you call them. They pursued Benedict and now they're harrowing me."

"Cosmonaut Carla. That's one thing I never thought of her as."

"Whatever she is, I want to find her – and fast."

*   *   *

"So, George gets a night with Marilyn?"

Now that he'd learned about Marilyn Monroe Barney had re-christened Kaliska with the obvious sobriquet.

"Somehow don't think he's her type."

In the canteen, Cosima was sitting nearby with Catherine.

"They were always going to be away tonight Barney. It was planned as a first overnight from base."

"Okay Miss Top of the Class. We know you have privileged access to our illustrious leader!"

Catherine rolled her eyes and drank her tea. Bringing some vegetables into the kitchen Barbara Moon placed them in a rack.

"Somehow Barney things never change with you. Moon life seems to have no effect on your rumbustious nature."

"Oh, I don't know Mrs Moon. I think it's important to be more sharing caring in our galactic existence. How's the fruit and veg coming along?"

"Very nicely thank you. With no pollution peas and tatties are growing a treat."

"Moon's market garden. Start a colony."

"People have thought about it."

Having finished her two-pupil class with Lilian Bekes and Amy Moon, Denise Mullins wandered in.

"Wouldn't you miss the trees and rivers let alone the sea?"

"Nah. Only Netflix and Prime. Got to talk to Podric about that."

"Got to talk to Podric about what?"

Entering, Podric took a bottle of water from a fridge.

"Media content available on this junket. Can't get my favourite shows."

"Peppa Pigs off now or are you more a Bob the Builder fan?"

Lobbing her question at Barney, Amy went over to a fruit bar and selected some plums and a banana. Lilian helped herself to a chocolate nugget.

"He's more of a Clanger."

"No down time Barn, we're off in a couple of hours."

Podric turned to go.

"The peace of the Lord passeth all understanding."

Not registering Barney's wistful quote, Podric turned back.

"Oh, and make sure you dig out those extra rations plus equipment spares. Who knows what we might find. I'll see you at the workshop."

Catherine got up and headed for the door. Passing Barney, she said.

"Discretion shall preserve thee; understanding shall keep thee."

Barney was oddly rueful. Cosima looked at across at him.

"Very biblical all of a sudden."

Barney smiled, put his tray in a stack and went out.

"It's being here. Astronauts speak of feeling moved in space. Miniscule, fragile – aware of human frailty."

Denise Mullins sipped her coffee. Sitting at the far end of the canteen, Lilian Bekes looked up from a game of poker she and Amy were playing on their tablets.

"What are they gassing about Accy?"

"Oh, life, the universe and the meaning of everything."

"That all. Right waste of time. Raise you fifty."

Upping the stakes, the two girls resumed their game.

Chapter 25
Dallas 2
22nd November 1963

The short flight from Carswell Air Force Base, Fort Worth to Love Field, Dallas had been uneventful. Light rain falling earlier in Funkytown (one of the nicknames Fort Worth is known by) twenty minutes later the wheels of Air Force One touched down thirty odd miles away in glorious sunshine. There had barely been time on the short flight for the president to straighten his tie and Mrs Kennedy to adjust her pink Chanel suit before the Boeing 707 was taxiing on to the pan. It was 11.38am Central Standard Time.

The previous evening JFK had been in an unusual mood – assassination much on his mind. Although recognising the need to travel to Texas in order to heal rifts that existed amongst the Democratic elite there and shore up a consolidated drive for his re-nomination in 1964, Kennedy wasn't comfortable making the trip considering it a reactionary place and as he put it, nut country. Talking to his wife as they dressed that morning he brought up the subject of death again. "It would have been easy last night Jackie. I mean it. There was light rain, and the night, and we were getting jostled. Suppose a man had a pistol in a briefcase." Making a gun shape with his fingers, Kennedy 'fired' at the wall. "Then he could have dropped the gun and the briefcase and melted away in the crowd." JFK had also been shocked to read a full-page advertisement in *The Dallas Morning News* accusing him of treason. The ad demanded the president be tried, and justice meted out. With these chilling thoughts in his mind JFK stepped outside his hotel and made a warm impromptu speech to a crowd standing in the rain. The president then went to the Hotel Texas ballroom and addressed the local Chamber of Commerce at a fund-raising breakfast, his last event before leaving Fort Worth.

The plane stopped. Seconds later the front door opened and military aides along with members of the press disembarked. Then the aft door was swung out and with a brief smile to his wife President and Mrs Kennedy stepped into the Dallas sunshine. After a lively airport welcome the Kennedy's climbed into the open-topped Lincoln behind Governor John Connally and his wife Nellie. Followed by a stream of vehicles including Vice-President and Ladybird Johnson, Texas State dignitaries and a squad of secret serviceman, the motorcade set off for the six-mile trip into downtown Dallas. Time of departure – 11.53am CST.

Such was the allure of the president and Jackie's magnetism people stood waving roadside on Mockingbird Lane as the motorcade drove away from Love Field; still more were along Lemmon Avenue. By the time the Kennedys reached the lower end of North Harwood Street heading downtown into Main, residents had turned out in their droves to see the couple. Although Dallas was a hotbed of dislike for JFK – some said hatred – many didn't feel that way and were eager to catch a glimpse of their handsome young head of state and his glamourous First Lady.

The motorcade slowed to a walking pace. A right turn into Houston Street and a left on to Elm – at Dealey Plaza vehicles were travelling at no more than three or four miles an hour. Accelerating away from the corner, the Texas School Book Depository on the right and the plaza on the left, occupants in the specially adapted Lincoln convertible smiled and waved. The crowds responded. When the first shot was fired there was no massive bang – more like a car backfiring. Many bystanders only became aware something was amiss when the president stopped waving and put his hands to his throat. Governor Connally also hit, rolled forward. A second or two later the President's head snapped back, and Kennedy's brains were blown out of his head. His wife began scrambling onto the trunk of the Lincoln gathering up matter before being pushed back inside the car by security operative

Clint Hill. Jackie clutched pieces of her husbands' cerebrum. The rear section of the president's head had been shot away. It was 12.30pm CST.

Hill stayed on board the Lincoln shielding the occupants as best he could as the presidential limousine sped off. Police motorcycle outriders cleared the way in front as the car accelerated down the remainder of Elm Street making a right on Stemmons Freeway up to the Medical District and Parklands Memorial Hospital. Taken to Trauma Room 1 and worked on briefly, the hospital pronounced John Kennedy dead at 1.00pm CST.

By 2.00pm local time JFK's body was removed from the hospital and the hearse carrying Jackie Kennedy and her slain husband set off for Love Field where the president had landed a little over two and a half hours previously – vital, charismatic and very much alive. Pulling up beside Air Force One twenty minutes later there was some difficulty getting the casket carrying the slain president's body aboard the aircraft. A cabin section had to be cut in order to accommodate the tragic load.

When Jackie Kennedy boarded the presidential plane, confusion reigned. Anxious to get out of Texas and fly Jack back to Washington no one could explain why the aircraft didn't take off until it became apparent Lyndon Johnson after making a number of phone calls announced he would be sworn in as 36th president whilst they were still on the ground. Requested as a witness Jackie wearing her bloodstained clothes stood beside LBJ as he took the oath. Minutes later, SAM 26000 finally got airborne.

Depending on who you were the two-and-a-half-hour flight to Andrews, the Air Force Base outside Washington DC that Friday afternoon was one of either indescribable tragedy or shocked anticipation. One presidency was at a brutally abrupt end, another unknown one about to begin.

Dark as the lights of Washington appeared below him, the captain of Air Force One, Colonel James Swindal brought the aircraft in to land at 5.59pm Eastern Standard Time.

Learning of his brother's assassination whilst at home with his family at Hickory Hill in McClean, Virginia Bobby Kennedy had immediately left his house for the air force base. Now waiting hidden in the back of an army truck – as Air Force One taxied to a stop steps appeared. Bobby moved quickly to the plane's front door. When it opened, he immediately walked inside. Barging through the cabin brushing past the new president who he didn't acknowledge in search of Jackie, Bobby was in an acutely distressed state. Although clearly she was as well, it was Jackie's instinctive understanding of the nation's shock that enabled her to rise to the heart-breaking occasion with decorum. Quickly sensing how in controlling the style and content of proceedings during the next few minutes, hours and days she could manipulate and potentially romanticise her late husband's presidency promoting the Kennedy White House as some kind of twentieth century Camelot which would become so linked with his image, Jackie now orchestrated events.

Stipulating that she would accompany her late husband's body from Air Force One, floodlights came up as the casket surrounded by JFK aides was lowered to the ground via a mechanical loader. The casket moved away from the plane revealed Jackie and Bobby Kennedy looking anguished and forlorn. It was an image that seared into people's minds. Of the new President, his wife and aides there was no sign as, still aboard the aircraft, they waited to disembark. To the worlds eyes they were invisible and at least temporarily, irrelevant.

The casket having been placed in an ambulance, Jackie and Bobby got into the vehicle which sped away to Bethesda Naval Hospital where it would remain overnight. Crossing the airfields perimeter, the dead President's body wasn't simply being taken to a military destination it was passing into history.

The distress felt at John Fitzgerald Kennedy's assassination wasn't so much the loss of what the young man had achieved in his short life, but what he might have. That such a vibrant and youthful leader with so much still to give his country and the international community had been removed from it so violently shocked America. It also shocked the world.

Chapter 26
Stormy Travels

Clad in their spacesuits setting out from Alamo Ridge in Romulus all initially went well. Podric and Barney crossed a sizeable section of the Sea of Tranquillity and entering the Theophilus region headed for the Delambre crater at the edge of which George and Kaliska had radioed in their position. There not being much traffic about (well none!) Calypso's tyre marks were quite clear only occasionally being lost when the vehicle traversed rockier terrain. It was as they approached the highlands not far from the craters of Theon Junior and Senior that dark went to light and a strange storm began.

Barney Sturridge may have been a difficult friend of Podric's but when Barney knew he was likely to be going on a lunar adventure, he read up extensively about what could be experienced on the selenic satellite. Driving the rover, Barney stopped the little vehicle and pressed a couple of buttons. Seconds later a stylish Perspex cover protected them. The boys stared out at the fine redolith that was all around.

"You make this?"

"No Podric. It grew."

Barney sighed.

"You could admire the ingenuity, the engineering skill that created this designer cabriolet."

"I admire it."

Barney laughed and peered through the screen.

"On the cusp of night and day, it's that positive negative thing. Won't last long. Electrostatically charged dust's being pushed across the terminator sideways."

"Who's been reading up then?"

It was Podric's turn to activate technology and a video link with Kaliska and George was established. The scene in the Cabstar was busy – Kaliska down loading data while George prepared a meal. Barney leant over Podric's shoulder.

"Domestic bliss mate."

Looking up at the camera Benedict smiled. Podric adjusted a picture setting.

"George, we're twenty point two miles from you. It shouldn't take us long now even with the escarpment."

Kaliska turned into shot.

"Hi Podric."

"I'm here an' all."

Barney waved. Kaliska shrugged.

"Yeah."

Barney shrugged too.

"Whatever."

Kaliska was all business.

"You'll have seen the weird signals traffic."

Podric tweaked one of the small monitors in front of him.

"Yup."

"Mean anything to you?"

"Yup."

Podric didn't enlarge. Kaliska hesitated.

"Is there anything we should do?"

"No."

Again, he didn't expand. Kaliska looked a little frustrated.

"Okay. As long as you're aware.."

The view in front of Romulus abruptly changed. As quickly as it had appeared, the strange transient phenomena vanished. Barney engaged drive.

"Rock 'n roll."

The lunar vehicle moved forward.

"Weird signals huh? You know all about them, then."

"Uhuh."

"Gonna tell me what they are?"

"Oh, the usual little green men. Eyes on the road now BS. Busy junction ahead."

"Yeah – 'lunar rock strikes driver at intersection. Tail back in space."

Romulus traversed an incline. Barney continued.

"Still, you could always take your test here. Like I said, quiet enough even with your limited driving skills."

"Meow."

*   *   *

Given they'd flown across the Atlantic in their separate private jets, the idea that Secorni's head would share a limousine driving down to Hampshire with Pasaro's CEO might seem unlikely. Nevertheless, after both had drawn blanks trying to make contact with any of the people they wanted to, Fred Schepesi and Cy Zaentz decided they would travel to Drinkwell together. Fred had been there once before. Buying Podric's latest game but frustrated at not being able to put the boy under contract, Fred opted to pay his wunderkind a surprise visit. Failing to meet because Podric was at school, Schepesi had gone round to Archie's house and spent an illuminating hour with the games' creator at the Lighthouse. For all the man's arrogance Schepesi found him surprisingly vulnerable.

Knowing the route Fred's driver Hector Railston guided the Mercedes off the M3 into the English countryside. Behind him the two executives enveloped in their leather seats checked their phones. Having dealt with his messages, Zaentz slipped his mobile into his pocket and stared out at the countryside.

"I love England."

"Too small for me."

"Anywhere's too small for you."

Schepesi chuckled. Approaching Drinkwell he became more reflective.

"'Never understand why a kid with so much talent lives in a little place like this when he could be hanging out on the Coast with me spending his millions."

"Maybe that's why he stays here."

Zaentz was dead pan. Schepesi gave a snort. Zaentz said.

"That how much you're paying him?"

"Could be. Royalties. 'Games through the sky."

"Is he aware of the money he's got?"

"Search me."

They pulled into Briony Close. Railston got out and went to the door.

"For a kid he's a strange bird. Money doesn't seem to bother him much though don't think he's a Mickey Mouse negotiator. Minor he maybe but he's major in dealings."

No one being at home Railston was returning to the car when he was accosted by Mrs Rajpundit from across the road. The chauffeur chatted to her for a second or two then got back into the limo.

"Got yourself a date?"

Railston smiled.

"The lady was just saying the household's away for the moment."

"That would seem apparent. She know how long?"

"Thought about a week, sir."

Schepesi grunted.

"These people are always goofing off. Head round to that other address, the sprauncy Englishman's Disney fortress."

"The Lighthouse I think the address is."

"If you say so Hector. Let's hope its shining bright and someone's home. Unlike my colleague here, I find the lack of sidewalks gives me the creeps."

The Mercedes edged out of Briony Close and headed off across the green to the smarter side of the village.

* * *

Deep in the Virginian countryside the Director was standing in his bunker conferring with several personnel working a bank of computers. "What's the trace on those signals?"

The lead operative tapped some keys and further data appeared on his screen.

"It's difficult sir. The encode's complicated."

"Well uncomplicate it fast."

Walking out of the tech room, the Director returned to his office. A few minutes later the agent code named Lodestar appeared. He placed a single sheet of paper in front of the Security Chief.

"Report on the signal. The firewall block leads one way then another, diverting all the time."

Lodestar sat down. The Director scanned the paper.

"For God's sake. We've got the most sophisticated decoding equipment on the planet. Are you saying you can't read it?"

"I'm saying that reading infinity is going to take a little time."

The Director thought for a moment. "Explain."

"The divert self-perpetuates so when it looks like its nailed, it's already propagated."

"Jeezus. What kind of a brain figured this baby out?"

"One that we need to get hold of."

"'Didn't come from that slime ball games executive we had in here that's for sure."

"No. But he's a lead. 'In the UK now sniffing out something."

"What glue do those limey's snort?"

"He's with the head of Pasaro – and they're not doing a merger."

The Director got up and paced around.

"So, what are the heads of the two largest electronic play play outfits doing in LL?"

Aware the Directors use of initials stood for Limey Land – the more relaxed Lodestar, sat back. "Let's recap." He scratched his nose.

"A team of writers or whatever they're called making these things were tasked to come up with a computer game they called *Moon Landing*. To stimulate the challenge, the brief from the commissioning company stipulated it was to be created so that a player could only use 60s technology." Lodestar stretched.

"The reason our predecessors pulled the guys game was that

working on it – in the process whether inadvertent or otherwise, these folk somehow got too close to understanding our space progress."

"Or lack of it."

"Issues getting key parts of the Apollo program to work and potentially exposing that."

The Director didn't respond.

Lodestar continued.

"The service feared that if the lid did come off – 'In God we Trust' wouldn't look too worthy."

The more logical Lodestar was, the more agitated the Director became. "Now we're getting these signals. "

Lodestar suddenly sat forward and snapped his fingers.

"It's a game. We're being played. These signals aren't coming from the lunar surface, they're being bounced via EME."

"Why?"

"To make us think they're on our trail."

"But how? How would they be able to do that using a computer game?"

"I don't know but it doesn't matter."

Lodestar stood up.

"What does matter is we've got to get to these guys whoever they are. Benedict's the key. It's the tail on Schepesi and Zaentz that'll lead us to him."

"You sure about that?"

"A damned sight more sure than trying to decode an infinity signal that's a deception." Lodestar left the room. The Director sat down.

"A computer game that uncovers a nation's secrets. What kind of a game is that?"

He might well have asked, but the security services hadn't yet begun to fathom the intricacies of Podric Moon's alternative world.

Chapter 27
Two Meetings

As it turned out Alannah Brodie's visit to her homeland had been brief. Because notice of her little holiday was sudden, the relatives and few friends she had in Ireland were either away or had prior commitments. Although she spent some time travelling around looking into the 1916 Easter Rising (Alannah had broadened her studies researching Erin's early twentieth century struggle) working in England the housekeeper felt strangely discontented. She decided she didn't feel animosity for contemporary Britain though her Gaelic blood temperature rose when reflecting on the history of the Anglo/Irish conflict. Foreshortening her trip, Alannah crossed the Irish Sea to Holyhead driving back to Hampshire. Arriving at Drinkwell with a stack of books on the subject, she looked forward to studying them and learning more about the origins and attitudes that led to such nationalist animosity.

Entering the Lighthouse Alannah found the place in darkness. Her employer, Podric and George Benedict in Wales with Dog, obviously the rest of the family and friends engaged in this latest computer adventure would surface when it suited them. Meanwhile, she kept the door to the tower firmly locked. They could go off on their weird trip if they liked. Whatever it was it wasn't an Irish story – the only topic of Podric's other reality Alannah had an interest in. Getting into bed that night Brodie thought about the boy's birthday – the night Podric had shown her those early twentieth-century April days in Dublin. The memory was still with her – as vivid as it had been when she'd been caught up in the adventure. The family being away would give her plenty of time to study the reference volumes she'd acquired. Sitting in her little private sitting room the following afternoon it was exactly what Alannah was enjoying.

She sensed rather than heard a car come down the drive. Being alone in the house was the one time she missed Dogs' boisterous enthusiasm. Whilst Alannah didn't doubt the Irish Wolfhound would be worse than useless if an intruder was determined Dog's size and behaviour gave one comfort. Putting down her book, she went through to the kitchen and checked the CCTV. Standing on the step was a smart man the housekeeper recognised. Behind him was an enormous limousine. Alannah opened the front door. Hector Railston said.

"Good afternoon ma'am. We've met before."

"I remember."

They smiled. Alannah continued.

"No doubt your boss is looking to see the doctor but I'm afraid he's away."

"Would you excuse me?"

The chauffeur turned back to the car. An electric window slid down and after a few seconds two doors opened and two men got out one of whom Alannah identified. Fred said.

"Ma'am. We've met. Fred Schepesi. I came by a while back and met with Dr Light."

He put out his hand.

"My colleague Cy Zaentz. In the neighbourhood, we went by young Podric's address but he's not home either."

"No. They're both out of town."

Looking around, Schepesi laughed.

"That's a good one. Ma'am – I wonder if we might have a word?"

"I can't imagine how I can help."

Schepesi and Zaentz glanced at each other before Schepesi continued.

"Rather than stand on the doorstep, would you care to come out to tea? There must be somewhere nearby."

"But they don't serve what I like."

The four people stood there. Zaentz cleared his throat.

"You'll likely be aware we have business interests with your employer and his young partner."

Alannah made no response. Zaentz hesitated.

"We really want to know if all is well with them."

The housekeeper's eyes narrowed.

"What do you mean?"

"There have been some problems recently we can't figure out."

"What sort of problems?"

Again, Secorni's leader hesitated.

"It may sound a bit crazy but National Security problems."

Alannah sighed.

"Does this have anything to do with Mr Benedict?"

The two men glanced at each other.

"Likely it does."

"Oh, faddle. We can't stand here all day. Come in – all of you." Whatever this was to do with Brodie had an instinctive feeling that the chauffeur anyway wouldn't let any harm come to her. Call it Irish instinct – but computer people were a strange breed, and she wouldn't rely on them!

*   *   *

Coming over the brow of the escarpment running up to Delambre crater, Podric and Barney spied the CabStar. Beside it was parked Benedict and Kaliska's lunar rover and trailer. Stopping alongside, they decided to make an immediate start fixing Calypso. It was Barney who took charge. Taking out a small diagnostic scanner, he plugged the device into the appropriate socket on the rover.

"Quicker if I sort this. You go and check out the love nest."

Opening the small portable decompression chamber door, Podric stepped inside closing the seal behind him. The unit's air supply gradually stabilising, Podric checked a meter on his suit and removed his helmet. He then opened the second door and entered CabStar's living quarters. Kaliska and Benedict had seen Romulus approach and Podric's reception was a warm one. Kaliska handed Podric a steaming paper mug.

"Arabica fan I recall.."

Static on the comms system – Barney's image appeared.

"Someone's got a heavy foot. The brakes are shot."

Aware Barney knew she was driving Romulus when the rover broke down Kaliska shrugged.

"The people servicing my Merc said they'd never seen such under-worn discs. A light touch they said."

"Yeah, but the way those Kübelwagon's are built.."

"How long?"

Podric sipped his coffee.

"Couple of hours."

"I'll be out shortly."

Podric checked some data on a device.

"Want us to press on?"

George Benedict seemed tense.

"Sure."

Podric had another sip of coffee.

"Reckon it's there?"

He looked up at Benedict.

"What – Eagle's descent stage, the flag and some bits and pieces?"

Draining his drink and putting the paper mug in a self-sealing bin, Podric turned to leave.

"Wikipedia says so. Besides, it's all part of the adventure George."

* * *

"So, you read a lot of history?"

Sitting in the Lights' drawing room, Cy Zaentz turned over one of Brodie's books on the Irish uprising.

"A particular subject by the look of things."

Fred Schepesi finished another scone.

"I can see why you like stayin' home. These beat anything the

Big Bagel can offer."

A last mouthful of almond, cherry and pistachio covered pastry disappeared. Schepesi continued through a mouthful.

"This family are fortunate to have you Ms Brodie. Sure, I can't lure you Stateside?"

Things seemed relaxed. Alannah had insisted Hector Railston be included having tea and he was now in her sitting room watching a television show. Things paused. Brodie decided she would wait for the men to begin; it was Zaentz who led.

"You mentioned George Benedict."

Alannah didn't reply. Zaentz looked as though he had a decision to make.

"My company was put under a lot of pressure to persuade George to make contact with your employer who he used to partner professionally."

The housekeeper was going to ask the obvious question but decided to maintain her silence. Zaentz continued.

"I could go into a long explanation about how and why this came about but-."

"We think something's happened here."

Schepesi cut in with his New Yorker bluntness.

"Some new game Light's come up with or more likely boy wonder. Pasaro – my outfit – has taken their last couple of games."

Even with this new spirit of cooperation Schepesi couldn't miss an opportunity to flex some business muscle. Alannah said.

"But how would I know anything about this?"

The two men caught each other's eye. "Maybe you wouldn't."

"But I do."

Schepesi and Zaentz were mute. Alannah didn't know why she was going to talk to these people. Maybe she was making a mistake, yet she somehow felt it right. Alannah was aware there had been a lot of stress about the place recently which seemed to have started when George Benedict came on the scene. These computer games men being here, it was time to sort things out.

Before describing the most amazing experience of her life, one thing Alannah decided she would not do is tell these two American computer games CEOs that not two hundred feet from where they sat ten people were experiencing the transient state that was Ultimate Alternative Reality. There was something particular about that – almost sacred. Alannah picked up the book Zaentz had flicked through.

"It was Podric's birthday..."

Chapter 28

In and Out

Calypso was fixed. Podric and Barney stood back from their handiwork.

"Not bad. The brake system needs a proper overhaul, but it'll get them home."

"That's good because you're driving it back."

"Eh?"

Barney turned to Podric. Unable to see one another's expression – space helmet visors blocked out the other's eyes, the visors plastic coating reflecting the viewer rather than the viewed – Barney went on.

"We're going on together aren't we?"

"Change of plan. I'm staying here for a bit. Want to do some checks. You're going back with George."

There was something in Podric's tone that suggested he'd brook no argument. For all Barney's bravaggio their relationship was particular; the bigger boy knew when the other was serious. Minutes later Benedict appeared suited and booted.

"We're not continuing then."

"Not this time. I'm not happy with the rovers and there's some things I want to check on while I'm here."

"Can't I help?"

"Better you get back. The service departments got work to do."

Barney and Benedict climbed aboard the rover and a short while later Calypso was heading back to base.

* * *

In the Mercedes limousine Fred Schepesi and Saul Zaentz stared out at the passing countryside. For once the glass partition between the chauffeur and passenger section was sealed off.

"Have I been dreaming?"

Zaentz was muted. For several seconds the normally ebullient head of Pasaro didn't reply. When he did he too was subdued.

"Stacks up."

Schepesi sprawled in his seat and sucked air through a gap in his teeth.

"I've known Podric's been playing me for a while."

Schepesi stroked his stubbled head.

"Ain't one for superlatives using the word genius – but if the kid's not one he's the next best thing."

Zaentz didn't comment. Schepesi continued.

"He had trauma. Aviator dad killed in a freak flying accident. The boy idolised his pa who'd got him into computer games."

Reaching into a small cabinet at their feet, Schepesi took out a bottle of water.

"You'll have read about his skills. He's beaten more people of any age group than anyone alive."

Fred swigged his water from the plastic bottle.

"With his dad gone the boy lost interest. I knew there was somethin' going down, but it figures now – the whole Light bit."

"Father figure?"

"Hmm – yeah, well... Reckon in the end maybe some mutual need."

Zaentz helped himself to a bottle of water from the minifridge.

"In his day Archie Light was a considerable writer."

"Made you a lot of mazuma."

"Sure did. Then again he could be an arrogant bastard to work with."

Schepesi chuckled.

"Podric told me. Reckons half the time he's the adult."

"No surprise there."

Zaentz swigged his H_2O.

"So, this state... Living in the game. What d'you reckon?"

For a while neither man spoke. Then Schepesi said.

"If it was anyone else.."

Schepesi had some more water.

"We're meat."

Zaentz turned to look at his rival. Schepesi took his time before continuing.

"If it's a quarter the experience the leprechaun described can you imagine what it'll do to the industry? Overnight everything else is obsolete."

He slipped the near-empty water bottle into a slot beside him.

"Who's going to want to play a game conventionally if they can live in one – live inside the adventure and experience it that way. Non compare ain't in it."

Zaentz was thoughtful.

"So why if MoonLight have got this – what did she say – Ultimate Alternative Reality – have they not announced it?"

"That my friend is a very good question and leads to another. Your being pressured by agency evil eyes about this writer of yours – you said he was the guy who was involved with the game that got shut down."

Zaentz said.

"George Benedict, yeah. What's that got to do with living in a parallel universe?"

Ignoring his fellow CEO, Schepesi went on.

"And the feeling's been that maybe Georgie and this team stumbled on something trying to create the game the government powers that be didn't like."

Schepesi was on a roll.

"Moon stuff, wasn't it?"

"*Moon Landing*, yuh."

"*Moon Landing*! And the game was going to be played using only '60s technology. Right?"

"Pretty much its whole point 'cept George couldn't get it to work."

"Couldn't get it to work.."

Schepesi was intense.

"You're a security agency bent on hiding something – what if this alternative stuff of Podric's somehow threatens exposure?"

"Where's the link?"

"Benedict. You got him to his ex-business partner, Light's new one. It'll be what they're after."

Zaentz shrugged.

"How would a computer game be linked to America's Apollo space program?"

Schepesi cracked his knuckles.

"I don't know but there's a hell of a lot of crazy shit flying around right now."

Schepesi unscrewed the top of his bottle of water and finished it.

"If I'm a tenth accurate going down this road the issues with this alternative reality and MoonLight affecting our market ain't nothin' to the hornet's nest that's going to stir up in Maryland and Old Virginny. What those Good Ol' Boys don't understand they don't like and when they don't like they get sore."

"This is one mite lot of supposition."

"Whatever it is the keys got to be with Podric and his compadres."

The two men were silent for a while then Zaentz said.

"Do you believe Ms Brodie didn't know where they were?"

"Dunno. Don't care. What were we gonna do, put her on the rack? What she offloaded today's already a game changer."

Zaentz looked at Schepesi.

"Very funny. So, how do we get to them?"

"We don't. We leave messages and wait for them to get in touch."

"Think they will?"

"I know they will."

"You seem very sure."

Schepesi screwed the top back on the empty water bottle and tapped it against his knee.

"I said Podric's a clever kid. You're tellin' me Archie Light's an egomaniac. George Benedict sounds a mess. They'll get in touch."

"Are we going to help?"

"Screwing those secrecy bastard's balls in computerised knots? Why not? I want into this alternate world. Don't you?"

*   *   *

Working away in the CabStar Podric and Kaliska were immersed in statistics. Rubbing her eyes Kaliska relaxed.

"Why did you send George back?"

Podric spooled through some data.

"Because he's on the edge."

"What do you mean?"

"He's cracking up."

Kaliska thought about this.

"I haven't really been in the picture."

"No. You're more preoccupied with Dallas."

Kaliska smiled. Podric continued.

"He's cracking up in the real world."

Kaliska swung round to face her client.

"In that case you'll not want to press ahead with things here in Ultimate Alterative Reality."

Podric appreciated his lawyer's intelligence. She continued.

"You didn't really want to check anything did you?"

"It's not a priority."

They looked at each other.

"Why are we here?"

"In UAR? Adventure and to provoke things in the reality world. Are you okay coming out temporarily – you at the Lighthouse me in Wales?"

"Why?"

"I need to check what I set up is working. It's to do with George."

Kaliska's eyes narrowed. Podric continued.

"We can make a detour en route."

*   *   *

"Well, here I am."

It was night. Located in a side room adjacent to the morgue at Bethesda Naval Hospital Washington DC the late President Kennedy sat wearing a casual shirt, slacks and loafers. On seeing Podric and Kaliska he smiled.

"It's begun. No autopsy and rumours are flying around."

Although he smiled, the horror and sadness were profoundly chilling. Kennedy said.

"Where do we go from here?"

JFK attempted to maintain his sangfroid though the scene was unimaginably mournful. Podric tried to be matter of fact.

"The game we're currently in that you're linked to is called *Moon Landing*. We're checking out of UAR for a little while, but we'll be back. We're closing in on a lot of things."

"Like?"

"Your assassination, the moon landings.."

Kennedy shrugged.

"Good luck with that."

He sighed.

"First time in my-."

JFK checked himself.

"After life – I find myself in other's hands."

"Your legacy won't be forgotten."

Approaching Kennedy, Kaliska was intense.

"But my life's been taken."

Restless, JFK stood up.

"It was quick though. I'll say that."

However lightly he spoke it was impossible not feel profound sadness.

"Didn't Jackie do a great job."

The way Kennedy spoke, it wasn't a question.

"Her efforts President Kennedy have only just begun."

Chapter 29
Revelations

Sitting up in a bedroom in Bwthyn Anghysbell the Welsh cottage the Lights rented, Podric depressed the microchip in his left wrist disengaging UAR. Stretching and getting up – on his way downstairs he looked in on Archie and George Benedict. Archie was in the main bedroom and George in a single one. Both were still in Ultimate Alternative Reality and appeared Zen-like in their preternatural state. Dog lay on a rug near the hearth in the living room. He too was apparently in a caninely ethereal condition. Lunar Dog. Wasn't man's best friend the first animal to go into space? In the kitchen Podric put on the kettle.

They hadn't been in UAR very long but Ultimate Alternative Reality not having any bearing on real time it always took a little while to accustom oneself when returning to reality. Fishing out his iPhone Podric didn't have many messages but there were two from Fred Schepesi. The second was strange. Apparently in attempting to track Podric down he and Cy Zaentz had been to tea at the Lighthouse and met Alannah who was the greatest pastry maker in the world! Fred and Cy together. Something was going on.

Texting Kaliska checking she was okay it was no more than forty minutes later that the lawyer called back. Emerging from the same state as Podric, she had monitored her more numerous companions before taking the lift to the first floor. Unlocking the tower, she'd walked across the flying glass hallway to the main house and met Brodie. Kaliska explained that Podric had asked her to come out of UAR. The housekeeper had a story to tell. When Brodie had finished the lawyer reached for her phone.

"Sitting down?"

Nursing his tea looking out at the Brecon Beacons Podric said.

"Alannah's told the computer gurus about UAR."

This spoiled her news but Kaliska just said.

"They called you."

"Left messages. Fred didn't say that – just that they'd had tea at Archie's."

"Joining the dots Podric. Why aren't you in my legal team?"

There was a pause in the conversation before Kaliska continued.

"If your plan is working these guys are going to be tailed."

"We have to work on that being the case."

"So how do we get to them? Any contact is going to be compromised."

Podric chuckled.

"There needn't be any physical contact."

Kaliska waited. Podric continued.

"They're both programmed."

It was Kaliska's turn to laugh.

"Back in then?"

"Not the recent game or *JFK and His World.*"

More silence, then Podric said.

"I think the original *Moon Landing.* I've got all George's codex."

*   *   *

"I don't know why I'm feeling like this, but everything's crowding in on me."

Still in UAR Archie and George Benedict were sitting in the Lunar Station café.

"Small wonder."

Archie got up and placing his empty coffee mug under a machine's dispenser turned to Benedict.

"Look George the longer this goes on the more it's obvious the whole thing stinks. It's a set up. You contacting me. Compromising my relationship with Podric, compromising Podric himself."

Benedict was subdued. Pressing the coffee refill button Archie said.

"That's some grudge you must have against me to do what you did. But Podric, what did he ever do to you?"

Archie checked his coffee measure.

"When you betrayed us to the agency, frankly I'd have thrown you to the wolves."

He stared down at his ex-games partner.

"You don't owe your existence in this adventure to me though George. You owe it to Podric."

"Why's he doing it?" George was sullen.

"Like me, he doesn't trust you and reckons it's better to have you in UAR where we can keep an eye on you."

"Why does he want to do that?"

Archie looked at Benedict. "George. You are not that dumb."

Archie gave a snort and picked up his coffee.

"Haven't you begun to get a handle on what Ultimate Alternative Reality can do yet? Apart from give us great adventures we appear to be inside people's worlds at the time they were living them. That gives us a unique insight."

Archie added some sweetener to his coffee. Benedict said.

"So Podric's using UAR to flush people out."

"Haha George. You're paying attention. That's exactly what I'm saying – nailing these bad boys."

Archie stirred his coffee. Benedict said.

"Do you really think the moon landings were a con?"

"Oh and did Stanley K shoot faked images of astronauts on the moon in a studio and who murdered Kennedy? It's conspiracy wonderland."

Archie sipped his coffee and continued.

"I don't know George and I don't particularly care. I don't think Podric does either. What excites us is the cover up. From where we're coming from that's more interesting than one giant step for mankind or who pulled the trigger."

Pressing a remote button, Benedict activated a sliding window in the café. The Earth was massive behind the moon's curvature.

"What are you going to do with me?"

Sipping his coffee Archie looked at his ex-partner.

"Do you know George I really don't know. Your betrayal killed something in me."

Archie had some more of his lunar coffee. It wasn't bad.

"People think I'm a bullshitter and maybe I have been in my time, but you of all people ought to know that I never wanted to take credit for anything I didn't do. If my name was put to a game, I'd earned the right for it to be there."

"So, it's up to Podric then." Benedict closed the window.

"Since I've known him that's usually the way things are."

*   *   *

"For chrissakes Podric, I've got to have this!"

"If you do I do Fred. After all we're in my company's HQ."

If Schepesi was excited, Zaentz was hyper.

"What's that got to do with anything?"

"It has to do with the fact that coming into Ultimate Alternative Reality Podric's put us inside a game Secorni commissioned."

"Podric's my protégé. Pasaro gave him the breaks!"

The person they referred to was standing in Pasaro's computer lab with Kaliska Monroe. Podric having revised George Benedict's near completed game giving it the title *Moon Landing – 1984* (on hearing the title 'Fitting year' had been Kaliska's only comment) Secorni's offices in Silicon Valley circa 1984 were very different. Women wearing power suits with shoulder pads à la Dallas and men with mullet haircuts and Miami Vice style outfits were much in evidence. Podric looked across the computer assembly plant.

"Hard to remember how crude things were then."

"What about twenty years previously? Computer dark ages."

Schepesi and Zaentz approached. Podric said.

"Your Head of Europe's experienced this before."

Talking to Cy Zaentz, Podric walked along the lines of early computers.

"It was in the first adventure. Listening to Archie rail about

Saul I profiled him in."

Zaentz was attentive.

"He actually met Archie and me on the Rock of Gibraltar in 1793. Archie was a lieutenant in the British navy, and I was a midshipman. Prendergast was the captain of an American privateer. It was a Secorni game we fell into – one that Archie wrote – *Napoleonic Wars.*"

"I can't begin to imagine how you came up with this?"

Zaentz was genuinely amazed.

"I don't give a goddamn about how you came up with it. I don't give a goddamn about George Benedict and the crazy secret service. I've got to have this thing. We've got to put it out!"

Podric turned to Fred. Taking the man's arm, he led the executive a little away.

"You think this is good Fred, this experience?"

Podric was courteous and continued.

"Different – being inside a game."

They stopped.

"Given we're not actually playing *Moon Landing – 1984* I inserted a Preparation option to the Menu which is why we're here. Background to how it was made. Gamers love that. If I do this."

Podric activated *Moon Landing – 1984* and the games Menu appeared at the top of Schepesi's eyes. As the CEO watched Podric moved the cursor across various options/levels of play.

"You can see the games challenges – Testing, Lift Offs, Orbiting, Landing Attempts and Rate of Play variations."

Clicking on Lift Off – Schepesi suddenly found himself in a cramped Saturn V capsule dressed in a spacesuit vibrating on the pan at Cape Canaveral. The sensation was indescribable as the giant rocket climbed into the sky. Every bone in Schepesi's body was jolted and sweat ran down the inside of his suit. He was living the experience.

Podric clicked out of the game. Schepesi was visibly affected.

"That's what you get inside a game in UAR."

Podric let go of Schepesi's arm and went on.

"When you get back to your hotel, have another think. The

very few privileged participants all recognise the experience as being unique. It blows one's mind and I think is life changing. Other people say so anyway. I can see it's affected you."

Podric looked at Schepesi full square.

"Now that you're one of us – no we are not going to release Ultimate Alternative Reality to the masses because we want it kept for ourselves. As part of our select little club, you will too."

They walked back to Kaliska and Zaentz. Schepesi was slightly unsteady.

"Where to from here?"

Zaentz seemed more au fait with the situation than Schepesi was but then he hadn't just been blasted skywards from Launch Complex 34 at Cape Canaveral!

"You're being tailed right now by the people who threatened George. The way to sort these bad boys is bring them in and confront them."

"And... how will you do that?"

Podric moved his wrist. Zaentz nodded.

"Ah."

"The problem is I don't have data on the dark forces movers and shakers which I'll need to create their profiles."

"I might be able to help you there. Haven't got a depth of material, but I have got images."

Zaentz activated his cell phone.

"It's a download. I grabbed them while I was in their company."

"Sloppy security wasn't it?"

"They took my phone and watch but for some reason, not my wallet. I always carry a small Dictaphone in it for emergencies. It comes with a lens and these guys were... preoccupied."

"Even so. They really on top of their game?"

Podric transferred the images into his own phone. Zaentz half-smiled.

"Sometimes when you're up close to the big guys they forget you in their arrogance."

"Is that so?"

Zaentz and Podric looked at each other. Zaentz said.

"You'll have a problem getting much on them though I can tell you the older one was the character who leant on us bringing in George Benedict."

"Everyone's got data somewhere Mr Zaentz. Everyone."

Kaliska spoke with a certainty.

"Good luck with that then."

Stupefied by what he'd experienced in Ultimate Alternative Reality, Fred Schepesi had largely been left out of the conversation. He looked at Podric intensely.

"When can I go in again?"

Podric smiled and turned to Zaentz.

"By the way, Carla's with us."

"I figured as much."

Preparing to disengage from UAR Podric moved his right index finger across his left wrist. Zaentz continued.

"Tell her I look forward to seeing her again."

"You can tell her yourself."

"I don't mean in reality."

Zaentz smiled. Podric also smiled and said.

"Ah, I heard that as a PA she's out of this world."

Chapter 30
Lunar Wales

The little dining area at the back of the cottage looked more like a computer control room than somewhere to eat a meal. When Podric and Archie decided to go into their *Moon Landing* computer game facilitating Ultimate Alternative Reality from Bwthyn Anghysbell Podric had ensured they'd brought everything with them they'd need by way of computing equipment. The cottage dining room became a mini-Lighthouse computer lab.

Aware that the Security Services hounding George Benedict would have tabs on Archie and likely Podric himself normal communication would be dangerous. Podric had immediately switched off the device after speaking to Kaliska and changed its sim card. Deciding the lawyer should stay at Drinkwell to keep an eye on things (plus if he needed anything he didn't have access to she could encode it to him over the ether) Podric felt comfortable communicating with Kaliska via electronic mail. He was confident that the firewalls at the Lighthouse and the system in front of him were sufficiently protected from the likes of Cheltenham or Langley.

Studying visuals of The Director and Lodestar Podric worked on their images analysing every element of the two men's faces in microscopic detail. Kaliska had also been conducting her own forensic research but they were still some way off being able to accurately identify the agents. Concentrating on his work, Podric became aware of movement above and half a minute later George Benedict appeared. Podric looked round.

"Wasn't aware you knew how to get out."

George shrugged.

"A lifetime writing games, guess you pick up something."

Benedict peered out of a back window and gazed at the mountains.

"What you and A L have created I never could have but first rule for a games writer is listen and learn."

"I must tell your ex-partner."

Benedict laughed.

"He's yours now."

Sounds were heard above. Podric worked away. Hesitant, Benedict began.

"Podric-."

Turning away from the screens, Podric said.

"Like a cup of tea?" Benedict shrugged.

"I'd kill for one but I'm quite capable of plugging in a kettle."

Podric got up.

"I need a recharge."

Podric was making tea in the kitchen when Archie came downstairs. The games creator noticed two mugs were out. He said. "You heard me."

"I did but this is for George."

"How did he get here?"

"He's been watching and learning."

The boy and man looked at each other. Archie reached for a third mug hanging off a hook. Podric said.

"Safe to leave everything was it?" Archie answered.

"It was... necessary to come out. Doubly so now."

Another look between the two. Archie continued.

"Besides, I can be back in the drop of a hat. Your girlfriend and my daughter are well in control. Big mates these days."

Benedict appeared in the doorway.

"Those images you're looking at."

Podric turned. "What about them?"

"I've seen one of them."

"Which?"

"The younger – on the righthand screen."

Re-entering the dining room George and Podric went over to the computer screens. Benedict indicated Lodestar's picture. Podric said.

"Where did you see him?"

"He was the American officer who came to check on your mother and me when we supposedly strayed into a military exercise area not a couple of miles from this house."

"Never forget a face huh, George? Time for your UAR plan then Podric."

Archie sipped his tea. Podric said.

"Thanks for bringing ours Archie. By the by, your housekeeper's told Fred and Cy about Ultimate Alternative Reality."

*　*　*

"You look done in."

Preparing food in the Lunar Station kitchen with Charlotte Light, Barbara Moon saw Barney enter the café.

"Sweating over the bloody rovers!"

Leaving her recipe, Barbara walked round the counter. Barney helped himself to a beer. So did Barbara.

"You brought George back."

"Yeah." Opening the bottle, Barney had a swig. Barbara took the top off her beer and poured some into a beaker. She said.

"Podric's staying out there then." Barney shrugged. "Says he wants to check data." Mrs Moon sipped her liquor. "But you think there's another reason."

Sturridge wiped his mouth. "He's worried about the old guy."

"Archie?"

"No, Benedict!"

"What makes you say that?" Barbara had some more beer. Barney sighed.

"The back story to his turning up a few weeks ago. People after him."

"Yes?"

"It's strange how he just appeared Podric's mum."

"I like George."

"Bully for you."

Barbara had some more beer. Although she had an eccentric personality, since losing her husband and having to bring up two children on her own Barbara had learned wisdom. She decided to change the subject.

"Hungry?"

"You cooking?"

"No. Charlotte is. She's much better than me."

"Untrue but. What's on the menu?"

"It's Mardi Gras and we're making pancakes. Fancy a crepe?"

"How many you talking?"

"We could feed the five thousand."

"Should be enough then."

*   *   *

"She's meat!"

"No, she's not Archie. It was bound to come out sometime. Alannah's done us a favour."

Podric finished a beer.

"How's that?"

"Fred and Cy were always going to be blown away by UAR. Now they've been in they understand why we want to keep it to ourselves. As long as they experience it from time to time there's no problem. In fact, I think they've got off knowing about it, knowing its there."

It was evening and Podric, Archie and George Benedict were sitting in front of the fire in the living room at Bwthyn Anghysbell. The remnants of a couple of bottles of red wine Archie and George had polished off stood beside them. Benedict was looking at a photograph of Lodestar. Podric said.

"My mum was there that night when you saw the American officer wasn't she?"

"So were you."

Benedict was uncomfortable. Podric continued.

"Yes, but I only glimpsed someone wearing an American officer's uniform. You might recall I had other preoccupations."

"Dating were you?"

Archie was arch.

"Driving."

Finding this amusing, Archie said.

"Mastered double de clutching yet?"

Retrieving Lodestar's photograph from Benedict, Podric studied it.

"I think she'd like to be around for this."

"What do you mean?"

"We've got to reel in this dude. Cy Zaentz recognises the older guy who he calls The Director. It was the senior man who pressured Secorni in the first place and Cy's agreed to act as lure, but we want both of them."

"If Americans are involved and they're in the UK at least we know where they'll be hubbed out of."

Archie finished his wine.

"And that's."

Checking his phone Archie activated Google maps. Finding the location in Gloucestershire, he showed Podric.

"How come?"

Archie closed his phone.

"Trust me. If it's an American operation and they're coming in to look for George its likely that's where they'll be based – at least temporarily."

"How do you know this?"

"Because it's one of two or three shared airbases the US has in the UK which they use for a variety of operations including bringing their under-cover people over."

"It could be one of the other two. They don't know where we are."

"That's not the point. It's nearest Cirencester."

Podric didn't get it. Archie said.

"GCHQ – UK spooksville. Shared information."

Podric put Lodestar's photograph in a file. Benedict abruptly stood up.

"They'll head here but not just for those reasons."

Archie and Podric looked at him.

"Soldier spy knows this place. He was part of the SWAT team your mum and I escaped from. We didn't stumble into that exercise. It was part of a back-up plan."

Chapter 31
A Cabinet Meeting

"We're gonna support Khánh and commit more troops to South Vietnam."

Early into 1964 and several months after John Kennedy's assassination the new president Lyndon Johnson was presiding over a cabinet meeting. Outwardly, LBJ claimed to still be finding his feet but few witnessing his bullish mood would agree. Johnson's combativeness honed by a lifetime battling and persuading the Senate and Congress – his Texan drawl may not have had the urbane sophistication of Kennedy, but Johnson was an effective politician. That however seemed at odds with a cabinet that was still largely Kennedy's. Amongst the dozen or so men sitting at the table many had served under JFK and to them for all the new president's robust behaviour, Kennedy's shadow was a long one. It was the day that Jack in Ultimate Alternative Reality and unseen to anyone else, stood by a far window, an arm crooked, an index finger against his cheek. The dead president was in thoughtful mood. A cabinet member spoke up.

"Do you think that's wise Mr President?"

"Damned right I think it's wise! We've got to show these monkeys who has the muscle here. Our policy is to flush out the Viet Cong and drive communism from South East Asia."

Several people in the room raised an eyebrow.

"I only question the strategy Mr President. Right now, regime change down there seems to be operating by rote."

"Good point, Bob."

Referring to Secretary of Defense Robert McNamara, JFK turned towards his ex-cabinet. Johnson said.

"Another damned good reason thing's need straightening out."

"I'm not convinced."

It was a voice LBJ dreaded. The elephant in the room left over from his brother's presidency, Bobby Kennedy as Attorney General was a constant reminder to Johnson of the Kennedy torch and an unwelcome thorn in the new chief executives' side. For all his bluster and hardnose bullying tactics Johnson could be surprisingly sensitive and even now Jack Kennedy's mantle affected him. Every time he looked at Bobby an image of the man's elder brother flashed before him.

"It was Jack's policy Bobby."

"Policy is a fluid thing. It can change."

JFK walked behind the row of men sitting around the table. Even more restless than his brother Bobby Kennedy sat forward.

"After the Bay of Pigs my brother became mistrustful of the military and wary about making any overseas commitment that involved US troops."

"He raised the number of our people in the region."

McNamara's voice was neutral.

"They were peacekeeping. At the time of my brother's death there was no major US military commitment."

RFK's voice was raw.

"Sadly, we cannot say what President Kennedy would or would not have done."

Larry O'Brien, a JFK stalwart serving in the new administration was gentle. Standing behind them JFK fiddled with his PT109 tiepin.

"Listening to this, I'd have got the hell out."

Johnson sat forward.

"Well son, as Larry says that sadly is something we'll never know. But this is my administration now and my gut tells me we go in and we go in big."

JFK sighed. The cabinet was silent. Secretary of State Dean Rusk cleared his throat.

"Mr President, there's a final item on the agenda or do you

wish to discuss South East Asia further?"

Johnson was looking at a brooding Bobby Kennedy.

"That is?"

"NASA progress."

"How's it comin' along?"

A change in the meetings tempo, Johnson seemed suddenly distant. Rusk said.

"Frankly Mr President it's way behind schedule."

Yet another Kennedy initiative, Johnson was underwhelmed.

"Gonna cost us big."

"Not as much as a war."

Bobby was pushing it. Jack put his hands on his brother's shoulders. Johnson sighed. It was a sighing day.

"Look Bob, I appreciate how you feel. Believe me I do but we have to act here."

"Why? Why not wait a while, get more reports in from our people on the ground and see how things develop?"

Bobby didn't say that caution was his brother's preferred method of doing things but several people in the room got the inference. Johnson said.

"Because if we don't act dammit, we cause a vacuum and if we cause a vacuum Hanoi's little jungle buddies are gonna get active."

Johnson leaned in and faced RFK.

"We've got to nail this Bob and we've got to nail it now!"

The cabinet was silent. Secretaries of state fiddled with their blotters. Finally, Rusk led again.

"Er, so the Apollo program..?

"Right now, I don't give a longhorn's shit about the Apollo program."

Intense, Johnson sat back.

"Oh... Get hold of the kraut."

"von Braun?"

"Yeah. Have him in for a meeting."

Dean Rusk made a note.

"That about wrap everything up then for today Mr President?"

The Secretary of State seemed keen to bring the session to a conclusion.

"'Guess. Gentlemen.'"

This being permission for cabinet to conclude, members began filing out. A NASA brochure lay on the cabinet table containing artists impressions of space flight. Johnson picked it up. Labor Secretary Willard Wirtz was one of the last to leave. Johnson said.

"Think we can deliver this cockamamie dream Bill?"

Johnson appeared deflated.

"It's a tall order Mr President but then President Kennedy shot for the moon."

Johnson sighed.

"Some say he got too near the sun."

"Wouldn't know about that, sir."

"No. Thanks Bill."

Alone in his cabinet office, Johnson ruminated.

"Lonely isn't it, Lyndon?"

John Kennedy walked along the far side of the cabinet table.

"Your predecessors whose ranks I've now joined, reckoned it's the loneliest job in the world. We've all coveted it along the way going right back to him."

Kennedy nodded at a picture of George Washington hanging on the far wall.

"But no one can teach another how to be president. It's the office that counts."

Kennedy began walking towards the door. On the back of the NASA brochure was a picture of JFK and underneath his famous quote.

"We choose to go to the moon in this decade and do the other things, not because they are easy, but because they are hard, because the goal will serve to organise and measure the best of our energies and skills, because that challenge is one that we are willing to accept, one we are unwilling to post-pone, and one which we intend to win."

Johnson dropped the booklet back on the table.

"God Jack, if I hadn't seen you shot I'd say you were right here in this room. You've never left. The shadow you cast is a damned long one."

Kennedy looked back.

"It'll fade Lyndon. Life moves on. Just don't screw up."

He went out.

Chapter 32
An Emergency and
Rendezvous with Spies

Ambulance lights flashed through the night. The emergency had been sudden and had taken place whilst Cosima was helping Miss Mullins teach Amy and her friend Lilian Bekes in Lunar Class Morpheus 9 – a lesson on planetary alignment. Clearly Cosima's weren't as racked with pain she was rushed to hospital with acute appendicitis. Given she was in Ultimate Alternative Reality both her father and Podric immediately re-entered the state releasing Charlotte who accompanied her daughter to Wendbury hospital from the Lighthouse.

After establishing that his daughter wasn't in danger and physically being in Wales, Archie decided to stay in UAR's Lunar camp for the moment. Sitting in the small library which served as a classroom (Amy and Lilian Bekes were ostensibly finishing their homework) Ultimate Alternative Reality's creators talked to Podric's mum and Catherine.

"So, you think I should come with you and George."

Barbara spooled through Amy's homework remotely on a tablet device.

"I'd like you to witness things."

There was little argument against Podric's reply.

"Will you bring us all out now?"

Catherine sat back. Podric said.

"Had enough?"

"No. I'll miss Cos but it's such an interesting experience being in this environment."

Barbara looked up from the iPad.

"People don't want to leave. They feel its liberating being here

– out of this world."

She smiled at her son and continued.

"Like your sister and her friend. They're getting a lot out of it."

"And Barney."

Catherine's tone was firm.

"He's really putting in the hours Podric."

"Hmm... But neither Archie or I will be here if anything goes wrong.."

"That's a bit melodramatic. I'm not completely UAR illiterate and neither is thuggee..."

Although Barney's bullyboy tactics at Wendbury High had long gone Catherine's euphemism for her father's tenant had somehow stuck. Podric said.

"Like your *Civil War* riverboat adventures.."

"Ha. Not just sharp with the cards either."

Archie who had been reading a paper, cut in.

"I'll stay."

He turned to them all.

"We shouldn't take our minds off the bigger picture – why we're doing all this. Everyone coming out now isn't in the script."

Dog appeared and seeing Archie bounded over. Acting irritable, the games creator attempted to fend off his pet.

"On the other hand..."

*   *   *

It was a similar evening to the windswept night Corporal Podric Moon had been at the wheel of his mother's Land Rover Defender. This time he was in the back of the vehicle and approaching a military base, not escaping from it. His mother was driving, and George Benedict sat beside her. Podric said.

"I could have driven."

"I know darling. Very proud of you passing first time."

Changing gear, Barbara didn't expand on the fact that getting her own licence had taken Podric's mother four attempts.

Barbara had come out of UAR the day before in the Lighthouse. After a coffee with Kaliska and Alannah, she left Drink-well to rendezvous with her son and George Benedict who had departed Wales for the meeting in Gloucestershire. Pulling up at the security barrier a guard appeared. Barbara opened her window and George leant across producing an ID card. The female guard inspected it and re-entered the admissions office.

"Bit like old times Podric."

Having been married to an RAF officer for eighteen years military checkpoints didn't bother Barbara.

"'Cept we never had to wait."

"Do you think they'd speed up if I flutter my eyelashes?"

An RAF officer appeared.

"That's not-. You're not Barbara Moon by any chance?"

Barbara leant out.

"Do I know you?"

"Groves, Brian Groves. I was AOSC OPS at Wildenrath when Sean was there."

The guard returned and seeing the driver engaged with one of her superiors, walked to the far side of the Land Rover. She handed George back his card. The barrier came up. Barbara engaged gear.

"Can't recall you I'm afraid. You'll have to excuse us – we're meeting some spies."

She accelerated away.

"Oaaah. Groper Groves – fancy seeing him. Sooo creepy."

The Defender made its way across the base and entered the American sector. Although within the overall UK base area, the US Tactical Wing was a separate entity. Passing through its security, George quietly called out directions and they arrived outside a non-descript block. George, Barbara and Podric got out and walked to the entrance which was code locked. Benedict tapped some keys and a release was activated. Entering the building, they approached another door. Also coded, Benedict punched some more numbers into a wall device unlocking it. They entered a lift and descended to a basement. The lift door opened directly into a self-contained sealed unit complete with its own domestic facilities. At a table on his cell phone sat the Director. Seconds later, the man Cy Zaentz called Lodestar appeared. That had been the deal. Caught unawares by Benedict making contact with them, the security services were suspicious. However, believing he was the link to accessing the knowledge they so desperately craved these secretive people accepted the computer man's terms providing the rendezvous was on their territory. Benedict having no issue with that, the arrangement was made.

"You are?"

The Director not being one for courtesy, addressed Barbara.

"I'm... with them."

"Er, yeah, sure you are, but why are you here?"

Barbara walked around the basement.

"I was with Mr Benedict that night several weeks ago when you were playing marine captains."

Barbara stopped and gave Lodestar a long look.

"I suspect you're a man who's used to playing a lot of roles."

She turned to Podric.

"And he's my son."

"Cosy. So what are you doin' here?"

The Director addressed the computer games champion.

"I'm the guy who'll take you to your dreams."

Unslinging his backpack, Podric didn't say 'or nightmares'. The two goons could make their own call on that soon enough. Under their cynical eyes, he took out his laptop.

"Huh. Why doesn't this surprise me? A kid."

The Director was dismissive.

"So, whadya got?"

"That Mr Agency Director you're about to find out."

Chapter 33

Bargain Basement and Celtic Times

"Yeah? Right now I'm underwhelmed."

The Director turned to George.

"If these two are part of the deal Benedict, it had better be some revelation."

The Director wasn't a happy man. Podric said.

"Oh, we're that alright."

Podric was preoccupied with activating his laptop. The Director said.

"And had to bring your mum."

"Something like that."

His laptop sorted, Podric sat back.

"We knew you'd worked on turning George. We've known all along."

Barbara hadn't. The agents tensed. Podric ignored them.

"If you'll pay close attention."

He turned to Lodestar.

"You'll want to be seated sir."

Podric waited for the man to sit down. The Director giving his colleague a nod, Lodestar found a stool. UAR being fully prepped with the two agent's details Podric activated Ultimate Alternative Reality.

The word normally used to describe the journey the Director and agent Lodestar experienced – a visitation that included the development of the V2 rocket, rocketry research with Wernher von Braun and Sergei Korolev, the development of Vostok and Soyuz space rockets, John F. Kennedy and the American political inspiration for adventure into space – NASA, Saturn V and the

Apollo program: Stanley Kubrick with a metal jacket full of *Dr. Strangelove* connotations – would be 'kaleidoscopic'. But that multifarious word couldn't do justice to the sensations the two men experienced. This is because Ultimate Alternative Reality is the greatest mind set invention ever realised.

The Director and Lodestar didn't just witness these people and the activities they were involved in – they *lived* with them. Working alongside an exhausted and ill-fed Jewish labour force the Director and Lodestar experienced the brutal behaviour of Nazi overseers at the Mittelwerk factory at Nordhausen. They *felt* the crack of a bullwhip on the prisoners backs living in the nearby Mittelbau-Dora concentration camp.

At Peenemünde and Baikonur, they experienced von Braun and Korolev's tension. They observed close up and personal their president's 'We choose to go to the moon' speech in 1962 at Rice University and were with von Braun again at Cape Canaveral that fateful day in July 1969. As for Stanley Kubrick Podric had placed the agents in *2001: A Space Odyssey* – HAL advising that 'whilst he continued to have great confidence in the mission, he couldn't allow them to jeopardise it'.

As has been explained, Ultimate Alternative Reality time and real time have no equivalent and monitoring them, Podric brought the two men out of their alternative reality state at the end of the sequence he'd programmed. Both were in shock. To say they sat stupefied in the basement was an understatement. The Director and agent Lodestar were shattered. Packing up his laptop, Podric glanced at them.

"Whilst you won't exactly understand what you're dealing with, perhaps gentlemen you'll at least now give me and my friends a little more respect."

The Director's look was baleful. Lodestar simply stared into space.

"This sample was just a beginning because to paraphrase President Kennedy 'we choose to go to the moon not because it's easy but because it's hard'."

Putting his laptop into his backpack, Podric turned to go.

"No doubt we'll meet again. Meanwhile, I hope you're both less underwhelmed now. Maybe you'll even have plenty to think about..?"

As his mother and George headed for the door, Podric looked back. Both security people remained where they were completely numbed by the experience they had just lived through.

* * *

Travelling back into Wales after the meeting and sitting in The Griffin, the pub in Felin Fach a few miles from Aber Village the mood was strangely melancholy. It was Podric who bought his mother and George Benedict drinks, and it was Podric who was in the brightest spirits. Sitting by the big open fire at the same table he'd sat with Archie on that fateful day when they'd discussed the remote programming of their invention – a precursor which led them into their adventures in The American Civil War – Podric was even drinking the same beer, a pint of Purple Moose. Another sat in front of George. His mother had a large Gin & Tonic.

"What do you think George? Interesting isn't it?"

"I don't know what to say."

Podric looked across the top of his diminishing pint.

"Hope it's not that disappointing."

Referring to the beer, Podric smiled.

"Go on. Try it." Benedict did so. He smiled wanly.

"You really know about what you said?"

Podric put down his glass and sat back in the kitchen chair.

"It stood to reason. They tracked you down. They compromised you. Between them and a pressured Secorni, they must have promised you all kinds of stuff to blow Archie away."

Podric rotated his beer glass.

"They didn't really know much about me or Ultimate Alternative Reality, but they smelt something was out there and were getting increasingly paranoid."

"But you know don't you."

Benedict looked at Podric who met his gaze.

"You told us you were a turncoat, but you weren't turned George, were you? You've been one of them all along."

Podric finished his drink.

"I've got some calls to make. I'll leave it with you to line up the next round."

* * *

"She's being sick everywhere. Terrible. Miles has been over. He's been a real help."

Although it was dark, Podric sat at an outside table in the Welsh pub garden listening to his friend Billy Johnson describe his pregnant girlfriend Carol Jensen's morning sickness. Podric had a pang of remorse. So preoccupied had he been with his latest adventure Ultimate Alternative Reality's creator had temporarily lost touch with his school friends and he felt it. How were Miles, Norris and Billy? Billy certainly had a lot on his plate. Podric sighed.

"I've got some stuff to sort Billy, but I'll be back soon."

"No problem Pod. You sound tired. All that gadding about."

"Yeah."

"Still on your moon trip?"

"Uhuh."

"Wish I was with you."

"I wish you were too."

"Plenty of adventures?"

Podric didn't say that he'd experienced more in *Moon Landing* than ever before.

"Some."

Billy chuckled.

"That's why I love you Podric."

There was a pause.

"You're still me best mate. You know that."

They rang off.

Re-entering the pub, Podric found his mother alone. A fresh pint of Purple Moose and some crisps were on the table. Benedict's glass was empty, but he was nowhere to be seen. Barbara was looking at the clip on her iPhone Podric had saved for her of Sean's last message to their son.

"Call of nature?"

Podric nodded at George's empty chair.

"He's gone out."

The way his mother said it was flat.

"Where?"

"'Don't know. 'Said he needed some air. Didn't you see him?"

Shaking his head Podric sat down and picked up his pint of beer.

"You're a bit remote mum."

Barbara put down her mobile phone. Podric sipped his pint.

"I thought you liked him."

"I thought I did. He's a lost soul Podric."

"He's been under a lot of pressure."

"You seem very relaxed about him in the circumstances."

Podric had some more Purple Moose.

"Ha. George doesn't faze me. I feel sorrier for Archie and... you."

Mother and son sat in companionable silence then Barbara said.

"Strength's important to me."

Podric flicked a beer mat. Barbara continued.

"Your father wasn't as deep a file as you are, but he had steel."

"Were you thinking of something deeper with George?"

For a few seconds Barbara looked into the distance.

"Perhaps. Maybe... Do you think we should go and look for him?"

Podric didn't immediately answer his mother.

"If I'm not mistaken, he'll right now be with his people."

"You mean we've been followed?"

"Pretty certain."

Podric munched a crisp.

"I think it's time things were brought to a head in this adventure."

"I'm sure they will be soon enough. You'll be leading us to an extra-terrestrial climax but there's something I'd like to do in your game before that."

Barbara sipped her G&T.

"The experience I'd like isn't in space."

Podric waited.

"I'd like to meet President Kennedy."

She had another sip of her drink.

"I know he's in your game because he inspired America's space program."

"What is it about people wanting to meet President Kennedy?"

"Two reasons. The first – Mr Kennedy brought a sense of style to politics – class if you like and I'd like to see that close up."

Barbara finished her drink.

"It may not be very important in the greater scheme of things, but it seems a dimension that's sadly lacking today."

"Don't you think behind the scenes he'll have been just as grubby as the rest."

"Probably, but he didn't seem to be."

Podric shrugged.

"Could just be a shrewd politician. And the second."

"The second is whatever he was or wasn't President Kennedy gave people a sense of hope. A genuine sense that there could be a better world."

"What about his reputation?"

"Oh, I know all that. I'm not saying everything he did was so good, but I've always thought there was something about him. Anyway, if I've got the chance to meet him in Ultimate Alternative Reality I can't believe that part of his character is going to be very important."

Podric had some more beer. He said.

"Since meeting him on this adventure, I've wondered whether his legacy and the whole Kennedy aura wasn't seriously stimulated because he was cut down in his prime. He can't ever grow old. He's frozen in youth."

"Uhuh. It's that sense of loss – that things could have gone in a better direction with him around than they did. Check out

YouTube."

Podric finished his drink.

"Where would you like to meet him?"

Picking up her phone, Barbara reactivated Sean's little piece talking to her son. Sent from his RAF Ops Room just before his last flight, Sean's Irish smile seemed to broaden as she looked at him.

"A couple of months before he died President Kennedy went to Ireland. I think I'd like to see him there."

Podric didn't press his mother as to the location's significance but just said.

"Where did he visit?"

"Oh, Dublin and his family came from County Wexford. It's the other side of the country from Kenmare Bay.."

"'Doesn't matter mum."

Podric looked at his mother steadily.

"You'll see him wherever you want."

Chapter 34
UAR Lunar Travels
and the Emerald Isle

Sitting beside Archie Light in Romulus the second lunar rover, Denise Mullins adjusted one of the on-board cameras. Several days out from their base at Alamo Ridge, they were the furthest anyone had travelled on the moon. Given their adventure had come about almost randomly – Miss Mullins as Podric still called her, wandered into the workshop at the only time Barney Sturridge wasn't there and Archie happened to be. Their conversation turned to the locations of the Apollo landing sites. Archie said.

"If you went exploring which one would you head for?"

Denise Mullins thought for a minute.

"How does your upward buoyancy fair when equalling the weight of the fluid your body displaces Dr Light?"

Archie laughed.

"From memory, it can't do otherwise. 15 was the first mission one of these was used. He tapped the rover.

"It is in our game anyway..."

Now bouncing across the Mare Vaporum heading towards the mountainous region known as Montes Archimedes, the journey had been remarkably uneventful. The rover pulling its neat trailer made excellent progress across the terrain at times reaching speeds of nearly fifty miles an hour.

"Goes pretty well."

"Not quite as smooth as my Faciella. I'll see if Sturridge can fine tune the suspension next time."

Whilst not secretive – planning for the trip had been almost casual. Denise had told Catherine Halliday that Archie was keen to go exploring but Catherine had been largely unresponsive. When Barney heard he laughed.

"What, drive a rover? Bit different to his Facel V's!"

Looking around at the lunar scape this was the type of UAR adventure Denise found incomparable.

"Only thing lacking is wind in your hair."

Denise laughed. Archie changed down.

*   *   *

Watching a black and white television screen of his visit to Ireland, President Kennedy stood in the parlour of the Dunganstown cottage his Irish forbears had relinquished when they set off for America to make a new life for themselves a hundred years previously. Knocking on the door Podric Moon entered and said.

"Good memories of your Irish trip?"

The president looked round.

"Hi Podric. Family. Origins. Beginnings... Leaving here the only way was up."

Kennedy paced around the little room.

"So, I'm back here now but it's after my demise."

"This adventure is building to a climax. My mother wanted to meet you."

"The power of mothers."

They watched a grey-haired woman cross the little compound. Kennedy said.

"My cousin Mrs Ryan."

"Gather she's formidable."

The president laughed.

"She can't see us. Correct?"

"Unless I program her into the state – no, she's not aware of your presence."

"Though some people have felt it."

Podric looked at President Kennedy, who continued.

"Always wondered about ghosts."

Restless, the president was like a caged animal in the tiny room.

"Not sure being one now suits me very well."

Kennedy appeared to take hold of himself.

"So why Ireland?"

He looked out of another window. A man and a woman stood chatting a little away from the cottage. The man wore an RAF uniform.

"That your mother?"

"And my dad. She's alive but he's like you."

"Dead you mean."

"And Irish."

"I see. I recall your father was killed in a flying accident."

Podric nodded. The president's expression saddened.

"I lost a brother and sister the same way."

"Your family's certainly had its fair share of tragedy."

"If you call it fair."

Kennedy looked down.

"Knowing what I know now I remain reluctant to suggest we're cursed but it's hard not to avoid that conclusion."

JFK turned to Podric.

"Mind if I see your mother outside?"

Podric shrugged. The president walked to the door.

"And your father. Guess he's programmed as you call it."

Podric nodded. Seconds later he watched the president go out and chat to his parents. With obvious humour the three strolled across the paddock. In spite of the meetings warmth Podric felt it was a sad scene.

*　*　*

"How much further do you think?"

Parked at the bottom of a steep incline Archie Light and Denise Mullins were studying an electronic map of the lunar surface on one of the on-board MacBooks. Punching in some data Archie said.

"This will take a bit of time. There's a route round that way I think."

He pointed to what looked like a less boulder-strewn area. Checking their seat belts, Archie engaged drive and they set off. Attempting to circumvent the Montes Archimedes range, Archie was quieter now as he concentrated on the tortuous challenge before them. Romulus seemed to be doing well edging its way along when all of a sudden a rockfall appeared out of nowhere pushing them downhill on a bed of shale. Wrestling with the wheel, Archie's driving skills were valiant but try as he might, he couldn't get the rover out of the slide. Gathering speed at an alarming rate, they quickly parted company with the trailer as the little buggy was swept along. Larger boulders appeared and seconds later the kart turned over. Denise Mullins saw the lip of a crater rushing towards them then they were falling into a black chasm and she lost consciousness.

*   *   *

Barney Sturridge and Stanley Kubrick were in the lunar workshop. The director had been helping Barney run tests on various pieces of equipment.

"What was the reading?"

Barney's voice came over the intercom. Sitting in the control room Kubrick replied.

"Stress 13.05, vibration 44.8."

"Still too high. Give me five."

Watching Sturridge make some adjustments to lunar rover Remus, Stanley Kubrick tweaked a remote camera. Possessing a powerful lens, it meant Barney viewing his work on a monitor could see some intricate electronics far more clearly than his naked eye was able to. Barney said.

"That's good. Pan left a bit."

Kubrick did so.

"Thanks Stanley."

Casually appreciating the film-making skills of one of the

greatest directors of all time, Barney continued his work. Suddenly a piercing noise came through on the workshop scrambler ...
--- ... / ... – ... . -- . ... The Mayday signal! The emergency automatic call from Romulus appeared in the form of pre-recorded squawk and automatically gave the grid reference of the vehicle's location. Rushing to the control panel Barney checked data.

"Go-. They're several hundred miles away."

"Are the on-board cameras working?"

As ever Stanley thought visually.

Punching keys to activate the remote links, screens came up but they were all blank.

"What the hell's happened to them?"

Kubrick looked out of the workshops panoramic window at the lunar scape.

"If its that serious, no point in trying to do anything from here. How good are you at getting in and out of UAR?"

Smart as he was, Kubrick had already worked out the criteria. Barney said.

"We've got to get hold of Podric."

*   *   *

"She just wanted to talk to him."

Sean Moon and his son were sitting in the Dunganstown cottage's rustic garden. Barbara and JFK walked in the distance talking animatedly.

"She looks happy enough. No doubt falling for his famous charm."

"Thought that was you."

Sean laughed.

"Well... We're both Irish!"

The deceased air force officer sat back.

"How's this adventure been? Guess you're working things up to a climax now."

"Every UAR experience has given participants different horizons but this one's new."

"Wonderful you've created alternative reality."

Father and son enjoyed a second's companionable silence.

"Wish you were back really though dad."

Sean sighed.

"Yuh. Well, that can't be but look how incredible this is. You've given me a life beyond the grave and that is something that isn't available to other people."

Barbara and JFK began to head back towards the cottage. Sean and Podric watched them for a moment then Podric said.

"This has been an interesting dimension. He inspired the whole space race thing."

"Yeah."

"But seeing him now..."

Podric fell silent. Sean stood up and walked round the table.

"Knowing you you'll have done some research. Jack wasn't scheduled to be the chosen one in his family. That honour was going to his big brother who was sadly killed like I was."

Sean put a hand on his son's shoulder.

"It was the best thing that ever happened. I don't mean Joe Juniors death or mine, but that Jack stepped into his shoes."

Sean nodded at the US president.

"Joe would have been a disaster."

"Why?"

"Too hot headed. He'd have put too many peoples noses out of joint whereas our Jack's self-effacing diffidence.."

Sean removed his hand and walked a few paces away.

"In a way Podric you're standing in my place now and I often think how wonderful that is."

Father and son were quiet then Sean continued.

"Sometimes Podric a person is just special. Others try and analyse it and good luck to them but invariably there isn't any accounting for it. The persons just got that something."

"Like you have dad."

Sean laughed.

"Ha. I'm just a tuppenny ha'penny fighter jock."

A UAR notification appeared at the top of Podric's eyes. Using his index finger as cursor, he spooled through the games menu. Sean continued.

"I think you've got a point about President Kennedy being all the greater in death. Certainly, the event itself did the enshrining."

"Dad I have to go! Something urgent's come up in the game."

Podric stood. Indecisive for a second he made up his mind.

"I can leave mum here with you for a while."

"Is everything alright?"

"It's Archie. He's gone missing on the moon."

Sean looked concerned. Podric continued.

"His lunar rover's disappeared."

Chapter 35

A Lunar Rescue and No Appendix

Back in the real world in Bwthyn Anghysbell, Podric clicked out of *JFK and His World* and immediately clicked into *Moon Landing*. In seconds he established what had happened – Archie and Denise Mullins were at the bottom of an unknown caldera near Archimedes Crater, their lunar rover a right-off. Podric put the game on pause and temporarily exited UAR.

Walking round the cottage, he checked on the state of his mother and business partner. Both insentient in Ultimate Alternative Reality his mother's expression was serene, Archie's tense. Perhaps experiences in UAR permeated a person's subconscious? He should analyse it someday – but what to do now? He could stop the games action and make everything alright in seconds. Knowing he had that option gave Podric a sense of security. Equally, one of the things about UAR was its potential to enhance people's sense of worth. This was particularly true where Barney was concerned. Catherine was also still in *Moon Landing* and Barney would right now be telling her about the disaster. Ever since their previous adventures in *Civil War*, Podric had concerns about not being inside a game when anything critical happened. Criticised for being a control freak – maybe in more ways than one it was decision time?

Taking a last look at his mother – he could let her stay happily in *JFK and His World* for a while, but the decider was George Benedict. This was a real-life issue and a situation Podric knew would require all his talents. The matter was further complicated by the fact that Podric, his mother and Archie as well as Archie's Irish Wolfhound, Dog were physically in Wales. Podric made his decision.

Reversing his mother's Land Rover to the front door he dragged a mattress off a spare bed and put it in the back of the Defender. Then he managed to pick up his mother and with several stops, carry her to the vehicle of her dreams. Podric knew that the next challenge was the big one. Archie was a solid 6ft 2ins weighing 190 pounds. How could Podric get his sentient business partner into the back of the Land Rover? It would be a story that passed into folk lore. Pulling the mattress off the bed complete with a somnolent Dr Light, Podric dragged the mattress and its passenger to the landing and down the stairs. Taking another breather, he made the rest of his bizarre journey in stages. The most difficult part was getting Archie into the Pride of Solihull's rear. Recalling there was an old door in the outhouse, Podric brought it round to the Land Rover and set it up as a ramp. Then dragging the mattress with its dead weight towards it, he got a tie under it and winched the door up inside the vehicle. His last task involved Dog. Also in a UAR state, the animal wasn't easy to shift. Using the door again, Podric got the tie round it and rolling Dog on top hauled the platform up to the Defender. He then swung Dog into the passenger seat.

His herculean efforts finally completed Podric made himself a cup of coffee and activated UAR for a break! Repositioning *Moon Landing* – Catherine was managing the Alamo Ridge base and Barney and Stanley Kubrick were heading off for the crater with the necessary equipment for a rescue operation. Podric reflected that it was a pity he hadn't had the kind of kit they had at their disposal. Sipping his coffee, he took out his phone.

*   *   *

Sitting up in bed minus her appendix, Cosima Light fiddled with her cell phone.

"I'm bored."

"That's a pity. Taking a bit of exercise, you've got to have at least a week of not doing much."

Sorting out clothes of her daughters Charlotte put some recently completed ironing in one of Cosima's chest of drawers. She picked up a photograph of Archie and herself, a gap-toothed Cosima between them.

"God, your first day at Farn Hill."

"Miserable bloody experience that was."

"What are your plans darling?"

Charlotte hung a blouse on a hanger.

"Will you stop doing that mother? It's getting on my nerves."

Charlotte put some T-shirts away.

"Well, what are they?"

Cosima sighed irritably.

"I don't know."

Charlotte turned and headed for the door.

"Your A levels are this year – presumably you'll want to go to uni."

"And read ancient zoology? Waste of time that'd be."

"Mock me if you want but giving yourself a goal makes sense, believe me."

She went out.

"A goal. Afrikaans anthropology or Siberian social sciences? No way."

Cosima got up. Wearing some trendy jimjams, she tied a kimono loosely round her waist and walked on to the landing. Strolling across the walkway linking the house to her father's tower, Cosima stared out at the afternoon. She loved the fact that he'd had the glass-sided connection constructed. Some thirty feet from the ground it gave one a space-like feel looking out at the garden and open countryside below. Tapping the security code into the tower's door mechanism, Cosima entered and pressed for the lift. Everyone in UAR being in the theatre below, she arrived at the top of the building to find the den empty. Hearing someone in the lab, Cosima crossed the room and put her head round the door. Kaliska glanced round.

"Up already. How are you feeling?"

"Bored." Kaliska smiled.

"You have to allow a little time to heal."

"Don't you start mama-san two."

The two women looked at each other. They had an intimacy but also now a separateness.

Kaliska's phone vibrated. Taking Podric's call she wasn't on for long. "Podric's heading back from Wales."

"Lovely. Riding to the rescue is he?"

Cosima put her hand on Kaliska's shoulder.

"What's up?"

"George has gone missing again."

"Becoming something of a habit isn't it? Don't tell me he's made off with the mad bird woman this time – or p'raps her feathered friend?"

Not finding this amusing Kaliska shrugged off Cosima's touch.

"He didn't say except that it was serious."

Cosima turned away. Kaliska said.

"Make sure security's kosher around the house. I'll check on them downstairs."

"You really think George is going to show up here? What's he going to do if he does?"

"That's not the point. If he appears he won't be alone."

Chapter 36
Reality? What's Reality? 1

Coming to at the bottom of the crater Archie Light didn't feel as though he was experiencing an accident in a computer game. He *knew* his lunar buggy had been swept over the lip of a crater. That was the reality of UAR! He was in total darkness.

Managing to sit up Archie's body ached, and one leg was badly twisted. His breathing laboured, Archie reached around his right thigh where several tools were clipped to his spacesuit. He tried to find his emergency torch, but it was missing. Looking down at the luminescent gauge on his wrist, he still had half an hour's oxygen. All of a sudden a pinprick of light flickered a dozen yards away. The small beam caught his visor, then reflected on to the torch owner's helmet.

"Archie?"

In his stupor, Light had completely forgotten his comms system!

"You okay?"

Denise Mullins laughed.

"Never felt better. You?"

"Can you shine that around? Let's see if we can see the rover."

Denise Mullins did as he asked. Slowly panning the torch, after seconds of nothingness the end of her little beam picked out a twisted pile of metal. It didn't make comforting viewing. For all Barney Sturridge's strengthening work, Romulus's frame was a mangled wreck. Archie said.

"Shine your beam vertically."

Denise did so. The tiny light ran out into infinity. They were in a black abyss with no geographical reference point. Denise said.

"What's our air supply like?"

"Twenty-five minutes. There should be an emergency supply on the rover."

Using Denise Mullins beam to guide him, Archie crawled over to the smashed buggy. Groping around the wreckage he couldn't find the additional oxygen supply tanks but did find one of the on-board torches which was much more powerful. Shining the beam more closely on the damaged vehicle he discovered that neither of its spare life support systems were in great shape.

"Archie. My air supply's suddenly dropping."

"Can you make it over here?"

Denise didn't reply. Archie shone his torch at her. Denise killed her beam. Getting up, she limped across to him. Archie immediately started work taking a feed from one of the spare life support systems. A couple of adaptors were broken but removing bits from one to the other, he prepped a linkage to Denise's. Archie said.

"This alternative reality alternate enough for you?"

Miss Mullins chuckled.

"Hmm... Guess the Mayday signal will have gone out."

"It's automatic."

While Archie worked on their air supply, Denise looked through other bits of wreckage. One of the MacBooks was completely destroyed. She couldn't find the other but discovered her iPad in a personal bag she'd carried on board.

"Might this help?"

Glancing round, Archie said.

"Give me a minute."

He twist locked an adaptor into one of the PLS systems then working round the back of Denise's, removed an outer covering.

"You get half a minute's supply when I disconnect."

"Could this be an adventure you get us out of?"

"Thought UAR did it for you."

"Just checking."

"Want me to try?"

"Could be an option in 30 seconds."

"I'll bear that in mind. Ready?"

*   *   *

"I dunno. All the data's in the old fella's computer lab or whatever it's called."

Sitting in an unmarked SUV parked in a side road near Wendbury High School Carol Jensen looking very pregnant was spilling the beans. School winding down for the year, she and Billy had gone by to drop off some books. Coming out of school they were approached by a member of the agency's surveillance team.

"Say, you wouldn't know if this is the right school where some kid's been developing a new computer game, would you?"

"What is it to you?"

Billy was guarded.

"I'm with people in that line. Could be interested."

The agent appeared relaxed.

"What for game development or information?"

Billy took Carol's arm. The agent said.

"Likely there's money in it."

Ignoring this, Billy and Carol continued along the street. Rounding a corner, Carol stopped.

"I left some of my sports kit in the locker room."

"Do you need it?"

"I need to wash it."

"I'll go back." Billy was considerate.

"No, I'll go. Also, I want to see if I can find Miss Mills. She needs team details for the last match this term."

"But you're not playing."

"I'm still captain, Billy."

Turning back to the school, Carol said.

"Head for the café. I'll have a latte."

Back at the school gates, Carol spied the man across the road in a side street. He was talking to some people in a parked SUV. Minutes later she was singing like a bird.

"You're not a computer games player yourself then?"

"Can't stand 'em."

The Director and agent Lodestar maintained neutral expressions.

"Well guess that's it information wise. Thank you Miss.."

"Carol."

"Thank you Carol. Can we drop you anywhere?"

"No. Thanks. Just..."

Carol looked at the men.

"Oh, sure. Kobal."

The agent who had met Carol by the school gates reached for his wallet.

*   *   *

Hands groped through sawdust that lined the bottom of Ivy Bickerstaff's bird cage. Whatever was being searched for, wasn't found.

"You'll be looking for this."

Standing in Mrs B's living room, George Benedict turned to face Ivy who held the little grey rock broach. Eamon sat on his mistresses' shoulder. Using his powerful beak, the bird snatched it from her.

"My boy found it. You'll remember nothin' much escapes his pryin' eye."

Eamon fluttered off and landed on the back of Ivy's old sofa.

"Hide it did yer? Must be an important bit of rock."

George looked concerned.

"Cuppa tea George? And you be quiet Eamon."

*   *   *

Sitting in a café half a mile from school, Billy was reading a paper. His coffee finished Carol's latte stood untouched. Carol arrived flushed. Billy put down his paper.

"It'll be cold now."

Drinking it quickly, Carol said.

"No worries."

Billy eyed his girlfriend.

"All okay with the teams?"

"Oh, er, yeah."

Carol finished her cold coffee.

"Your kit was cleaner than you thought then."

Having no kit bag with her, the mood suddenly changed.

"Or maybe the guys in the SUV offered a cleaning service?"

"Bastard!"

"Not me Carol."

Billy got off his stool. Carol said.

"Snoop then."

Billy picked up his bag.

"I knew you were lying."

Carol put two fifty-pound notes on the counter. Billy glanced at them.

"What did you tell them?"

"None of your business."

He looked at her steadily.

"I think you know that it is."

There was real tension now. Carol turned away.

"Bloody computer world – it pisses me off."

"Whatever has Podric's computer stuff got to do with you..?"

"It's not me. It's you!"

Carol was vehement. Her attitude left Billy gobsmacked.

"Huh?"

"You're more interested in what Podric does than me."

"You must be nuts. What's whatever Podric does got to do with us?"

"You just want to do stuff with him, go off on his games adventures."

Billy was dumbfounded by her attitude, but he was also angry.

"What did you tell those guys Carol?"

Realising her boyfriend was cross with her Carol looked surly. Billy continued.

"You didn't tell them about what Podric's developed, did you?"

Carol didn't reply.

"My God."

Billy was furious.

"You've betrayed my best friend."

Billy was astounded at Carol's betrayal.

"For a hundred quid."

His anger boiled over.

"You stupid fu-. You!"

Billy headed for the door.

"Billy. Billy!"

The predominant force in their relationship, for the first time ever, Carol was alarmed.

"Billy!"

He turned back and sweeping the money off the counter pushed it into her lap.

"Enjoy your thirty pieces Carol. I hope it buys you something good."

"We need that money for the baby." Carol was defiant.

"Don't give me that. You've always known I would earn for that."

"Past tense. So you're walking out on me now."

"After what you've done, sure I'm walking out on you."

Billy found it difficult to hold back his fury.

"Oh, I'll provide for our baby – I said I would, and I will. But as for you – I don't want to see you again – ever."

"That's stupid."

"Is it? Is it stupid to betray a friend and lie? I don't want to live my life with a woman like that."

"You don't mean it."

"Don't I? Try me."

And with that we walked out of the café.

* * *

"So why d'you come sneakin' in here like some guilty schoolboy?"

George Benedict and Ivy Bickerstaff were having tea on Ivy's veranda. Watching Eamon fly around, Benedict appeared agitated. Ivy continued.

"And why'dyou bugger off like that?"

Ivy wasn't aggressive. Quite apart from being the village eccentric, she was nobody's fool.

"It's a bit of a story."

"Not in a hurry."

"Will he land soon?"

"When he's ready, or I tell him."

Ivy poured George another cup of Earl Grey from her old fine bone china teapot. Although it had seen better days, its image was unusual. Logs on fire at its base, the lid was a head and shoulders of the devil complete with horns and fork.

"I'm in a lot of trouble, Ivy."

"Good trouble or bad trouble?"

"Is trouble ever good?"

Ivy sat back and rolled her tongue round her lone tooth.

"There's trouble that yer deserve and trouble that yer don't. Which is yours George?"

George didn't reply. Not having touched his second cup of tea, he watched transfixed as Eamon swooped and climbed. Mesmerised by the bird, the vista of fields Ivy's tumbledown bungalow fronted on to had been a rural idyll for him.

"This is the only place I've been at peace for a long time."

A whistle from Ivy brought Eamon into land on the picket fence in front of them. "Give it to him, Eamon."

Eamon cocked his head and didn't seemed too inclined.

"Go up to 'im George. He always liked you. Take some of these."

Fishing into an old canvas bag that hung from one of the arms of her chair, Ivy took out some seeds and nuts which she gave to Benedict. The bird's food in George's palm, Eamon released the little moonrock broach re-gurging it neatly into George's hand. Then angling his neck, his powerful hooked beak collected some dry fruits from the man's fingers.

"That dun't answer the question but you've got what you came for."

Benedict turned over the odd little badge. Ivy said.

"Drink yer tea now and you can be on your way.."

"Don't you want to know what I did?"

Eamon flapped up beside his mistress and took some more food from her.

"Reckon it's bad trouble George."

Benedict looked lost. Ivy continued.

"Which means the only chance you've got is to somehow make it good. Otherwise it's the teapot for you."

Chapter 37
Reality? What's Reality? 2

Sitting at the bottom of the moon crater, Archie Light had discovered that they'd somehow ended up beneath an overhang which deprived them of any view above. Once he'd secured Denise Mullin's air supply and checked his body over more thoroughly, Archie was able to hobble around. Emerging from under the protruded lava he looked up at the stars. The heavens always wondrous to him, this wasn't a time for reflection. Although anyone coming in search of them would be guided by Lunar Station's GPS system, Archie figured it wouldn't do any harm to make them as visible as possible. Returning to Denise and the broken Romulus, Archie first ran out a cable with the buggy's intermittently flashing beacon. Then he collected some items from the wrecked rover (emergency rations and several water bottles) and created a camp. Finally, he supported the schoolteacher to the new location and made her as comfortable as he could.

Denise Mullins wasn't in great shape. Although Archie had managed to stabilise her air supply, she was using much more oxygen than normal and his own was getting low. Archie knew that if help didn't arrive shortly he'd have to abort the UAR adventure. This left him with an acute sense of disappointment. For the first time in this adventure Archie understood how NASA must have felt looking down the barrel of such potential failure. Whether one believed the Apollo program made it to the moon or one didn't – the phrase generally attributed to Gene Krantz, Apollo Flight Director and lead on the Apollo 13 mission that 'failure was not an option' resonated with Archie. There was something about surviving a challenge within the UAR experience that was all important to him. Sitting down on a rock Archie decided he would give it another fifteen minutes by which time things would be getting very near the edge safety wise. Having done all he could, Archie realised life had always been like that for him. It was risk that drove him – his spur...

* * *

"You've brought him all the way back like that? And Dog. You must be crazy!"

"And mum. Dropped her at home. She was easier though."

It was getting dark and Podric having driven from Wales, parked his mother's Land Rover in the Light's drive.

Cosima, Charlotte and Kaliska stood looking down at Archie's inert form.

"And he was in UAR at the cottage."

Podric answered Charlotte with a nod.

"How the hell did you manage it? Dad's not exactly a light-weight. I'm tempted to prod him – Lord Fauntelroy all tucked up."

Cosima was caustic. 'Hardly little' was her mother's retort.

"Is it really that important not to interrupt them?"

As usual Kaliska was more interested in Ultimate Alternative Reality's process. Podric folded up a blanket he'd covered his mother with.

"Stopping off at the motorway service station and checking on them, Mum's wasn't critical, but it was important she was left undisturbed in UAR. Archie and Miss Mullins are at the height of their adventure. As for Dog..."

Everyone smiled. Kaliska said.

"We haven't discovered the Apollo sites yet."

Kaliska appeared preoccupied.

"No, we haven't but who said anything about *Moon Landing* being finished? There's things we need to do outside the game just now."

Using a couple of broom handles and a duvet cover they rigged up a make-shift stretcher and prepared to move the insentient games creator.

"Probably best if we put him in one of those bunks in the tower."

"You make it sound as though your father's being confined darling."

"Ha. Throw away the key shall we? What about old Baskerville here? Do we take him too?"

Depositing Archie and Dog in the small sleeping quarters that were situated opposite the games creators mini computer museum, they left man and man's best friend out to the world.

"Still don't know how you got them into the Land Rover. Superhuman are you Podric?"

Poking Podric in the ribs, Cosima returned to the house with her mother. Kaliska and Podric climbed the back stairwell into the lab.

"So – things to do in the real world..."

Glancing at a couple of VDU screens, Podric made an adjustment. Kaliska continued.

"Any news on George Benedict?"

Turning to her Podric smiled.

"You'll know when I know."

Podric twiddled with his mother's car keys. Kaliska said.

"Oh, by the way a friend of yours came by.."

"Which one?"

"Billy is it?"

"I have a friend called Billy."

"He seemed concerned. Said it was important and he had to see you."

That was unusual for Billy.

"Did he say what it was about?"

Kaliska shook her head. Podric stood up.

"You okay here?"

"Well..."

He smiled.

"Don't worry. You'll be back in for the finish."

Podric placed the pc he'd been adjusting on standby and continued.

"If you need somewhere to sleep they've plenty of spare beds over at 5 Star Lightville."

"I quite like it here. Anyway, there's a spare bunk downstairs."

They laughed.

"Good luck with that then."

Outside in the Land Rover Podric checked his phone. Sure enough, there were several messages from Billy.

*   *   *

At the Archimedes Range on the moon a fellow school mate and a famous film director peered over the lip of the unmarked crater. Romulus's beacon flashed intermittently far below.

"Okay, we have a plan Houston."

The incorrigible Barney turned away. Stanley Kubrick continued to stare into the crater and said.

"They're not responding."

Barney grunted. Carla Logan arrived driving Remus. Barney directed her to position the rover transversely. Placing rocks round its wheels he then moved Calypso up to the crater's edge. Paying out cable Carla clipped Calypso and Remus together. Barney said.

"They said you were efficient."

Concentrating, Carla took her time replying.

"You ain't seen nothing yet."

"Jazz Singer, 1927."

Barney turned to Kubrick.

"And Stanley don't get me into another fine mess."

Unable to see facial expressions through their reflecting visors, the three astronauts nodded to each other. Kubrick said.

"Your film studies are really coming on."

Clipping on a harness Barney turned to Kubrick.

"What were you going to make after *Eyes Wide Shut?*"

As Barney edged nearer the craters edge, Carla eased the cable winch as Kubrick checked its pay-out. Kubrick said.

"I was planning a Pinocchio motion picture."

Disappearing over the side, Barney laughed.

"A family film of lies and deceit. Bit of a problem growing a nose inside this lot."

* * *

Back home with his mother laid out on her bed, Podric sat in the kitchen with his friend Billy.

"Thought I'd better come and tell you."

"Thanks Billy."

Getting up from the table, Podric took a couple of beers from a pack on the counter. Billy said.

"You don't seem so angry with Carol."

"Carol's desperate Bill. She'll know she's done wrong and if you want my advice, you've now got your trade off."

Billy said. "That's a bit cynical Pod."

Podric shrugged and taking a piece of paper from his jeans pocket, handed it to his friend. Opening it, Billy stared at the information.

"I said no Podric."

Billy's expression hardened. Podric was bland.

"That's tough 'cos it's done."

"But I can't ever pay this back to you."

"No you can't nor will you be. It's something called a consultancy fee."

Billy looked at Podric suspiciously. Podric walked round the kitchen.

"Look Billy, I've made some dough with Lord Archibald and I'm okay. More to the point, I happened to have created something that's better than anything else on earth, so I don't need to spend it on much. UAR beats fast cars and beautiful women."

"You'd better not say that Pod."

Podric laughed.

"Yeah, okay I've got a beautiful girlfriend, but it's an exotic lifestyle all its own."

He swigged some beer.

"So I've had to figure – how's my life going to pan out? What else would I ever need or want?"

"Kids? A family?"

"Exactly! And you're ahead of me on that. Okay, maybe you wouldn't have quite planned it like this, but it's happened, and you've stepped up to the plate. But not only are you going to do that you're going to stay on at Wendbury, get whatever you get in 18 months time and if that means university, marketing men at MoonLight need plenty of qualifications."

Billy was near to tears.

"Come on Bill – we're talking tomorrow here. We're talking about the future!"

Parting forty minutes later, Billy said.

"And those guys she told.."

"Oh, they'll be making their appearance. Now with your info, I've got a pretty good idea where and how."

Chapter 38
The Beginning of the End Game

"Come in George. I've only just got back."

Sitting in their Romany caravan parked in the Light's orchard Carla Logan was towel drying her hair. George Benedict appeared. He was tense and a little dishevelled.

"You look as though you could do with a drink."

Carla reached into a cupboard and took out a bottle and two little glasses.

"Red wine or rum?"

Opening a bottle of tequila, Carla poured a glass and handed it to Benedict.

"Reckon you'd better have this."

George took it and knocked it back. Carla ran a comb through her hair.

"Bottle's there."

Helping himself, George slumped into a chair. Carla said.

"Been busy, have you?"

"What do you mean?"

She sat down and poured herself a drink.

"It's all out now George."

George didn't respond. Carla continued.

"Compromised to get hold of the one thing they want – an ultimate alternative reality that does what it says on the tin."

She sipped her drink then continued.

"As far as the people you got into bed with are concerned – of more importance to them is its life revealing potential."

George gulped down his second tequila and muttered.

"Ultimate Alternative Reality.."

Carla said.

"Its concepts been gnawing away at you, has it – though I've wondered if what really troubles you is your ex-Secorni partner?"

Benedict snorted. Carla continued.

"What was it – jealousy?"

"Of him? Tcha."

"Rumour had it you had the hots for his wife."

Carla's course risked foundering on unchartered rocks.

"The way he treated her.."

"They seem pretty united now. Apparently they found each other again through UAR. More conventionally, the sales of MoonLight's games have gone into orbit."

George drank.

"It won't be thanks to him."

He refilled his glass and said.

"He's good at using people. I'll give him that."

"But you betrayed him and it's not strictly true, is it? Him not being a great games writer..." Benedict's face grew darker.

"Digging through files at the office, I found some interesting anomalies."

Carla stood up and hung her towel over a wooden drying rail.

"Like the fact you sabotaged some of Archie's codex destroying elements of the games you and he were creating. Was that so you could be seen riding to the rescue when they didn't work?"

Benedict was out of his seat and looked threatening. Fearless, Carla was face to face with the man.

"Don't even think about it, George. Don't-even-think-about-it."

Benedict backed off. Carla poured herself some tequila.

"The company knew more about you than you thought."

She sipped the rum. They were both drinking quickly.

"As to your version of *Moon Landing* – when dealing with the Feds Cy was suspicious they were in possession of inaccurate data which had to have been deliberately planted. He wanted to face them down, but the pressure was so great even Secorni didn't have the bottle. Big brother and all.."

"They think they're protecting us."

"Yeah... Doesn't answer the question though, does it? Their cover up and your betrayal."

Carla didn't yet know he was actually one of them – an undercover operative. Benedict drank some more and said.

"What do you think I should do?"

Carla put the stopper on the tequila bottle.

"What do I think you should do..?"

She looked at him for several seconds.

"If you want to earn any self-respect there's one thing you guys have in common. How does that English saying go – play up play up and play the game. I'd find Podric and fast."

"You think he's my best bet."

"I think he's your only bet."

*   *   *

Moon Landing in play – a rocket is prepped on the pan at Cape Canaveral. Viewed through a monitor – in the top right corner of the screen seconds and milliseconds of a countdown rapidly advance.

Lift Off!

The rocket begins to climb into the sky. Its trajectory pre-programmed, it arcs away from the earth's surface.

Another player in action. Docking 60 miles above the lunar surface, a CSM is manipulated into position releasing its Lunar Module for an attempt to land on the moon. The manoeuvre tenuous, the LM finally unlocks but seconds later, its descent faulty, it spins away from the moon's surface.

Points are lost.

A player tries to guide a rover across lunar terrain. Out of control, the vehicle hits a boulder. Upending itself, only sheer luck lands it back on all four wheels. Not that it makes much difference. Seconds later it vanishes.

So does AP18. The voice of Houston tracking the rocket loses contact and it disappears.

The game is terminated.

Screens to black.

Rebooted – another challenge begins, and play becomes more frenetic. A thousand miles above the moon's surface, an advanced SLS rocket docks at a Lunar Gateway. Its LM disengages and begins to descend. Closing on the selenic surface, its mountain ranges and craters are prominent. Approaching an area known as Theophilus 'Apollo 11' flashes up on the VDU screen and whatever was there is no more. Moving on to Copernicus, 'Apollo 12' is supered up and the same thing happens. The player zeros in on Ptolemaeus. 'Apollo 14' then Archimedes and 'Apollo 15' Mare Nectaris and 16, Descartes Highlands. All are reached before finally arriving at Posidonius and 'Apollo 17'. Any traces of landings are expunged. The player has beaten the clock and wins!

* * *

Sitting in his mother's garden studio, Podric removed George Benedict and himself from *Moon Landing.*

"God, I felt, I felt-."

"As though you were on it. Yup, that's UAR George. It's so real you may as well have been."

"But the Apollo sites – they never made it."

"We were playing a game George."

"That's the one thing I don't get about Ultimate Alternative Reality – playing a game and living inside one."

Podric looked at Benedict and smiled.

"They're two distinct elements. When in the UAR state one is always in a games' existence. If one wants to play it as game, it's a Menu option. Playing the game in the state, you get all the benefits of UAR's reality which is why its Ultimate."

"As simple as that?"

"As simple as that. It's called 'Game Activation' though I don't often use it."

"Why not?"

"I told you. Once upon a time I played so many games I got sick of them which is why I wanted something different."

Podric got up from the battered wicker chair he'd been sitting in.

"What UAR gives me is meeting John Kennedy, Abraham Lincoln and Napoleon Bonaparte. Getting under their skin so to speak. Then I like to see how they are in situations in their time – live a life alongside them."

"So the game itself is incidental."

Benedict picked up a mug of coffee. Podric said.

"That'll be cold."

Taking his own mug and collecting Benedict's, Podric hesitated at the shed door.

"If it is ancillary to a gamer it's only because UAR offers so much more. Having said that the motely crew that have been UAR programmed are pretty n00b (computer speak for newbie).

Will that do for your masters?"

He headed for the house.

"Podric, I-."

"Mr Benedictus. Sputinski 5 to mission control – this is Amy Arcana. Come in please."

It being the morning after Podric's return from Wales everyone was back from the Lunar Station. Wearing a spacesuit, Amy roared into the garden.

"Benedict man – are you earthling or moonite?"

Contemplating this unusual question George Benedict wasn't quite sure but he now made a decision that by his own determination would be irrevocable.

"I'm going to be from a planet you've never heard of."

"Negative. You come from Star XVII – the Upright Star. You have good health, hope and inspiration. With my middle name I'm the Major in tarot."

Chapter 39
Ill Lit by Moonlight

Sitting in their basement hideaway in the US section of the UK airbase where they had undergone Podric's Ultimate Alternative Reality experience the Director and agent Lodestar stared at screens in a little control room. They were advised that their National Security's computer system had been hacked and that higher powers were withdrawing them from their operational assignment.

"The firewalls... It's like – that cannot be!"

"What the-?! How..?"

No replies – just instructions. Their link shut down, the Director turned to his colleague.

"If you're thinking what I'm thinking."

Lodestar didn't respond. The Director continued.

"Have to be preemptive."

Lodestar nodded.

"Let's bring it on."

*   *   *

The state-of-the-art Italian coffee maker installed in the groundsmen's shed aka GCR had been paid for from Podric's computer games earnings. Podric hadn't advertised the fact, but its arrival was a powerful new allure. It being the day before the end of the school year Catherine had completed her final term in the Lower VIth and it was a time to relax. She'd partly come into school because back from her lunar adventure she wanted to revisit her academic studies. Unlike most of her fellow students, Catherine was already acquiring work for her next years' courses! In anyone else she'd have been thought of as a swat, but Catherine somehow managed to avoid this sobriquet, casually dismissing her scholarly keenness as a way of passing some time in the summer holidays. Most of her friends didn't believe it, but that didn't bother her.

The luxury of having that first macchiato was however frustrated as coming out of the school library Catherine had met a distracted Carol looking very pregnant wandering around in a distraught state. Going to the common room to talk, Catherine's coffee had cooled as she listened to a distressed Carol.

"I know I shouldn't have done it, but..."

Her eyes red from crying, Carol sniffed into a tissue.

"It's your boyfriend's computer games – that's all Bill ever wants to do – have those games adventures."

Drinking her near cold coffee, Catherine said.

"Carol, if you remember, Billy hasn't been in any of Podric's recent adventures because of being with you."

Carol wiped her eyes. Catherine continued.

"What you did wasn't good – like trying to get back at Billy for some reason."

"'Said he never wanted to see me again."

Deciding on a refill, Catherine got up. Neither girl spoke as she prepped the machine. Then Catherine said.

"Billy's a good guy Carol and I'm sure things can come right."

The coffee machine began making delicious sounding noises. Carol wasn't mollified.

"You all want him to stay on at school, but he can't if he's going to earn money for us."

"Well only you can decide whether you put that in jeopardy."

"Thanks for the support!"

Carol snapped with aggression, but Catherine remained cool.

"I suggest first you'll need to get your relationship back on track."

Carol said.

"What does Podric think?"

"What you've just said – that Billy should stay on and take his

A levels."

"I don't mean that."

"Oh... I don't know Carol. Boys don't always get stuff."

Catherine was short. Carol said.

"What do you think I should I do then?"

"Right now? Nothing. I think you should wait a little and let the dust settle."

"Easier said than done." Catherine produced two new coffees.

"Leave it with me. I'll see what I can do."

* * *

It was late evening when the unmarked convoy moved out of the military base. The vehicles weren't service vehicles but specially adapted long wheelbase SUVs. It was a several hour trip to their destination and moving through the English countryside they travelled at a good pace.

By the time the convoy arrived at Drinkwell it was the middle of the night. Militarily organised, they came to a halt in a field on the outskirts of the village not far from Mr Godiver's store. Disembarking, the passengers were dressed in quasi combat gear. Fanning out through woods they moved stealthily towards the Lighthouse.

Archie's property backing on to a stream, the cadre's main concentration arrived at the top of the drive. Night vision glasses were donned, and small arms made ready, but the team would never need their sophisticated visual equipment as halfway down the drive floodlights came on and the whole property lit up like a Christmas tree. Standing eighty feet from the house the figures stood frozen. Music blared out from speakers - The Beatles 'All You Need is Love' and Archie's electric garage doors activated. His Facel Vega's had been removed replaced by tables, chairs and a projector screen on which were images of the Director and agent Lodestar. The music mixed through to Archie's voice.

"Wonderful sentiments - seats are in front of you gentlemen."

Their masked faces twitching, the uninvited guests looked at each other. Archie's voice continued.

"The Director and his colleague agent Lodestar are invited to the tower. The rest of you help yourselves to refreshments."

For all their professionalism the perpetrators completely wrong footed, were hesitant. Signs and monosyllabic instructions were exchanged. Most of the unit entered the garage while the two men whose presence was requested approached the Lighthouse. Admitted, the garage doors were lowered, and the unit was securely housed.

Chapter 40
Revelations

The mood in Archie's den as the Director and agent Lodestar were brought in was one of subdued excitement. Introduced by Barbara Moon who Podric wanted to have present, the only others in the room were her son, Archie Light and George Benedict. Archie directed the men to two additional chairs that he'd procured.

"Would you gentlemen care for a drink? Your colleagues have coffee available, but we have something stronger if you prefer."

"Coffee will be fine."

The Director was neutral – indeed everyone appeared to be. With emotions running high, perhaps it wasn't surprising communication was bland. It didn't have to be said that the attempted burglary thwarted, the US agents were pretty certain their security systems had been hacked by those in this room.

"So you did the impossible."

The Director again. Podric gave the two men their coffees.

"Not difficult if you can work out the codes."

George Benedict tapped his fingertips. Looking at him the Director said.

"Your decision to renege?"

It was barely a question. Benedict said.

"Pointless debating lies."

The Director snorted.

"That's allegiance for you. As a soft operative, you were happy enough to take the assignment. Getting your own back, you said. Deserved his comeuppance for all those years claiming the glory you said."

Podric asked.

"Soft operative..?"

It was Archie who replied.

"Sub rosa agent; one who has other employ."

Looking at the games' creator, the Director cleared his throat.

"You're well informed."

"Amazing what you learn writing computer games."

Archie sipped a scotch and continued.

"From our point of view, we're only interested in you because of your many cover ups over the years. Whatever your deal with George only affects us because of personal friendship and betrayal. As for your attempted break-in to steal our UAR drives-."

"UAR?" The Director wasn't napping. Podric said.

"Ultimate Alternative Reality – the state I took you into."

"Takes computer codex to a new level, one you're unlikely to understand." Archie's confidence irritated the Director who wasn't having it.

"You expect me to believe that? With all the systems technicians available to me – one tired old second rate computer games writer and a kid?!"

Archie was about to remonstrate but Podric put up his hand.

*   *   *

The Platform Gateway positioned 1000 miles above the lunar surface – *Moon Landing* had planned for a multi-faceted docking point. The station was able to not only manage localised descents to the moon but was positioned to dispatch spacecraft into deep space from earth orbit – probing missions to Mars and beyond. Sitting in an informal de-briefing area, Podric Moon and Archie Light sat opposite The Director and agent Lodestar.

"So, it was a cover up."

Archie eyed the two US National Security agents.

"No. Yes. NASA had issues.."

"Which were?"

For the first time since Podric had any dealings with The

Director, the man looked uncomfortable.

"Things weren't working right."

"You're damned right they weren't!"

Archie exploded. The Director spoke flatly.

"There'd been failure after failure. The pressure was on to deliver."

"They believe they got there."

Lodestar cut across the conversation. Podric asked.

"What do you mean?"

"NASA thinks it landed on the moon."

Lodestar was harder than the Director.

"Manned crew, six times."

Podric stared at the agent.

"Wait a minute..."

He turned to look Lodestar full in the face.

"The way you're talking – The National Aeronautics and Space Administration thinks its Apollo missions landed on the moon, but your inference is that you know better."

"You learn quick."

Lodestar appeared indifferent. Incredulous, Podric stood up.

"The arrogance of you people."

He walked a little away.

"You mean to tell me that you faked data even to your own aeronautics agency?"

"Like I said, you're gettin' it."

Running a hand through his hair, Podric laughed at Lodestar's contemptuousness.

"And you did this so America wouldn't lose face."

"No holding you back now."

Lodestar sat resting his western boots on the spine of a chair.

"'Truth is – what is the truth? Only someone's perception of something."

Wearing a Stetson, he tilted it forward.

"Hohoho... Getting a bit Kafkaesque aren't we? Analysis of being, perception and reality.."

Getting up Archie tipped the hat right over Lodestar's face.

"Anyway, what if your fudges were wrong? What if they did walk on the surface?"

Straightening his hat Lodestar said.

"I'm tellin' yer – it was fixed. Ain't from the lone star state for nuthin.'"

Lodestar laughed. Archie said.

"Like you fix everything else, huh? Could be that Texas has a lot to answer for."

"Meanin'?" Lodestar sneered.

"Meaning you creature of darkness – that as we're talking states, we could leave you in this one – our state. We could leave you in it for as long as we want."

Podric added. "Though eternity might be a bit soon."

"What do you mean?"

No cynicism from the Director now; he was concerned.

"You know you're in our alternate state. You know what you can see, feel and experience. You might think this is a fantastic adventure but equally you might find the out of body experience is one you don't want to stay in forever."

"You could leave us like this?"

"Certainly. Your bodies are back in the Lighthouse and I'm sure we could find an appropriate resting place for them."

The Director was fascinated.

"Can your alternate reality really discover things?"

"It did a minute ago."

The intelligence operative and UAR's youthful inventor took each other's measure.

"Maybe I underestimated you?"

He looked from Podric to Archie who said.

"Surely not. Remember I'm just a tired old second rate games writer!"

Podric added.

"And I'm just a kid!"

The scene paused. The four people looked out at the heavens. The moon beside their space station and the Earth nearby, other stars were scattered across the galaxy. Podric said.

"Time for you to meet some of your forbears."

Podric prepped his wrist and checked out UAR's menu at the top of his eyes. Able to see what Podric was doing from the menu in his own eyes the Director was transfixed. He murmured.

"Like?"

Archie smiled cynically.

"J. Edgar and James Jesus suit you – along with the president who met his bloody end in your colleagues state and his good ole' boy Texan successor."

"Quite a party then."

Lodestar was his truculent self. Looking into Lodestar's face, Archie said.

"Remember pal, just say the word and that option to leave you up here forever is wide open."

Chapter 41

More Revelations and a Passing

The fob activated Archie's garage doors and electronically raised them. The agents released George Benedict flashed an ID card at the leading operative.

"You can return to base."

The man briefly eyed George who continued.

"I'll wait for the Director."

Minutes later the drive was deserted. Barbara Moon and George Benedict walked along a path to the orchard where three Facel Vega's had been hidden as well as Barbara's Defender. The feeling was melancholy.

"So you were part of it all along."

Benedict didn't reply. Barbara said.

"You're some actor George."

"Like a drink?"

Barbara looked across at the gypsy caravan parked at the far end of the orchard. Its doors were open, and the interior soft yellow light bathing it was romantic.

"No, I don't think so."

Taking out her Land Rover keys Barbara moved towards her vehicle.

"You'll be heading back to America soon."

Barbara unlocked the Defender. George said.

"I've decided against that."

"You work for them.."

They looked at each other.

"There was way more to it Barbara."

"I'm sure there was."

Barbara opened the driver's door.

"At least you tipped us off."

She took her phone out of her shoulder bag.

"About tonight, I mean."

"Your son was the first to work things out."

"He usually is."

She got into her Land Rover and put the key in the ignition. Benedict looked up at the night sky which was clear.

"Podric and I talked about it. He wanted to take them into UAR again – give them a final bit of education."

"And you?"

Closing the drivers' door, Barbara slid the window open.

"It's over for me Barbara – in this world or any other.."

"Bit melodramatic."

George smiled.

"You've been very kind and I'm grateful."

Barbara was going to say that he had a funny way of showing it but refrained. Benedict leant forward and kissed her cheek.

"You and your children are amazing."

Turning on his heel George walked back up the path towards the Lighthouse. For a few moments Barbara watched him go then starting the Defender, she began negotiating her way along the orchard track that led to a five-bar gate and the road beyond.

* * *

"Who are these guys?"

J. Edgar Hoover was his usual aggressive self.

"They're part of your Truth Making Free, Defending Our Nation, Securing the Future with Fidelity, Bravery and Integrity crowd Mr Hoover."

Podric smiled.

"That's some trip you're on kid."

"Guess not if he's into mottos."

James Angleton was his usual considered self.

"Covers most of the security services."

Standing on the sixth floor of the Dallas Book Depository beside Podric and Archie, The Director and agent Lodestar looked across the grubby floor at the late FBI and CIA directors and the late President of the United States, John F. Kennedy (Hoover and Angleton had been the heads of their respective security organisations during JFK's presidency).

"What are they doing here?"

Hoover was persistent, enquiring about the Director (a title he himself was known by) and agent Lodestar. Podric said.

"Learning from those who went before."

Hoover snorted and turned away.

"Haven't we seen enough of this?"

Hoover glanced round the shabby 6th floor with its grisly memories.

"It's a museum now."

Podric moved his right index finger over his left wrist and activated UAR. The locale transformed the seedy store area into a brightly lit 21st century museum commemorating 22nd November 1963. It featured a display of memorabilia and large black and white mounted pictures. Activating UAR again, Podric switched back to the rundown depository with its shoddy half completed repairs. Standing on the spot Lee Harvey Oswald had aimed his Mannlicher-Carcano rifle at him JFK was genuinely admiring.

"That's one heck of an invention, Podric."

Leaning against the window frame the president looked down on Elm Street below. Flashing through his mind was the crawling motorcade – thousands of people waving, the brightness of the day. If his death was in part due to the slowness of the vehicle he travelled in Kennedy realized how close the Lincoln had been to accelerating away towards Stemmons Freeway – the route it would carry his dying body to Parkland Memorial Hospital where he would be pronounced dead. The president turned back to the leaders of two of his country's security bureaus.

"Well, here we are. I see Rowley's kept a low profile."

The president referred to the head of the Secret Service. Directly responsible for his safety the day of his assassination, that arm of America's security services had maintained a low profile in the wake of Kennedy's murder. JFK continued.

"I've read all the reports. Chief Justice Warren's commission seems to conclude my expiration is the work of a lone assassin. Other semi-official documents and the more farfetched appear to suggest everything from Cosa Nostra involvement to an agent assigned to protect me in Dallas accidentally discharging his weapon. It wouldn't surprise me if Mother Hubbard's goose hadn't taken a pot shot."

JFK took a last look at the view below.

"Frankly gentlemen it seems to me my demise was at the least a comedy of unfortunate errors that resulted in quietus."

Thus did Kennedy describe his death. Hoover started to remonstrate but JFK stopped him.

"Director, assigning blame and debating responsibility in our after life is futile. Whilst our hearts beat you considered me a spoilt spoon-fed kid and I regarded you as a mean son-of-a-bitch. Perhaps we were both wrong. I suggest we let history be the judge."

He nodded to Hoover then Angleton.

"Mr Angleton."

The late president began to move away.

"Podric. Podric! Where is that kid when you want him?"

*   *   *

Podric clicked out of UAR. He and Archie stood in darkness by the window watching George Benedict take his leave of the Director and agent Lodestar in the drive below.

"Think it had an effect?"

"Time will tell."

"George?"

They saw Benedict cross to the hedge and take the path to the orchard.

"He wants to go into UAR."

"What do you mean?"

"He wants to be left inside a game."

"What?! Like we threatened those goons – forever?"

"That's what he said."

"He can't be serious. Absolutus inifinitus?"

"You and Latin."

Chapter 42

In and Out the Party

To celebrate the end of the school year Podric invited his UAR afficionados to a *Moon Landing* party at the moon's Lunar Station.

"Where else?" had been Barney's cry.

"Now our adventures are out of this world!"

Although the atmosphere aboard the Spacecruiser was celebratory, looking around at his school friends and UAR compadres Podric spied several holes. Sitting beside her son, Barbara Moon said.

"George said you knew..."

"Hmm."

"For how long?"

"A while – at least suspected."

Podric was thoughtful.

"When you'd got lost and ended up in that barracks that night – maybe you don't remember George excusing himself from your interview. He'd been trying to gather UAR info and was rendezvousing with the Americans reporting in. Then when we met those two agents where they'd briefed him with those admittance codes – whatever he was up to there had to be some trade off."

"He seems eaten up – lost."

Barbara sipped some Spacecruiser decaff. Podric said.

"Well he might. Apparently he's been a soft operative forever. He had a career games writing but he's always worked for the agency."

Podric swigged some water and continued.

"At the time *Moon Landing – 1984* was being worked on Mr

Zaentz had stipulated using '60s technology was part of a player's challenge. When at their California base with him and Fred, I checked out with some writers who worked on it. They reckoned they could have got the game to function with the technology available. It was George who sabotaged it."

Approaching the moon, Barbara looked out of the window.

"Which was the complete opposite of what he said."

"Yeah. Sorry mum, he's a snoop. Talking of which."

Podric turned round to see Fred Schepesi and Cy Zaentz chatting to Denise Mullins and Carla Logan. Addressing Carla, Podric said.

"Thinking of going back?"

Carla Logan smiled. Cy Zaentz said.

"I'm doing my best."

"Podric, I'm in. So long as we get trips it'll never be marketed." Fred Schepesi was his avuncular self.

"What about you changing companies Podric?"

Cy Zaentz was stirring. Fred Schepesi snorted.

"Over my dead body – or yours!"

Podric smiled. "We'll be arriving shortly. Enjoy the party."

The Spacecruiser passed over the Sea of Tranquillity where the world had been told the Apollo sites were located. Gazing down, the moon looked as untrammelled as its four and a half billion-year-old age belied. Dropping closer to the surface skimming over the terrain Alamo Ridge appeared – Lunar Station on its far side.

*   *   *

Inside the Lunar Station the party had already begun. Moving through the crowd Neil Armstrong was talking to President Kennedy. Film director Stanley Kubrick was deeply engrossed in a conversation with the ill-fated Apollo 1 commander Gus Grissom.

"Just viewed your movie. Wish we'd had what your ship looked like. Way ahead of anything available to us." (At the time of Grissom's death, the director was in production with *2001: A Space*

Odyssey). Kubrick acknowledged Grissom's compliment. Gus concluded wistfully.

"Yeah – way ahead of reality."

Other astronauts present included Alan Shepherd, Ed White and Roger Chaffee. All now dead – in the games world they were animated, larking around in high spirits.

"Difficult experience for you to describe being the first man to place a footprint on another planet."

Kennedy was speaking to Neil Armstrong who appeared tongue tied.

"You set the sights sir, had the vision."

"Political wasn't it, Mr President? No disrespect."

Grissom cut in.

"None taken."

Kennedy laughed.

"'Can't let us navy men have all the glory."

Gus chuckled at the president's deflecting reply.

"Mind if I ask you a question, sir?"

"Shoot."

Aware of JFK's assassination the rumbustious astronaut for once looked embarrassed. Kennedy's smile broadened.

"Ha. Takes a bit of getting used to."

For a moment the two men stared at each other, then Kennedy said.

"Guess it was quick for both of us."

Normally bluff, Grissom smiled shyly. It was endearing.

"I read a lot about you being a World War Two hero – saving your crew in the Pacific. That took courage, sir."

Kennedy wasn't having it.

"You likely also read Colonel, my response that I had little choice. They rammed my boat."

Grissom laughed. JFK continued.

"Everyone here has shown acts of courage – some of great endeavour. If I've contributed to that.."

As JFK continued talking a spacecraft descended.

"Setting sail on an untried mission to an unknown celestial

body – a challenge we're able to accept, one we aren't willing to postpone and asking God's blessing on the most hazardous and dangerous of adventures ever undertaken by man – seeking His guidance of our efforts, then His will be done."

*   *   *

Sunset at the Trout & Eel was the nicest time of the day. Sitting in the garden by the weir, Carol had apologised to Billy, but the boy found it hard to overcome her betrayal. What had been a difficult hour looked to become even more so when Carol spied Podric. Having clicked out of UAR, Podric was very much back in reality emerging from the pub carrying a tray of drinks. Carol's heart sank. Podric put the tray down on the table.

"Your poison's Bacardi & Coke I think. I know you're pregnant, but I'm sure a single will be okay, and I got extra Coke."

Podric passed the drink and the additional can to Carol. He turned to Billy.

"Didn't have to guess what you're on."

"Pod. How did you know we were here?"

Podric and Billy picked up their pints.

"I didn't. Spied you when I was parking Wombat."

"Wombat?"

"Yeah, I know – terrible isn't it. What mum calls her Beetle."

"But you got her that fancy Land Rover."

"Yeah, which means I get Wombat. Some trade!"

They sipped their beer. Carol looked at Podric suspiciously and said.

"Coincidental then – Bill and me having this chat and you turning up."

Podric had another pull of his Hop Old Original.

"Did Billy tell you he won a contract?"

Billy looked a bit embarrassed.

"Oah, Pod.."

"That'll be something of yours then will it? Tryin' to buy him now, are you?"

"Not as I sit here. Billy knows that."

Podric put down his drink.

"Carol, you know what you did, and you know why you did it. I don't agree with it - particularly as it affected me but it's over. For what it's worth I don't hold it against you."

"Very big of you Podric."

Billy did not look pleased with his girlfriend's attitude - or would she be ex? Podric was cool.

"When all of us heard about you being pregnant we were concerned for you both. Apart from your being best at sports in the school, obviously Billy's also got talents."

Podric smiled and looking at Carol, continued.

"It's just that people - and not just me - think that if you can, you should both be at Wendbury and finish A levels. After that, who knows?"

Podric rotated his beer glass, a habit he had. Reverting to her sullen attack mode Carol said.

"Good speech. Long time preparing it, have you?"

Unfazed, Podric replied.

"I thought with the stress of all this, maybe things weren't being thought through enough."

"Well you know what you can do."

Carol spat out her words. Billy stood up.

"He's right Carol."

Billy finished his beer.

"Podric has helped me and I'm going to work for his company after I've done my A levels. I told you I'd provide for the kid, and I will."

"What about us - you and me?"

"I'm going to get another drink. Pod?"

Podric shook his head. Billy headed for the bar. Carol burst into tears.

Chapter 43

Loose Ends

Driving back to Drinkwell later, Podric had left Billy and Carol at the pub. Not convinced his intervention had achieved anything except increasing Carol's antipathy, he was surprised to see George Benedict sitting on the village green bench. Pulling over, Podric parked his car. As he approached Benedict, George said.

"Not going to check everyone out? Presumably they've gone in from the Lighthouse."

Sitting down, Podric didn't reply. George said.

"Don't say you came back for me."

Podric shrugged. George continued.

"You know what I want."

"Eternity's a long time George – or so we're told."

Benedict laughed.

"It'll suit me."

"You don't know that."

"I've got nothing else."

They looked across the village. Podric said.

"You know I can't do it George."

Benedict looked at Podric sharply.

"I know you can."

"That's not what I mean. You can go in from anywhere – back in the States, it doesn't matter. But to live you have to come out."

"I don't want to. That's why I want infinity."

"Then I can't help you."

More silence then George said.

"What if I said I would – at least from time to time..?"

"Right now, I wouldn't believe you."

"But if I swore?"

Podric didn't reply. George went on.

"This is my most precious possession. Officially, only twelve were ever struck."

George opened his hand revealing the little grey rock broach. He handed it to Podric who turned it over. Underneath the clasp was the 'many called, few chosen' motto.

"If you believe they got there – that's a tiny piece of the eight hundred and forty-two pounds brought back."

"Something tells me I shouldn't ask how you came by it."

"The twelve had a few more struck. It was a gift."

"Even so, surely the services you rendered ran counter-."

Benedict cut in.

"Podric, my beliefs about Apollo are my beliefs. The original *Moon Landing* game didn't prove anything."

Podric looked at Benedict icily.

"That's as maybe but not only did you not write it, you deliberately corrupted it. From the moment you appeared in our lives everything you've said to us has been a pack of lies."

Pre-announced by Eamon Ivy Bickerstaff wandered into view across the green. The macaw began circling overhead. Benedict said.

"Well, anyway, I want you to have it."

Archie's ex-partner began to shake.

"Can't you help me Podric? I'm desperate! I just want to escape myself, everything.."

Podric studied the broach.

"It could be said George that's pretty weak."

Podric stood up.

"I don't need to help you. You conned us, all of us. You betrayed Archie, my mother took you in. You're a liar and a cheat."

Both the boy and man seemed frozen. Finally, Podric sighed.

"If – and it is an if, I help you I'm doing it to get rid of you. Understand?"

Benedict nodded. Podric tossed the little broach in his hand.

"Bit ironic really if I give you access to UAR it being the ultimate gift."

Podric silently read the Latin motto to himself.

"I'll look after this for you but I'm only doing so because if it is that important to you, you'll come back and collect it. That's the deal."

Benedict was very tense. Podric looked at him and said.

"Agreed?"

Benedict muttered that he did.

"Abuse it George and I'll block your returning inside."

"You can do that?"

"Trust me."

Podric gave a hollow laugh. Eamon landed between them. Podric stood up.

"Go and have a cup of tea with Ivy and I'll see you at the lab later."

"Isn't it a bit crowded?"

"They're in the theatre. The lab's the one bit of the Lighthouse we never go in from. You won't either. When I've checked out you know what you're doing, you'll be on your way – physically I mean."

Podric turned to Ivy.

"Mrs B – time we had some more adventures."

"Oh yes Podric. I've been thinking about that. Quite fancy old Rome – those togas."

"You were great in *Napoleonic Wars* Ivy. I'll see what there is to explore.

"*Imperium Romanum* looks good and *Praetorium*.

Podric laughed.

"Didn't know you followed computer games?"

"Lots about me you don't know young man."

"You're on. I've just about done with space."

Ivy chuckled.

"No, you haven't. Plenty more adventures for you in the *Final Frontier*."

* * *

The doorbell of No 5 Briony Close rang. Prepping some UAR material in his bedroom, Podric craned to see who was visiting but the small porch blocked his view. Going to the door he was amazed to find Miles Willoughby and Jane Cartwright with Billy and Carol and Norris Widget on the step. Jane said.

"Reckon this is a surprise – even for you!"

It was. Inviting them in, Podric offered coffee and beers.

"So you're thinking, what's with the change of mind? How's this come about?"

The normally reticent Miles was exuberant. Podric poured him a beer.

"Whose change of mind and what's come about?"

Jane Cartwright laughed. Podric noticed Billy and Carol were quiet – even shy. He gave a coffee to Carol and a beer to Billy.

"There's something you can do for us."

Carol's voice was little more than a whisper. Podric said.

"Might this something have to do with adventure?"

They nodded.

"They want to go into your other world Podric. We all do."

Jane was excited.

"Would it be alright Podric? How I am..."

Carol looked at her enlarged body.

"Maybe it would be better if it was afterwards."

"Hmm... But I want Bill to go."

"Carol, there'll be plenty more adventures."

Podric was considerate. Carol was intense.

"It's important now Podric. It's important!"

There was an air of desperation in her voice.

"Then we'd better make sure it's nothing too earth shattering."

"The moon isn't it – your latest quest Podric Moon?"

Jane smiled. Podric looked at them all. He'd have to help Billy and Carol and the other three coming along wouldn't hurt. Whatever it was that had changed Carol's mind left him no choice.

"I have to go out for a while. Make yourselves comfortable. We'll go in from here."

*   *   *

Lit only by the banks of computer screens in Archie's lab Podric and George Benedict sat back. Now programmed and briefed, under Podric's tutelage George had been into Ultimate Alternative Reality a couple of times coming out under his own steam. Benedict said.

"So, it's Rome and Caesar next."

Podric didn't reply.

"Those Legions and Cohorts – games at the Colosseum's going to be a blast."

"Time you were on your way George."

Benedict turned to Podric.

"I know you think I failed you, failed everyone."

George stood up.

"You haven't asked me why."

"Do you know George I don't really care. Whatever you say, it's likely not to be the truth."

Podric began returning the computers to standby. He went on.

"Oah you'll have had your reasons. Belief in what is it, Uncle Sam? National Security – for the greater good – all that."

The computer screens reverted to a glow. Podric continued.

"You being a Brit, they must have recruited you a long time ago. Anyway, you're out of our lives now."

Benedict had pulled himself together. There was a hardness about him and for the first time, Podric realised the man was callous. Podric turned to leave the room. In the half-light Benedict looked sinister.

"I'll just tell you this. You've spooked them, freaked them out Podric. They're terrified of the exposure your creation could cause."

Podric sighed.

"National Security wouldn't have known about UAR George if you hadn't told them."

Benedict gave a hard laugh.

"If you think that you're naïve. Archie certainly doesn't."

Podric stood up.

"Okay, well I'm sure you're both right."

He picked up his bag.

"It's turned out well though. Your actions have worked to our advantage. I put your associates into UAR and allowed them to view the world I've created because I want them to realise I'm watching them like I will be you. It's an insurance policy to ensure you and your buddies stay in your box."

Podric moved to the door.

"You now have the ability to enter UAR at will. We'll see if you deserve it. Doubting that, I've blocked your admittance to any space related games. Right now, George that's access you cannot have."

"But-."

Podric had a foot on the fire escape stairs.

"Take it or leave it."

Outside the tower, Podric took out his car keys. Benedict appeared. Podric said.

"Train, boat or planing it?"

"I'm trying for the rural ride... Ivy said she could find a horse to pull the caravan."

"Ha. Good job Carla's moving out then."

Podric unlocked Wombat's door.

"Whether or not you're a bad man George, you're a sad one."

"You saved me, Podric."

Taking the little moon rock badge from his pocket, Podric clipped it to his denim jacket.

"Make sure you collect."

Starting the VW Podric didn't want to be around George Benedict anymore. He was tired of him and his lies.

Chapter 44
Goodbye to All That

Motoring away from the Lighthouse that night, Podric felt empty. At his lawyer's request he had taken his friends into the world of the 1960s. Always on the lookout for adventure, Podric realised that a decade of such expectancy for America had rapidly disintegrated. JFK had been shot in November of 1963, Martin Luther King early April in '68 and the younger Kennedy brother Bobby in June of that same year. As the country slid into a mire America became gripped in its overseas conflict with North Vietnam and with its violence at home. Rounding out the 10 years, anti-Vietnam protests and Civil Rights disputes culminated in the Kent State riots which involved the National Guard opening fire on protesters killing several students and wounding others. Although the Watergate building wasn't burgled until June 1972 and Richard Nixon wouldn't resign as President of the United States until August 1974, he had won the presidency from Lyndon Johnson taking office in January '69 and was the president to end the decade.

The one uplifting event America and the world could celebrate took place in July of that year when Armstrong and Aldrin walked on the moon, but now even that seemed tarnished. Sitting in his car outside his house in Briony Close Podric studied the little badge of grey rock George Benedict had placed in his keeping. Of course it mattered if mankind was cheated. Apart from the con it would represent failure for those men and women driven in their task to fulfil the challenge laid down by the leader who inspired his country to achieve it.

And what of Kennedy? *Moon Landing* incorporating the years

JFK was in the White House had certainly taken Podric on a rollercoaster ride of adventure throwing up as many questions as it answered. But thinking about Kennedy Podric could only admire the man's attitude to his death. According to the late 35th president, apportioning blame for his demise didn't amount to much. Losing his life on that bright day in Dallas brought an end to his charmed existence. Privileged as it was – Kennedy had needed a degree of fortitude to sustain his physically vigorous image. Frequently in pain, he struggled daily with ailments that affected his damaged body. It had been a well-kept secret.

This latest adventure had also taken Podric and his friends into the world of Stanley Kubrick. Unpleasantly tied to lunar machinations the film director had been challenged by powerful corridors in the American government and had decided to depart his native shores for Britain making it his domicile.

If Kennedy and Apollo were forever bound together so was George Benedict's involvement in this UAR adventure. It was George who had appeared in their lives apparently a victimised innocent but actually someone embedded in the National Security Service planted in their midst in an attempt to reveal the secrets of Ultimate Alternative Reality.

Podric had pressured the games writer and Benedict ultimately fell on his sword. Telling Podric that real life held no meaning for him, UAR's inventor had released Benedict into his alternate world. He would be free now – removed from the shackles of those who controlled him, spending his existence inside Ultimate Alternative Reality in a state with no end. Was that desirable? Was it the ultimate form of escapism or was it a void for lost souls..? That was something Podric would have to monitor.

Getting out of Wombat, Podric locked the VW. Inside No 5 Briony Close his friends awaited their adventure. He would provide it for them, but this would be his last trip into *Moon Landing*. It was time to part from the game and leave Earth's satellite to its peace – not that it's solitude would remain. Podric knew that whatever had or hadn't happened, one day the moon would be a busy jumping off point for man's efforts in deep space exploration. That *Star Trek* slogan – mans' final frontier. It wasn't really. A person's imagination beat that. It was limitless.

Chapter 45
A Lunar Farewell

Looking round the party guests Archie Light noted Podric's arrival in the company of several more of his school friends. Mingling with the Lunar crowd, Archie was pleased to see his sister-in-law Dinah de Vries with her husband, Count Leopold. Considerably older than his wife, the count's style was mannered and courtly.

The scientific community led for America by Wernher von Braun and for Russia, Sergei Korolev, political figures in *Moon Landing* included Lyndon Johnson and Richard Nixon. Having told President Kennedy about his son John Junior's youthful demise, Podric thought long and hard about a final inclusion. Seeing JFK talking animatedly to Catherine Halliday, he decided the time was right for this additional participant to appear. Preparing the link, Podric then temporarily placed it on Standby.

"So, where's the source of all our troubles?" Archie was reflective.

"If you mean your ex-business partner – right now he's escaping the world's ruthless clutches in a gypsy caravan."

Archie smiled but remained concerned.

"So you set him free."

"With inhibitors – space games being one of them."

"That's why I can't see him here."

Standing on a balcony, the two surveyed the scene below. Watching Kaliska Monroe being chatted up by JFK, Archie said.

"What do you think about this one?"

"*Moon Landing?*"

Podric looked up at the Lunar Station's panoramic screen and the moon's surface.

"Our adventures only get better – witnessing people's thoughts as they experience what they went through."

Podric watched Neil Armstrong and his colleagues.

"It's great to come face to face with the movers and shakers of another time. That does it for me. I think it's endlessly amazing."

Kaliska laughed at something Kennedy said. Archie turned to Podric.

"Couldn't you have told her all this at the outset?"

"I did but it made no difference. Besides, how cool is it for her to know the man she's always longed to meet and otherwise never would have."

Archie nodded.

"So what's next then maestro?"

"Why don't you choose for a change?" Archie smiled.

"Ha. I quite like leaving that in your idiosyncratic hands. For me, the surprise makes it part of the fun."

Podric shrugged.

"Ivy fancy's Rome. Julius and the Conquest of Britain."

"You're going to select an adventure because the village eccentrics interested in something?"

"Can you think of a better reason?!"

Podric's reply had feeling.

"She's as much right to an idea as any of us. Anyway, we'll see."

Heading for the melee below, Podric said.

"Got your big speech ready?"

For a second Archie looked blank then his face cleared.

"You mean the one where I tell everyone how you've changed my life, given me a renewed sense of purpose and generally helped make me a better person." Podric turned back and smiled.

"I was thinking more of something complimentary!"

* * *

Sitting in an African desert Barney Sturridge watched apes' aggression. Bones flew and the sky lit up with the 'Dawn of Man'. Clicking out of the 2001: A Space Odyssey computer game, Barney found Stanley Kubrick in the Lunar Station's astrodome staring at the moon's terrain. On the edge of a nearby rock formation a plain headstone-like shape protruded. Barney said.

"Could be the monolith."

Kubrick didn't reply. Barney continued.

"What do you think then?"

"About what?"

"All this. The meaning of life. Everything."

Kubrick smiled.

"You're referring to the state we're in."

"Bit different to films, huh? Being able to live in another world."

"Only wish it had been around when I was."

"You were a pioneer in your time."

Kubrick didn't reply. Barney said.

"It's been great to have met you Mr Kubrick."

Kubrick faced Barney.

"Mr Kubrick now is it? What happened to your irreverence?"

Barney laughed.

"I've learned a lot."

"Not as much as I have."

"Want to stay in UAR? I could ask Podric."

"I haven't lost the power of speech Barney. I can talk to your friend myself."

They had another look at the vista.

"We always want more. Whatever our life span, it's never enough.."

"Then you're in the right place. The ultimate form of an alternative reality. With your interests – galaxial adventures are where you belong."

*   *   *

The lunar party was in full swing, Carol Jensen suddenly felt a twinge. Breaking off his conversation with the late Gene Cernan, Billy was immediately attentive. Carol said.

"I think it's coming Bill."

Billy looked around but couldn't see Podric. Catherine and Cosima appeared.

"We'd better get out of here."

"Where's Podric?"

"He went off with President Kennedy."

"Can your dad get us out?"

Cosima looked doubtful.

"What about the medic centre?"

"Having a baby in UAR? Our minds are disengaged from real life Cosima. We're in Ultimate Alternative Reality – remember?!"

Catherine was tense. Cosima moved to help the groaning Carol.

"Well if you can't get her out, can you think of a better alternative?"

No one could so they took Carol to Lunar Station's infirmary.

*   *   *

"You're leaving us then."

Surrounded by racks of spacesuits and helmets, President Kennedy and Podric stood in the spaceship kit room. Kennedy said.

"Thank you for the experience Podric. It's been interesting."

"I'm sorry if you didn't get more from it."

"I got plenty from it. For an out of body experience it's unique."

Kennedy picked up a portable life support pack.

"Amazing what mankind's accomplished, but this was always going to be just a beginning."

"I think for you, UAR's been unfulfilling."

JFK inspected an oxygen purge pack that sat on top of a PLSS unit.

"If I felt unfulfilled in real life Podric, I was hardly going to find gratification in your alternative reality."

The backpack combination holding Kennedy's interest, he looked across at the boy.

"It was always my problem."

Though they didn't know it this was a similar sentiment to

Kubrick's. Perhaps it was life's common denominator – people wanting that little bit extra? In Kennedy's case that would be a lot. Leaving the storeroom, Podric and JFK headed back to the Lunar Station's central building. Podric was thoughtful.

"Though you inspired all this I didn't think you'd want to stay here."

Kennedy laughed.

"I have a choice in your brave new world?"

Walking along a gallery Podric said.

"Archie met you sailing offshore in your boat. I thought perhaps that would be a better-."

"Resting place..?"

JFK smiled and like Stanley Kubrick, gazed out at the earth and the galaxies further beyond.

"Sailing about Nantucket Sound? There are certainly worse places to be cast adrift though I'm not sure Podric if I want to be left roaming around anywhere in one of your worlds. Whilst it's held some fascination for me we are of our time."

"But yours was cut short."

"Yes, and it's unfair. There's always inequality in life. It's how it is."

Kennedy smiled. He'd made a variation on that statement before. They moved on.

"At least you gave me the opportunity of airing some of my thoughts and taking a look at things to come."

"Plenty of which aren't too satisfactory."

Kennedy looked at UAR's young creator.

"That's with you to change. My arena gate got closed."

Podric studied the Alamo Ridge and a moon buggy parked below.

"So 'Victura' and Nantucket Sound doesn't appeal?"

"I didn't say that. Any chance of a ride on one of those before we go?"

They went on their way.

Chapter 46
Cart before a Baby

Carla Logan having quit the gypsy caravan parked in the Light's orchard for a return to her London flat before attending the UAR Lunar party, George Benedict began preparing the Romany vardo for the open road. With most people in *Moon Landing* he didn't hurry the work – indeed he wasn't certain whether Ivy Bickerstaff's promise that she would find him a nag to pull the caravan would materialise. It was a delight when the following evening a Connemara pony 'Aengus' arrived at the Lighthouse delivered by Ivy's horse contact. Irish himself, Seamus Rafferty brought Aengus to the door. Seamus struck lucky because Alannah Brodie opened it. Epitome of the four leaf clover, Alannah took him round to the orchard. The moment he saw the gypsy caravan the poitín was brought out and the night quickly dissolved into a tripartite blur. Benedict finally managed to enquire what he owed the equine procurer, but Mr Rafferty became furtive and assured George that it was all taken care of. Enquiring no further, on waking the following morning, the computer games man discovered Alannah Brodie was packed and ready to go. She announced that she was coming with him!

*   *   *

Lunar Station's medical centre was busy. Carol positioned on a hospital bed, Billy held Carol's hand and Jane and Sally were in attendance.

"Where is Podric?"

Billy was agitated. Jane said.

"We sent Miles and Norris to look for him."

Gowned up, Catherine and Charlotte Light appeared. The baby having begun life's most important journey, hiding her apprehension Catherine made an inspection.

"You think it's okay having a baby like this?"

Jane was nervous.

"How do I know but that's what's happening!"

Extremely preoccupied, Catherine and Charlotte were managing the birth when Archie showed up with his daughter.

"Did I hear-?"

Charlotte waved them away. Sally said.

"I've read about women using alternative medicine – TM, mantra and stuff to clear the headspace."

Adjusting her mask, Catherine looked up at her friend who continued.

"Never know, might start a whole new method. Leboyer out, UAR in!"

* * *

Re-entering the party with Podric, President John F. Kennedy met Count Leopold de Vries and his wife Dinah.

"Mr President. 'Knew your sister-in-law. Prince Stanislaw and Lee were old friends."

Kennedy was well aware of the European high society circles his wife's sister had moved in. Leopold continued.

"Indeed, I was so happy to see them attending the event this evening."

Kennedy looked across the room to see Prince Stanislaw Radziwill talking to several astronauts. Taking a closer look, he saw Stas's wife Lee appear. Alongside her svelte and elegant was another woman. It was his own wife Jackie. Kennedy turned to Podric who was talking to some other guests. Catching each other's eye, both smiled.

"Podric. You've got to come now!"

"What is it?"

"Carol – she's having her baby."

Collared by Norris Widget Podric was incredulous.

"What in U-? Er, wow. Are you sure?"

"No, Pod – winding you up. Come on!"

Hurrying round to the medical centre, they discovered Billy holding his new born. Others stood by enchanted.

"What do you think Pod? Me star child."

Podric was amazed.

"Er, well – incredible Billy. Is it a boy or a girl?"

"Girl 'o course."

The way Billy said it, he seemed surprised Podric hadn't thought it wasn't obvious.

"Have you got a name for... her?"

"Sure have. Catherine thought of it. When she explained about the goddess – only one moniker."

Returning to Carol's side, Billy started making baby noises.

"Little Luna - my beautiful baby girl.."

Podric looked at his girlfriend. Catherine said.

"Before you say anything, I did not box set *Call the Midwife!*"

Chapter 47
Luna's Irish Eyes

When learning that George Benedict would be leaving Hampshire in the caravan Podric was certain he would head for Ireland. Where else could offer such peace and Trá Ros Beithe on Éire's west coast was the perfect place to physically escape. Its remoteness would be a safe locale to enter Ultimate Alternative Reality far away from prying eyes.

Parking the vardo in a field outside the hamlet of Rossbeigh, Aengus had pulled it along the lanes and byways of Country Kerry and now stood munching some well-earned pasture. Atlantic rollers were breaking gently against the nearby shore and Podric was pleased to see George preparing supper. Viewing the errant computer games writing agent in UAR Podric felt that his father would be a good person to keep a weather eye on Benedict. Already programmed into *JFK and His World* Sean wouldn't judge the man but could act as a cypher monitoring Benedict's troubled condition. Besides, George Benedict was the first person Barbara Moon had been attracted to since Sean had been killed. With Sean around laying a few things to rest might not be a bad thing.

There was another reason.

When he could Podric always wanted to help his mother. Even though Sean had been killed eighteen months previously, he knew she missed him as if it was yesterday. Barbara and Podric being in UAR at the Lunar party, Podric removed his mum from *Moon Landing* and re-programmed her into *JFK and His World*. Although his parents' existence together these days was only transitory in Podric's alternate reality state, it was the best their son could manage. The one character Podric hadn't bargained on seeing was Alannah Brodie though her appearance didn't surprise him.

Watching his parents cross the field and approach the caravan arm in arm, their arrival on the scene seemed natural. Barbara and Alannah were obviously pleased to meet up. It was hard not view the rendezvous as anything less than idyllic.

*   *   *

Making coffee in the kitchen Podric and Jane Cartwright heard a baby's cry coming from upstairs. Jane said.

"How did all that happen? I mean delivering a baby in a parallel state."

She and Podric looked shellshocked. She continued.

"And your girlfriend seemed to be in charge. I mean how could that work?"

"In UAR we can all be anywhere. Maybe she was with us in spirit."

"That's a bit existential Podric. Maybe she's trying to tell you something?" Jane smiled and had some coffee. Podric said.

"I'm going to have to go round to the Lighthouse and check everyone's back."

A dazed Billy came in.

"Pod, Carol wants to see you."

Extraordinary though it may seem, an hour or two later Miles, Jane, Norris, Billy and Carol clutching the world's most beautiful new addition were on their way to the Lights. No one believing Carol would be with them, her retort had been mild.

"Mum went to work after having me. Dad wasn't keen but she said a gearbox needed changing on a car they were servicing, and she didn't trust him with it."

Her friends didn't know quite how to take this. Carol continued.

"'Sides I'm only sitting around drinking bubbly."

Podric had put several bottles of champagne his mum had left over from Christmas into the boot of his car. Everyone packing into Wombat they all set off in the VW. Arriving at the Light household Cosima let them in and another party rapidly ensued. Carol showed off little Luna in the living room and Dog got in people's way. Everyone was in high spirits.

"Well that's the-."

Archie waved his champagne glass.

"Nothing UAR can't handle now!"

Muttering something about how nature had to have taken its course, Podric looked dubious. Standing nearby Sally said.

"'Told you – not only have you created an alternative reality you've also got an ultimate birthing method!"

Knocking back some champagne, she giggled.

"Just so long as you don't go getting any ideas."

This was spoken by Catherine who appeared at Podric's side. His girlfriend was less inebriated than her friend. Podric said.

"We can't work that out. You seemed to be in charge."

"I felt I was there and all of us knew she was having it alright."

Sipping her drink Catherine continued.

"Maybe you delivered her."

Podric went pale. "Men don't normally get broody do they?"

"Look at him."

Catherine nodded at Billy.

"That'll be a football team."

"What, a female club?"

Podric put down his glass.

"Something I've got to do."

He walked over to Billy and half a minute later, the two stood in Alannah's little study.

"We always seem to come in here when something significant's happening. Apart from my being a dad, there is something significant is there Pod..?"

Podric looked at his friend.

"*Moon Landing*'s been great Billy, but you top it."

"How d'you mean?"

"Whether we've all been cheated – the moon and stuff – Luna's arrival is fact."

Moving a little away, Podric looked out at the view. It was one that was special to him.

"In our adventure she's a star child."

He turned back to face his friend.

"You know UAR was recently challenged by Archie's ex-business partner."

Billy muttered that he'd heard something to that effect.

"George got into trouble and helping him, he gave me something telling me it was his most precious possession. I said I'd look after it for him but not having got a present for your daughter – whatever I got her could never match this. That is, if you believe... Anyway, I'm giving it to Luna."

"Won't he be upset?"

Billy was concerned. Podric said.

"What I'm giving him – he'll want her to have it."

Podric took out the little piece of moon rock and handed it to Billy.

"'Wouldn't have a clue if it's really moon rock or any old piece of olivine basalt but it doesn't need checking because Luna's real and that's all that matters. In our minds, she came into this world on another satellite which is why it's a special gift."

Billy studied the rock and read off the tiny inscription 'multi autem sunt vocati pauci vero electi'.

"How's your Latin?"

Billy shrugged.

"Great."

"Then you'll know what it means."

*   *   *

Back in the living room, Podric watched a thoughtful Billy reunite with his girlfriend and baby. Nodding to Catherine she and Podric left the party. Making for the Lighthouse, on their way up the stairs they passed the enormous black and white studio photograph of Cosima. Catherine stopped.

"Do you think I should have one of these done?"

Podric looked back.

"Bigger."

Catherine laughed.

"Might just do that. Had an effect on you."

Crossing the gallery to the tower, instead of going up to the top floor Podric headed for the rear of the building where the work sleeping quarters were located. Occupying a bunk Barbara in *JFK and His World* was still in Ultimate Alternative Reality. Looking down at his mother in repose, Podric saw that her face had a slight smile.

Climbing the interior fire escape, the den was empty. Catherine went to the kitchen area and activated the Gran Gaggia coffee machine.

"Want one?"

"Wouldn't say no."

In the lab Podric fired up the bank of computers.

"Ready?"

"Wha-?"

"I'm only making an adjustment."

Sitting in one of the Eames chairs, Catherine checked the UAR menu at the top of her eyes.

"You've got a thing about Ireland."

Busy at the computer bench, Podric pulled up George Benedict's details. His UAR profile had a block on admission to any space games. The computer whirred and hummed.

"I'm keeping that piece of rock George gave me – I've given it to Luna. It can be his gift to her as thanks for setting him free."

With a click Podric undid the block. Catherine watched the game change from *JFK and His World* to *Moon Landing*. She said.

"Resent him?"

"No. I think infinity is where belongs – for now."

"Isn't that a contradiction in terms?"

They laughed. Catherine looked at her boyfriend.

"He's a learning curve Podric. Justice done is about right."

Podric raised an eyebrow.

"Praise indeed."

Catherine exited Ultimate Alternative Reality and sat back.

"What about you?"

"What about me?"

"Games, plans, ambitions... At seventeen, what is there left?"

She smiled. He smiled. Returning the computer to standby Podric spoke in an American accent.

"With the job I've got to do, you can follow. Where I'm going you can be a part of."

He got up and came over to her.

"I'm no good at being noble Catherine, but it doesn't take much to see that with UAR around the problems of this little world don't amount to a hill of beans. Someday you'll understand that kid."

Catherine laughed.

"Some paraphrase. *Casablanca* wasn't one of Kubrick's."

"Uhuh. Neither was *Gone with the Wind* but then 'tomorrow is another day'!"

*   *   *

HAIL PODRIC!

Podric Moon's Adventures
with
Julius Caesar and the Roman Empire

Chapter 1

An Unwelcome Announcement

"Breast cancer's not the end of the world darling."
This announcement from his mother did not fill Podric Moon with joy. Having already lost his aviator father in a freak flying accident some eighteen months previously, news of his mum's recent health check immediately caused her son concern.

They were sitting in the kitchen of 5 Briony Close having breakfast. Not long returned from their latest Ultimate Alternative Reality adventure – the unique mind pathway state Podric and his computer games writing partner Dr Archie Light had invented – Barbara's medical result was an unwelcome surprise. She'd had the test almost randomly. One day at work a mobile unit had arrived at the industrial site Tweeney's Waste Disposal was located and along with most women employees Barbara had availed herself of a mammary screening. It being conducted several weeks ago she had actually forgotten about it.

Largely because of Podric's incredible alternative reality creation the Moon family's lives had recently begun to regain some happiness. Out of this world excitement in UAR – *Moon Landing* had delivered what it said on the tin and their experiences in this latest adventure had been extraordinary – celestial roamings enchanting the privileged participants. To Podric his mother's revelation brought things back to reality with a bump. Barbara put down the letter.

"It just says the count is high and I need another test."
"When will you have it?"
"I'm to call the hospital and they'll make an appointment."
Finishing her coffee, Barbara got up and put her mug in the

dishwasher. Getting herself ready for work, she called back from the hall.

"Did you see those cottage details have come through?"

Podric didn't reply. His mother had been making plans for them to rent a cottage in Northumberland for a week's holiday. That would be okay. Barbara invited Podric's girlfriend Catherine Halliday and one of Amy's friends to go with them, but she also planned on extending an invitation to her parents to visit for a couple of nights. 'It's a big farmhouse and we ought to see them darling.'

As far as Podric was concerned there was no ought about it. His grandmother Oona Fosdyke wasn't too bad. Erratic and smothering, Podric could survive a couple of hours in her company but the loathing he felt for his grandfather was pathological. Gerald Fosdyke was an anathema to Podric. His voice, his manner, his attitude – Gerald's whole presence his grandson found repugnant. How the man could be his mother's father was beyond even Podric's imagination. And inviting Oona and Gerald to spend a few days with them on holiday. His mother had to be losing it. Podric turned to his mum. Barbara had put on a gilet and was about to leave the house.

"Mum. This is crazy. You've had this letter. You've got to be seen straight away."

"I will be darling. I told you I'll call the hospital."

"Today. You'll call the hospital today!"

Barbara looked at her son and realised how deeply her news had affected him. She came over to him.

"I'll call them this morning."

She kissed his forehead and turned to go. Podric said.

"Mum we've got to talk."

"Yes darling..?"

Barbara picked up her car keys from a bowl on the kitchen table.

"Not just about you being seen privately."

Turning to go out the door, Barbara stopped. Making himself some more coffee, Podric said.

"How quickly do we know when you can get an appointment otherwise?"

He looked at his mother.

"You should be seen privately. We've got the money. In fact, that's what I want to talk to you about."

"Not now darling, I'll be late for work."

"Living here. My games returns. Archie reckons there's a quarter of a million in MoonLight's account."

Barbara walked back into the kitchen.

"Podric, I know you've made a lot of money and I'm thrilled for you."

Distracted, Barbara went over to the French doors that opened on to their little garden and her studio shed.

"It's more than wonderful. I'm so proud of you darling – and not just because of your computer games success."

Barbara appeared more intense talking about her son's achievements than her recent news. She went on.

"Since dad was killed you've helped me so much, more than a mother has any right to expect. I know a big part of this is because of UAR. Having another world to escape into has saved me. To even feel that I'm seeing him, being in his arms – it's been a lifeline. That's got nothing to do with money. It's given me a happiness I never dreamt I could have again."

Barbara turned back to Podric.

"But your computer games earnings are something else and I'm not sure I'm best equipped to deal with the kind of commercial success you're achieving. It's beyond my paygrade darling. I know you've got people, professional people to advise you about what to do with your money – investments and things but if you need more help on that front we should get it."

Barbara came over to her son.

"The point I'm trying to make probably not very well is that it's your money darling, not mine. You've earned it. You've already spoiled me, buying me my Defender but the idea of you paying for a new house for us I can't get my head round."

The kettle clicked off. Podric said."You'll have to let him go sometime mum."

Mother and son looked at each other.

"But UAR – you created it because of him."

"I know. I will too. Sort of."

Referring to Sean Moon, Barbara's late husband and Podric's father, his mother was unable to speak. Podric said.

"You'd better get to work otherwise Repulsive Ralph will be jumping up and down."

Fighting back tears, his mother smiled.

"And you'll make that call."

Podric was forceful. Barbara just about managed to say 'promise' and left. Pouring water on his instant coffee, Podric watched his mum drive off in her Land Rover. It didn't seem such a big deal to have given her a car and he knew how much she loved it, but things were going to change and Podric felt it was right that they should. What his mother said was true – he had earned his money and the people he wanted to benefit from it most lived in this house.

About to go into the downstairs loo with a computer magazine the land line phone rang. His sister not yet having risen, Podric thought of letting it go to answerphone, but something made him answer the call.

"Hullo."

"Is that Podric? Podric Moon?"

"Who's calling?"

"It's Sergeant Paxman."

Barbara having left the house just minutes before, Podric was immediately concerned something had happened. The police calling now – it couldn't be that quick. Paxman went on.

"How are you?"

"Okay."

Podric was pretty sure the force weren't ringing to check on his health. Paxman said.

"Sorry to bother you, it's about a neighbour of yours. Well anyway, she lives in Drinkwell."

Podric didn't react.

"You know Mrs Bickerstaff."

"Yes."

"Quite a character."

Paxman paused.

"She's had a stroke."

"Oh, I'm sorry to hear that."

Podric genuinely was. He was fond of Ivy.

"How er, serious is it?"

Podric didn't know that much about strokes except that they could vary in acuteness. Paxman said.

"She's in hospital. She asked us to tell you."

"Er, right."

There was a thud upstairs and doors opened and closed.

"It appears Mrs Bickerstaff doesn't have any relatives. She wanted you to know where she was."

Podric considered what to say. Did he offer to help in some way? What sort of assistance might be required?

"What's happened to Eamon?"

"Her macaw?"

Paxman sighed.

"He flew off. Went crazy when we were putting his mistress into the ambulance. Oscar tried to catch him, but the red one wasn't having any of it."

Podric thought he heard the sergeant chuckle.

"Constable Ravelious has got a couple of budgies but dealing with a bird of paradise is a bit more than his avian skills run to."

Footsteps on the stairs announced the days arrival of Podric's sister Amy. In a state of post slumber, Amy opened a packet of cereal that was on the kitchen table. Continuing his conversation with Sergeant Paxman Podric said.

"Was Mrs B at home?"

"Found on the village green. Daughter of your village's other computer kahuna. Out for a run she was. Went off looking for the bird."

Cosima searching for Eamon. Podric still found her sharing caring attitude challenging.

"So what should I do?"

"Nothing really. As I said, Mrs Bickerstaff just wanted you to know what had happened and where she was."

Seconds later Paxman rang off. Speaking through a mouthful of Cheerios, Amy said.

"Curepen mon bro?"

Amy's preoccupation using odd words particularly Romany ones irritated Podric that morning. Asking her brother if he had a problem, Podric replied.

"No, kəns."

Romany for concern, Amy gave Podric a long look.

"Hmm... Learning the chib then are we? No need to get buli on me."

"Voi fi la fel de buli pe tine și îmi place și este timpul să începi să crești."

Podric went out. His speaking in a Romany patois suggesting to his sister that she started to grow up surprised her.

"Oah, nnukwu umunne."

Amy finished her Cheerios.

"He can't speak Igbo."

Her utterance disclaiming big brothers in an African dialect, Amy had been trawling language websites. Alighting on this Nigerian one, the phrase 'Brothersmunna niile bu ndi nzuzu na otu ubochi m ga-abu adaeze' particularly appealed to her. But whether she really felt her brother was an imbecile and that one day she would be a princess was something only Amy could determine.

*   *   *